Sadie's War

A Supernatural Uprising Novel
Book 1

Jayelle Cochran

Cochran Novels, Indianapolis, IN

This is a work of fiction. All of the characters, places, and situations (both personal and political) are the result of an overactive imagination. Any and all similarities to reality are pure coincidence and fiction.

SADIE'S WAR: A SUPERNATURAL UPRISING NOVEL: BOOK 1

Copyright © 2014 Cochran Novels
All rights reserved.

Published under Cochran Novels, Indianapolis, IN 46241

First edition printed February 2014,
    added Gutter Glossary March 2016
    added Tara's Escape, Chapter 1 preview June 2016

ISBN-13: 978-0615967721
ISBN-10: 0615967728

http://jayellecochran.com

Printed in the United States of America

It was obvious that whatever was going on, it wasn't going to have a good outcome...

It seemed as though Sal wasn't even afraid of what was happening. Sadie thought about all the times Michael had called Sal 'bad news'. He said she was a bad person, and that she had once threatened to kill him and Chloe. Now Sadie wondered if what he told her had been an understatement.

"You're starting a war," Fester saud as Sal began to walk away.

"BINGO!" she called back and didn't miss a step.

"Bitch created a willing army of Supernaturals, and is making sure they'll all be loyal to her," he said with disbelief.

"Yeah, an why I gettin a feelin she gonna throw our lot under a bus?" Michael asked with his voice trembling.

"Because she has heavy hopes that this'll also give her some political gain. You basically told us that she's some sort of prodigy. I don't doubt that she truly does have a plan for everything. A sad story can be used to sell votes and gain influence. Who knows what she'll do with us after she's done."

Michael swore. Chloe continued to cry and it sounded as though she was also trying to be quiet. This was not a good place for the empathic child. Sadie wanted to comfort her, but wasn't sure Michael would want her near his sister after the damage she had already caused. The hopelessness of their situation was as infuriating as it was frightening. All her fault...

Fester and Chloe, they both needed to live through this. If they were hurt and Sadie could have stopped it...she wouldn't be able to live with the added guilt. Her heart was simply too heavy with the feeling already.

The Supernatural Uprising Novels

Sadie's War
Tara's Escape
Sarah's Nightmare

Dedications

This novel has been made possible by the friends and family who have supported my love of writing since the beginning. Whenever I doubted myself and wanted to quit, these wonderful people ensured that I never gave up.

Frankie Cochran, my husband and biggest supporter. He refused to let me quit, even when it was what I thought I truly wanted.

Orion and Kieriana, my two beautiful children who are always ready for any fantasy tale!

Nicole A. J. Haeussinger, my best friend who showed me a new way to create stories. Without her influence, this book might not have been written.

Ed D., a good friend and the first to read Sadie's War. Ed helped me to keep my momentum during the final rough draft.

Jody and Gene Kim-Eng, two great friends who always were willing to listen to me babble and offered some much needed advice.

Ian S. Caldwell, a friend who drove me insane during early editing, and at the same time showed me how to look at my work from a different persepective.

Claudia Taake, my amazing editor who was a huge asset with the Gutter dialect and her professionalism saw me through the final stages.

I love you all!

Chapter 1

"That there been Tom spot."

Sadie lifted her head in the direction of the woman's loud raspy voice. "Are you talking to me?" she asked.

"Yeah I talkin to ya, girlie. Ya shit sittin in Tom spot. Ya ass gotta get gone."

"Sorry," she said as she began to pack up her things. It was her first night on the streets and Sadie didn't know that there were rules about where everyone slept. "Where do I get to sleep?"

"Ain't knowin, ain't carin," was the only response she was given. Sadie pushed away the overwhelming worry about how she was going to live outside. With her lips held tight, she packed up her sleeping bag and picked her cane out of her backpack. When she let the cane unfold the woman began to speak to her in a gentler tone. "Wait, I...I ain't got no clue ya been blind. Tom ain't gonna get mad ya stayin his spot one night. Hey, come back!" It was too late. She had already begun to walk down the line of homeless, away from 'Tom's Spot' and the woman who told her to move.

It wasn't that she hadn't been tempted to accept the woman's offer. However, her sudden change in tone made Sadie suspicious. Her mother had always taught her that kindness was never free and there was always a price to pay. There was no way that she was going to stay to find out what the loud woman, or 'Tom', would want for letting her sleep in that space. It would be safer to find somewhere else to sleep for the night.

Using her cane to guide her around the corner, Sadie tried to focus on which street she walked beside. The streets here were given either a number or a letter, and that made knowing where she was a little easier. Since this was her first day Downtown, she didn't actually have a clear picture in her mind as to where she was and the direction she faced. Determined not to panic under the circumstances she found herself in, she focused on searching for a place to rest. Panicking would do her no good in this strange place and the next day would bring with it plenty of time to get used to the directions here. All she could do now was cope with the new rules, large amounts of space, and immense crowds.

Downtown seemed at times to be far more dangerous than her parent's home had been. This was exasperated by the added difficulty of crossing the streets. Earlier in the day, it had taken Sadie several attempts before she knew how to safely navigate a crosswalk. There were a few fast moving vehicles that had almost hit her, and more than a few harsh words thrown her way, before she knew what to do. It seemed as though there was always something to be wary of and far too many things that she had yet to understand. What she had managed to learn thus far caused her to wonder if she would survive living outside.

Though a bit overwhelming, the strange noises and smells were easy enough to cope with. It was the people she encountered with whom she had the most difficult time learning to manage. Throughout her life, she had only known her parents. Now she was surrounded by people she couldn't comprehend. She didn't know how to respond to them, and they in turn didn't know how to respond to her. Their strangeness was more than a little frightening at times. So long as they left her alone, she felt that she would be alright.

Sadie found an empty patch of sidewalk, and laid out her sleeping bag. Folding up her cane, she leaned against the wall of a building and closed her eyes. With her body and mind weary from the long day, she slid down the wall until she sat in a heap. Her legs were sore from walking more than usual and couldn't support her weight any longer. Exhaustion began to set in and she yearned for a long night's rest.

It wasn't long before her stomach growled and she grimaced at the sensation. An entire day had passed and she still didn't know where to find food out here. Until she did, her belly would remain empty. With any luck, she would be able to find something to eat tomorrow. She wasn't sure how long she could endure the hunger.

The air held a bitter chill and Sadie shivered. She wondered if this was what autumn felt like and how far winter would be. Since she had never actually experienced the seasons before, she could only imagine what they were like. It didn't seem cold enough to make ice, so it seemed safe to assume that it wasn't winter yet. How would she keep warm when the weather drew colder? There were no sources of heat that she could find, only the chilling breeze that caressed her face and pulled at her hair. She couldn't imagine what it would be like for the air to be colder than it was now.

Slowly, Sadie slipped into her sleeping bag. She had reached out for her backpack to use as a pillow when she noticed that someone had walked up to her. Her hand froze as she waited for whomever it was to speak. Groaning from exhaustion, she hoped they wouldn't force her to move again. Her body was too tired to do anything other than sleep at this point. There wasn't much time to worry about such things before the sound of a paper bag crumpling came from directly in front of her face. The bag shook again and brought with it the unmistakable smell of food. Her stomach growled and she clutched her belly.

"Take it," a man said and she heard the bag shake again.

Hesitantly, Sadie reached out for the food, unsure if this was a test of some sort. The bag that was pushed into her hand felt warm and she swiftly brought it to her chest. "Thank you," she murmured. With the bag held in one hand, she reached for her backpack with the other to give the man some money. Her mother had left her with a few dollars to pay her first debts. Food, she had been told, would be her highest debt now that she no longer lived at home. The man moved away before she finished and she stopped in confusion. "I didn't pay you yet," she said as she turned her head in his direction.

"You don't have to," he said softly and continued to walk away.

Sadie was as confused as she was grateful. With the sleeping bag wrapped around her legs, she sat up and leaned against the building. Unashamed of her own hunger, she devoured the greasy meat between bread and what seemed to be cut-up potatoes. She had never been given odd food like this, though she didn't really care. It was enough simply to have something in her stomach.

It confused her that the man hadn't taken her money. You always had to pay for kindness in one form or another. This was a fundamental rule her parents had taught her ever since she was small. There was always a price and never an exception. Yet, this man gave her food and asked for nothing in return. The thought made Sadie fearful of him, more so than the others. If the man didn't take something now, would he insist on payment later? There were too many ways for someone to collect a debt. Worried about what he might ask of her, she decided that she would sleep somewhere else tomorrow. She was too weary to move now.

The food sat uneasy in her stomach. Slowly she lay down and placed her head upon her backpack. Curling up as much as the sleeping bag would allow, she waited for the air inside of it to warm up. Why hadn't he taken the money? Pushing such thoughts aside, she snuggled further into her sleeping bag. Tomorrow was a new day with plenty of time to worry about unpaid debts.

Although sleep had pulled her eyes closed, the sounds of the city swirled around and danced uncomfortably through her mind. Sadie had no idea what time it was, though it had to at least be night by now. The warmth of the sun could no longer be felt, and the air had cooled considerably. Yet there were still a lot of people walking around. Vehicles buzzed by, occasionally honking their horns. Music played from somewhere nearby and people laughed at things she couldn't fathom. There was no way to shut out the noise and she wondered how she was going to find rest.

Eventually, exhaustion won over the overwhelming sounds, and Sadie fell into a deep and restless sleep.

The chaos of the street echoed in her dreams, and her deepest fears revealed themselves. Her mind was full of turmoil as painful memories swirled around with a fear of the unknown. Among the torment that raged in her mind, she heard a baby wailing in the distance. Her heart broke at the sound and pain tore at her from the inside. The nightmares seemed to have no end until Sadie finally awoke. At first she lay still with her body and mind gripped in fear. It took a moment before she realized where she was and remembered how she came to be there.

That was when she smelled eggs. The scent seemed to come from somewhere close to her face. Hesitantly, she reached out her hand. The moment her fingers brushed the paper bag, her heart went into her throat and she pulled her hand back. That man must have come back and given her more food. Sadie wanted to cry. What did he want from her? Unsure of his motives, she decided not to take the offered food. She didn't want to increase whatever debt she already had with this man. If she was quick to leave, then maybe he could be avoided.

Sadie struggled to escape from her sleeping bag as quickly as possible. Her nose tickled when some of her hair brushed against her face. She ignored the annoying strands and rushed to pack up her things. Her breath came out hard, and her heart felt as though she had been running. Without knowing when the man may come back, she needed to leave as soon as possible. There was no time to waste.

"Aren't you going to eat?"

Sadie froze. His voice sounded like the man from the night before. A burning heat rose up in her stomach, and her pulse quickened further. He was still there and refused to allow himself to be avoided. How cruel her fate to hand her such misery. Nervously she licked her lips and tried to steady her breathing.

"No," she said quietly as she rolled up her sleeping bag.

"Why not?"

"Because I don't have anything other than a little bit

of money to give you for it."

"I don't want your money." Sadie heard the food-man shift his weight.

"What do you want?" Her voice almost came out as a whisper. Her hands and body trembled as she fumbled with the ties to her backpack. She knew that if the food-man planned to hurt her, then she must be prepared to run away. There was no way to tell how dangerous he could be.

"I just want you to eat," he said sadly.

"And after that?"

"I don't want anything from you."

Sadie could hear his clothes rustle and shoe scrape the sidewalk as he turned to walk away in the same direction as the night before. "I don't understand!" she called out after him. There was no response as his footsteps carried him away into the chaos of Downtown. The sound of the traffic ensured that she couldn't hear him for long. The city moved on around her, and she was left to sit in stunned silence.

Unable to ignore her hunger, Sadie quickly reached out for the bag. Perhaps if she left this area for good after her meal, then the food-man wouldn't be able to find her again. After that, the food truly would be free. Her fear of what the food man would demand easily overrode how wrong she felt to not pay the debt. She reasoned that it would be better to save herself the agony and simply leave for good.

Sadie needed to learn more about this unusual and intimidating Downtown place. She wasn't sure she wanted to, but her survival depended on it. Her mother never explained the rules, and she didn't trust anyone enough to ask. She wanted to go home, though that place was far more dangerous than Downtown could ever be. How was she going to manage such a task? She blinked back the tears that threatened to fall. Now was not the time to cry.

With her hunger satiated, Sadie brushed her hair back into a pony tail. Anxious to move on, she finished attaching her sleeping bag to her backpack and pulled out her cane. She needed to find a restroom and then learn how to properly get food. Neither was going to happen if she continued to sit on the sidewalk.

In her distress, Sadie found herself wandering aimlessly until she accidentally bumped into a woman. Hastily she asked where she could go. Ready to burst, she rushed in the direction the woman told her. The directions led to a store with restrooms. There had been no time to repay the woman and she made it just in time.

Sadie was proud of herself when she was able to buy some water at the store as well. The clerk seemed happy to help and his kindness was repaid with her purchase. She reasoned that in a store they needed to be kind so you would buy their products. Such reasoning allowed her to feel far less suspicious of the clerk than any others who might offer assistance.

The rest of the day crept along rather slowly. Sadie's mother had given her a cardboard sign when she dropped her off the day before. Her task, she was sternly told, would be to hold the sign. The money she received as payment would buy items such as food and water. Always one to obey her mother, she found a spot to sit in and dug the sign out of her backpack. The indentation near the top told her which way to hold the flimsy board. A small tin box, also given by her mother, was placed on the ground in front of her feet. Hoping that she did everything properly, she carefully reviewed her mother's instructions in her head.

Once she was satisfied with her setup, she allowed herself to relax. She used her rolled-up sleeping bag as a seat and leaned against the side of a building for comfort. The shift of the sun from one side of her body to the other notified her when several hours had passed. It seemed that so long as the sun was around, then she would easily be able to tell the passage of time. The temperature shifted between morning and evening with the weather starting off cool, warming up during the day, and then finally cooling off again. While this method of telling time seemed interesting at first, it quickly became bland and her interest waned after the second day.

To ward off the monotony that followed, she listened to the conversations of the people who walked by. While a few gave her dollars or coins, most paid her little attention and she was content with that. After her near-miss with the food-man, Sadie didn't want anyone else to give her more than her due.

Listening to these strange people actually helped her to understand some of the world of Downtown, and what to expect. Hopefully this, too, would help her to survive this place. Unfortunately their words would sometimes cause fear to rise and showed how dangerous this world could be.

"There's a new shop down on fifth. They have the cutest little dresses!"

"Hey, get ya hearin? Chris got nabbed by them cops. Jackass been gettin into trouble all o'er. HA!"

"That bitch picturin I gonna be lettin her fuck 'round, she gettin pound on!"

"Cherry ain't so bad. Her sister gonna fuck ya up true."

Most of the people here had a strange way of talking, though they were easy enough to understand. There were times, unfortunately, when Sadie wished that she couldn't understand them at all. They all sounded angry when someone was well, or happy when someone was hurting. Most people were only interested in what they could get from others. They preyed upon each other and reveled in causing pain or grief. There were several occasions when people laughed specifically at her, as though her blindness was somehow amusing. Some were even angry about her in particular. She couldn't understand where the animosity came from, though their comments still stung.

"Get ta lookin at her, man. Maybe bester ya gone an get her datin ya. It ain't same, cause she ain't never gonna get seein ya face!"

"Fucking bums been gettin them angles. Blind? Please! Bitch ain't never gettin nothin from me."

People here were just as cruel as her parents. It was easy to imagine that everyone must be like that wherever you go. Their cruelty and selfish behaviors intimidated Sadie, and she wanted nothing to do with any of them. There were a few instances where someone would wish her well as they handed her money. It was rare, however, and the only time she heard anyone say something nice. Perhaps it was what they were supposed to do when they paid her; just as the store clerks were nice when she paid them. It was simply the way of things out here.

For several days, life continued without incident. Convinced that it wasn't safe to pick a permanent location just yet, Sadie tried not to stay in the same spot every day and night. Instead, she built up a daily routine that allowed her to take care of herself and do her job wherever she found herself. She learned about various places to buy food and was happy how simple such a task was to accomplish. When she had the extra money, she could also get herself and her clothes clean. Her desire for cleanliness was almost as strong as her desire for solitude. With no way to escape the crowds, at least she could be clean whenever possible.

After a while Sadie began to feel comfortable with her situation. Living on the streets definitely seemed safer than living at home. On the street no one hurt her or forced her to do things she didn't want to do. For the vast majority of the time, she was ignored and that gave her a certain amount of comfort. She had figured out how to get what she needed to survive and was content to continue life in this manner. Here, she finally felt free.

A gentle breeze blew across her face one morning as she sat with her sign. Smiling, she turned towards the breeze and closed her eyes. The air felt good as it brushed her cheeks and pulled playfully at her hair. The sensation reminded her of something she had only done a few times at home.

Long ago, she learned how to feel the shapes of everything around her when playing with the air. To Sadie, this was as close to seeing the world as she would ever be able to achieve. For reasons she couldn't fathom, her parents would become angry when she did this. Their cruel punishments could still be felt even now. Would someone become angry with her out here? Air moved more freely outside than it did inside, and she doubted that anyone would notice if the currents were to shift.

Still she worried. Playing with the air wasn't without risk. When listening to people around her, Sadie learned about people called 'Police' and 'Cops' who would stop others from breaking the law. It wasn't hard to figure out that 'law' was another word for 'rules' and she was terrified of disobeying them. If playing with air was against the law, then she could potentially find herself in a lot of trouble. On the other hand, she reasoned that it would be safer to know more about the world around her. Eventually, she decided that it would be a good idea to at least learn if anyone would be bothered by her playing with the air. Her survival might depend on the information she could glean.

Leaning against the wall behind her, Sadie concentrated on the air currents. Gradually, she began to feel where the air touched a surface and where it flowed freely. When the air was pushed around by movement, it was recognized as swirls through space. It didn't take long for her to have a 3D model of the immediate area. As more and more objects came into focus, she found herself smiling proudly. At first she could only tell the general shapes of people walking by. Eventually, more came into focus such as a box-like object between her and the street. The street itself was difficult to detect due to the amount of air pushed about by the vehicles. When they were still, however, it was easier to tell where they were and the general shapes that created them.

Sadie smiled widely. This, she realized, would definitely make crossing the street easier. While playing with the air did cause it to move about her in an unnatural manner, nobody seemed to notice. Listening to the city while she held her sign had grown dull. Now that she could easily see her surroundings, it should make her days somewhat interesting. Maybe there was more that could be done with the air if she practiced dutifully.

That night, as Sadie waited for sleep, she actually felt happy. It was a new sensation and one that she hoped to feel again. It was now possible to see what went on around her without facing any consequences for using the air. Her parents couldn't hurt her here; they were gone from her life now. At first she had been horrified that her mother left her in this insane place. Now, she knew it was something to be grateful for. Her life was better here.

A shiver ran through her body, and she wondered if she could somehow warm up the air around her. The weather had become steadily colder each day. The air sometimes stung her skin from the temperature and it didn't feel safe. Without the courage to ask someone where to go, Sadie was worried about what she would do when winter finally came.

She knew she would need to find out or face the possibility of freezing to death.

Chapter 2

Sadie had never been so cold. Even through her layers of clothing and the sleeping bag, the bitter morning chill crept in to bite at her bones. She shivered and tried again to warm the air around her. It was futile. Only moving would warm her frozen flesh. Before she could rise, however, the sound of footsteps approached. Her breath caught in her throat and she waited for whomever it was to continue on. The sound of a paper bag being placed close to her head made her pulse quicken. Had the food-man found her again? She hadn't heard him in weeks! Fearful of what he would demand from her now, she remained absolutely still and hoped that he would quickly leave.

Cautiously she moved the air around her, feeling for where he could be. From what she could tell, he simply stood beside her prone body and looked down. The dreaded bag of food was on the ground, about the same distance to her head as the one from all those weeks ago. She watched as the food-man moved in the direction of her feet and leaned against the wall a short distance away. She couldn't tell if he was watching her.

Sadie wished she could sense more details when she felt with air. The man standing by her feet seemed much taller than she, but she really couldn't tell much else about him. Many people wore thick clothing and she didn't know what shape their bodies might be underneath. If only she were able to see more with air, then she would be able to avoid people like him in the future.

It took a while for her to realize that he didn't plan on leaving any time soon. Eventually, she opened her eyes and sat up. Acting as though she hadn't noticed the food-man, or the bag, she continued with her morning routine. Unable to trust him, she continued to feel with the air while she brushed her hair. He barely moved other than occasionally putting his hand to his mouth and then exhaling heavily. The motion was accompanied by an unpleasant odor and she crinkled her nose. Downtown people were always acting strangely.

As she rolled up her sleeping bag, she could feel the food-man turn towards her. "Your breakfast is getting cold." She was surprised to hear a soft and gentle tone to his voice.

"I don't want any, thank you." she said quietly, turning her head slightly in his direction.

"You have to be hungry; hungry and cold."

Sadie was hungry and cold. The smell of the eggs and biscuit in the bag made her mouth water. "I'm fine," she lied.

"You didn't eat anything yesterday."

Sadie stood up and faced him, putting her backpack on as she did. "You were watching me?" she asked, her suspicions rising.

"I noticed you sitting with your sign, and later on noticed you hadn't moved until it was almost dark."

The fact that the food-man had been watching her flooded Sadie with anxiety. Her ears filled with the whooshing sound of her racing pulse and her breathing felt labored. She was now more on guard than usual. Everyone she encountered was someone to fear, yet the food-man seemed to frighten her the most. Not only did he insist on increasing her debt with him, but he just told her that he could watch where she went and she would never know.

"What do you want from me?" she asked as she shivered, more from the fear that had risen up than from the cold morning air.

The food-man sighed. "I don't want anything from you."

Although his voice sounded gentle and sad, Sadie didn't believe him. She said as much before turning away and hurrying down the street, her cane moving almost wildly before her. As she walked, she continued to reach out with the air to make sure he wouldn't follow. Thankfully he bent over, picked up the paper bag, and walked in the opposite direction with his head bent down. Sadie was glad he didn't follow her, and tried unsuccessfully to put him out of her mind. Perhaps now that she had outright refused his food, he would finally leave her alone.

What could he possibly want from her? Sadie knew that she had done nothing worthwhile to be shown such kindness. Yet, this was the third time he had given her food. Her lack of money rarely allowed for such luxuries. The food-man was right. She hadn't eaten the day before, nor had she eaten the day before that. Her stomach growled painfully at the reminder.

Now that she was safely away from him, she wished she had taken the food after all. Her stomach hurt from constant emptiness. She ate less now than she did back home, and her body suffered as a result. Lately she seemed to be paid less and less for her job. What little money she had now wasn't even enough to buy water. Thankfully she had thought to save a bottle and filled it up with the foul tasting water from a bathroom sink. It was disgusting and horrible but she was desperate. After she found a spot to sit with her sign, she dug into her bag and brought out the water. Careful not to drink too much, she took a sip and grimaced. She needed it to last all day and would have to conserve as much as possible.

Shivering from the sharp bite of the cold air, Sadie pulled up her hood. She rarely covered her head but today was an exception. The cold air made her ears sting and she wondered again what she would do for warmth. Heating the air around her wasn't working as well as she had hoped. There were fewer people on the streets the more harsh the weather became as well. Even those who usually slept there seemed to find somewhere else to go. With no idea of where they went, Sadie was left to follow on with her routines. The solitude she had long desired had come and she knew it wasn't good.

Sadie sat with her sign and let her mind wander for what must have been twenty minutes before a man came over. "You no sit here!" he yelled. He had a thick accent that Sadie had heard before, but couldn't name.

"Sorry, sir. I'll leave," she said and reached for her things.

"Wait a one-two. I show you where you sit."

Sadie gathered up her things and waited for the man to show her where to go. It wasn't long until she heard him call out to her, "Oi! Over here!" He was some distance away. Carefully she made her way towards him, clicking her cane around to make sure she didn't trip on anything. She didn't want to stir up the air again just so she could feel her way around. Without anyone to tell her the specific laws, she still wasn't sure if controlling the air went against them. It wouldn't be wise to risk bringing attention to herself. Her cane did an adequate job anyway.

As soon as Sadie neared where the man with the accent had called her from, she felt the hair on the back of her neck stand on end. Something didn't seem right. The man had been near where she now stood, she was sure of it. But now there were no sounds to tell her where he was, and she wondered where he had gone. Using her cane to locate the wall, she realized that she was standing in front of an alley.

"Hello? Sir?" Sadie called out but heard no reply.

An uneasy feeling fell over her and she quickly decided to find somewhere else to sit for the day. When she turned to go back the way she had come, strong hands grabbed her from behind. One hand was on her shoulder, the other hand across her mouth. She struggled and tried to scream as she was pulled back into the alley. The man's breath was hot on her neck as he let go of her shoulder to grab at her breasts. The motion caused her to remember her father and the lessons he gave her. Sadie began to panic as fury and terror were fueled by the memories. She couldn't bear to experience that ever again!

A desperate scream tried to escape only to be muffled by the man's big hands. He chuckled at her vain attempts to break free. It reminded her of how her father sounded when he would come for her. Her mind flooded with the memories of those horrifying nights. The streets were supposed to bring her freedom from such torment. She was away from her parents and the home that was her prison for so long.

This man wasn't her father. This man had no rights to her body. She owed him nothing as he had given her nothing. She wasn't about to allow him to take what he wanted, for free or at all. No matter what happened from this moment on in Sadie's life, she knew that she would never again endure the agony her father had placed on her so many times before. Her freedom held a value that no one could match, and she would defend it with every ounce of her being.

As the fury inside of her grew, her fear loosened its grip. By this point the man had her pinned against one of the walls of the alley. One hand continued to cover her mouth while his other hand groped and grabbed at her body. Her eyes stung with unshed tears as she called upon the air in a way she never had before.

The air currents shifted violently around her, and a furious wind blew the man away to thrust him against the opposite wall. The air was pushed out of his lungs as the sickening sound of bone breaking was clearly heard across the alley. The sheer force of calling such wind had taken a lot out of her, but there was no time to rest. Ignoring her fatigue, she used the air to see what was around her. She needed to know where he landed and what he was going to do next. It was surprising how much detail she could detect this time. Never before had the air shown her anything so clearly.

Slowly and deliberately, Sadie walked over to her cane and picked it up. She kept watch on the man and could hear him moan in pain. Without hesitation, she moved swiftly over to him and harshly pressed her cane into his neck. When he began to choke she relaxed the pressure slightly.

"Try that ever again and I will kill you." Her voice sounded hollow and cold. She didn't even recognize it as hers. Quickly she turned and walked over to where her backpack had been tossed aside. She didn't remember when it was pulled off of her and shrugged before she picked it up and put it back on her shoulders. The man rolled over and began to stand up with his hand held onto his side.

Sadie turned her face towards the man as he swayed. "You'll stay there a while if you know what's good for you." Once again she didn't recognize the sound of her voice. She refused to allow herself to worry about that now and instead moved through the alley, swinging her cane back and forth as usual. When she neared the entrance, the man had begun to move in her direction.

Immediately she pushed another strong force of wind at the man. The gust blew him up against what she figured was a dumpster by the foul stench emanating from it. Sadie resisted the urge to wince at the unpleasant sound of his body impacting with the harsh metal. Once again, the force used to create such wind took a lot out of her. She made sure not to let this weakness show as she strolled out of the alley and onto the sidewalk.

Her stride was wide and quick as she moved away from the horror she had almost endured. Never in her life had she used air in such an aggressive manner. She wasn't even sure how she managed to do so. What bothered her the most was how she sounded when she spoke to her would-be attacker. Her voice didn't sound the way it should. She almost spoke out loud to herself, to see if it had returned to normal.

Afraid that her voice was still not hers, she decided to stay silent. Her anxiety wasn't so much about what had almost happened to her. The man was no longer a danger and therefore easily put out of her mind. She was far more afraid of herself at this point. Throughout her life she had always been the only person she could trust. For someone who relied on what they heard to distinguish between one person and another, not recognizing her own voice was terrifying.

Her pace slowed as she put the alley and what that man had tried to do behind her. Using the air to see, she was able to avoid moving cars and other people. She tried to put her fears to rest with the knowledge that she saved herself. Regardless of how her voice had sounded when she did it, logically she knew that she was still herself. Not even the wind could take that from her.

Exhaustion crept in and she knew she needed to rest soon. As her weariness grew, she reluctantly released her hold on the air. Once more she was blind as the shapes of those around her could no longer be felt. She continued to walk, unwilling or unable to decide on a place to sit for the day. Her mind whirled about and she realized that Downtown truly was safer than home. At home she wouldn't have been able to force her father away in the same manner as she did that man. At home she would have been severely punished for refusing him at all.

The thought gave her little courage, however, as she realized she couldn't do what she had done in the alley out here on the streets. The Police and The Cops might come to hurt her then. To keep her secret, she knew that she would have to be more careful in the future. She not only had to worry about someone seeing her play with the air, she also had to worry about what her wind could potentially do to an innocent – if any existed.

Sighing, Sadie finally stopped walking. She almost lost track of where she was, and it took her a moment to get her bearings. As far as she could tell, she had walked seven blocks and had a good idea of where that placed her. The stores on this street didn't mind when she sat near their door with her sign. If she sat near an entrance then she would be able to feel the heat coming from inside the store when someone opened the door. She was likely to earn more money when sitting in such a location as well. It was far better situation than the one she just came from.

Sadie leaned against the wall of the nearest building and yawned as exhaustion washed over her. Today she would go to sleep earlier than usual. First, she desperately needed to try and make some money with her sign. Sadie didn't think she could go another day without eating. If the food-man came tonight then she would accept the food he offered. Her hunger was strong enough that she didn't care about debts or payment. She just wanted to eat!

The food-man didn't come, however. Instead Sadie worked until she had enough money to buy some food. After dinner she found a good spot to go to settle down for the night, even though the sun could still be felt. It had been an eventful day for Sadie. If the rest of her week went smoother, then she would be pleased.

As her eyes grew heavy and sleep began to envelope her, Sadie hoped to avoid another encounter with anyone even remotely interested in her for a long while.

Chapter 3

Nearly two months had passed and with them came a steady increase in cold weather. The days had become unbearable and the nights were worse. Sadie knew she had to find some sort of shelter soon. The weather would only become more severe the longer she waited. Alarm ran thought her when she discovered that during the night she had nearly frozen. Her face and ears were numb and little bits of ice clung to her eyelashes and eyebrows. Her concern for her body increased when she realized that she couldn't feel her fingers and toes as well. When she tried to move, her muscles stiffened and her joints ached.

There was no doubt in her mind that she couldn't sleep on the sidewalk anymore. The search for shelter had been put off for too long, and now she found herself needing it desperately. First, she needed to get her body moving and that wasn't going to be easy. Sadie finally realized how dire her situation had become. Painfully, she brought her hands to her face and cried for the first time since she arrived Downtown.

Fighting the anxiety that tried to take hold of her, Sadie struggled to get out of her sleeping bag. There were few pedestrians who braved the outdoors lately and so she was keenly aware of a stranger's footsteps as they approached. Her breath caught in her throat when the stranger paused mere inches from where she struggled. Anxious for them to either speak or move on, she listened intently as their shoes shifted on the pavement. She heard a sad sigh before a large gentle hand touched her shoulder. Without the strength to do more, she could only flinch in return. Sadie was unused to the touch of another and couldn't fathom what this stranger would want.

"You can't sleep out here anymore. Ya have to know that by now."

The sound of the food-man's soft voice was a shock

to Sadie. It had been so long since she last heard him that it seemed he had forgotten all about her. Apparently she was wrong. Her throat was sore from breathing in the cold winter air and she could only respond with a solemn nod.

"C'mon. We need to get you warm."

The food-man placed his hands under Sadie's elbows to help her stand. She jumped at his touch but reluctantly accepted his help. An intense pressure had begun to build in her head and she wasn't sure if she could stand on her own. Once upright she felt disoriented and her thoughts were hazy. The sense of helplessness that overcame her mixed with her desire to find warmth. When the food-man let go of her to gather her belongings she began to sway.

"Are you feeling OK?" he asked.

Sadie brought a trembling hand to her forehead but didn't say a word.

"It's OK. We'll get you inside. C'mon."

The food-man placed a firm hand under her elbow. She didn't object as he led her away, nor did she think about taking out her cane. The fog in her mind had grown and she couldn't think about anything. She unintentionally leaned into the food-man as they walked. It was difficult to keep herself upright. The bite of the cold winter air stung her skin and her desire to be warm was all that kept her feet moving. She focused on every step she took in an effort to stay conscious.

Without warning, the food-man paused and she lost her footing. He released her elbow and wrapped his arm around her waist as she began to collapse. Sadie's belongings fell to the ground with a thud. She allowed her head to roll back as a sense of relief flowed through her body. Falling was always a bad idea. The food-man gently placed a hand on her forehead and swore.

"Fuck me, you're burning up! Stay with me, girl. We're almost there."

His words barely registered as now he was only a voice in the distance. With her mind in a haze, he didn't seem real. She did wonder where she was for a brief moment. In her current state, however, she wasn't even fazed. Instead she allowed herself to be half led, half carried, into a building that was...somewhere. A small pang of fear gripped her as she crossed the threshold. *Is it safe?* She pushed the thought out of her mind and chased the fear away. The knowledge that soon she wouldn't be cold gave her the strength to continue.

The air inside, however, was hardly warmer than outside and Sadie felt her heart sink. The disappointment nearly caused her to give up and she missed a step.

"Just a little further, girl. I can't carry you and this stuff too. Just stay with me. OK?"

Sadie managed to nod a little. Exhaustion flooded her body and the only thoughts in her mind were for warmth and sleep. Her head hung low and bobbed with every fumbling footstep. A heaviness dragged her body down and her legs felt stiff under her body weight. Each step took an eternity. The food-man continued with his soft encouragements, though she hardly heard him.

"That's it. There's a few steps here. C'mon, you can do it."

Sadie tried to lift her foot up onto the first step but couldn't. The food man swore as she slowly passed out.

When Sadie awoke there was a bed beneath her and the weight of heavy blankets pressed down upon her body. She had no idea where she had been taken. A shiver ran through her from the cold that seemed to still cling to her bones. Her muscles ached and her hand trembled as she reached to touch her forehead. Gently she took off the damp cloth which had been placed there. With a strong desire to learn about what happened, she forced herself to sit up.

"Hello? Is anybody there?" Her voice shook with trepidation.

When there was no answer, that familiar fear rose within her belly. She tried to remember how she got to this place and couldn't. All she could recall was the food-man telling her he would get her warm. She was disappointed in his lie.

A door opened suddenly and someone entered the room. "Hey, you're awake." It was the food-man.

"It's just as cold in here as outside," Sadie said as she pulled off the blankets and began to swing her legs off of the bed.

"It's warm in here, truthfully. You're just sick. Ya have a fever and shouldn't get out of bed yet." The sound of water sloshing in a container was heard as he placed something down nearby.

Ignoring his suggestion, she continued to rise. "I have to use the restroom."

"Here," he said, "let me help you."

He was soon at her side and placed his hand firmly under her elbow. The ease at which he touched her was unnerving and she jumped in spite of herself. She felt his hand on her forehead and flinched again. There was no reason for him to touch her like that.

"Easy there...just checkin your fever. Seems to have gone down some but you're still pretty hot."

As she stood, she found she felt a little unsteady. Ignoring the dizziness that threatened to overcome her, she asked for her cane. The food-man let go of her elbow and soon she heard zippers open and close.

"It's in the left side pocket," she said, assuming it was her backpack which he searched. A moment later she heard the familiar clicks of her cane as it opened.

"Here you go," he said. She was grateful when the cane was gently placed in her outstretched hand. "I'm Fester, by the way."

No one had ever introduced themselves to her before. Sadie hesitated before giving her name. If she didn't answer him then he may become angry with her. Would he hurt her then? The thought sat uneasy in her mind. "Sadie," she finally said at a near whisper.

"C'mon, Sadie. I'll show you where the bathroom is." Food-man Fester took up her free hand and she flinched yet again. "Easy there. I'm just going to lead you is all."

Sadie heard the door open and allowed herself to be led. The same odor that she had smelled when people put their hands to their mouths repeatedly wafted from the next room. She wondered what they could possibly be doing that would cause such an unpleasant odor.

As they continued into the room, she heard someone swear.

"Jesus fucking Christ, Fester! She been blind too? The fuck!" This other man sounded as harsh as his words.

"Shut the fuck up, Michael," Fester said softly and continued to lead her to the bathroom. When he stopped he said, "The bathroom's on your right. Do you want me to show you where everything is?"

"Thank you, I'll be fine."

Sadie reached out to feel for the doorway to the bathroom. As she eased herself into the small space she heard heavy footsteps coming from the direction of the other man. Feeling nervous about the stranger's sudden movement, she swiftly closed the door behind her. The ensuing argument between Fester and this Michael was audible through the thin wall. The contrast between the two men was unmistakable. Michael's tone was harsh and he spoke the way most Downtown people did. Fester spoke in a way that was easier to understand and with a hint of sadness behind his tone.

"We all gonna get fucking sick an it gonna drop on ya head, Fester."

"I told you, I don't think she's contagious."

"Yeah, when ya ain't got no clue 'bout a thing, I gonna get ta worryin."

"Don't. It'll be fine."

"I ain't able ta 'ford fucking missin works, man."

"I said, 'It'll be fine.'"

There was a brief pause. Sadie heard Michael's heavy footsteps through the wall as he paced. "Ya gotta get mindful, Fester. It ain't just ya ass be livin up in here. I gotta be keepin in mind 'bout Chloe same. The girl ya got up in there ain't keepin here."

"If I leave her out there then she'll die, Michael! I can't do that!" It was the first time she had heard food-man Fester raise his voice. The sudden change in his tone made her flinch. "Fuck! Don't ya get it?"

"Oh I get it. I get ya gone all wrapped up in ya head, so's ya ain't never seein hows ya getttin the rest us in riskful danger from bringin her up in here!"

As Sadie flushed and washed her hands, the sounds in the bathroom muffled the argument outside. She had barely paid attention anyway. She knew she couldn't stay here even before Michael had said so. The rest didn't make a difference. Did he say that she was a danger to these people? It was probably better that she didn't know more. When she opened the door, she was glad to hear that the two men had stopped arguing. Michael let out a sound of exasperation before his heavy footsteps carried him away.

"Don't pay him any mind," Fester said softly before taking her hand. She tried in vain not to flinch this time and allowed herself to be led back into the bedroom. Once inside, he led her to the bed and gently took her cane. As she sat down, she heard the man zip her backpack shut.

Sadie almost asked for her things so she could leave. The heaviness which coursed through her body, followed by the pressure in her head, told her that she should lie back down instead. Once this fever went away, then she would leave. She didn't want to make her debt with Fester any higher than it already was. It would be impossible to repay him for what he had done, let alone what he might try to do in the future. The thought of having to pay such a large debt increased her fear. What would he ask of her?

"C'mon, Sadie. You should lie down and try to get s'more sleep. Don't worry about what Michael said. OK?"

Sadie nodded as she lay down and closed her eyes. Fester laid the blankets over her, and pulled them up to her neck. While still afraid, she knew that there was nothing she could do about her current situation. The hatred she felt for her weakness burned with a passion as hot as her fever. Rest and warmth were the only remedies.

The sound of water sloshing around startled Sadie. Opening her eyes, she remembered that Fester had placed something with water down earlier. She listened as he wrung out a cloth and placed it on her forehead. Once more, she flinched uncontrollably. Closing her eyes again, she found that the cool water on the cloth actually felt good against her aching forehead. She swallowed and winced at the soreness in her throat.

"I can't pay you for this," she whispered hoarsely.

"Don't sweat it," Fester whispered. "Just try and get some sleep."

Sadie nodded and listened as he moved to the door and out of the room. Unhappy that she was stuck in this place, she couldn't ignore the weariness that had fallen upon her. At least the bed was far more comfortable than the sidewalk she had become accustomed to. By the time she heard the door close she was already drifting off to sleep.

Chapter 4

Sadie awoke to the sounds of both men arguing. Even though they were in the other room, she could still hear them perfectly. The only explanation she could think of was that the door must be open. Moving slowly so she wouldn't make a sound, she gingerly got out of bed. Her body was finally warm and her head felt normal. It was time to leave. Hopefully Fester wasn't going to ask too high a price for his debt. She wasn't sure how she would handle such a situation.

"No no no no NO!"

"Michael, please! She won't last out there. Let her at least keep here for the winter."

"Fester...I wanna get ta helpin the girl. We just ain't able ta get feedin 'nother fucking trap, s'pecially with money all fucking tight this year. We near ain't got none ta feedin we own selves, an keepin the damn heat steady."

"Fine, then she can have my share."

"Ya ain't gonna get fucking crazy an shit."

"Crazy would be sending her out there. Crazy would be allowing her to die of starvation. Crazy would be allowing her to freeze to death, when we coulda actually gone done a thing 'bout it!"

"What goin on up in here with them shits, Fester? What be 'bout the chick been gettin ya all wound up?"

Sadie paused in getting herself ready. She hadn't paid much attention to the conversation until this point. Now she was curious about what Fester had to say. Why was he trying so hard to help her? When he didn't answer Michael, Sadie went back to getting herself together. She continued to move silently so as not to interrupt.

"Fester," Michael said after a moment, "she just 'nother runway kid stuck in the Gutter."

"So am I."

Even from this distance, Sadie could hear Michael

sigh. When he spoke again his tone was gentle. It was something she hadn't expected from him. "Look, I get ya be carin 'bout her. But we just ain't got no money for them shits."

"If you would let me get a job, Michael, then we would have more money."

"I done been tellin ya, it morer true ya gonna get ta feedin ya brain. 'Sides, who gonna get ta hirin a fucking goth punk same ya ass?"

"Lots of people would, and I can do both! If ya all worried 'bout me bein found out, I can go back to what I did 'fore."

"No!" Michael's tone was back to being harsh. "If the cops nab ya– "

"I can outsmart the cops."

"No! We ain't gonna fucking share no more words 'bout them shits! We ain't that desperate."

"I am."

Sadie was ready to leave but paused before opening the door. Fester sounded so sad, so defeated, with that last statement. Why was he desperate? What was it Michael didn't want him to do? The questions continued to build in her mind. She shook her head to clear her thoughts. None of it mattered since it was time to go. As she walked through the doorway, the sounds she heard meant that both men had turned to face her.

"What's all this?" Fester asked. She heard his footsteps as he neared her.

"I'm better now. Show me where the door is and I will leave."

Sadie flinched as she felt a hand touch her forehead. "Easy, it's just me. You still have a slight fever."

Sadie feared that he would try to get her to stay. Her debt was high enough. "Just show me where the door is and tell me where we are. I'll be fine."

"Sadie..." Fester whispered.

"I don't want more debt with you." She tried not to tremble and nearly failed at keeping her voice steady.

"'Sadie' been ya name?" Michael sounded unexpectedly gentle when he spoke to her.

"Yes."

"Get ta listenin, Sadie, it night an it snowin up heavy out there. Keep here for a night, an if ya wantin, in the mornin we gonna help ya get on, an find ya homeless shelter ta keep for winter. K?"

Sadie considered what Michael had said carefully. If they could help her find shelter then she would be able to survive the cold weather. Perhaps staying one more night would be worth the added debt, assuming she ever found a way to repay them. With no other viable option, she decided to agree. Cautiously, she nodded her head.

"C'mon," Fester said as he guided her back into the bedroom. "Let me help you with your stuff."

Sadie allowed herself to be guided. When she felt Fester slide off her backpack she couldn't help but flinch again. He needed to stop touching her, but since she was leaving she kept silent about the discomfort. Instead she took off her coat and turned to face him. "Can I..."

"What is it?" Fester asked gently.

"I'm afraid to ask after all you've done."

"Go ahead and ask. You don't have to be so 'fraid here, ya know."

Sadie was already in so much debt, a little more couldn't possibly make much of a difference. "I was wondering if I could wash myself and my clothes. It's been a while." She felt heat rise in her cheeks from embarrassment.

"Are you sure you don't want to eat first? You've been in bed for half a week and haven't had a thing to eat."

The mention of food made Sadie's stomach growl. She was extremely hungry, but after overhearing the argument she didn't want to ask for food. Instead, she shook her head and ignored her empty belly. "I just want to be clean," she said

"OK. Let me get you something to change into." Drawers slid open and closed nearby while she grabbed her bag of toiletries from her backpack. "Here, they'll probably be big on you but it should work for a one-two."

Sadie held out her hands and Fester handed her the clothes. She held the clothing, and her bag, close to her chest. "Where do I go?"

"The bathroom. C'mon, I'll show you."

Fester gently took her elbow in his hand and guided her towards the bathroom. She couldn't hear Michael and wondered if he was still in the room. It was tempting to use the air to see. Fearful of making Fester or Michael angry with her, she resisted the urge. Sadie still felt that it was best to keep her ability to play with the air a secret. By tomorrow these people wouldn't be in her life anymore.

As he led her to the bathroom, Fester told her where the faucet in the shower was and how to turn it on. "Do you want me to do it for you?"

Sadie shook her head. "No, thank you. I can do it."

"OK. Well there's a clean towel on the wall to the left."

"Thank you," she said as she eased into the bathroom. After she put her things on the sink, she carefully closed the door behind her. Then she felt around the bathroom for the towel and shower. She managed to turn on the shower without too much difficulty, and undressed while the water warmed. The three layers she wore made her feel too warm and she anxiously peeled them off. Layers were great for when it was cold outside. In the home, however, they were stifling.

Sadie wrinkled her nose at the odor that emanated from her body now that she was no longer covered. The smell was worse than she initially thought and her desire to get clean increased tenfold. She grabbed her shampoo and soap out of the bag and climbed into the shower. The warm water felt good on her skin and she took a moment to enjoy the sensation.

As she bathed, Sadie was dismayed with how thin she had become. It felt as though she had been gradually shrinking. Now her bones noticeably poked through her skin, and she could hardly feel any muscle on her arms and legs. She knew that the past week she had spent in bed didn't help. The day before Fester found her, she hadn't eaten anything either. That was far too long to go without food, and she wasn't sure when she would be able to get more. She needed to find a way to eat soon; her body couldn't possibly grow any smaller.

The air in the bathroom was warm from the steam, however it still felt cool against her wet flesh. Wishing to enjoy the warmth for as long as possible, Sadie quickly dried her body. Tomorrow she would have to be cold again. Even if she found shelter, she had heard Michael talk about paying for heat. She knew that she wouldn't be able to heat whatever shelter they helped her to find. She didn't know how to do so in the first place. Even if she did, how would she get the money? Never before had she needed to worry about heat. Now she found that missing information to be dangerous. Her parent's lessons had never prepared her for living on her own. Forcing such thoughts from her mind, she continued to get dressed.

The clothes Fester had given her to wear were far too large for her body. The pants had a drawstring on them which she pulled as tight as the fabric would allow. Even so, they fell down whenever she let them go. Carrying her things and holding up the pants seemed like an impossible task. The shirt was so big that the neckline fell off her shoulders. She felt clever when she managed to use her hair-tie to secure it. With no other way to improve the fit of the clothes, she opened the door and reached for her cane.

Michael whistled and Fester swore as she exited the small room. "Fester?" She took a few ginger steps in his direction.

"Yeah, I'm here," he said as he moved over to her.

"The pants are too big. I can't carry my clothes to wash them, and hold up the pants."

"Don't sweat it. I'll get your clothes."

Sadie once again thought about her increasing debt. "I can do it. I just need something to hold up the pants."

"I said, 'Don't worry about it.' C'mon, sit at the table and let me get ya a thing to eat." Sadie heard Michael walk towards them as Fester gently guided her forward.

"I...I don't have any money, Fester. I can't pay for the food."

"Will you stop with that! I keep on telling you, I don't want your money."

Sadie was confused and frightened. If he didn't want money, then what did he want? Kindness is never free. She knew that beyond a doubt. So what was it that Fester truly wanted in return for all that he had done? Her body shook as possibilities floated around in her mind. Most of them were horribly unpleasant and the idea that she might have to...to...*it's too much!*

They didn't walk far before Fester placed her hand on the back of a chair. Trembling, she pulled out the chair and sat down. Her hunger was to the point of being extreme. While she didn't have money, her body couldn't afford for her to turn down food either. Silently, she folded up her cane and placed it in her lap. She had no choice but to accept what he gave her, despite her inability to pay.

Michael walked over to Fester and whispered. Although she wasn't close to them, she could hear him clearly. "Fester, get ta listenin, I ain't got no clue she been heavy bad. She gonna keep here. We gonna picture a thing out."

"Thanks, Michael." Fester said.

Sadie tried not to panic at Michael's words. If she stayed here then her debt would not only be with Fester, but with Michael as well. For all she knew, she already had a debt with Michael for staying while she was ill. His words echoed through her mind. *'I ain't got no clue she been heavy bad.'* What had she done that had been bad? Sadie hated her confusion with a passion and decided that no matter what, she had to leave in the morning. She couldn't afford this. None of it.

A plate was placed before her on the table and a fork was gently pushed into her hand. "Eat," Fester said softly, "it's spaghetti."

Pulling herself closer to the table, Sadie began to eat. Fester's footsteps headed towards what seemed to be the bedroom she had stayed in. As far as she could tell, she was alone in the kitchen. With her hunger as it was, she found it difficult to eat slowly. The spaghetti was delicious. Grateful for the food, she felt that whatever debt she might have to pay would be worth it. Maybe.

One thing was for certain. Sadie never would be able to pay for any of this. If Fester demanded that she pay him in one of the horrible ways, then she would do whatever she could to stop him. She knew that she would never pay a debt that way again. *Never!*

Chapter 5

Sadie had nearly finished her spaghetti when she heard movement from behind her. She paused and listened as her clothes were gathered up. She knew that she should be the one to wash them. It wasn't fair to let Fester do it for her. Plus, she really didn't want him to. It was her responsibility, and she had enough debt with this man to last her a few seasons. She wondered why he kept helping her when she had told him repeatedly that she couldn't pay for it.

"Ya gonna get ta washin ya beddin so's ya launderin." Michael called from the other room.

Sadie heard Fester walk back towards the bedroom. This was yet another thing to add to her debt: Fester had to wash the sheets because of her illness. The fact that she wasn't clean while sleeping in there didn't help. When she started making money again, she would have to make sure she saved up for bathing more often. She disliked the filth that clung to her body and the odor which assaulted the senses.

Sadie heard the sheets rustle as they were tossed on top of her clothes. She sat and listened as Fester moved through the kitchen and pulled something out of a cabinet. The jingle of coins sounded as though they were in something made of glass. Standing up, she let her cane unfold while holding onto the pants with her other hand. He was not going to add her laundry to the debt.

Sadie turned towards Fester. "Let me wash the clothes," she said.

"Ya sure? You still need to rest a one-two."

"Yes, I'm sure."

Fester sighed. "Uh...OK. Why don't you come here and hold the door while I grab everything. I'll carry the clothes for you."

She walked in the direction of his voice. There were a few distinct clicks as he unlocked the door. When it was fully open, she held it with her foot while he gathered everything. Fester grunted as he carried the clothes passed her, and she followed him out of the home.

"Uh...I don't know how to show you where to go. Both of us sort of have our hands heavy full."

"Just direct me with your voice. I don't need to be led around by the hand all the time."

"Yeah, I guess not. OK...come this way. Steady, there are about 4 steps you have to go down. A little further. Yeah, right there. Mindful of the step."

Sadie was fascinated with how carefully he guided her with his words. She knew how to navigate steps and how to keep from bumping into things. It wasn't as though this was a first for her. Yet, he insisted on warning her of every obstacle as they walked to the laundry room. He was so thorough that she almost didn't need her cane to keep from tripping over something. His concern was amusing.

"What are you smiling at?" He asked as she heard a door open to the left.

"You don't need to warn me about everything," she said.

"Right. Sorry. Here, can you hold this door open?"

Sadie reached out for the door with her cane hand. Feeling where it was, she held the door open with her foot again so that he would have enough room to pass. The musty odor of laundry detergent and dust wafted from the laundry room. One of the machines was going through its cycles when they entered, and the floor felt gritty beneath her bare feet.

Fester opened two of the washers while she folded up her cane. Holding the pants and cane in her left hand, Sadie began to put the clothes in the washer. She didn't want him to have to do that for her as well and shooed him away when he tried to help. Fester chuckled and she turned to face him.

"What's funny?"

"Nothing, it's just that most people would be more than happy to let someone else do their laundering. Yet ya seem to insist on doing it yourself."

"It's my responsibility."

Fester didn't respond to the statement. Instead he asked, "So, how do you measure the laundry detergent if you can't see what you're doing?"

Sadie thought it was an odd question. "I use my finger to let me know when the cup is full."

"I get that," Fester said as he closed the lids to the washers. "Ya know, Michael said you can keep here. You don't have to go to a shelter tomorrow."

"I'm still going."

"Why? I know we don't have much but it's better than the shelter."

Sadie hugged herself with her right arm, her left hand still held the pants and cane. She knew that this conversation was bound to happen eventually. They were due for it. Finally, they were going to discuss payment, and then she would know exactly what she owed these men. Closing her eyes tight, she took a deep breath and tried not to tremble as that familiar feeling of fear steadily rose up within her.

Fester's steps were almost completely muffled by the sounds of the washers as he stepped in close to her. "Please...please stay."

Sadie took a step back. "Fester, I can't afford the debt I already owe you. I can't owe you anymore."

"What is with you?" Sadie heard the frustration in his voice as he walked first away from her and then back towards her. "I keep telling ya that you don't owe me a thing. I don't want anything from you. I just want to help."

Sadie said the quote she had heard many times in an almost monotone voice, "'Kindness is never free. There is always a price.' I haven't repaid you for your kindness. For the food. For staying here. For everything. I don't have anything to give you for it all."

"Sadie, where did you learn that kindness is never free?"

She hesitated before responding. "My...my parents...they taught me that lesson many times." Her voice shook with fear and she inhaled deeply. "I can't afford any more debt," she whispered.

Fester stepped close to her again. "Your parents were wrong, Sadie. Kindness can be free. You really don't owe me a thing. I would never ask anything from you that you weren't steady ta give."

Sadie tried not to tremble and to keep her voice steady. It wasn't easy. "What about Michael?"

"Michael, too."

She didn't know how to respond. *'Kindness can be free.'* Was that truly possible? He said her parents were wrong. She never imagined that her parents could be wrong about anything. Throughout her life, whatever they said had been concrete. They backed up their truths with harsh lessons. Even during her time Downtown, Sadie had never experienced anything that would suggest they were wrong. Except, that is, for Fester.

She jumped as she felt him touch her arm lightly. "Listen, Sadie. Just do me a favor and keep it in mind. I really don't want you to leave."

"Why?" The word came out as a faint whisper. She didn't trust her voice.

"Because I don't want to see you suffer no more. Just...just keep it in mind. OK? Will you at least do that?"

Sadie nodded.

"Good. C'mon. Let's go back to the apartment. You came without your shoes, and its chilly up in here."

Again Sadie nodded. She turned around, opened up her cane, and left the laundry room without any guidance from Fester. Her mind reeled with all that had happened thus far. It seemed as though the people of Downtown were just as strange inside their homes as they were on the street. The two of them walked back to the apartment in silence, which was fine because Sadie had never liked to talk anyway. Things had become increasingly confusing and more frightening than she was ready for. Her world had just been turned upside down and she wasn't sure what to do about it.

At the moment, she wasn't sure about anything.

Chapter 6

When they were back in the apartment, Sadie headed directly for the bedroom. Her mind was still swirling and she continued to hear Fester's voice float about in her head. *'Kindness can be free.'* She had never considered the possibility that kindness could be free. It sounded absurd. Her mind was buzzing so much with what Fester had said that she almost didn't hear Michael call out to her.

"Hey, Sadie. C'mon an get ya sittin with us o'er here for a one-two? Huh? Ya ain't gotta stick to them cramped room there."

His voice was gentle and Sadie didn't know what to make of it. Usually when he spoke to Fester, his tone was loud and harsh. She couldn't decide if the gentle tone he used was genuine or if he was deliberately trying to gain her trust. The fact that he was so inconsistent with the way he spoke made her instantly not want to trust him, not that she ordinarily would anyway. Trust just wasn't something to give another person. Not wanting to be rude, she turned towards him.

"OK," she said. "Where should I sit?"

"A chair, to ya right an ta me a lil."

Sadie felt for the chair with her cane. As she moved towards it, her cane hit something in-between the chair and where she had heard Michael. Carefully, she sat and avoided banging her legs on the object in front of her. The chair was comfortable enough, though the fabric felt rough beneath her fingers. Sadie folded up her cane and put it in her lap. She heard Fester move and sit somewhere to her right. Slowly she took a deep breath.

"So Sadie," Michael said, "get ta tellin us a story 'bout ya ass."

"I don't know what to say," she said softly.

"Well, get startin on easy shits. Same bein, where ya done comin from?"

Sadie sat completely still. No one had ever asked her where she was from. Likewise, no one had ever told her. "I...I don't know," she finally said.

"How do you not know where you're from?" Fester asked her. His voice sounded disbelieving.

"I just don't," she said.

"K, I get it. Ya ain't got no clue where ya done comin from," Michael said, "How old ya then?"

Again, Sadie didn't have an answer. "I don't know that either."

"Wait! Get ta holdin them crazy shits a God damn one-two." Michael's voice was low but he didn't sound pleased. Sadie wondered if she had done something wrong without knowing it. "I gettin ya ain't got no clue where ya done commin from. The hell ain't ya got no clue how old ya got?"

Sadie flinched. "I just...don't."

"K, when ya birthday?" he asked.

Sadie felt uncomfortable with these questions. Her confusion had built upon itself and again she felt that familiar fear rise up in her belly. Perhaps if she sat still and didn't reply then they would grow bored and stop asking such strange things.

She heard Fester shift his position. "Sadie, do you know your birthday?"

She shook her head 'no' and licked her lips nervously.

"Fuck me," Michael whispered. "Ain't nobody never get ta tellin ya?"

Sadie shook her head again. She could tell by Michael's tone that something about this was wrong, though she couldn't understand why. It would've helped if she at least knew what a 'birthday' was. Her parents had never told her about a birthday. No one on the streets had ever asked her about it. The same with where she was from. All she knew was that she wasn't from Downtown.

"When was the last time you celebrated your birthday, Sadie?" Fester asked gently.

"Fester, I...I don't know what a 'birthday' is."

A chill went up Sadie's spine as both men swore softly. She really didn't understand what was happening, nor why they seemed so upset with her. Her confusion brought about a special kind of pain. She hated admitting when she didn't know something that was seemingly obvious. What should she do now? No one had asked her these types of questions before. It was an entirely new experience, and one that was highly unpleasant.

An uneasy silence fell over the room. Sadie's fear crept up her body, filling her with dread. She listened to the sounds the two men made in the ensuing silence. They moved about in their seats, but she couldn't guess as to what they were doing. If they were outside, she would use the air to see them. She knew that wasn't possible while in the apartment. There wouldn't be a way to hide the unnatural air currents inside the room.

In the quiet of the apartment, Sadie heard someone approach from the opposite side of the room. The footsteps were so soft that she had hardly heard them at all. Out of habit, she turned her head slightly towards the newcomer's direction.

"Michael?" The girl's voice was soft and unsteady.

Michael swore under his breath, and Sadie heard him get up from his seat. "Chloe," he said gently, "ya s'posed ta be in bed."

"I was, but I gettin nightmares."

"OK," Michael said with a sigh. Sadie heard him walk over to Chloe. "I gonna get ta sittin with ya ass for a one-two."

"Who her?"

"Oh, she Sadie. She gonna keep with us for winter." Chloe sounded happy as she said, "Hi, Sadie."

"Hello," Sadie said softly.

"Chloe," Michael said, "Sadie ain't gonna be seein ya wavin to her. C'mon, get on back ta bed."

Sadie listened as the two of them moved off into another room. She suspected that was the direction of Chloe's bedroom. Michael used the same gentle tone with Chloe as he had done with herself. What was it about her and Chloe that caused him to change how he spoke? Who was this 'Chloe' person anyway? She had heard the name mentioned before, and now found herself curious.

"She sounds small," Sadie said, hoping to alter the conversation.

"She is small," Fester said.

"Who is she?"

"Michael's little sister."

"Oh."

Neither she nor Fester spoke for several minutes. Sadie was thankful for the silence. It would've been unnerving to expose yet another subject she was unfamiliar with. What was a 'sister'? She also felt that more questions would've been overwhelming after their recent conversation. It was difficult to understand why these concepts had been important in the first place. The men's reactions were excessive from her perspective.

"Sadie," Fester asked softly, "didn't you ever get to wonderin how old you were?"

"No, not really." She heard Fester sigh. "I don't really see why it's so important. How old are you?"

"Sixteen. My birthday is in March."

"I...how old do you think I am?" Sadie was unsure if Fester would be able guess.

"Honestly, you look like you're 'bout fifteen or sixteen," he said.

"OK." Sadie said, satisfied with the answer but confused by his sad tone.

She didn't know people could tell how old she was by looking at her. It was something she had never imagined was possible. Obviously there were times where her blindness put her at a huge disadvantage. There seemed to be more to learn about the world than she had originally surmised, and even more she needed to learn to detect. She detested her lack of knowledge. It was easy enough to figure out information based on what others had said while nearby. But, now she was being presented with ideas which had never been mentioned around her. It made her feel far too uneasy.

"Hey," Fester said, "your clothes should be ready for the dryer."

"OK"

Sadie stood and opened her cane. She was careful not to bump into the object in front of the chair. It was probably a small table like the one her parents owned. She resisted the urge to reach out and inspect it further. There wasn't a need to know more about the furniture in the apartment since she was leaving in the morning anyway. Fester stood with her and they both headed for the laundry room in silence. Sadie discovered that she was actually curious about this age thing.

"How old are Michael and Chloe?" she asked.

"Michael is about to turn twenty and Chloe just turned nine."

Sadie opened the washing machine and listened for where Fester opened the dryer. She was glad to hear the creak of the dryer door opening had come from behind her. It would make it easier to transfer the clothes from one to the other. As she had done earlier, she folded up her cane and held it in her left hand along with the pants.

"Nine sounds very young." She said absently as she gathered the clothing.

"It is young. Chloe's still a child."

Sadie couldn't figure out why Fester continued to sound sad. She felt perplexed by all of it, and tried not dwell on the matter. There would be plenty of time for that later. For now, she wanted to focus on not dropping any of the laundry on the gritty floor.

It was difficult to find the opening to the dryer because the door was higher up than she had anticipated. Usually she would feel for it with her left hand, but that was busy holding up her pants. She managed, and the two of them finished the laundry relatively quick.

Sadie wondered what Fester thought about. Her curiosity of him had begun to grow and she wanted to know why he was sad. The thought of asking terrified her and she kept her questions to herself. Throughout her life, she had learned that it was usually better to not speak unless asked a direct question. Since waking up from her fever, Sadie had found herself talking more than usual. It was odd and made her feel uneasy with herself. Asking Fester a personal question was probably unwise and so she kept her mouth shut.

When they were back in the apartment, she quickly went over to the bathroom and gathered her shampoo and soap. As she walked through the main room, she heard Fester and Michael whispering furiously on the other side. They were too far away for her to clearly make out what they were saying, and she figured that was probably the point. So she let them be and made her way into the bedroom.

After putting her things back into her backpack, Sadie dug out her hairbrush and sat on the bare mattress. She crossed her legs so she was comfortable and began to brush her hair. Her mind wandered as she worked at the pleasant task. The shirt she wore began to slip off one of her shoulders like it had earlier. Surprisingly the hair band had fallen off, and she absently wondered where it wound up.

As she brushed her hair, Sadie tried to understand Fester. She remembered all the times he had given her food and had never taken anything in return. Much of what he had said tonight echoed through her mind. *'I don't want to see you suffer no more.'* *'You don't have to be so 'fraid here.'* *'Sadie, do you know your birthday?'* *'I keep on telling you, I don't want your money.'* *'I just want to help.'* He wanted to help and she couldn't understand why. Michael had asked, *'What be 'bout the chick been gettin ya all wound up?'* Try as she might, she couldn't figure him out.

Sadie took one of the extra hair bands off from the brush's handle and put her hair up. She felt uncomfortable with it down like it had been. The shorter hairs on the front of her head always fell in her face, tickling the tip of her nose. As she finished with her hair, she heard a gasp from behind her. Her back had been to the door and she turned to face whomever was there.

"Sadie!" Fester exclaimed from the doorway, "Oh my God!"

"What? What's wrong?" Sadie asked with growing alarm.

"You're back! What the hell happened?"

Sadie heard Fester move swiftly across the room and the mattress moved suddenly. He crawled onto the bed and sat behind her. Gently he moved her hair and touched where the neckline had exposed her flesh. She jumped at his touch and her fears increased.

"What are you doing?" She asked.

"It's just...your back! Your shoulders! What happened to you?"

Sadie's confusion added itself to her growing fear. Michael's heavy footsteps approached the bedroom. "What do you mean?" she asked, worried that something had happened to her without her knowledge. "What's wrong?"

Michael was at the door now and he let out a slow whistle. She felt the mattress move as Fester shifted his weight. Frantically, he called Michael over and showed him her shoulders and back. She flinched hard as one of them pulled the shirt collar away from her body.

"My God!" Michael sounded shocked. "Them shits been coverin plain cross her back!"

"What?" Sadie was on the verge of panic at their reactions to her back.

"Ya fucking scars, Sadie. Where ya done gettin them scars?" Michael asked.

"You mean the bumps?"

"Yeah, Sadie. 'The bumps'."

The realization of what they saw dawned on her. She let out a sigh of relief now that she knew nothing was actually wrong. Her back had bumps and ridges all over it. She could feel them when she bathed and knew exactly what they were from.

"They're from my mother's lessons," Sadie didn't know what the big deal was. Surely they had them too. "Like how she taught me that kindness isn't free. It was my payment."

"Your payment for – is this what you thought I would do to you if you didn't pay me for the food?" Fester sounded upset.

Sadie turned towards him again and frowned. "It was one of the possibilities."

Michael let out a sigh. "Them shits done been

worser than I been picturin," he said softly.

"Sadie," Fester said softly. His voice sounded even sadder than before. "Sadie, I'm never, ever, ever, never gonna do nothing like that to ya. Not ever. Never!"

"You...you wouldn't?" Sadie was confused.

"No," Fester whispered. "Never."

"She lookin not sure," Michael said. "I ain't believin, she true findin them words confusin. Shit!"

Michael's loud footsteps moved away from the bed and out into the other room. He swore a few more times before he was finally quiet. She didn't know what to think about their reactions. Michael seemed angry. Fester seemed sad. They both had sounded shocked. Sadie couldn't understand why.

She had assumed that her life was normal. Before, she thought that everyone had grown up the same. In the span of one night she had learned how wrong she truly was. What else in her life was wrong? What else was unusual? How often would she find herself this confused? The fear she usually felt had changed. Now, not only was she afraid of being hurt, but she also realized that her situation was far worse than she had thought.

"You know you didn't deserve that, right?" Sadie thought she heard Fester's voice crack. "You didn't deserve any of that."

Sadie didn't say anything and instead faced forward, her head bent. Her mind swam with all that she had learned that night. Suddenly feeling exhausted, she closed her eyes. The men's reactions made her uneasy. She was confused, worried, and didn't know what to expect. Not knowing how to proceed, she came to realize that it might be best if she stayed with them for a while. She didn't believe for a second that their help truly was free, but she did realize that she needed it. There had to be a way to repay them, and she would endeavor to discover what that was.

"I'll stay." Sadie's voice was unsteady as she spoke. The words terrified her.

"What?" Fester asked.

"I said, 'I'll stay.'"

Sadie feelt the mattress move as Fester shifted so that he was seated next to her. "Thank you," he said. She heard him sniffle.

"Are you getting sick?" She hoped she hadn't given him her illness.

"No, I'm fine. Probably some winter allergy."

Sadie suspected that he wasn't being truthful. His breathing sounded uneven through the sniffling. If he wasn't sick, then he was crying. She reasoned that he couldn't be crying. Crying was for when things were seriously bad, and right now things seemed alright. So that meant he was sick. Sadie again hoped that it wasn't she who had made him ill.

If Fester told her the truth about never hurting her, then she wanted to make sure she never hurt him either.

Chapter 7

After a few minutes of listening to Fester sniffle, Sadie had begun to feel restless. Purposefully, she stood up and headed towards her belongings. The small size of the room allowed her to find the backpack without the aid of her cane. After she put her brush in the bag, she stood and leaned against the wall. The silence that had fallen over them brought with it an uncomfortable tension. Not wanting the awkward silence to continue, she felt the urge to speak.

"Are you sure you're OK? You sound like you have a cold."

Fester let out a short laugh. "Yeah, I'm fine. Hey, let's go back on to the living room."

Sadie nodded and felt around the bed for her cane. It took only a moment to find it before she left the bedroom. She heard Michael blow out air and smelled that unpleasant odor again. Smoke filled her lungs and she coughed involuntarily.

"What is that?" she asked, her voice strained.

"Sorry 'bout them shits," Michael said. "I gonna get ta switchin on them vent from the kitchen. It gonna get the fucking smoke gone."

As Sadie made her way to the couch, she listened to Michael head towards the kitchen. It wasn't long before she heard the whir of a fan. When she and Fester sat down, she folded up her cane and silently placed it in her lap. She was nervous and didn't know what to expect. A few minutes passed before Michael sat across from them with a sigh.

"Sadie," he said gently, "ya gotta get ya shit ton o' help. Pro fucking help."

"Michael!" Fester sounded offended.

"It gotta be tellin, Fester. She gotta get her a shit ton o' serious fucking help, 'cause all the shit done to her. Sadie, ya even gotta clue how fucking heavy ya situation got?"

Sadie nodded. "I think so."

"I ain't sure ya do. Ya ain't seein what we be seein whens we got eyes on ya. If Fester ain't gone an get ya whens he learn ya freezed, ya be fucking dead 'fore now. Ya get them shits? Dead. Ya done been freezed ta dead. An ya seemin so's ya gonna break in bits. Ya ain't seein how crazy fucking bony ya got. It plain ya been fucking starvin ta dead, Sadie! An ya back! What them piece o' shit assholes done ta ya? Fuck!"

Michael's outburst made Sadie flinch. She heard him get up and begin to pace about the room. Shivering in spite of herself, her eyes filled with tears and she told herself not to cry. There was no need to cry.

"I know things are bad." Sadie winced at the unsteadiness of her voice. "I know I almost died. I know I'm starving. My eyes can't see my body, but I can feel it. I know how skinny I am. I can feel my bones where they shouldn't be. What I don't know is what I'm supposed to do now. Nobody really told me what I'm supposed to do."

Tears spilled out of her eyes. She began to understand now why both men were so upset. For some reason they didn't want her to die, and neither did she. Something about her bumps, her scars, alarmed them. She thought again about what Fester had said in the laundry room. *'I don't want you to suffer no more.'* They were angry that she had been hurt. So many things were confusing and made little sense. For the first time in her life, Sadie thought about asking someone for help. She was still afraid.

"I know my life is wrong," she said, "I know that. But please understand, I don't know what to do. I don't know how to ask for help. I was never allowed to ask for it. I've been told what to do my whole life. No one tells me now and so I just don't know. There's so much that's strange to me and I hate that! I need someone to tell me what I'm supposed to do now that I'm alone. I...I can't ask for help. What else am I supposed to do? I'm trying to survive on my own, but I really don't know."

Sadie put her hands to her face and sobbed. The tears flowed so freely that it felt as though they would flood the room. Her pain poured out of her as she cried. When Fester touched her hands she flinched again. She wished he would stop touching her so freely. He spoke to her in that same soft gentle tone but with more force behind his words than before.

"Sadie, listen to me. Listen carefully. We will do what we can to help you. K? But, you're going to need to trust us. Do ya think you can do that?"

"I don't know."

"Can you at least try?"

Sadie nodded her head. "Yes, I can try," she lied.

Fester breathed out a sigh of relief. "Thank you."

Sadie stopped crying, though the shaking continued. For her entire life, the only thing she trusted was the knowledge that at any moment someone would come to hurt her. Now, Fester asked her to trust them. She wanted to believe that she would be safe, but that seemed unlikely. These people seemed nice but that could easily be as false as any other lie that one could tell. No, the truth was that she couldn't possibly trust them. It was a fact that she would keep to herself for now.

"It done gettin heavy late, kids." Michael sounded as exhausted as Sadie. "We gotta get sleeps."

"Yeah," Fester said, "I'll go get the laundry from the dryers." Sadie started to get up to go with him. "No, Sadie. You should stick there. Michael needs to talk to you about a thing."

Michael swore under his breath. "Yeah," he said reluctantly, "we gotta share words. I ain't fucking likin them shits. If ya gonna get ta keepin here, then there a thing I guess ya gotta learn 'bout us."

As she waited for him to continue, Sadie heard Fester leave the apartment. Michael paced about the room and several long sighs escaped his lips. Whatever he had to say was obviously difficult to reveal. Finally he sat down next to her.

"It my lil sis, Chloe," he said slowly. "She been a... sensitive kid. Ya get it? She been gettin ta feelin all them shits 'nother peoples be feelin. Them fucking emotions an whatever. It what them callin 'empathy', an she ain't picturin how ta control them shits. Ya get it?"

"She...she can feel what I feel?"

"Yeah. She gettin bad dreamin tonight, an I picture it cause ya be gettin so damned 'fraid. Even sleepin she gettin steady ta feelin emotions. Thing been, ya done been gettin a shit ton o' shit put on ya ass. I ain't got no clue hows ya life musta lived. I sayin it 'fore an I sayin it 'gain: ya gotta get ya pro help, girl. An up in here on the one-two, ya gotta get learnin ta controlin them damned emotions."

"Control emotions?" Sadie turned towards him. "What do you mean?"

"Fester an me been knowin how it done an shit. We gonna teached ya same. Laters. We gotta get ta sleep. It just...I ain't never gonna get ta lettin my sis be hurtin an shits. I fucking gotta get ta keepin her riskless. Ya get it? Ya gotta get so's ya ain't gonna be damn 'fraid, so she ain't gonna be neither. Ya get it?"

Sadie nodded in understanding. "Empathy."

"Yeah. Empathy."

"How did she get it?"

She heard Michael shift again. "She done been fucking birthed with them shits. She one o' them damn Supernaturals. Ya ain't never tellin us story ta nobody neither. Them be sure for true words, Sadie. Ya ain't never sayin a thing ta fucking nobody."

"Why? What's a 'Supernatural'?"

Michael sighed heavily. "Supernaturals been peoples who done been birthed with power, Sadie. Them ain't all that usual, an them gov'ment...them done been gettin all wound up doin experiments on 'em. Them lovin ta get 'em hurtin. I gotta get steady ta doin whatever it takes so's Chloe gonna be clear them fucking shits."

Michael stood up and slowly walked away before Sadie could stop him. She found that she didn't want him to leave yet. There was so much she needed to know. Was she one of those Supernaturals too? Perhaps the men could help her to understand why she could control the air. Up until now, she thought she was all alone in that endeavor.

The thought made her pause. They were already helping her so much, and she didn't want to burden them any further; especially since now she had to worry about some government and their experiments. She definitely couldn't ask for help with something so dangerous. Besides, she didn't trust them. If Michael thought her wind would make Chloe unsafe, then he would make her leave. She didn't want to go back out into the cold; she didn't want to die.

Fester came into the apartment and Sadie heard the click of the lock. Soon after, he dropped the laundry onto the floor near her. She heard the rustling of fabric as Fester separated the sheets and blankets from the clothes. Determined to do the rest by herself, she scooted towards him and felt for the pile.

"What are you doing?" he asked.

"I'm trying to grab my clothes so I can fold them."

"Oh...here."

Fester moved the pile so that it was under Sadie's hand. She heard him head towards the bedroom and assumed that he went to put the sheets back onto the bed. While she folded the laundry, she thought about everything that had happened that night. It had been one of the most intense nights she had ever experienced. Even though she hadn't been awake for all that long, her mind and body were exhausted.

She placed the folded clothing on the couch and grabbed something to wear. It would be nice to be able to walk without her pants falling down. She left her cane on the couch with the clothes and walked over to the bathroom. The apartment was small and didn't have much furniture. It was a relief to no longer need to use her cane constantly.

When she came out of the bathroom, she heard Fester moving about in the living room. Cautiously, she walked in with his clothes in her arms. Her own clothes were loose on her body but at least the pants didn't fall down whenever she let them go.

"You can have these back," she said.

"Oh, thanks. Just give me a one-two. I put your

clothes in your bag, I hope ya don't mind. The bed is made up so's you can go to sleep whenever ya done. I'm just fixing up the couch for me. I...uh...put your cane on the coffee table."

"I'll sleep on the couch."

"Don't lose your mind, Sadie," Fester said as he took the clothes from her.

"Fester, I can sleep on the couch. I don't want to take your bed from you."

Fester sighed. "It's OK, Sadie. Seriously, go sleep in my room. I'll sleep out here. It's fine."

His persistence annoyed her, and her face felt hot with the anger that began to rise. "No, Fester, it's not fine! You said you didn't want to take things from me. Well, I don't want to take things from you either. I'm not going to take your bed from you. I can sleep on the couch."

Sadie didn't know what had come over her. Never before had she spoken so forcefully. She had grown tired of Fester doing everything for her as though she couldn't do any of it herself. Michael was wrong; she wasn't going to break. She desperately wanted them to stop treating her as though she were made of glass. They needed to realize that she was more capable than that.

"Ok," Fester said after a moment. "You can sleep on the couch."

"Thank you."

Feeling victorious, Sadie smiled and moved towards her prize. To keep from bumping into the coffee table, she used her foot as a guide. After feeling for the pillow and laying her head down, she pulled the blanket up to her chin and let out a sigh of contentment. Relief filled her now that she was able to sleep indoors. The couch was far more preferable to the sidewalk. She knew that by morning her body would be thankful as well.

"G'night, Sadie," Fester said softly. She heard him turn off a switch.

"Good night, Fester."

Sadie lay there for a while before sleep took her. It was apparent that her life had just changed dramatically.

She didn't know what to expect anymore. For the first time that she could remember, she wasn't terribly afraid of the unknown. She smiled and closed her eyes. Hopefully that feeling would last. It didn't seem likely though. These people were very strange. Still, it was nice to have hope for once.

Maybe Fester was right. Maybe she really didn't need to suffer anymore.

Chapter 8

When Sadie awoke the next morning, the only noises she heard came from outside. They were a distant reminder of the street. Although the sounds were muffled, her sensitive ears could easily pick up the cars going by. Nothing was to be heard from inside the apartment and she assumed everyone was probably still sleeping. She rolled over onto her back and stretched. Letting out a peaceful sigh, she relaxed into the couch and let her mind wander.

It had been only a short while ago that she had been freezing to death and near starvation. Now such unpleasant matters no longer plagued her mind with worry, doubt, and fear. She was safe from the dangerous weather and people outside who may try to cause her harm. Her body was surrounded by a blissful warmth that chased the winter chill from her bones. Best of all, her belly was full and she suspected that food would no longer be an issue. The security of this home was an exceptionally welcome respite from what life had granted her thus far.

As she rolled back onto her side, some of her hair fell in front of her face and tickled her nose. Sadie brushed the hair away, but it was persistent. It was as though these strands of hair had a mind of their own and were intentionally antagonizing her. After the third time the hair fell to tickle nose, her annoyance with her misbehaving locks had grown. She let out a frustrated sigh moments before a tiny mischievous giggle came from directly in front of her face. The sound caused her to frown with worry.

"Who's there?"

"Guess!" A small voice said.

"Chloe?"

The giggle turned into cheerful laughter which eased Sadie's concern. She couldn't understand why Chloe showed such genuine happiness, but liked it all the same. There was another quality to the laughter that she couldn't quite grasp, and it filled her with an unusual sense of joy. It reminded her of when times were gentle. With her parents, it was rare that Sadie was allowed to experience such moments. That this child laughed with carefree abandon brought a wide smile to her lips.

Michael's heavy footsteps were heard as he swiftly entered the room. "Chloe, I been tellin ya, let Sadie sleeps."

"It's OK," Sadie said with a wide smile. "I'm already awake. Apparently, Chloe finds something funny about that." The comment brought a renewed fit of giggles from the younger girl.

Michael let out a grunt as he walked over to Fester's room. He banged loudly on the door which caused Sadie to jump in spite of herself. "Fester! Time to get up, man."

A very clear "Fuck you!" came from the bedroom as Michael continued to pound on the door. Not understanding what was happening, Sadie cringed at the noise. Something had to be wrong for the harsh man to bang on Fester's door in such a way. Without warning it opened harshly, hitting the wall with a thud. "The fuck, man!"

"Got calls from Dan. I gotta get ta works, an I gotta be havin ya eyes on Chloe."

"Thought it was your day off," Fester said groggily.

"I fucking tellin ya, bro, Dan callin. José gettin all sick, an I gonna get ta takin the damn o'ertime."

Fester let out a series of swear words as he shuffled off towards the bathroom. Michael walked into the kitchen, and soon the sounds of dishes and other items being moved about could be heard. Everyone was awake and starting their day. Sensing that this must be the usual time to rise, she stretched once more and then sat upright. Something suddenly bounced on the cushion beside her, causing her to jump before freezing in fear. Chloe's giggle reassured Sadie that it was she who had caused the cushion to move. Instantly, she let out a sigh of relief.

"Guess what, Sadie!"

"What?"

"It snowin last night!" Chloe sounded excited, though Sadie didn't understand why.

"I know."

"Wanna get playin in it after breakfast?" Chloe asked as the cushion moved again.

"Play? In the snow?"

"Yeah! It be fun!"

Fester shuffled loudly out of the bathroom. As he moved across the room, it sounded as though his feet never left the ground. The man didn't seem to wake up easily. Chloe jumped off of the couch and ran in his direction. Sadie was again startled by the sudden movement.

"Fester! Fester! Fester!" Chloe's excited tone baffled Sadie.

"What? What? What?"

"We gonna go out after breakfast? Pleeeeeease! I wanna get playin in the snows with Sadie!"

Sadie felt around the coffee table until she found her cane. It was her turn to use the bathroom. As she walked across the apartment, she could hear Fester groan.

"It's too early for that, Chloe. Maybe after lunch. We'll see."

Chloe whined with disappointment and objects were placed on the table. As Sadie walked into the bathroom, she heard Michael tell Chloe it was time for breakfast. Closing the door, she shook her head with disbelief. She couldn't understand the enthusiasm of the child. Her confusion was deepened by the suggestion that they play in the snow. While she knew what snow was, she had never experienced it before. She couldn't imagine how one would play with it. Then again, she didn't have much experience with playing at all. Growing up, she was rarely allowed to.

Chloe's voice was barely muffled by the thin wall as she asked Fester question after question about Sadie. It was obvious that she had somehow caught the girl's curiosity. Listening to her tone, she wondered if this was what childhood was supposed to be like. Happiness, excitement, curiosity, play... These were things she hadn't experienced much at home and she liked that Chloe was able to. With a slight smile on her face, she carefully walked out of the bathroom.

"Sadie," Michael called from the living room. "I get ta sharin words in a one-two?"

"Sure," she said and headed towards his voice.

"Get ta listenin," he said quietly, "Chloe gettin heavy curious 'bout ya. The kid gonna maybe get ta askin a shit ton o' questions. Ya gotta be fucking mindful what ya sayin ta her."

Sadie frowned and began to feel nervous. "What do you mean?"

"I sayin, I ain't letin her get ta fucking picturin ya past yet. She been easy young for them shits. Ya able ta be sharin words with her. Just...just I ain't want ya tellin no story 'bout any bad shits. K?"

Sadie knew by now that her past bothered the two men. The fact that Michael wanted her to keep it from Chloe was a little confusing. Based on the men's reactions from the night before, nearly everything in her past would be considered *'bad shits'* by them. It was obvious by his tone that this was something important to him, so she nodded. The least she could do was obey his wishes as a guest in his home.

"Good. Thanks." Michael moved away from her and called out, "I gettin gone. Laters!"

As the front door opened and closed, Sadie made her way to the couch. Her mind wandered and she thought about Chloe. Obviously, Michael was protective of the girl. That was something Sadie could almost understand. What bothered her was that if she hadn't been too young to experience her past, then why was Chloe too young to know about it? She couldn't make the connection between Chloe's age and the knowledge about her past, so she put it out of her mind for now. Regardless of the reasons behind his request, she would do what Michael asked. Truthfully, she would prefer the past to stay in the past. Not talking about it suited her just fine.

When her cane tapped the side of the coffee table, Sadie put it away. She moved over to the couch and started to fold the blanket. The men were helping her by letting her stay with them for the winter. The least she could do was pick up after herself.

"What are you doing?" Fester asked as he came over to her.

Sadie thought it was obvious. "Folding the bedding."

"Here, let me do that." She felt a tug on the blanket that she held as Fester tried to take it from her.

"I can do it, Fester. Let go."

"Don't sweat it. Go eat. There's a bowl of cereal all ready for you on the table. I'll take care of this stuff."

Sadie's face felt hot from frustration. "I'm not helpless, Fester. I can fold the bedding."

"I get it," he said softly. "Just go eat."

"Fester..."

"Go, Sadie. Your cereal is gonna get soggy."

Sadie's anger added itself to her frustration. Remembering what Michael had said the night before about her emotions, she figured it would be best to let Fester have his way. An argument would only get her more upset. Not fully understanding how empathy worked, Sadie didn't want to take a chance of hurting Chloe with her frustration. She let go of the blanket and turned to pick up her cane.

"Thank you," Fester said as she moved towards the kitchen. Sadie didn't respond.

Once again, she found herself completely perplexed by Fester. Would he try to do everything for her all winter? She understood a little about why he gave her food on the street. She understood why he had brought her to his home. She thought she understood why he wanted her to stay. These things were all made clear to her last night. What she didn't understand was why he insisted on folding the bedding. It was the same with washing her clothes and who was to sleep on the couch. He even tried to help with something as simple as walking down a hallway.

It felt as though Fester believed that she was incapable of performing simple tasks. Did he truly feel that way? She knew how to take care of herself. Her parents had made sure of that. There were plenty of chores that she could do on her own. She knew that she hadn't fared so well out on the street. But in a home, it was different; in a home she knew what needed to be done and how.

Finding the kitchen table wasn't terribly difficult. Sadie had only been to it once, and so she wasn't entirely sure where it was. The apartment was small enough that she didn't have far to walk and soon she felt her cane hit one of the table's legs. Still frustrated about the bedding, she refused to ask Fester which side of the table her cereal was on. So, she felt around until she found it and then sat down with a sigh.

The cereal was too sweet for her, but she didn't want the men to become angry with her for not eating. Food was expensive and wasting it wasn't wise. So she ate slowly and let her mind wander. Fester made her feel helpless and she couldn't understand his motives. It tended to frustrate her more than anything else. Did she miss something? Was there a rule here she didn't know about? She realized no one had told her the rules of the apartment. She would have to remember to ask later, when she wasn't so upset.

"Sadie?" Chloe asked timidly. Sadie wondered if something was wrong.

"Yes, Chloe."

"Ya K?"

"I'm fine."

"Why ya so mad at Fester?"

Sadie put down her spoon and sat back in her seat. "He wouldn't let me fold the bedding."

"Yeah, but, why ya soooo mad at him?"

There were many reasons why she felt angry. After her conversation with Michael, however, she didn't want to speak them out loud. She finally settled on "I don't know."

Sadie heard Chloe's feet slide across the floor as she slowly shuffled towards her bedroom. Her behavior was confusing at best. Why did Chloe sound so timid? Did she think that Sadie was going to hurt her or Fester? While that would've been her reaction to anger, she didn't realize that someone as happy as Chloe would also react that way. Sadie feared anger because it usually meant that there would be pain. Did Chloe fear it for that reason too?

With a deep breath she tried to calm herself. It didn't work. That familiar feeling of fear steadily rose up within her. She wondered if the men had lied. Was it as safe here as they made it seem? Logic would say that if the men weren't violent, then Chloe wouldn't be afraid when Sadie became angry. Perhaps Fester didn't want her to be able to take care of herself so that she would remain helpless. If that were true then what could he possibly be planning? Did he want something from her after all? The possibilities that floated about in her mind were terrifying. What did he want?

Not wanting Chloe to feel her fear, Sadie tried even harder to control herself. The problem was that she hadn't yet learned how. Fear was such a common emotion for her that she didn't know if she would ever be able to master it. Sometimes fear was even a comfort. Even so, she didn't want to hurt the girl in any way by sharing these emotions. The thought of hurting Chloe, however, caused Sadie to become even more afraid.

Fester's footsteps came towards her and she stiffened in her seat. "Sadie?" He sounded concerned. "Sadie, what's wrong?"

"Nothing, I'm fine," she lied. She went back to eating her breakfast.

"Sadie, I can see on your face that you're 'fraid. I don't know what's got you so spooked but you need to calm your mind. Chloe will feel you if you don't."

Sadie didn't say anything. She continued to eat as though Fester hadn't spoken at all. She didn't want to talk to him right now. He was the one that she feared. Muffled sounds of Chloe crying came from the child's bedroom. Sadie turned her head in the direction of the sound. Now it was her turn to be concerned.

Fester swore. When he spoke his tone was gentle and his voice soft. "Sadie, please calm down. Please. Take deep breaths. Think of something you love or something that makes you happy. Anything. You just need to calm down. Please, Sadie!"

Fester's footsteps moved quickly away from the table and towards the direction of Chloe's room. A moment later she heard a gentle knock on a door. With the door open Sadie could fully hear Chloe's crying. The sound caused sadness to mix in with her fear, and she knew she needed to learn how to control herself for the girl's sake.

"Why she so 'fraid? Why Sadie so 'fraid?" Chloe asked over and over in between sobs.

"Shhhh. It's OK, Chloe. It's OK. C'mere. Just keep your mind on what I'm feelin. K? Just focus on me. It's OK. It's gonna be OK."

Sadie sat at the table and focused on her breathing. While taking slow deep breaths, she tried to think about something that made her happy. At first she couldn't think of anything. Happiness wasn't something she experienced often. For a while, memories of the unfamiliar emotion eluded her. Then she remembered how she felt when she heard Chloe laugh. Sadie had to block out the sounds of the girl's sobs, much as she had on the streets at night, to focus on the memory.

It wasn't easy to do, but the fear began to subside and a lighter mood gradually came over her. All she could think of was Chloe laughing this morning and how it had made her feel. A tear rolled down her cheek as she began to feel guilt for making the child cry. Knowing that wouldn't help her, Sadie pushed the guilt aside and again focused on the memory of Chloe's laughter.

Eventually Chloe's sobs began to lessen and Fester continued to speak calmly to the girl. Sadie took another deep breath and tried to rid herself of the remnants of the fear. It was difficult, and in the end she couldn't get rid of it completely. Hoping that it would be enough, she stood and headed in the direction of Chloe's room.

This area of the apartment was still new to Sadie. Gently she swung her cane back and forth, hoping not to bang into anything. She didn't want to break their possessions or knock one of them over. When she reached a wall, she felt around for Chloe's door. Using

Fester's voice to guide her in the right direction, she found the room and then stood inside the doorway. Their clothes rustled, and she assumed that they had turned towards her.

"Are you OK, Chloe?" Sadie asked.

"Y-y-yeah," Chloe said in a shaky voice.

"I'm sorry, Chloe. I don't know how to control my emotions yet."

"Why ya so 'fraid, Sadie?"

Sadie knew she had to choose her words carefully. "It's hard to say. I'm afraid a lot."

"But...but why?"

"Lots of reasons. Sometimes I think of something and get scared, like today."

"Chloe," Fester said softly, "some people just get 'fraid easy. Sadie is like that. OK?"

"K," Chloe said, seemingly accepting the explanation.

Sadie felt relieved. Fester was obviously better at answering questions than she was. As she turned to leave, Chloe ran over to her. She jumped as the girl threw her arms around her and hugged her tightly. It was the first time Sadie had ever been embraced. At first she didn't know what was happening. Feeling the girl's arms around her body caused her to go still. It was difficult not to be nervous and she didn't know what was expected of her. Finally she placed her hand on Chloe's back.

It was surprising that the girl wasn't as small as she had thought. Chloe's head was about even with Sadie's shoulder. It only went to show that she truly didn't understand the whole age thing. For some reason, she had thought that someone who was about 6 years younger than her would've been smaller. It was one more thing that Sadie had yet to understand. Would she always be confused? When would the world make sense?

For the rest of the morning she focused on keeping any upsetting thoughts from entering her mind. It was easy to watch what she said around Chloe since she didn't talk much to begin with. Until she learned to control her emotions, however, Sadie would have to watch what she thought as well. Her thoughts influenced her emotions all the time, and the last thing she wanted was to make Chloe cry again.

It was difficult. Sadie's thoughts had been her only companion for most of her life. She was used to being in her head more than in the real world. Now she had to learn how to control them until she could master the emotions they inflicted. It seemed like an impossible feat, and she was tempted to leave because of it. Not wanting to die on the streets was the only thing that kept her on the couch.

Instead of letting her mind wander as she usually would, Sadie focused on finding a way to pay back the men. They had said that they required no payment for their help. She still wasn't sure how true that was. Unable to trust them, and highly doubtful that she should, it seemed best to find a way to repay her increasing debt.

Even if they were telling the truth, she always had to pay her debts. They might not recognize that she had one with them, but that didn't matter. It wouldn't be right to stay with them all winter and not give them something for their troubles. The problem was, what could she do? There were no possessions that she could offer them for trade. Nor did she have any money. Pain wasn't an option and neither were acts in the bedroom.

Sadie's mind flashed on how helpless she felt when Fester insisted on folding the blanket. The memory gave her a brilliant idea. She could pay back the men and at the same time be able to show them that she wasn't helpless. Her payment would solve two problems at the same time. She couldn't wait to talk to Fester!

Chapter 9

For most of the morning, Sadie sat on the couch with Chloe. The girl watched something called 'cartoons' on the television. The strange noises made Chloe giggle from time to time. Sadie tried to understand what was going on, but it was impossible to tell. She found it utterly confusing, so she sat and let her mind wander rather than figure out what the strange noises meant.

She thought about her payment and had frequently considered talking to Fester about it. Every time she tried, her own nervousness held her back. What if he said 'no'? She didn't want to feel helpless, nor did she want to spend her time listening to the TV. Random sounds weren't entertaining despite what Chloe might think. It wasn't long before her boredom had begun to give way to restlessness. She couldn't stand it any longer. Nervous or not, she needed to talk to him now.

"Chloe?" she asked.

"Yeah?"

"Where's Fester?"

"I'm right here," he said softly. He sounded like he was on the other side of the coffee table.

Sadie took a deep breath. "I want to talk to you about something."

"She feelin nervous," Chloe said.

"Yeah, um...Sadie, let's go into the kitchen to talk." She heard him stand up from the chair.

Taking a deep breath to calm herself, Sadie also stood and headed for the kitchen. She had a good idea where the table was. Until she was positive about the location of everything, however, she would have to use her cane. When she reached the table she heard Fester pull out a chair and she did the same.

"OK." Fester's tone was low and gentle. "What's up?"

Sadie started to feel afraid. With the way he sometimes treated her, she wasn't sure how Fester would react to her idea. It seemed like he thought of her the same way he thought of Chloe, as though she were a child who needed to be taken care of. It was important to show him that she was more capable than that. After another few breaths to calm her emotions, she still wasn't ready to speak.

"Sadie, what's wrong?" Fester sounded concerned.

"Nothing's wrong. I'm trying to calm myself. I want to talk to you and I'm very nervous."

"It's OK, Sadie. You don't have to be nervous. You can talk to me 'bout anything."

"It's just...it's my payment."

Fester let out a sigh. "Sadie, I keep telling you. You don't owe us a thing."

"But, I do, Fester. I owe you a lot. It doesn't feel right not paying you in some way."

Sadie heard Fester lean back into his seat. "Alright. What did you have in mind?" he asked.

Letting out a sigh of relief she said, "I want to do the chores for you."

"What do you mean, Sadie?"

"I want to do the housework. I can wash the dishes and do the laundry. I can clean the apartment. I can make the beds. I can even cook a little."

"You can do all that?" Fester sounded surprised.

Sadie tried not to be annoyed by his tone. "Yes."

Fester was silent. At first she wasn't sure if she had upset him in some way. For a while the only sounds she heard were the cartoons mingled with Chloe's giggles. She tried not to let her mind wander as she waited for him to speak. Her patience had begun to wear thin when he took longer than she expected.

"Ya know," Fester finally said as he shifted in his seat. "If you can do the cleaning true, then that'll help us out tons."

Sadie smiled widely. "Thank you, Fester. I can begin as soon as I learn where everything is in here. That shouldn't take too long."

Fester stood up and moved about the kitchen. By the sounds Sadie heard, he was making something to eat. Confused by his desire to make food so close to their last meal, she stood and opened her cane. The sooner she felt her way around the apartment and learned where everything was, the sooner she could begin to pay the men back. With a smile on her face and a light mood to her heart, she began to walk towards the living room.

"Sit, Sadie. I'm almost done with lunch."

"Lunch?"

"Yeah," he said. "Go ahead and sit back down."

Sadie sat, though she was confused yet again. She had heard the word 'lunch' a few times while sitting with her sign. Unfortunately, no one had said enough for her to be able to learn what it meant. It was infuriating for her to admit when she didn't know something. She let out a sigh as she realized there was no way to avoid asking.

"Um, Fester? What's 'lunch?'"

"Oh, we're just having sandwiches."

"So, it's food then?"

Fester stopped what he was doing. "Sadie, you mean to tell me that you don't have a clue what lunch is?"

Sadie shook her head and nervously licked her lips. Heat rose in her cheeks and she shifted her weight. Fester had the same tone that he had used the night before when they spoke about birthdays. The fact that he was surprised about it bothered her more than she was willing to admit. Once again, she was reminded that she didn't know enough. She felt wrong and that was unsettling.

Fester let out a sigh. "It's food you eat in the middle of the day." She heard him go back to making the lunch.

"I...I don't think...I can't eat it."

There was a distinct sound of a utensil being placed harshly on the counter and Sadie flinched. "Why not?" Fester sounded upset.

Sadie was terrified by the change in him. She froze, afraid to answer. He sounded upset with her, and the way he placed the utensil down indicated that he was angry too. Usually such a reaction meant that pain would shortly follow. Forgetting that she was in a safe place, Sadie braced herself for whatever was to come. No matter what, she would find a way to keep herself safe if he attempted to hurt her. As she heard Fester's footsteps approach, her body began to tremble.

"Sadie?" Chloe's tearful voice came from the living room.

When Fester moved near her, Sadie raised her voice to him. "If you hurt me I'll hurt you!"

Fester stopped where he was and Chloe began to cry. "Sadie," he said softly and gently, "I would never hurt you. Please believe me. I'm not going to hurt you. Never." When Sadie didn't respond he said, "You need to calm down, Sadie. We can talk about this but first Chloe needs you to calm your mind. There's nothing for you to be 'fraid of up in here. Please, please calm down."

Fester quickly moved into the living room to comfort Chloe. It took a few minutes for his words to sink in. It was difficult to believe him and she didn't know if she could. What she did know was that the empathic child needed her to calm the fear that was building inside. She began to take in slow deep breaths as tears rolled down her cheeks. Chloe's cries made Sadie try harder.

Little by little, her fear began to subside. She tried to think about Chloe's laughter but it was difficult to focus on. Every time she heard Fester speak softly to the child, she remembered what had frightened her in the first place. This unraveled any progress she had begun to make. There had to be another way.

Maybe if she could convince herself that Fester wasn't a danger, then she wouldn't be so afraid. Unsure of what else to do, Sadie focused on every kind word he had ever said to her. The first memory to surface in her mind was what he had said after he saw her scars. *'I'm never, ever, ever, never gonna do nothing like this to ya.' 'You didn't deserve any of that.'* Did he truly mean what he said?

Sadie not only thought about the words, but also the emotion that showed through his voice. He had sounded so sincere. His tone matched a great sadness that seemed to come from knowing she had once endured such pain. She could tell that Fester didn't like people being hurt. The concept was new to her and she didn't fully understand his reasons.

Her thoughts were interrupted with the realization that her fear had subsided more than she thought was possible. She heard Chloe sob softly from the living room while Fester continued to soothe her. The way he interacted with Chloe had also caught Sadie's attention. She turned her mind back to how he would quickly rush to her whenever she was upset. Likewise, Chloe behaved as though she had complete and total trust in Fester. Neither of those would've happened if he'd been anything like her parents.

Sadie began to feel that perhaps she was safe after all. Even if she didn't understand it completely, she knew there was hope for her future. All she had to do was trust, and that wasn't going to be easy. Sadie had never trusted anyone other than herself before. No one had given her a reason to. Fester did say that she needed to trust them so that they could help her. It seemed doubtful that she would be able to learn how, or that it would be wise even if she could figure it out.

When Chloe had stopped crying, Sadie noticed that her own fear had subsided as well. For the second time that morning, she had somehow hurt Chloe. The guilt was starting to eat away at her. Her fear always made the child cry. Did it cause her pain? She didn't want to harm the girl, yet she continued to do so simply by being afraid. Again she considered leaving, but the cold outside kept her where she was.

"Sadie?" Chloe asked.

Sadie had been lost in thought and hadn't heard the girl approach. She turned her head towards her and said, "I'm sorry, Chloe."

"It K."

Sadie jumped when she felt Chloe's arms wrap around her. Not knowing what to do, but feeling as though she had to do something, she placed her hand on the girl's back. It was surprising that Chloe had wanted to touch her after what she had done. The hug helped to make Sadie's heart feel a little lighter. The girl wasn't angry with her, and still wanted to be around her. Did she deserve such treatment? It was doubtful.

Fester walked slowly into the kitchen and continued to make the lunch. Unused to eating so often, Sadie wanted to tell him that she couldn't eat more food. If she refused then he may become angry again. His anger would definitely trigger more fear. In turn, that would hurt Chloe, and she wanted to avoid such at all costs. The problem was that her belly was still full after eating the night before, and again this morning. Having more so soon didn't seem like a good idea.

"Eat," Fester said as he put a plate in front of her. "No words. You need it."

Sadie felt the plate and the sandwich. It didn't seem like a lot of food, but she still didn't think she had room. Not knowing what else to do, she folded her hands in her lap and tried not to worry.

"Fester, we gonna go out after lunch? I wanna get playin in them snows with Sadie!"

Fester sighed. "I guess."

Chloe let out a squeal of delight. Sadie smiled at the sound, though she still wasn't sure how to play with snow.

"Why ain't ya eatin none, Sadie?"

"My belly is full, Chloe. I don't think I can fit it in."

Fester swore softly. "Sorry 'bout that. I wanted you to eat so badly that I forgot your stomach would've shrunk from starvation. Here, I'll take your plate. Maybe we can put it in the fridge until you're hungry later."

"Thank you."

It was surprising to Sadie how understanding Fester had been. From the way he had sounded when he made the food, she was sure he would be furious with her for not eating any. He seemed to love to give her food, and that was definitely something she would never understand. Why did he want her to eat all of the time? Thinking back to the night before, Sadie was reminded of how Michael had said that she was starving to death. Was he afraid that she would die if she didn't eat constantly?

Throughout her life, she went through periods

where food was scarce. At home, she couldn't eat if she was being punished, or if it was part of a lesson. It happened often enough that she was used to the lack of food. On the streets, she didn't have enough money. She knew that she had been starving, but didn't think it posed a threat to her life just yet.

The fact that Fester and Chloe were both eating a second meal in the same day as though it were normal baffled Sadie a great deal. She had always assumed that a person usually ate once per day, and twice when you hadn't eaten the day before because of a punishment. On the streets she learned that food was expensive and the men were low on money. It surprised her that they would eat so much.

Sadie was convinced that she would never understand these strange Downtown people. They were as odd as any other.

Chapter 10

After lunch, Chloe ran into her bedroom to get into her snow suit. Sadie wasn't sure what that meant and wondered if she would need one too. She reasoned that if she did then Fester would say so. Instead, he had only told her to get her shoes and coat and then handed her a pair of gloves. As she sat at the table, she wondered what the snow would be like. When she heard Fester come over towards her, though, she stiffened.

"We need to share words," he said softly.

Sadie nodded. Chloe had been hurt by her emotions this morning. Surely the men would punish her for such an action. They wouldn't physically hurt her, so perhaps he was going to tell her that she had to leave. With a deep desire to not be sent into the cold, she swallowed hard and held back her tears. Regardless of how she felt, it wasn't her decision and she needed to respect that. Fearful and unsure about what to do, she sat and waited for him to continue.

As he sat down in the seat beside her, Fester asked, "Sadie, are you a Supernatural?"

That wasn't what she had been expecting. "I think so."

"Why didn't you tell us?"

"I was afraid that you would send me away. I was afraid that Michael wouldn't want me around Chloe."

"Why would you think that? You know we accept that Chloe is a Supernatural."

"I know. I just didn't want to be sent back into the cold."

Fester sighed. He seemed to do that a lot. "Sadie, listen to me. In this joint, having a power isn't a thing that's gonna get you kicked out. We're not going to send you into the cold."

Sadie turned towards him. "You won't? What about how I've hurt Chloe today?"

"How did you hurt Chloe?" Fester sounded alarmed

which confused Sadie since he had been there both times.

"With my emotions. I am afraid almost all the time, Fester."

Fester let out a sigh of relief. "Don't worry about that. You'll learn to control it and then Chloe will be fine."

"Are you sure?"

"Yeah, Sadie. I'm sure."

"OK." Sadie felt a wave of relief wash over her. She truly didn't want to return to the streets.

After a moment Fester asked, "Your power has to do with air, doesn't it?"

"How…how did you know?"

"The last time I had brought you food, I saw the air shift around you. The currents weren't following a natural pattern."

"You were able to notice that? I thought no one did." Sadie said as her heart began to beat faster.

"I notice things a ton easier than other people, Sadie." After a moment Fester said, "I'm a Supernatural too. My power is a bit different though. It basically turned my brain into a super computer."

"A what?" Sadie asked.

"I notice things that other people don't. I can record in my head everything I see and hear. I can understand everything I read. My brain can just do things that no one else's can. It's the same as a computer."

Sadie didn't know what a computer was. It must be significant for Fester to mention it in such a way. Thinking about her own 'power', she couldn't help but worry that others might one day discover what she could do. He did say that he noticed things that others don't. But last night Michael said that Supernaturals were in danger from some sort of government. That made her nervous. Before she could dwell on it further, Chloe came running into the room.

"I all ready!"

"We'll talk more about this later," Fester whispered as he stood.

With Chloe jumping and bouncing around them,

they all headed out the door. It was odd for Sadie to be going out into the cold again. Knowing that she would be warm later made her feel happy and safe. A small smile played across her lips and her steps felt lighter as they headed out of the building. When a blast of freezing air hit her face she took a step back. It was far colder than she remembered, and she knew that Michael had been right. If Fester hadn't found her, then surely she would've frozen to death. Even Sadie knew that no one could survive such weather for long.

Fester offered Sadie his arm to hold onto. She was reluctant to take it at first, thinking that he was treating her like she couldn't walk on her own. When he said that it'll help her know where they were going, she saw the logic in his offer and cautiously put her hand in the crook of his arm. A few steps later and she was glad that she did when she felt her foot slip.

"Careful," Fester said, "there's some ice on the ground."

Sadie nodded and they continued down the sidewalk. There was a certain quality to the air that she hadn't experienced before. It was crisp and didn't smell quite as bad as it did when she had slept on the streets. The ground they walked on was also different. Aside from the patches of ice, she also noticed that there was a somewhat crunching sound – though it was a crunch she could also feel through her shoes – when they walked. The ground beneath her shoes felt very uneven as well.

"Fester, why does the ground sound and feel so different?" she asked.

Fester let out a chuckle. "We're walking on snow."

"Oh."

As someone who had never experienced snow, Sadie found herself highly curious. She couldn't wait for them to get to the park so she could touch it and see what it was like. From her mother's nicer lessons, she had learned that snow was tiny bits of ice that fell from the sky in the winter. She hadn't been able to imagine such a phenomenon and was happily anxious to learn more.

Chloe had been unusually quiet as they walked. Sadie had expected the child to talk or laugh and wondered if everything was alright. She could hear the crunch of Chloe's footsteps and knew that she was on the other side of Fester. Not wanting to embarrass the girl, she decided that she would ask him about it later. After all, if Sadie didn't enjoy when others pointed out that she did something strange, then Chloe might be the same way.

They had walked only two blocks before they reached the park. Sadie realized that the fence bordering the park was where she had slept her last night on the street. She had no idea that there was a park there, or that she had been so close to the food-man's home. Although she did notice there was a fence instead of a wall, she had always treated it the same way she did the buildings. It was nothing more than something to lean against.

When they entered the park, Sadie heard Chloe run on ahead. Surprisingly, she didn't hear her giggle or laugh the way she had expected. The crunch of the child's feet took her away and before long Sadie couldn't tell where she was. When Fester guided her over to a bench, he told her to wait until he brushed off the snow. She waited patiently for him to finish and then asked where Chloe had gone.

"She's not far. She's forward and to the left, 'bout twenty feet away," he said.

"What is she doing?"

"She's doing what we came here for. She's playing in the snow."

"Yes, but what is it she's doing?

"Making snow angels."

Sadie decided not to ask any more questions. While she didn't know what 'snow angels' were or how they were made, she was reluctant to show Fester her ignorance. There was already far too much that she didn't know. To admit to yet another thing she was clueless about would be embarrassing. Instead, she took off her glove and reached for the ground. The snow felt cold and wet as it melted on her fingers. She couldn't understand the appeal.

Chloe's footsteps were heard as she ran towards them. "Sadie! Sadie! C'mon play with me!"

Sadie jumped when Chloe grabbed her hand and pulled her off of the bench. At first she wasn't sure what to do since she had never played with snow before. Even so, she decided to give it a try and allowed Chloe to lead her away from Fester. Before she could go far, he gently took her cane and told her there was nothing to bump into. Without her cane she felt a little unsteady.

Sadie nearly cried out in shock when her foot first went deep into the snow. Her calf stung from the snow's cold wet bite. Bits of ice made their way into her sneakers as well. The sensation of pins and needles surrounded her feet, and she wanted to cry out in protest. Chloe continued to giggle as she pulled her further into the snow. Not wanting the girl to stop laughing, Sadie didn't voice her discomfort. The snow could be endured so long as Chloe continued to make that beautiful sound.

"Chloe, how do we play in snow?" she asked.

Chloe laughed. "Ya just playin!"

"Can you teach me how? I've never played in snow before."

Chloe stopped pulling Sadie. "Ya ain't? K. First I gotta show ya 'bout makin a snowball."

At first it wasn't easy for Sadie to make one. She had a difficult time feeling the shape of the snowball through her gloves. She tried not to get frustrated and was glad that Chloe was patient with her. The child seemed to really enjoy the instruction and after a while Sadie started to actually have fun. When Chloe suggested a snowball fight, Sadie felt it wasn't a good idea. She couldn't see Chloe, so she wouldn't know where to throw the snowballs. She knew she could use the air, but she was afraid to after what both Michael and Fester had both separately told her.

"I got it!" Chloe said, "We gonna get playin Marco Polo in snow!"

"How do you play that?"

Chloe explained the game and Sadie thought it

would be fun to try. Even with Chloe yelling 'Polo', she still had a hard time hitting her. Every now and then she heard the smack of the snowball against Chloe's snowsuit. When she did, both girls were overly excited. For the first time in her life, Sadie experienced what it was like to laugh with joy. It was an unbelievable feeling that she never wanted to go away. There was nothing that could make her want to stop feeling this happy. Playing was better than anything she could have imagined it to be.

Eventually, Sadie's feet began to hurt more than she could withstand because of the snow that had made its way into her sneakers. She asked Chloe to take her back over to the bench so she could sit for a bit. The girl made a sound of disappointment but did as she was asked. When she reached the bench, Sadie sat down and sighed. A wave of contentment had washed over her and her body relaxed against the seat.

"Have fun?" Fester asked.

"Yes," Sadie said with a wide smile.

"Chloe, why don't ya go back to playing? Give Sadie a one-two rest."

Sadie heard the sound of Chloe's feet trudging through the snow. Never before had she felt anything like what she had just experienced. She couldn't stop smiling. It was such a beautiful feeling and she found that snow was actually fun to play with. She didn't even mind the cold. Remembering that she wanted to ask Fester why Chloe had been quiet on the way to the park, she tried to figure out how far away the child had gone. If the girl was within earshot, then she would wait. As she listened, she heard the crunch of footsteps walking towards them. They didn't sound like Chloe's.

"Hey Fester. It's been a while." The woman's voice sounded pleasant and friendly.

Fester swore. "What the fuck you doing here, Sal?"

"Is that any way to greet an old friend? I thought you would be here. I wanted to come see you and say 'hello'."

"We ain't friends, Sal. Get gone."

"That hurts, Fester. So, who's your Asian friend?

Pretty blue eyes."

Fester sighed. "Sal this is Sadie. Sadie this is Sal. Now go away."

"Fester, I need to talk to you." There was a slight sense of urgency in her tone.

"I'm watching Chloe," Fester said with frustration.

Sadie wondered what was happening. He didn't even give her a chance to say 'hello' to this new person. Something seemed wrong by his tone and she couldn't fathom what it might be.

"It'll just be a minute. You can watch her while we talk."

"No, Sal. Get gone. Go away. I don't want to talk."

For a while no one spoke and for once that made Sadie very nervous. This Sal woman sounded friendly and nice, yet Fester wanted nothing to do with her. He sounded like he was angry that she was even there. It was unsettling to hear his voice take on such tones. With what little knowledge she had of people, she was oblivious as to what could be bothering him. All she could do was sit and listen. Swallowing, she tried to hold back her fear that the encounter had stirred within her. Chloe could be hurt if she became afraid again.

"I have a job for you, Fester." The woman said. Her tone had shifted and now she didn't sound as friendly.

"No, Sal."

"You're perfect for this one. The payout could even get you out of that rat's hole you're in."

"No, Sal!" Fester sounded even angrier than before. "C'mon, Chloe! Time to go!"

"Think about it," Sal said. "You know how to reach me if you change your mind."

"Fuck off, Sal."

Sal's footsteps took her away as Chloe's footsteps came near. As they walked back towards the apartment, she replayed the conversation in her head. The ease at which the woman's tone had shifted made her nervous. She had heard Michael shift his tone before, but there was something different about the way this Sal had done it. She couldn't tell which tone showed the real Sal and which was fake. What really bothered her was the thought that neither was true after the way Fester reacted.

Sadie had been a little frightened by his tone too. What was it that made him so angry with this new woman? She had said that there was a job for him. That meant that he could make money. With how little they all had, Sadie wondered why he wouldn't do the work. She remembered the argument she had overheard last night. Fester had said, *'I can go back to what I did 'fore.'* and Michael said, *'We ain't that desperate.'* Was this what they hadmeant? What was it about this work that caused Michael to be so adamant that Fester not do it?

The questions kept on building in Sadie's mind. It was tempting to voice them, but she feared hearing that angry tone in Fester's voice again. She didn't want him to ever have to use that tone with her. It wasn't like him, and Sadie preferred consistency. Plus, he sounded scary when his voice took on such tones. If he frightened her so soon, then Chloe might never forgive her for the pain it would cause. Perhaps even Michael would become angry because she hurt his sister. He was a harsh man and it wouldn't be wise to anger him either.

Sadie fumbled a step and noticed that her feet had become numb from the snow. She was glad that the apartment was close by. The warmth which awaited them there was a welcome thought. The sooner they reached Fester's home, the better her feet and body would feel. Thankfully, neither Fester nor Chloe spoke the entire way, and Sadie was happy for the silence. Their small excursion to the park had given her much to think about.

Chapter 11

By the time they reached the apartment, Sadie was anxious to warm herself. She rushed to the table and quickly kicked off her shoes. Once she was seated, she began to peel off the wet socks which clung to her painfully cold feet. From the kitchen table she heard Fester help Chloe take off her snowsuit. Desperately she rubbed her feet with her hands in an attempt to warm them.

Never in her life had she felt so frozen. She was sure that winter had come and gone while she lived at her parent's house. But, the home was always warm and so she hadn't experienced such extreme temperatures while there. It was surprising how quickly the cold had overcome her considering they weren't at the park for all that long.

Chloe's footsteps were loud as she ran into the living room. Soon after, the sounds of cartoons and the child's giggles filled the apartment. She wondered what the girl found so fascinating about the strange noises they made. It was impossible for her to tell and she knew that not even the air could show it to her. Not having any true interest in cartoons, she listened for where Fester had gone. Over by the door, it sounded as though he was shaking Chloe's snow suit. Sadie smiled slightly. The man seemed so strange. Uncertain of what he could possibly be doing to the outer clothing, she ignored his antics and continued to rub her feet.

"Sadie, why don't you take off your coat?" Fester asked, having finished whatever he had been doing.

She thought it was obvious but said, "I'm trying to get my feet warm first."

"Here," he said gently, "let me have a see."

Sadie tried not to flinch when Fester carefully took one of her feet and held it in his hands. Neither he nor anyone else, with the exception of her parents, had ever held anything other than her hand or elbow before.

At first she wanted to tell him to let go of her foot. It was uncomfortable having someone touch them with such familiarity. That was when she realized how much larger his hands were from hers. Instead of telling him to stop, she focused on how his hands felt. The few times they had touched, she hadn't bothered to pay attention. Now, as he rubbed her feet, she was keenly aware of their size.

When she had felt him with the air she had learned that he was much taller than she. Even so, she was surprised to find that his hands nearly covered her whole foot. Were they supposed to be so large or was it another thing that was strange about this man? It wasn't as though Sadie had been touched by many men, so she had no way to know what was normal about him and what was odd. For her, everything about him was different and unusual.

"Here," he said, "let's take off your coat and get you over by the heater. It'll warm your feet faster."

Sadie had a good idea of where the heater was. She could feel the heat emanating from the far side of the living room. Not sure of its exact location, she allowed Fester to guide her. The bottoms of her feet stung and her damp pants added to her chill as she walked across the apartment. As fun as it was, snow seemed to be an awful lot of trouble.

"Sadie, why didn't you tell me your feet were so cold?" Fester asked in an overly concerned tone.

Sadie didn't want to respond. When he placed her hand on the back of a chair, she gratefully sat. Slowly, she moved her feet towards the welcome warmth of the heater. Careful not to burn herself, she moved her feet as close as she dared. Fester's question made her feel foolish for not saying something at the park. She honestly didn't think it would be a problem so long as she was warm later. It wasn't as though she was used to being allowed to speak of her discomforts.

"Ya shoulda said a thing," he said, and started to move away.

"I'm sorry," Sadie said softly. "I didn't think it would be a problem."

Fester stopped moving. "You have to be riskless, Sadie. The snow is fun to play in but if you get too cold it can damage your body. Just...just be mindful next time."

"OK."

Feeling more foolish, she closed her eyes and leaned back in the chair. Allowing her mind to drift where it wanted, Sadie began to wonder if she would ever know how to do things properly. It felt as though she constantly made some sort of blunder despite her best efforts. There were so many things that she was never told; so much she had yet to learn. It felt as though nothing she did was right. From her words to her behavior, something always came up wrong. She wished there was a way for her to catch up with the rest of the world.

Thinking on this, Sadie reflected on how her mother had taught her Braille. She used to give her books to read so that she could learn math and science. They were the only books she had ever been allowed to have. She remembered how much she wished her mother would give her more. As though it were another harsh lesson, Sadie was never allowed to have more than were provided. Now that she was away from her, she wondered if she would be allowed to read again. Perhaps that would help her to understand the world a little more.

"Fester–" She hesitated. What if there was a reason she was never given more to read?

"I'm right here," he said from nearby.

"Where do people go to get books?" she asked.

"Books?" He sounded surprised. "Well, there are a lot of stores that sell them. You can borrow them for free from the library too."

Free sounded good. "Do they have Braille books at this 'Library' place?"

"Yeah, they do actually. You can read Braille, Sadie?"

She smiled proudly and nodded her head. "Can we go there sometime?"

"Yeah." Fester's tone was surprisingly happy.

"Maybe tomorrow when Chloe's at school."

It felt good to hear a happy quality to Fester's voice. Usually he sounded so sad when he spoke. She wasn't sure what made him happy, but that didn't matter. What mattered was that she had somehow said something right.

Satisfied with how much her feet had warmed up, Sadie stood and opened her cane. Her pants were almost completely dry as well, which eased her chill considerably. Now she was ready to pay her debt and start cleaning. She knew that it would be difficult at first since she didn't know the apartment as well as her former home. Obviously there was going to be an adjustment period as she learned where everything belonged.

As Sadie started to walk towards the kitchen she heard Fester follow her. "Finally hungry?" he asked.

"No." She felt a twinge of guilt at the mention of her uneaten food. "I'm going to do the dishes."

"Oh, uh, do ya want help?"

"You can help me find the sink," Sadie said with a smile. She was glad that he didn't try to force her to eat again.

Fester gently took Sadie's elbow and surprisingly she didn't flinch as harshly as she normally would. As he led her into the kitchen, her excitement began to grow. Finally Fester would know that she wasn't some helpless child. Yes, she had made some bad choices and was almost constantly confused. But, there were many things which she knew how to do on her own. It was time to prove it to him. She was going to start by doing the dishes.

When they reached the counter, Sadie folded up her cane and put it beside the sink. Feeling around with her hands, she was able to find everything that she needed. As she rolled up her sleeves, she realized that she had her work cut out for her. The men obviously didn't clean often. Not only was the sink overflowing with dirty dishes, but she felt bits of food stuck to the counters as well. She wondered if the rest of the apartment was this messy.

Fester had been silent while she searched about the sink. Once she started the water, he again offered to help. His insistence on helping her all the time was infuriating. She calmly reminded him that this was her debt and that she needed to pay it herself. If he didn't stop helping her, then her debt would never decrease.

The dishes didn't take long to do. She made sure they were clean by feeling for bits of food with her fingers as she scrubbed them. Once she was satisfied, she then carefully placed them on the drying board. As she worked, she listened for where Fester had gone. She couldn't hear him over the sounds of the water and Chloe's cartoons. Was he watching her? The thought made her be extra thorough with her chore.

"Impressive," he said from nearby as she finished.

"It's not hard to do."

Sadie wondered what was impressive about washing dishes. Now that they were clean, however, she really wanted to work on the rest of the kitchen. She had Fester show her where the cleaners were kept. They had to be reorganized so that in the future she would be able to find what she wanted without help. Fester stayed and they talked while she proceeded to clean the rest of the kitchen.

"Tell me about your power," he said.

Sadie didn't expect that and she paused. She had never talked to anyone about what she could do before. Finally she continued with her cleaning and said, "I can control the air around me."

"I get that. I mean, what can you do with the air once you're controlling it?"

"Oh. I've only learned how to do two things. I can create wind and if I focus I can also see."

"What do you mean you can see?" Fester sounded intrigued.

Sadie felt herself blush. "If I focus on the air around me, I can feel everything it touches. It allows me to sort of see what's around me without having to feel for it with my hands."

"Why didn't you do that to find the sink?"

"My parents used to punish me for using the air to

see, and I feel nervous using it where people will notice the air moving."

"You don't have to sweat it here, Sadie. If your power will help you see then you should use it when you can."

Sadie had finished with the kitchen by this point. She turned towards Fester. "I don't need to see all the time."

"I know. I just think that if you could do a thing that'll help you see then you should. It's better than being blind all the time."

Sadie frowned. His words upset her more than she would've expected. "What's wrong with being blind?" she asked defensively.

Fester sighed. "Nothing. I didn't mean it same as that. I just...oh never mind." He sounded disheartened.

Sadie walked away from him. She had planned on asking if it would be alright for her to control the air in the apartment so she could see where everything was. Now, she didn't want to use it at all. She had never wanted to use it all the time. There wasn't a need to since she could easily do things while blind.

As she explored and then cleaned the rest of the apartment, Fester's voice repeated his words in her head. *'If your power will help you see then you should use it.' 'It's better than being blind all the time.'* What was wrong with being blind? Sadie had been blind her entire life. If there was something wrong with it, then that would suggest that there was something wrong with her. Did he try to help her all the time because he thought her blindness made her wrong? The idea of it made her angry.

For the rest of the afternoon neither Fester nor Sadie spoke. She had planned on asking him about Sal, and finding out who she was, as well as why Chloe had been so quiet outside. But now she didn't want to talk to him at all. She felt more determined than ever to prove to him that, blind or not, she was more than capable of doing things on her own.

One way or another, Fester would learn that Sadie didn't need his help all the time...nor did she want it.

Chapter 12

By the time Michael came home from work, Sadie had cleaned most of the apartment. The bedrooms still need to be done, but she figured she could work on those tomorrow. When she had mentioned doing the laundry, Fester insisted there wasn't enough to wash yet. Satisfied with the work she had done, she had sat down on the couch to relax.

When Michael walked through the door, Sadie heard him whistle. "Fester, ya fucking get ta cleanin up the joint, man?"

"No," Fester said softly. "Sadie did."

"True? Sadie, ya done all them cleanins ya own?" He sounded disbelieving.

"Yes," she said. She tried not to be annoyed at his tone.

"Ya gone cleanin the bathroom same?"

"Yes."

"Good works!"

Michael sounded happy and that made Sadie smile. She was glad that he was pleased and that he appreciated what she had done. It was difficult and exhausting trying to find and clean everything. The men weren't exactly as neat as they should be. She heard Michael walk over to where Fester sat. The sound of someone being smacked caused her to flinch hard.

"What the fuck was that for?" Apparently it was Fester who was hit.

"It ain't right makin her fucking works her own self," Michael said

"She wouldn't let me help!"

"It's my payment," Sadie said softly. It wouldn't be right for Fester to be in trouble because of her debts.

"I sorry. Ya what now?"

Sadie sighed. Why didn't these men understand the desire she had to pay them back? "It's my payment for all the help you both have given me. I always pay my debts."

Sadie could hear Michael sigh heavily. "Sadie, ya ain't gotta-"

"I know," she said, holding up her hand. "I want to do it."

"K," he said with another sigh.

Michael's heavy footsteps took him towards his bedroom. Though she now knew where both his and Chloe's doors were, the inside of their personal rooms were still a mystery. There would be plenty of time to explore and clean them tomorrow. For now, she sat back and listened to the TV. Cartoons had been traded for something that had a lot of laughter and jokes. Fester would chuckle every now and then, but most of the time Sadie didn't understand what was funny. The jokes were as confusing as everything else. They spoke of things she had never experienced and she felt too foolish to ask anyone to clarify them.

Chloe came running out of her room. "Michael! Ya home!"

Michael let out a happy "Hey!" before Sadie heard him grunt. As she listened, she wondered if Chloe had given Michael a hug. The girl seemed to like to do that a lot. Shaking her head, she pondered why. Wrapping your arms around someone seemed like such an odd gesture. For Sadie it was another reminder of how much she didn't comprehend what went on around her. Hopefully that wouldn't be the case for long. Tomorrow would bring with it the chance to finally read again. It was exciting to know that soon she would have a better understanding of the world!

"Guess what we done today!" Chloe said excitedly.

"What?"

"We gone the park an Sadie an I plays in them snows! It got so much fun! Sadie ain't able ta see nothin, so's we playin Marco Polo, an when I yellin 'Polo' she throwin a snowball at me! I wishin we keep there longer."

Sadie smiled as she listened to Chloe prattle on about their day. She was glad that Chloe had as much fun as she did. It made her feel good inside. Fester chuckled at some of what Chloe recounted which also made Sadie feel good. She wished he were happy more. It was an easy emotion for the child, and it stood to reason that it should be easy for the man as well.

Soon Chloe's tale mentioned Sal and Fester swore in response. Sadie heard Michael's heavy footsteps as he moved quickly towards the living room. Sensing something was wrong, but no clue as to what that could be, she sat as still as possible and listened to the two men. It was difficult to not be afraid with the sudden change in atmosphere.

"Ya sharin words with them bitch 'gain?" Michael asked. Sadie flinched at his angry tone.

"No, Michael, it wasn't like that," Fester said.

"Ya gotta fucking stick far hell gone from her, Fester. An I ain't gonna fucking never get ta letin her nearer my lil sis!"

"I know. I couldn't do anything though. She fucking found me and came up to me. I didn't go find her!" Fester sounded defensive and that made Sadie nervous.

"Michael?" Chloe asked tearfully. She was upset and that bothered Sadie further.

"Not now, Chloe. Fester, the fucking bitch done been riskful news. Ya ain't gonna get ta messin with none them shits no more. I sayin last night, 'we ain't that desperate!'"

As Michael's tone became angrier and louder, Sadie couldn't help but be afraid. She tried to breathe through the fear like she had done before, but it wasn't working. Michael continued to yell, and that fueled her fear even further. Silently she wished that she was anywhere but in that room. It wasn't safe anymore.

"The fuck the bitch whore tryin ta get from ya?" Michael asked.

"She passed me work," Fester's voice was low.

"Ya got ta curbin the fucking pass ain't ya? Get ta sayin ya gone from them shits!"

"Michael?" Chloe asked again. She sounded as though she was ready to cry.

"Not now, Chloe!" he yelled.

Michael sounded like he was angry with Chloe

too, and Sadie couldn't understand why. She hadn't done anything but say his name. Had they only been pretending that it was different than her parent's house? Her mother or father would've been angry if Sadie continued to say their names. These people had made it seem like it was different here. Obviously they lied. Safety didn't actually exist anywhere!

As a means of survival, Sadie learned from an early age how to avoid the wrath of another. Wordlessly she made herself completely still in the hopes that she wouldn't be noticed. She was terrified of Michael now, and didn't want him to turn his anger onto her as well. She wasn't sure what she would do if he tried to hurt her or Chloe. Feeling helpless and terrified, all she could do was sit and listen as the men continued to argue.

"Course I curbed the pass!" Fester said defensively.

"Good! Fuck man! Shit! The fuck she get ta picturin where ya ass done been?" Michael asked.

"I don't know! She just found me."

"Michael?" Chloe asked as she began to cry.

"What?" He sounded frustrated and angry. Barely a moment later and his tone changed to one that was more gentle. "Hey, hey…I sorry lil one. I ain't meanin ta get so pissed. I gonna get ta calmin my mind. I sorry." He could be heard moving towards the child.

"It ain't just that, Michael. It Sadie. Ya scarin her," Chloe said as she cried.

Sadie closed her eyes and wished that Michael's attention hadn't been turned onto her. She was hurting Chloe with her emotions again, and couldn't calm down. There was no way to tell what Michael would do now that he knew she couldn't control herself. She didn't know if she could handle it if the loud harsh man focused his anger on her. Her body stiffened when she heard both men move in her direction.

"Sadie," Fester said softly as he sat down next to her. "Sadie, it's OK. Michael's just angry about Sal. He's not going to hurt anyone. OK? You're clear here, Sadie. Do you understand? You're safe."

Sadie held her breath, unable to answer. She could hear the wood on the coffee table creak. "Sadie,"

Michael said from directly in front of her. She wasn't sure if she trusted his gentle tone so soon after his angry outburst. "Fester tellin true story o'er here. I ain't never gonna hurt ya or nobody. I sorry. I gettin all freaked an shit, cause I be gettin fucking 'fraid from Sal. She ain't good ta get 'round. Get it? I ain't mad at nobody up in here, an I ain't gonna hurt nobody neither. Ya get them words, Sadie? Ya get it?"

Sadie's voice felt as though it were stuck in her throat. Her breath came out in uneven spurts and hot tears stung her eyes. It was a relief when Michael stood and headed over towards Chloe. He spoke gently to the child, comforting her the same way Fester had earlier in the day. He was calm now and she doubted he would hurt his little sister. As she listened, she found his voice and odd way of speaking to be almost soothing. While it worked for the girl, it didn't work for Sadie. The terror of what he might do weighed heavy in her mind. Tears rolled down her cheeks as she tried to stifle her fear for Chloe's sake.

"Hey," Fester said, "it's going to be OK. Just please try to calm down. Calm your mind for Chloe. Remember, you're safe here. OK? Clear and riskless. There's no one who's gonna hurt you. Sadie, can you hear me? Are you listening?"

It was difficult to do as he asked. She nodded slowly and tried to push the idea of Michael hurting her out of her head. She had to! It bothered her that she was easily frightened and she hated that her fear made Chloe cry.

It wasn't safe for her to be in this place. Constantly Chloe was hurt and constantly she felt that the men would retaliate upon her. The cold had been all that kept her from leaving thus far. Now thoughts of leaving the apartment and these people filled her mind with despair. The streets were so cold and she wouldn't know how to heat whatever shelter she was able to find. Regardless of the temperature outside, she should leave. Sadie would rather die in the cold than hurt Chloe again.

"I should leave," Sadie whispered.

"What?" Fester sounded baffled. "Why would you

say that?"

"I keep on hurting Chloe with my fear."

"Sadie, Chloe is OK and you're going to be OK too. If you go back out there...I don't want to see you hurt, Sadie. I don't want you to suffer and I really don't want you to die out there!"

"I can't keep doing this to Chloe, Fester." Sadie was still afraid but her voice was steady. "I have to leave."

"Sadie no!"

Chloe's footsteps quickly brought her over to where they sat. Without warning the child threw her arms around Sadie's neck. She jumped at the sudden contact and opened her eyes. Her heart felt like it went where her voice had been stuck shortly before. The girl's arms were wrapped tightly around her neck. Slowly she raised a shaking hand and placed it on Chloe's back.

Powerful emotions rose up within her and she began to sob along with the child. Chloe wanted her to stay after all the harm she had caused. With fresh tears spilling from her eyes, and a shudder that ran through her very core, Sadie's hold on Chloe matched the younger girl's intensity. No one spoke as they cried. There was no way that Sadie deserved to have anyone want her near them after the pain she brought to the child. Yet, they asked her to stay.

"Please! I ain't wantin ya ta get gone, Sadie!" Chloe said.

"I don't want to go either," Sadie's voice shook with emotion.

"Then keep here! Please, Sadie. Please!"

"I really don't want to continue hurting you, Chloe."

"It K, Sadie. I ain't mindin. It ain't hurtin true. Ya gotta keep here. Please, please, please!"

Sadie didn't want to leave the comfort and safety of the apartment. It was too cold for her to survive outside. While she didn't know what to think about Michael, she liked Fester and had a special fondness for Chloe. Their insistence that she stay filled her with emotions which she didn't fully recognize. A warmth gradually filled her chest and evicted her fears with swift efficiency. Her sobs began to cease and an unusual feeling of contentment washed over her.

"Ok," she said finally. "Ok, Chloe. I'll stay."

Chloe let out a squeal of delight and began to dance around the room singing, "Sadie gonna stick! Sadie gonna keep here!"

Fester exhaled heavily. "Thank you," he said softly.

Michael swore. "Them shits goin on heavy today?"

"This was the third." Fester said.

"Sadie, ya gettin 'fraid tons?" Michael asked.

"I'm scared less here than anywhere else. I'm usually scared all the time."

"Them shits ain't right," he said as he walked into the kitchen again. "Them shits just ain't fucking right."

Sadie turned her head towards Fester. "What did I do wrong?"

"Nothing, Sadie," he said softly. His voice held a strong sadness. "You didn't do anything wrong."

"Then what's not right?"

"What happened to you," he whispered. "What happened to you isn't right. What they did...what those fucktards did to you...it just...it's not right that you have to be so 'fraid." His voice cracked slightly.

Fester let out a shaky breath. Feeling as though she should stay silent, Sadie leaned against the back of the couch and began to wonder about him. The scars on her back had bothered him, but so did her fear. Was there something wrong with being afraid? Was it truly so unusual to them? A tear rolled down her cheek as she realized once again how far from normal her life had been. These people seemed to have never known fear and pain as she had. Or, perhaps they were simply used to hiding it so as not to upset the empathic child. For Chloe's sake, she tried not to feel sad. She swallowed hard, fighting back the tears that threatened to come anew.

"Hey, what's wrong, Sadie?" Fester asked.

Sadie let out a short and bitter laugh. "Me. I'm wrong, Fester. I'm all wrong."

Fester took one of Sadie's hands in his, causing her to flinch. "No. You're not wrong. You've just been too hurt is all."

"No, Fester. That's not all. I'm constantly scared and confused. I never seem to be able to do anything right. The world is too different. Everything around me is too strange. I just don't seem to fit right with anything. I really am wrong."

"Sadie?" Chloe asked with a sad tone that echoed how Sadie felt in her heart.

"I'm sorry, Chloe. I'm just sad. I'll try not to be." Sadie took a deep breath and tried to control herself.

"You're not wrong," Fester said. "You're just right. You can learn the things you don't know. I'll teach you if you want. Nobody knows everything, Sadie. Not even me."

"I don't want to know everything, Fester. I just want to know enough so I'm not so confused."

"You will," he said gently. "You will."

Sadie closed her heavy eyelids and continued to focus on her breathing. She had thought that Fester saw her as some helpless girl. She thought he saw her as wrong too. Yet, he said she wasn't wrong. He insisted that she was right. How could he know? The world revolved around her in a way that was constantly frightening. If she were right, if she fit with the world, then she wouldn't be constantly confused and afraid. Sadie was convinced that something was wrong with her and she desperately wanted to fix it. If she only knew how. With her eyes closed, and her hand still in Fester's, she had no doubts of her 'wrongness'.

The scent of food cooking wafted towards her. Once again they were preparing a meal. The thought of eating so much boggled her mind. Three meals in one day? It was something else that showed how wrong she was. For these people, eating so much was normal. For Sadie, it was as unusual as everything else. None of it sat well with her.

Even with Fester's help – if he could help her at all – Sadie knew that she might never understand this Downtown place or the people she now stayed with. These people, all of them, were far beyond anything she ever knew. Here was a home where no one was beat with objects or forced to do things in the bedroom. Even anger didn't bring the searing pain she had become accustomed to over the course of her life. Pain, it seemed, was almost completely unknown to them. For Sadie, the only pain she felt here came from her own emotions.

She had always seen her parent's home as a prison. Were her emotions and mind her prison now?

Chapter 13

The next morning Sadie awoke to the sounds of chaos and disarray. Loud noises filled the apartment as things were harshly moved about. Michael's stern voice was heard easily while he tried to get Chloe to move faster. Whatever they were preparing for, he was definitely in a hurry. After listening for a while, Sadie gave up trying to figure out what was happening. With a yawn and a groan, she sat up on the couch and stretched. Chloe came rushing over.

"Mornin, Sadie!"

"Good morning, Chloe," Sadie said sleepily.

"Chloe, get gone from Sadie an get ta eatin ya damn cereal. Where ya brush done gone? I gotta get ta doin ya hairs." Michael sounded overly impatient.

"I ain't got no clue," Chloe said innocently as she ran back into the kitchen.

Michael swore. "Sadie, ya see...er...noticin Chloe brush when ya cleanin or some shit?" he asked.

"No, but she can use mine if you want."

"Thanks," he muttered.

Sadie carefully made her way over to her backpack, which she had put in the corner the day before. Pushing aside her clothing and toiletry bag, she found her brush and headed into the kitchen. The apartment was small, and after cleaning yesterday she now knew the layout perfectly. It was a relief to no longer need the cane. She had never used it at home, except for when her mother made her practice. That was the day before she was brought Downtown.

Shaking her head, Sadie walked towards the kitchen. It wouldn't do her any good to start the day thinking about her parents. She had been so lost in her thoughts that she easily lost her balance when her foot caught an unfamiliar object. A bag of some sort had been carelessly left in the middle of the room. Her body fell to the hard floor with a thud, bruising her hip and her ego. Now the men might think that she was clumsy, as well as helpless and wrong. Michael rushed over and helped her up. Although she was grateful for his help, she couldn't stop herself from flinching harder than normal when he briefly touched her. She was getting used to Fester in small ways, but Michael was always too harsh for her to feel comfortable with his touch just yet.

"Chloe!" he yelled, "ya ain't gonna be leavin ya fucking book bag on the middle o' the fucking floor! Sadie be fallin over it an shit!" His obvious annoyance caused her to flinch again. She wanted to back up but was afraid of tripping over this 'book bag' again.

"Sorry, Sadie! I movin it."

"It's my fault. I should've used my cane." Sadie said as her cheeks grew hot with embarrassment.

"No," Michael said with a heavy sigh, "we gotta be fucking mindful is all."

Sadie quickly held out the brush. Michael muttered his thanks and the brush was removed from her hand. She felt guilty for getting Chloe into trouble. The girl didn't seem to be upset from Michael's harsh scolding. It was common for him to be loud and she seemed used to it. Regardless, it wasn't right for everyone to have to be extra careful because she couldn't see. This was their home, and she was only here until the weather warmed. They should be able to leave their belongings wherever they wished. It was obvious that now she would have to use her cane all the time to be safe.

She turned to grab her cane from the coffee table when she bumped into Fester. The sudden impact caused her to nearly lose her balance again. He muttered a tired sounding "sorry" as he caught her in his arms. He didn't linger, but instead headed swiftly into the bathroom. Sadie's face grew hotter and she rushed towards the couch. It would be better to busy herself there and stay out of the way.

Feeling as though she should do something to make herself useful, Sadie began to pick up after herself. As she folded the bedding, a wide smile began to form on her lips in spite of her embarrassment a few minutes earlier. This time no one tried to stop her. Perhaps they were finally getting used to the fact that she wasn't totally helpless. Or, she realized, they are too busy with whatever is going on to bother. Regardless of their reasons, she was happy to feel useful.

When she finished, Sadie sat on the couch and listened to the commotion that filled the small apartment. It was insanely confusing as everyone talked and moved about at once. Michael sounded as though he was far too frustrated, which worried Sadie. What if he hurt Chloe with his frustration? Chloe didn't seem to mind and instead began to complain about finding her homework. Fester tried to help Chloe find this 'homework' thing. Without knowing what else to do, Sadie waited and winced at the disorienting noise. She had to force herself not to cover her ears, fearing that would somehow be the wrong thing to do.

Suddenly Michael and Chloe called out "good-bye" and left. The silence that followed in their wake was pleasant to Sadie's overworked ears. Fester moved about in the kitchen and she went to join him. This time, she made sure to grab her cane. She didn't want to trip on anything else that had been forgotten.

"Have a seat," Fester said as she approached. "I'll make you some breakfast."

"You all eat a lot." Sadie said as she sat down and put her cane in her lap.

"No, truly we don't. We eat a normal amount." He paused in what he was doing. "Your parents didn't feed you much huh?"

Sadie shook her head. She ate more at home than she did on the street, yet it was definitely less than these people were used to. It was troublesome that they could fit so much in their bodies, while for her there was only room enough for small sporadic meals. Fester had said that her stomach had shrunk. Was it really supposed to hold so much?

"Explains why you're so tiny," he muttered, bringing Sadie back to the conversation.

"What do you mean?" She had never thought of herself as tiny.

"What? Oh...uh...sorry. Well, it's just that you're small, Sadie. You're so small for someone our age. You're very short and bonier than you should be. I think that you were malnourished while growin up. It would've stunted your growth some."

The word 'malnourished' confused Sadie. She could tell that it had something to do with food by the conversation. If she were to guess, it probably was something that happened if you didn't eat enough. But, was she really tiny? Was that why Fester's hands felt large to her and Chloe didn't feel as small as she would have thought? It was yet more proof of how wrong she was; proof of how she didn't fit with the world. Even her size betrayed her as an oddity.

When Fester brought the food over to the table, Sadie realized she wanted to know more. She didn't even mind the embarrassment of showing her ignorance so soon. "I never knew that eating was that important," she said.

"Yeah, well, it is. You need food, Sadie. Without it a person can't live. They become weak and eventually die of starvation."

His comment reminded her of what Michael had said the other night, *'It plain ya been fucking starvin ta dead, Sadie!'* She knew that a person could die if they never ate at all. Even though she had been starving, however, she didn't think that she was close to death. While she wasn't used to eating much, she did eat when she was able. Her body had been getting smaller to the point where her bones poked out through the skin. She knew it was because she didn't eat a proper amount, but now she wondered if it was also a sign that she had been dying.

Her parents never fed her as much as these people ate. While their lessons had caused her a great deal of agony, it had always felt as though they took care of her. Did they really not feed her enough? When she was on the streets, she ate even less than at home. Her bones didn't start to poke through until she was homeless. It had made sense to her that she didn't eat enough on the streets. Had she really not eaten enough her whole life? The idea was unsettling, and she felt as though they used a lack of food to hurt her as well. The reasons behind such a lesson eluded Sadie and she shook her head to stop from contemplating them any further.

There was no reason to think about the past now. Her parents weren't a part of her life anymore. Thinking about them served no purpose and would only remind her of the pain. If Fester would stop asking questions and making her think of new ones, then her mind would be free of her past completely. The present was so full of hope and she wanted to keep it that way for as long as possible. Eventually that hope would run out, but for now she could at least have her thoughts full of the pleasant things she had discovered.

It was a few minutes before Fester spoke again. "Do you still want to go to the library today?" he asked.

"Yes." The change in subject was a relief.

"We can go after breakfast if you want."

"OK."

Sadie was worried that if she said anything else then she would seem more out of place. She was tired of constantly being reminded how wrong she was. From not knowing her birthday, the scars on her back, and never having eaten enough...everything felt wrong. Last night Fester claimed that she was right. She wished she could believe him. Deep down inside she knew that he was either wrong or lying. As strange as Fester was, he had to see her wrongness. He was too intelligent to make such a mistake. Maybe he didn't want to admit it. Why?

Trying not to obsess over such things, Sadie turned her mind onto a more pleasant topic. What would the library be like? What sort of books would they have? Could she really borrow them for free? It was an odd concept for her. She knew beyond a doubt that everything had a price. There had to be something that they would want in exchange for the books. Sadie tried to imagine what it could be, but failed.

"Sadie? Are you OK?" Fester asked.

"I'm fine," she said.

"What's on your mind?"

"I'm wondering what the library will be like."

"Well, let's get dressed and I'll show you."

Fester sounded happy again. His voice was far more pleasant when filled with joy and not sadness. Sadie wondered what could have changed his mood so swiftly. Did she do something right and not know it? The conversation in her head replayed itself but she still wasn't sure. It was more important now than ever before for her to know what was right. She didn't want to expose her ignorance again so she focused on getting herself ready. The quicker she dressed the sooner they could go. Sitting and thinking won't solve her problems, but books might.

Soon they were out the door and on their way to the mysterious library. Fester had warned her that they didn't have money for something called a 'bus' and would have to walk for a while. She didn't care, and hoped that he would keep his unending questions to himself as they walked. There had been way too much talking lately. It wasn't normal for her. Besides, everything she said seemed to upset someone for some reason. She couldn't do anything right, and when she did do something right she couldn't figure out what it was. It was infuriating.

Unfortunately, it wasn't long until Fester broke the silence. "So, how did you learn Braille?" he asked.

"My mother taught me. It was one of her nicer lessons."

"I see. Did she give you books to read too?"

Sadie wished that he wasn't so curious about her. She truly didn't want to talk, yet she couldn't ignore him. With all he had done for her, ignoring him would be ruder than was warranted. That said, there was no reason she couldn't answer his questions as simply as possible. Perhaps her refusal to give him any real answers would bother him enough to shut him up.

"Yes," she said softly.

Fester seemed as though he was waiting for her to say more. When her silence held he eventually asked, "Um…so what sort of books did you read?"

"Math and science."

"Anything else?"

"No, I was only allowed to read math and science books."

"Was that all she taught you?"

Sadie sighed. "No. She also taught me how to do chores and take care of myself. At least, that's what she taught me in the nicer lessons," she said.

Sadie couldn't understand why Fester was so curious about what her mother had taught her. There had been both nice lessons, as well as ones that were harsh and painful and cruel. Some of the latter still plagued her with nightmares, as though her parents' torment continued even when they weren't around. There was no way that she would want to talk about those lessons. They were what she had actually been avoiding discussing.

"What about your father? You've talked about your mother and what she did to you. Did your father ever try to stop her?" Fester asked.

"No. He had lessons of his own."

Fester stopped walking and held Sadie's arm so she stopped too. She didn't want to talk about her father's lessons any more than she wanted to talk about her mother's. They were different but still held their own brand of pain. She didn't want to talk about her parents at all! Why was Fester always asking so many questions? Always with the questions!

"Sadie, did he—"

"I don't want to talk about the lessons." Sadie said calmly. She tried to keep her emotions from showing in her voice.

"OK. We won't talk about them." He sounded sad again. "But, Sadie, you're going to have to tell a story 'bout them sometime."

"Why? What does it matter?" she asked.

"It'll help you. Talking can help."

They started walking again. Sadie's mind was in a whirlwind of confusion and memories that she didn't want to face. She couldn't comprehend how talking about the past could possibly help her in the present.

Talking about it required thinking about it, and thinking about it reminded her of the agony she once endured. Some memories even brought back the pain so that she would have to experience it all over again. How could anyone think that would actually be helpful? Thankfully Fester didn't say anything else until they reached the library.

"Well, here we are," he said when they stopped. "There are a lot of steps. Why don't we take the ramp?"

Sadie nodded enthusiastically, her excitement was fiercely building now that they had arrived. She couldn't help but smile as Fester led her up the ramp. For the first time in a long time, she was going to be able to read! She was positive that now she would be able to learn more about the world she was in, and what was to be expected. Finally she would learn how to be right instead of wrong. Nervously she licked her lips as she walked through the door that Fester held open.

The inside of the library greeted her with warm air and the musty smell of old paper. The warmth felt good after the freezing cold that over ran the world outside. Her exhilaration continued to rise as Fester led her through the foyer. Immediately she wanted to use the air to see what it was like inside. Worried that someone might notice, she didn't dare try. The last thing she wanted was to get into trouble when she was so close to finding some real answers. It wasn't long before her cane touched something in front of her. Feeling with the cane, the object seemed to be quite long. She waited patiently for Fester to lead her around whatever it was. Instead he stopped walking all together.

"Excuse me," Fester said in a low tone, "but can you tell me where we can find books written in Braille?"

"Braille?" The woman's kind voice had an unusually high pitch, though her tone was as low as Fester's. "Oh…of course, follow me," she said.

Fester gently guided Sadie as they turned and headed in another direction. She noticed that the library was unusually quiet. People generally created a lot of noise to the point that the silence of the library was almost unsettling. No one spoke, and the few times she did hear someone talk they whispered. Every now and then she heard the sound of something that had fallen or pages turning. Off to the side someone stifled a cough, as though the sound would offend the other patrons. She found herself highly curious and a little fearful.

"Fester," she whispered, afraid to make too much noise herself, "why is it so quiet in here?"

"Library's are usually quiet," he whispered. "It's sort of a rule they have so people can read in peace."

Sadie nodded with understanding. The logic made sense. When she read at home it was quiet, but then again her parents weren't usually home when she read. If it had been noisy, like on the streets, then she might not have been able to concentrate on the information the books contained. It felt good to know about this rule. Breaking rules was something she avoided at all costs. The punishment was always harsh. Fearfully, she wondered what the punishment would be if someone decided to be loud in the library. Would it be painful? It was always best to know ahead of time.

"What do they do to you if you're loud?" she asked.

"Nothing. They would just tell you to leave."

"Oh." It sounded like an odd way to punish someone. "They don't hurt you?"

"No," he said sadly, "they just tell you to leave."

Sadie wondered why he sounded sad again. Did it bother Fester that she asked about the rules? Shaking her head, she knew that couldn't be right. He asked her questions all the time. Plus, it only made sense to ask about the rules of a new place. Poor, strange Fester. She feared that she may never understand why he did anything.

"Here is our Braille section," the woman said when they stopped. "Is there anything in particular you were looking for?"

"Oh," Fester said, "I don't know. Sadie, what sort of book did you want to get?"

"Well, what sort do they have?"

"We have hundreds of Braille books," the woman said, "If you would like there's a computer where you both can look up different subjects to see what's available."

Fester thanked the woman and Sadie clearly heard the click of her footsteps as she walked away. Her mind was too busy with the thought of rules to notice the strange sound of her walk before. What sort of person made a click when they walked, instead of a pound? She considered asking Fester about it but decided against that. Perhaps the books could tell her. It would be less embarrassing that way.

Fester guided her over to a table and they both sat down. She heard various clicks from in front of him and wondered what he was doing. The woman mentioned a 'computer' which is what Fester said his brain was like. Did computers make a low click when you used them? Oh why didn't she know more!

"Ok," he said, "so, what should we look up?"

"I don't know. I've only read science and math. I don't know what else there is."

"Well, there's a ton actually. You can read about anything you want really."

The idea that she could read about anything was a bit overwhelming. Her mind raced with possibilities, though she doubted there would be books on any of them. It seemed too simple. There was too much that she didn't know; so many subjects that she was sure her mother never told her about. Without knowing what to look for, she asked about the only thing she could.

"Are there any books that can tell me what life should be like?"

"What do you mean, Sadie?" Fester asked.

"I'm confused all the time. I want to know everything that I am supposed to know but don't. I don't want to be so wrong anymore."

"I told ya, you're not wrong," he said sternly before continuing. "Let's see though. Perhaps a novel? They tell stories and some of them could tell you a bit about what you're missing. There are so many different kinds. It seems they have a very large fiction section."

Keeping herself as silent as possible, Sadie sat and listened to Fester think out loud. Truthfully she would be happy with any book so long as it told her something new. Finally he found something he said she might enjoy. Without telling her what it was, he brought her over to a large and comfortable chair to wait in while he looked for the book. She took off her coat and waited patiently with her back straight and her legs crossed at the ankle. It was a position her mother had told her was proper. Without knowing more about the library, she felt that propriety was better than nothing.

"Here," he said when he returned. The book he placed in her hands didn't feel very large but it did have some weight to it. "It looks like it's a nice story. You might like it."

Curious about the title, she felt along the binding. "What's Christmas?" she asked.

"It's a holiday that's coming up. I thought you might like to read a story that had a thing to do with it. This way you know a bit about Christmas when it comes."

It sounded like a good idea so Sadie made herself comfortable and began to read. She wasn't too sure what a holiday was but refused to ask. The book would tell her, she was sure of it. Fester said that he was going to get some books for himself as well. She hardly heard him, her mind was engrossed in the story already. Fester chuckled softly as he moved away.

Slowly her fingers ran over the bumps that covered the pages. Memories of her mother's nicer lessons crept into her mind and she pushed them away. Not all of the nice lessons ended in a positive way. Here, in the comfort of the library, she didn't want to think of her parents. She came here to learn and that was what she was determined to do.

As Sadie read she was amazed at how different a novel was from the other books she had been allowed to have. It was far more enjoyable to read a story instead of only hard cold facts. By the time Fester returned, she was completely immersed in the tale. It told of a life so completely different from her own and she was entranced by the beauty of it.

Fester put down what sounded like a large stack of books before leaving to search for more. She wondered how many books the strange man had planned on reading. By the feel of the one book she held, she was going to be reading it for quite a while. Carefully she reached over to his stack and felt how many were there. She felt five large tomes. How long did he plan on staying at the library?

When Fester came back, he sat down with a sigh of contentment. She smiled as she realized that he must love to read. No one, she reasoned, would willingly take so many books if they didn't enjoy them. Perhaps asking to go to the library was what she had done right. It would explain why he sounded so happy when they talked about going. Absently she wondered if she would say something else right later, and that way she could learn about what else Fester loved to do.

It wasn't long before Sadie noticed that he had been turning the pages in his book quite fast. She couldn't imagine that someone would be able to read anything with such a pace. Even if he could see the words instead of feeling them, he shouldn't be turning the pages so quickly. She may not know much, but this she was certain about.

"Fester?" she asked.

"Yeah." He sounded distracted.

"Are you really reading that fast?"

"What do you mean?"

"I can hear the pages when you turn them."

"Oh, um, yeah I am," he said. "I only have to look at a page for a one-two and I have it memorized. Makes for fast reading."

Sadie was amazed. He did say he recorded everything he saw and heard. She didn't realize that applied to reading as well. *I can understand everything I read.* So, not only does he memorize it, but he totally understands it after a moment? The idea fascinated her more than she would've expected. The extent that Fester's power had influenced his brain finally began to dawn on Sadie. She knew she would never be able to understand the world the way he did, no matter how much she managed to learn. Trying not to become distracted by his power, she focused on her own book.

The story she read was about a young girl whom Sadie had trouble identifying with. The girl was happy, and her family was kind and gentle. It was such a stark contrast to what Sadie had grown up with. She wondered if what she read was how a normal childhood should be. Instantly she was enthralled by the way the characters interacted. The gentleness they showed one another reminded her of the people she now lived with.

It wasn't long before she realized that she truly did enjoy reading. It was no wonder Fester was so happy to come here. The library was peaceful and comforting. Sadie felt safe there, like she had at the apartment. Suddenly the world seemed a little less grim and a bit more secure.

There was hope for her future yet.

Chapter 14

It was nearly lunch before Sadie and Fester were ready to leave the library. Having finished his large stack of books, Fester told her that he had spent the last half hour thinking about what he had read. Learning such a vast amount of information in only a few hours had to be overwhelming. She tried and failed to imagine what it must be like to have such a powerful brain. Perhaps it was for the best. In her life there had been many lessons and experiences which she would rather not remember so easily.

While Fester obviously knew a lot, Sadie couldn't bring herself to ask him to help her learn more about her own ability to play with air. The book she read made no mention of Supernatural power or ability. If it were against the law to do such things, then it was understandable that a simple book wouldn't be able to tell her anything. Someone like Fester would know far more than anyone else. Yet, it was only a day ago that she admitted to him what she could do. Perhaps sometime later, when they were alone, she would find the courage. In the meantime, it would be wiser to stay quiet about the matter and focus on what was happening around her.

Curious to learn how they could borrow the book for free, she listened intently to his interaction with the woman behind the counter. True to Fester's word, the woman didn't ask for payment. Sadie couldn't help but feel as though they were doing something very wrong. As they left the library she felt her anxiety begin to rise. Borrowing the book meant a debt; nothing is for free. It was inconceivable that the library would let them leave without paying.

"Shouldn't we give them something?" she asked as they walked out. "We have to owe them a debt for the book. Why didn't they demand payment?"

"I told you before, libraries are free. 'Sides, we have

nothing to give them. Trust me, there's no 'debt' for borrowing a book," Fester said. When they reached the sidewalk he continued, "Listen, Sadie, I want to apologize. I shouldn't have brought up your parents earlier. I just...I want you to know that if you ever want to talk about your past...well...I'm here to listen."

Sadie didn't respond. It seemed strange that Fester would bring up her past, while at the same time he apologized for doing so. What a confusing man! If Fester was so upset about her past then why would he want her to talk to him about it? There was nothing for her to say about what her parents had done. Now that she knew how truly wrong her upbringing had been, she knew that there was nothing positive for him to gain from learning more. Once again she doubted the practicality in talking.

They walked in silence for a few blocks before Fester spoke again. "Hey, y'know Michael has his lunch 'round this time. Do you want to join him?" he asked. "He doesn't work that far away."

"Sure."

Sadie debated if she would eat with the men, or risk their reactions if she refused. Her stomach was still full from breakfast and eating so soon might hurt her belly. Then again, Fester always sounded sad when she refused his food. The trip to the library had been enjoyable and his tone indicated that he was still in a good mood. She realized that his happiness was more important than any discomfort eating would bring. It had become important to her that he keep that happy quality to his voice. Reluctantly she told herself that she would eat.

Michael worked in an area that Sadie had visited occasionally while living on the streets. For all she knew, they may have walked past each other before and neither of them knew it. Then again, she avoided the gas station where he worked. The amount of vehicles going in and out all the time had made her nervous. Chances were good that they hadn't crossed paths after all.

Sadie had to cover her nose and mouth with her

gloved hand as they walked through the gas station. The fumes that permeated the entire area made her stomach queasy. The place Fester led her to, an area he called 'The Garage', was far worse. There were more odors to upset her stomach, and the loud high pitched sounds of the work that went on there hurt her ears. She couldn't understand how anyone could tolerate it and was anxious to leave.

"Hey, Fester!" Michael could hardly be heard over the racket.

"Hey! Did ya get lunch yet?" Fester asked.

"Nah. Just 'bout ta grab a thing. I gonna get back in a one-two, an then we ables ta head out."

A high pitched sound suddenly burst its way through to Sadie's sensitive eardrums. Her cane dropped to the ground as she clenched her teeth and held hands to her head. The pain from the sound, along with the multitude of unpleasant odors, was too much to bear. Leaning into Fester, she blinked away the tears which stung her eyes. Her stomach lurched and she feared she would be sick. Michael needed to hurry.

Fester leaned over to ask if she was alright.

"I don't like it here," she said anxiously.

Gently he led her out of the garage and towards the street. "Better?" he asked.

"Yes, thank you."

"You sure you're OK?"

"It smelled very bad there, and the noise hurt my ears."

"Sorry about that," he said as he handed her the cane, "I didn't have in mind that it would be that bad for you."

Sadie took the cane but didn't respond. Fester seemed as though The Garage didn't bother him at all. Once again, something that was normal for them made her seem so wrong. How could he not suffer from those same odors and sounds? She shook her head, trying to clear away such thoughts. The day was going well and she wanted it to stay that way. Wondering about her wrongness could wait until later.

It was only a few more minutes before Michael

came out to join them. He suggested they go to a diner nearby for lunch. According to him, they sold *'the bester mother fucking burgers ya ever gonna get eatin.'* Content to allow the men to choose where they were going to purchase the lunch, she silently agreed along with Fester. As they walked the men talked about something that happened at The Garage. After a while Sadie stopped listening, even when the men laughed. She simply wasn't interested in anything having to do with that place. Besides, she knew that she probably wouldn't be able to follow the conversation anyway. If she paid attention, then she would again be reminded of her wrongness. It was easier and less embarrassing to simply allow her mind to drift.

After walking a few blocks, Sadie realized that the conversation wasn't the only thing she had ignored. She had no idea where they were. It had become almost second nature to backtrack in her mind how far they had walked and which turns they took. The ability to know where she was while blind had helped her to survive while on the streets. Even though she knew the men were aware of their location, she felt uncomfortable relying on their guidance. The moment she realized where they were, however, she stopped short. Her throat felt tight and her heart began to beat wildly in her chest. She fought the fear that instantly threatened to consume her. To panic now would be dangerous.

"Hey, Sadie...what's wrong?" Fester asked when she refused to move.

"Fester, what street are we on?" she asked.

"18th Avenue, why?"

Sadie fought hard to keep her voice steady and failed. "Are we halfway between E Street and F Street?"

"Yeah, we're heading towards F. Why? What's wrong?"

The alley! "We have to go!"

Sadie started to pull Fester back towards E Street. Her head swam and her heart felt like it would soon explode in her chest. The terror that filled her being brought her breath out in short, uneven spurts. The prospect of running into the man who had attacked her a few months earlier threatened to bring on an intense panic attack. Immediately, the air began to move in an unnatural way as she felt what was around her. The shift in the currents was anything but subtle as she pushed out further than ever before. It was important that she be able to see the entire street. She wasn't going to allow herself to be caught unaware again.

"Sadie, the fuck goin on up here?" Michael asked with alarm.

There was no time to comfort him. Pleadingly, she continued her attempt to pull Fester away from F Street and the alley nearby. He resisted, and she wasn't strong enough to force him to move. Both men insisted she tell them what was wrong first. Before she could explain herself, she saw four men come around the corner from E Street. The voice that called out to them chilled her bones far more than the weather ever could.

"Oi! Get ta lookin what we gone an findin on my block! Them bitch done gone brakin my fucking ribs yo! Ya gonna be payin for them shits!"

Sadie froze. Her fear turned to anger when his words registered. A few months ago he had tried to take something from her for free. What right did he have to insist on payment now? Obviously no one taught him properly about debt! Instinctively she wanted to shove him away with her wind, like she had in the alley. Out here in the open, such actions would be unwise. An innocent could be hurt, or she could be seen by the wrong people. Indecisive and unsure, she clutched Fester's arm tightly. She tried to suppress the terrible mixture of terror and rage that swirled violently within her core. For a brief moment she thought about Chloe and was glad the child wasn't there to feel her emotions.

The man in front took a few steps towards them and had barely raised his hand when Fester yelled, "Gun!" He threw Sadie to the ground and covered her body with his.

Sadie was aware of the actions around her thanks to her connection with the air. She gasped when a sudden burst of electrical energy shot out from

Michael's hand. It hit her attacker square in the chest and he instantly fell to the floor. The sickly smell of burned flesh mingled with the distinct aroma of ozone and caused her stomach to turn. The other men yelled out and raised their hands in response. The gesture was the same as the other one, and Sadie assumed that they had 'guns' as well.

Realizing that being seen was no longer a concern, she called upon the full force of her wind. The air around her shifted violently and she saw Michael stagger a little. There was no room for hesitation as she focused the terribly angry air at her attacker's friends. A narrow gust of wind hit all three men and blew them into the busy street behind them. There was a loud screech and the sound of metal scraping against metal as vehicles swerved to avoid the men's bodies. The air that swirled about in response made it difficult to see any further details.

"Run!" Michael yelled. "Go!"

Fester quickly pulled Sadie upright by her arms. Grabbing her hand, he ran in the opposite direction of the men they fought. She didn't resist and the two of them followed Michael, who led them around corners and weaved through the streets and alleyways for several blocks. Sadie ran as fast as she could, holding her cane high while she used the air to see. She was hard pressed to pay attention to the direction they headed and soon gave up trying. Getting to safety was more important. There would be time later to know where they were.

By the time they slowed down all three were panting heavily and it wasn't long before they stopped completely. A sharp pain stabbed Sadie in her side and her breath came out in uncontrolled spurts. It felt as though a fire raged through her lungs and she had to fight to keep from vomiting. Leaning against the wall, she relaxed her hold on the air and felt it move in a more natural pattern.

"Sadie," Michael said in between pants, "ya gonna get ta tellin me...the fuck...done goin on o'er there?"

Ignoring the anger and fear in Michael's voice, she

asked, "Is he dead?" Her own voice held that eerie hollow sound again and she felt numb inside.

"What? Fuck! Maybe. Oh fuck!" Michael said.

"Good," she said coldly, ignoring his obvious anguish.

"Sadie, what the fuck is going on?" Fester, too, sounded like he was on the verge of panic.

"He attacked me once; tried to do what my father used to do." Both men swore. "I used my wind on him to get away," she said, "I vowed never to let someone do that to me again. Never again. I still stand by that vow. I won't let it happen again!"

"Oh, Sadie," Fester said softly. The sadness in his voice tore at her heart.

"Ya power...ya done flyin three growed mans all in traffic with fucking winds. Shits, Sadie, ya ain't fucking helpless as ya been seemin, huh?" Michael sounded impressed.

"No, I'm not," she said firmly.

"What do we do now?" Fester asked.

"Get both ya asses fucking home. I gonna get Chloe from school laters, an we gonna figure them shits out when I home. For the one-two, just get ya asses ta home an layin low. Shit!"

"Michael, be mindful. They might be favoring eyes for us if anyone saw what happened."

"Same here, Fester. Now fucking get gone."

Fester took Sadie's elbow and she turned towards Michael. "I'm sorry," she said.

"Ain't no need."

Michael's footsteps began to move away as Fester gently pulled on her arm. The two of them walked back to the apartment in silence. Everything that had happened replayed itself in Sadie's mind. The hollow tone her voice took was concerning. It didn't sound like her. It sounded empty, as though it were not a part of her. It was the same after the incident in the alley. This time she had known her voice would return to normal, and so the tone wasn't nearly as frightening.

She almost smiled when she remembered what Michael had said. *'Sadie, ya ain't fucking helpless as ya been seemin.'* There was a glimmer of hope inside that they might finally treat her as though she were competent. If so, then Fester may stop trying to do everything for her. They couldn't possibly see her as helpless and wrong now. If only it had been different circumstances which allowed them to finally notice that there was some strength within her.

Sadie wondered if there was going to be a price to pay for what had happened. If she had simply paid attention to their direction, then they wouldn't have had to use their power. When she had lived on the streets, she managed to avoid the alley and her attacker without any difficulty. It only required for her to stay out of the area completely. Now, she may have put the only friends she had ever known in serious jeopardy, all because her mind had been distracted.

They'd been exposed as Supernaturals, and she feared that the government might try to hunt them now. The thought of someone performing painful experiments on Chloe frightened Sadie a great deal. She knew that if the government took them, then she may never again hear the girl's precious laugh. Whatever it took, such a thing may never be allowed to come to pass. Chloe needed to be protected.

Fester didn't take a direct route back to the apartment and Sadie didn't protest. He knew what he was doing. When they finally were home, she took off her coat and sat on the couch without saying a word. Fester, likewise, stayed silent. The sound of lunch being prepared reached her ears, and she decided the least she could do was to eat whatever he put in front of her.

"Sadie," Fester said eventually, "come eat."

Slowly she stood and walked into the kitchen. Worried that Fester and Michael were furious with her, she knew that strict obedience was needed. It was another lesson her parents had taught her; obedience in the face of anger led to a less painful result. She doubted that they would cause her physical pain. However, they may decide to hurt her in other ways. Perhaps it would be the same punishment as if she were loud in the library. While she didn't want to be sent away, she knew it was likely to be her price to pay for all of this. If she did whatever she was told, then they may decide to keep her. It was almost too much to hope for. The resulting anxiety twisted her stomach in knots.

Trying not to shake with fear, she sat in her usual spot. If Fester was going to send her away, then this would be the last meal she was ever given. Living outside would most likely lead to her death. It was a fitting punishment for putting these people in so much danger. When the plate was placed before her, she wordlessly began to eat.

"Glad to see you have an appetite," Fester said softly.

Sadie didn't respond. His voice didn't sound furious, and she wasn't sure what to say to him. Confused at the lack of anger in his tone, she did the only thing she could think of. She continued to eat. In the silence she heard Fester sigh heavily.

"You want to share some words about what happened?" he asked.

Was that concern in his voice? "No. It won't change anything," she said softly.

"I know but, Sadie…ya gotta at least be upset by all of this."

"I am upset."

"So then, let's talk about it."

Sadie put her sandwich down and leaned against the back of her chair. Fester wanted to talk. Always with the talking! Was he truly curious or would talking be her punishment? She couldn't understand the appeal, especially when it was about the past. There didn't seem to be any need for it as far as she was concerned. But, now Fester wanted to know about the man Michael had probably killed. She already told him what he had tried to do, and he was present for the rest. What more was there to talk about?

Sadie finally asked, "Why do you want to talk all the time? There's no point in talking about the past."

"Sadie, talking about things that have happened to

you can help you move past them."

"I don't understand. The past doesn't exist so there's nothing to move past. It can only hurt you through your memories. Talking about the past will make me remember the things that have happened to me. It'll make me remember the pain. That's not helpful."

Fester let out a heavy sigh. "Yeah, I know," he said. "You don't want to tell a story about your parents because it's painful. But, what about those men? I know you have to be freaked out by this."

"It's over, Fester. There's nothing more to say," she said firmly.

Once again, Sadie tried to figure out his motives. Didn't he know that she would feel the pain of her memories as though it were all happening again? Talking about the man in the alley would cause her to remember her father's lessons. Every time her mind turned to what her parents had done, the memories were accompanied by pain too. Fester was too intelligent not to understand that.

It began to dawn on her that there were more ways to hurt someone than what she had already experienced. Fester had said he would never do what her parents did. He said he would never hurt her. He had sounded so sincere and she had foolishly believed him. His words were all lies. He did want her hurt, by forcing her to remember the past.

Sadie felt like an idiot. Her precious trust had almost been given to a man who would use it to hurt her. It was obvious that there would always be pain whenever she was around other people. The only way for her to stay completely safe was to be completely alone. Yes, the cold outside may kill her, but a frozen solitary death was better than the dangers she faced here.

This new epiphany depressed Sadie and broke her heart. Something from deep within had stopped her from trusting Fester, and now she understood why. In his own way, the strange man was exactly like her parents. He wanted to cause her undue pain and agony, without the need to touch her first. Her parents had done all the work, and now he wanted to ensure their legacy of torture continued.

Once more, Sadie knew that she had to leave. There was no other reasonable option. This time, however, it was to protect herself rather than Chloe. When that man had attacked her in the alley, she made a vow to never allow anyone to hurt her again. It felt only fitting that she would enact that vow on the same day her attacker died.

Leaving her unfinished lunch on the table, Sadie stood and walked calmly into the living room. Upon reaching her backpack, she felt inside to make sure she had everything. A few objects, like her brush, sat on the coffee table. With her mind and heart numb, she picked up the items and packed them away. She tried desperately to figure out how she would keep warm for the rest of the winter. There had to be some safe way for her to find a warm enough shelter. The other people who lived on the streets had all found somewhere to go. There was no need to rely on the false kindness of her hosts any longer.

"Sadie, what are you doing?" Fester asked.

"I'm leaving. It's not safe here anymore." Sadie said, proud to hear an even tone to her voice.

"What!? What do you mean?"

Sadie stiffened when she heard him get up and come over to her. He was going to try and stop her from leaving and she knew she couldn't let that happen. Ignoring his presence the best she could, she swiftly headed towards her coat. Fester was very good with words; he had to be in order to hurt people through their memories. If she refused to answer him then she could leave safely and without any undue pain.

"What do you mean, Sadie? Talk to me, damnit! Why are you doing this shit?" he asked.

She shook her head and ignored the panicked tone in his voice. He seemed quite talented at pretending to be concerned, but Sadie knew better. Fester's vile plot had been exposed. Knowing his motives wasn't enough. With her vow strong in her mind, she knew that she had to do whatever it took to be safe.

"Sadie, will you just stop and listen? It's clear

riskless here. I promise! Just stop and tell me what has you so spooked!"

He had followed her around the apartment while she readied herself, though he made no move to stop her. Sadie was thankful for that. He was far stronger than she, possibly even stronger than her mother. If he tried to physically stop her then she would have no choice but to use her wind on him. So long as he didn't touch her, then she would simply leave and not blow him across the room.

The moment she picked up her backpack, however, it was torn from her hands. The sudden motion caused her to almost lose her balance. Sadie was furious! It felt as though he meant to imprison her here the same way she had been imprisoned by her parents. Would she never be free?

"Give me back my backpack, Fester," she said through clenched teeth.

"Not til you tell me what the fuck is going on!"

Sadie flinched at the anger and panic in his voice. It wasn't enough to stop her. She knew that Fester didn't want her safe and she couldn't let him hurt her. It wasn't an option and she needed him to realize that. Perhaps if she told him why she was leaving then he would know that he had lost. Perhaps he would let her go after all.

"You just want to hurt me in your own way, Fester. I'm not going to let that happen. I'm not going to let anyone hurt me. Never again! Now give me back my backpack or I'll use my wind and take it from you!"

"Hurt you? Sadie, I would never hurt you! Please believe me. It's true! I don't know why you think I would but I wouldn't. Sadie, don't you get it? I won't hurt you!" Fester said. His voice no longer held anger. Instead he sounded pained, as though her words had cut into him deeply.

"You do want me hurt, Fester." Sadie's voice trembled as she spoke. His tone was lying too, it had to be! "You don't want to hurt me yourself. You want my memories to do that. You want to hurt me with the past and I'm not going to let you!" she said.

"Sadie...oh Sadie..." She heard him sit on the

couch. "I'm sorry, Sadie. I had no clue that...I didn't know you would feel that way. I was just trying to help," he said sadly.

"You know that talking doesn't help, Fester. You have to know that! It doesn't change what happened. All it does is cause more pain; it will allow the torment to continue. I can't let that happen! Not again! The past belongs where it is. I'm not going to bring it to my present. I won't!" Her voice had risen far louder than she was used to speaking. She sounded strong and fierce. It took all she had not to smile with self pride.

"OK, Sadie. We won't bring your past to the present. I'm sorry," he said. "Telling your story can help but you're true. It won't help yet. I can see that you're not ready. I had in mind that...I thought talking about that man would be a good start. I thought if I could just get you to open up about it... I'm trying to help you, Sadie. I just...I ain't got no clue how."

When Sadie didn't respond he continued, "Please believe me. I would never hurt you. I don't want your memories to hurt you either. Please keep here. I promise, I don't want to hurt you. I would never hurt you. I won't ask you about your past till you're true and sure. Please, please, please keep here. Please?" His voice cracked after the last please and he sounded as though he would cry again.

Sadie considered everything he had said. As angry as she was, she still couldn't bear to hear Fester cry. The pained quality of his voice tore at her heart. It was strange. She never worried about how another felt until now. Why was she always concerned about how he sounded? Why did he make her feel this way? The unusual emotions that she felt around Fester pressed into her until she found she didn't want to leave him. With every fiber of her being, she wanted to believe that he told keenly the truth.

If he was serious and won't try to make her talk about the past, then maybe she should stay. It was far too cold outside, and she couldn't stand the thought of hurting him. The problem was, she didn't feel safe with him either. Holding onto her own arms, she hugged herself and tried to make a difficult decision. She was all ready to go out into the unbearable cold, but the apartment was comfortable and warm. She wanted to be alone, but these people – especially Fester – had begun to mean a lot to her. It may not be safe, but was outside actually better? She didn't really want to die out there.

"Alright," she said reluctantly. "I'll stay. But, I won't talk about my past, Fester. I won't feel that pain again. Never!"

"Thank you," he whispered. "We won't talk about it. Not unless you decide you want that."

Sadie allowed Fester to help her with her coat and he then lead her back to the table. Still numb from all that had happened, Sadie sat in silence. A sudden weariness fell upon her as the events of the day caught up with her all at once. Using her wind earlier took more energy than she initially realized. The anxiety, fear, and other conflicting emotions didn't help either. Leaning back in her seat, Sadie let out a yawn and rubbed her face.

"You OK?" Fester asked, sounding more concerned than usual.

"Just tired. Calling wind was exhausting."

"Yeah, they say power like yours and Michael's can do that. Why don't you finish your lunch and then take a nap?"

Sadie yawned again. "I still have some housework to do. The dishes need to be cleaned and the counters wiped down. The beds need to be made too."

"Don't sweat it. I'll do the dishes and the beds can wait."

"It's my payment, Fester. I have to be the one to do it," she said, annoyed at his offer.

"'Don't worry about it,' I said. Eat and then sleep. That's more true."

Sadie wanted to argue but felt far too fatigued. Obediently she ate what was left of her lunch. Neither of them spoke and the silence was welcome. Her mind swam with all she had to think about. If Fester was sincere about not wanting to hurt her with her memories, then there had to be some other logic. He was highly intelligent with a powerful brain. She couldn't believe that he didn't know that her memories would cause her pain. There had to be something else he wanted; some definite reason why he wanted her to talk all the time. The fog of exhaustion crept into her mind and slowed her thoughts. She tried to stifle another yawn.

This would all have to be figured out at some other time. Fester was extremely odd, and she knew that she probably would never be able to understand him or his motives. At the moment, she didn't feel safe, but she also didn't feel like she had a choice anymore. As soon as she finished her lunch, she stood and headed towards the couch. The nap Fester suggested seemed like a perfect idea.

"Why don't you sleep in my room?" Fester asked. "You might be more comfortable on the bed than the couch."

Sadie nodded reluctantly and turned towards Fester's bedroom. Sleeping in there would only add to her steadily increasing and overwhelming debt. However, she knew Fester well enough to know he would continue to press upon the matter, and she was far too tired to argue with him. When he followed her into the bedroom, she wondered what more he could possibly want. If he insisted on talking about anything at this point, she would use what energy she had left to hit him with her wind. The idea was only slightly amusing. When she reached the bed, she turned around to face him.

"Was there something else, Fester?" she asked.

"No, I just was going to help you," he said.

"I'm fine. I don't need help."

"I know you don't, but I want to."

Sadie sighed. Fester definitely seemed to have some issues. Why did he insist on helping her all the time? Couldn't he tell that she was more than capable of helping herself? Refusing to argue, she folded up her cane and sat on the bed. Aware that Fester was still in the room, she began to untie her sneakers. It was tempting to keep them on so she could fall sleep sooner. Her head longed to be nestled in the pillows. But, it would be rude to sleep on Fester's bed with her shoes still on. His sheets may get dirty.

"Here, let me do that." Fester said. Sadie heard his clothes rustle as he bent down.

"I can do it, Fester."

"Sadie, you're obviously exhausted. Humor me and take the pass. OK?"

Letting out a frustrated sigh, Sadie stopped untying her shoes and allowed Fester to finish them for her. She didn't argue when he covered her with the blanket as she lay down. Once again she felt that she would never understand him. Although he was correct when he said she was completely exhausted, she still didn't need help. There was no use trying to figure him out now. She had however long winter was for that.

Sadie had thought that after seeing what she could do, both around the house and with the air, then Fester would finally stop fussing over her. Obviously she had been wrong. He had to realize how capable she was, yet he continued to treat her like she was helpless and incompetent. Did he really think that she wasn't able to take off her own shoes and cover herself with the blanket?

One thing was for sure: Fester was a strange, strange man.

Chapter 15

Sadie woke to fingertips gently brushing her shoulder. Her first thought was that someone was about to try and cause her some amount of harm. For a moment she had forgotten where she was and almost thought she was on the street. Immediately she rolled over and grabbed the offending hand. It wasn't until Fester spoke that she noticed she was in a warm bed and relaxed.

"Easy, it's me. I was just waking you for dinner," he said.

"Sorry."

Sadie let go of Fester's hand and sat up. Her sleep had been fitful, but there were no nightmares. At least, none that had caused her any undue stress. All that flashed through her sleeping mind had been memories of living on the street and the few dangers she had found there. Although difficult to deal with sometimes, such dreams weren't all bad. It had been a while since she had experienced pain and suffering as she slept. The respite was still welcome.

Despite what had happened earlier in the day, Sadie knew that she felt safer here than she had anywhere else. No one had beaten her or forced their body parts inside of her. Her only torment seemed to come from her own mind. Even so, there was no way to tell how safe she truly was. Constantly, there were periods that felt like at any moment one of the men would hurt her. Every time she had been proven wrong. Instead of being a comfort, she had grown anxious that soon she would be proven right. The longer she stayed, the more fearful she became. Even to Sadie it seemed maddening.

As she rolled out of the bed, a bout of nervous energy began to fill her being. If it was time for dinner, then that meant Michael was home. He had sounded both frightened and angry earlier. Was he still angry with her for what had happened on the street? Although it had obviously been her fault, she hadn't meant to place these people in danger. Would he believe her? Could he forgive her? Such a thing didn't seem possible. His sister might be hurt because of one stupid mistake.

Realizing that she had no choice but to face him, Sadie reached for her cane. The sooner she was out there, the sooner it would all be over. Michael could very well be furious, but hiding in the room won't protect her. It would be better to go to him rather than vice versa. First, she needed to find that infernal cane. When she couldn't find it on the bed she began to worry. Would it be wise to make Michael wait or should she risk tripping over something? The last thing she wanted was to get Chloe or Fester into trouble with Michael because she was clumsy. Instead, she felt around on the bed, and then the floor, determined to find the missing cane.

"Want help?" Fester asked. He was still in the room apparently.

"No, I'm fine," she said.

"Are you sure?" He sounded amused, though she couldn't fathom why.

Sadie sighed and tried to not let her frustration show. "I'm fine, Fester."

"Well, if you're looking for your cane, it's not on the bed or the floor."

Annoyed by his mocking tone, she stood up and faced him. "Where is it then?" she asked. It was difficult to keep her voice calm.

"On the dresser," he said.

Sadie reached an arm out to feel for the dresser. It would've been easier to simply ask Fester for help, but she resisted. To show any amount of weakness now would undo everything she had worked so hard for. No, he needed to understand that she was capable of doing things by herself. That definitely included finding her cane on an unfamiliar dresser.

As soon as her fingers touched the long piece of furniture, she began to feel around for the mysteriously missing cane. Fester's dresser was covered with strange objects and she clumsily knocked many of them over. It was impossible to find her cane amongst the clutter. There was more than one cylindrical object and her hand kept picking up the wrong item. After a minute of fumbling around, she wanted to scream in frustration.

"Want any help?" Fester asked. He continued to sound amused, as though her frustration was a part of some private joke.

Sadie stopped searching and took a deep breath. "Why did you move my cane?" she asked through clenched teeth.

"I just didn't want it to fall off the bed and break, or for you to roll over onto it and hurt yourself."

"It wouldn't have broken or hurt me, Fester."

Fester sighed. "Yeah, that's true...here." The cane was pressed into her hand.

Sadie's face grew hot as her frustration turned to anger. "You had it the whole time?" she asked.

"No, it truly was on the dresser."

Sadie turned to face him. "Why did you really move it?"

Again, Fester sighed. "I don't know," he said, "I guess I wanted you to ask me for help for once. You always curb my pass for help and never ask for it."

"What's wrong with you?"

Sadie didn't wait for him to respond. Her anger had grown till she felt she would burst from the pressure. She wasn't in the mood for any more of Fester's nonsense and wanted to get away from him quickly. There was too much to worry about now that Michael was home. The last thing she needed was Fester making her feel worse. Attempting to contain her anger, she walked calmly into the other room. Soon she heard Chloe's tiny footsteps run over to her.

"Sadie! Sadie! Ya woked up!" Chloe said.

"Yes. Hello, Chloe," Sadie said softly.

"Why ya so mad, Sadie?"

"Fester hid my cane on me."

"Fester!" Michael yelled from the kitchen, "The fuck, man!"

"I didn't hide it! I just...moved it," Fester said

defensively.

Michael let out an exasperated sigh. "Just fucking get ya sitin an eatin, kids."

Sadie made her way to the table, careful to avoid Chloe's book bag. Thankfully it wasn't in her way this time. Without knowing how furious Michael was about earlier, she felt it would be best to sit at the table and eat whatever they gave her. Such had become a familiar routine with meals; the men would hand her food, and in turn she had to force herself to eat so they would be content. It wouldn't be wise to refuse food and risk the men's ire at this point. Wordlessly, she sat in her usual place and put her cane in her lap. Focusing on her breathing, she tried in vain not to be nervous. If she couldn't control her emotions for Chloe, then Michael might become more furious than he already was.

The smell of spaghetti made her stomach growl, and to her surprise she found that she was actually hungry. Eating so much still felt abnormal, but Fester did seem correct about her gaining an appetite. Would that make it more difficult once she was on the streets again? Hunger had only been a slight problem before. If she was now used to eating a lot, going back may be harder. It still wasn't clear if she would be forced to leave as punishment, however she didn't want to be caught unprepared. Her mind was uneasy from the turmoil that came with facing an unknown situation.

While they ate, Chloe prattled on about school. She didn't seem bothered by Sadie's mood and that was a good thing. Apparently, there were things about her day that were on her mind more than unpleasant emotions. Sadie tried to pay attention but couldn't follow what the girl babbled about. Without knowing much about school, she found herself confused by some of the terms that were used. School sounded like something that was normal for people to know about, and enjoyable to an extent for children. The fact that she couldn't follow the conversation only fueled her suspicions that she was wrong. Every day she found one more thing that illuminated the severity with which she didn't fit in with the world. After a few minutes, she stopped listening and focused on her own thoughts. At least her own mind was something she understood.

Michael hadn't mentioned anything about what had happened on the street. This made Sadie both happy and frightened at the same time. She had feared that he would be angry with her. Her actions had put everyone in danger, and it was no secret that Michael would do anything to protect his sister. He didn't seem like he would hurt her, though life had proven to her that one could never be sure. Her quarrel with Fester proved that as well. There were too many possibilities of what could happen to her now. Perhaps Fester should have allowed her to leave. Waiting for Michael to dole out her punishment was agonizing.

The men both talked with Chloe and asked her questions. Sadie tried to listen to everyone's tone to determine their moods. Each of them appeared to be in fairly good spirits and she eventually allowed herself to relax. If Michael wasn't angry now, perhaps he wouldn't be angry with her at all. Fester also hadn't been angry earlier. Of course, Michael could be controlling himself for Chloe's sake. That meant that she wasn't safe...yet. What would happen once the child was out of hearing distance?

Having finished all of her dinner, she put her plate in the sink. Fester had cleaned the dishes as he promised. She honestly wished he had left them for her to do. Why couldn't the man just leave things alone? Sighing, she walked into the living room and began to wonder about him again. What he did in the bedroom had seriously upset her. He claimed that he didn't hide the cane. Perhaps he was technically right. However, moving it to where she couldn't find it was just as bad. Why would he do that?

Sadie sat on the couch and it wasn't long before Fester came over to her. "Mind if I join you?" he asked.

"Go ahead," she said softly. Truthfully she didn't want him to, but it was his couch more than hers.

"Listen, Sadie, I'm sorry about the cane. It was a heavy bullshit thing ta do, I know. I honestly didn't think you'd get so pissed about it."

"It's OK."

"You sure? You don't look like it's OK."

"Fester...I like doing things myself. I don't like having to ask for help. Forcing me to ask for it wasn't right."

"True. It wasn't. Again, I'm sorry."

"Ok."

Sadie hoped that he wouldn't press the issue or continue to apologize. Leaning back into the couch, she wished he would simply go away and leave her alone. Her anger had been replaced with sadness by this point. Hiding her cane only proved that she couldn't trust him. What other sort of tricks would he play on her? She still couldn't fathom why he tried to trick her into asking for help. It was as though he was obsessed with helping her. The thought sat uneasy in her mind.

Sadie jumped when Michael yelled, "Chloe, get ta doin ya fucking homeworks in the one-two! I wanna see them shits when ya gettin done."

Heavy footsteps brought him swiftly into the living room. Having seen him with air earlier, she realized that he wasn't as tall as Fester but he was wider. Perhaps the slightly rounder size had made him heavy. He didn't seem much bigger so she couldn't tell. In truth it hardly mattered, she realized sadly. The time had come for him to reprimand her. Knowing his shape didn't change that.

Chloe was most likely in her bedroom with her homework thing. Michael must have waited until she was out of hearing distance so the girl wouldn't be upset by Sadie's punishment. Closing her eyes, she wished that she was anywhere else but on that couch. Slowly she took in a deep breath and tried to steady her wildly beating heart. By the time she heard Michael sit in the chair across from her, she was convinced that she was in serious trouble and perhaps mildly in danger.

"Sadie," Michael said gently, "why ain't ya never sayin ya been Supernatural?"

"You didn't tell me you were one either," she said, proud of herself for sounding so calm while her heart tried to escape her chest.

"True. I picture I oughta fucking done sayin a thing ta ya. Fester sayin 'fore ya done tellin him 'bout it, an he tellin ya 'bout him."

"Yes."

"Good, now we gotta fucking clue 'bout one 'nother. Question be: the fuck we gonna get doin in the one-two?"

"I watched the news. We weren't mentioned." Fester said.

"Good, it ain't meanin we fucking clear. There ain't been nobody on that block my eyes seein, but them dicks been flyin in traffic. Good moves by the way," Michael said.

"Sorry, Michael."

"Sadie, ya ain't gotta fucking get sorry. K? Them mother fucking pricks got what them been gettin comin! I worryin now 'bout ifs we gonna get rat out by 'em ifs thems livin."

"Do you think they're…dead?" Fester sounded as though he had trouble saying that last word.

Michael let out a heavy sigh. "I ain't got no clue. I ain't got no fucking clue, kid. What I gettin scarin the shit outta me be, I ain't none sure I care 'bout 'em bein dead or livin. I ain't never killin nobody 'fore, but I ain't never ever lettin them shits fucking hurtin ya kids neither."

All three of them were silent, each lost in their own thoughts. Sadie heard Chloe talking to herself in her bedroom. The child was oblivious to the danger which had been placed upon her. It was difficult not to be worried about the girl. Michael was concerned about the men they fought identifying them. If they lived they might tell the government who hurt them. What would happen to Chloe then?

"Sal." Fester said softly.

"The fuck ya fucking sayin?" Michael asked.

"We can ask Sal for help."

"No, Fester, we ain't doin them shits. Never. Them bitch been bad fucking news from birthed. We ain't gonna dare ask her for no help."

"She has the right contacts, Michael. She can give

us a pass if the fucking government is on to us!"

"Yeah, an what that whore bitch gonna fucking get from ya? Huh? Ya get ta picturin 'bout them shits?"

"I did. I can do the work as payment."

Michael swore loudly and Sadie went still. Anyone who frightened a man like Michael was someone to avoid having a debt with. It wasn't clear how Fester felt about Sal. He obviously didn't like her very much, yet he didn't sound scared when he talked to her or about her. It seemed odd that Fester wasn't afraid of the woman when Michael seemed terrified. Was Fester brave or did Michael know something more?

"Fester, get ta picturin them shits true with ya brain there. Ya ain't even fucking got a clue what the psycho bitch gonna get from ya."

"If it'll help us then it's worth it. No, don't give me that look! Michael, you took me in when I had nowhere to go. You and Chloe are fucking family."

"I get them shits, Fester. Ya been a fucking bro ta me an Chloe. But them gotta be some crazy assed shits ya talkin 'bout here."

"Yeah, tell me about it! Can't it be my choice though?"

"I'm sorry," Sadie said, "I'm so very sorry to the both of you. This is all my fault."

"The fuck them shits all ya faults, Sadie?" Michael asked.

"Michael, if I had been paying attention sooner, then I would've known not to go down that street. I've avoided it many times before. If I had done that today, then you all would still be safe."

"Sadie," Fester said, "that doesn't make this your fault. If that prick hadn't tried to...to...to hurt you, then you wouldn't have used your wind on him. Right?"

"That's true," she said softly.

"And if he hadn't pulled a gun on us, then Michael wouldn't have shot him with lightning."

"Fuck yeah," Michael said.

"So this isn't your fault any more than it's ours. The blame is on those jerks. Got it?"

Sadie nodded though she didn't agree. The fact

that the men didn't blame her was of little comfort. Deep down she continued to feel responsible for their situation. Now, Fester might have to take on a huge risk himself to protect them. Like Michael, Sadie didn't want Fester to work with Sal. She didn't want him to get hurt, or into trouble, because of her. Thinking about the danger they now faced fueled her guilt and fear. She wanted to cry. How could she have been so stupid!

"So, about Sal..." Fester said.

Michael sighed. "I ain't picturin it clear, man. Them bitch be full o' heavy fucking riskful danger. What we gonna get doin when she gettin ya ass hurtin or nabbed or worser?"

"I'll be mindful. I've told you already that I can outsmart the cops. 'Sides, the risk is worth it. Think about Chloe, man. We have to protect her."

Sadie heard Michael lean back in his chair. "I ain't fucking likin them shits."

"What will she make you do?" Sadie asked nervously.

"I don't have a clue," Fester said. "I've only worked for her a few times. The first time she had me run something across the border. Another time she had me hack into some corporate computer. It really could be anything."

"The fuck ya gonna get doin when she fucking sayin get ta doin a thing ya gonna regret?" Michael asked. He sounded more afraid and sullen each time he spoke.

"It's worth it to protect the girls."

"No. I ain't lettin ya fucking get ta doin them shits, man. Ya Supernatural brain gonna help us picture a thing. 'Sides, I gonna bet it good ain't nobody never seen us. I ain't seen nobody in that fucking block, an them assholes gotta be dead. Nobody picturin it been us."

"The probability is too high, Michael. You know I can tell when we're in real trouble and when we're not. You wanna know what story my brain has to say? Even if no one saw us, they will know that those shits were killed by Supernaturals. I mean how does lightning strike a man in the middle of a city and wind throw three men

346 feet back in clear weather? It's plain here, man. They're going to favor eyes for us. Now, they might not find us, you're true about that. But, I've already calculated all the factors, and it's more riskful danger than I like."

"Ya 'calculated all them fucking factors'? The fuck that tellin, man?" Michael asked.

"Shit, do I have to spell it out? Fuck, man!" Fester sounded frustrated and scared. He must have been hiding how he felt earlier. "There are a number of ways they can picture who we are: Traffic cameras, business security cameras, and anybody who saw three people running through the Gutter at 11:53 am. Not to mention the people in the cars that hit them. They may have also seen us run off. Add to that, if anyone looked outside their window at the right one-two, they could've seen what we did, too."

"Them shits gettin fucking paranoid."

"Bullshit, Michael! You know me better than that, man. I was able to rememery every camera we passed and anyone who favored our way. It's not paranoia to think that any one of those people or the cameras could easily ID us enough for PSI to find who we are and where we live! I went through the math and tried to figure out what our truest chances are. Trust me, I don't want to take Sal's pass for work. But, without her we have a 73% probability of being caught by a PSI Team. Out of that 73, we have a 28% chance of being taken in for experiments and a 72% chance we're dead, if we fight. Do you want more or are you good? I can go into more fucking details if you fucking want, Michael!"

"Fucking shit! Nah, I good. Ya fucking statistics gettin ta creepin me the fuck out."

Listening to Fester and Michael argue did nothing to ease Sadie's fear. With Fester's power, he was able to figure out that they could all die because of this. She understood enough about math to know the significance behind the statistics he had told them. It sounded as though they were most likely going to die, and it was all because of her. While the men had been arguing, she had hoped that Michael could talk Fester out of working for Sal. Tears stung her eyes with the realization that there was no way for him to avoid it.

Fester let out a heavy sigh. "I know you hate it. But, if Sal helps us that'll increase our chances of walking away from this to 88%. It's way better than anything we can get on our own," he said.

"Fuck! I true ain't likin them shits!" Michael continued to swear before finally conceding. "K...get ta callin the cunt. But, ya gettin her tellin a true story, an ya gettin good picture in ya mind what she gonna get from ya, 'fore ya go take them pass. Get it?"

"Yeah, I will. Don't worry."

Michael let out a snort. "Fuck that shit. Worryin what I done been doin, bro."

Sadie felt the couch cushion shift as Fester stood up. She desperately wanted to grab his hand and beg him not to call Sal. Michael's fear was enough for her to know that no good could come of this. There had to be another way for her friends to keep safe from PSI and the government. Fester seemed so sure that Sal could help them, and it was his choice as he had said. How could he trust the scary woman and how could Sadie trust him? Their future was devastatingly uncertain and there was no trust to be had for anyone at this point. Yet, none of them had a choice. She shuddered at the thought.

The tears that threatened to fall had built up and were about to spill. By the time she heard Fester's bedroom door close, her body had begun to tremble. Michael's heavy footsteps brought him all about the apartment as he paced. The movement bothered Sadie further. He only seemed to pace when he was very worried or upset. Thanks to her, fear could be added to that list. A few tears fell to wet her cheeks despite her efforts to hold them back. If only they hadn't gone down that street!

"I'm sorry," she said, "I'm so very sorry, Michael. I didn't want to put you all in danger. Especially Chloe." Her voice cracked slightly and she hugged herself.

"Sadie, ya gonna get ta stoppin them shits. We gone an fucking tellin it ain't ya faults," he said firmly.

"I know. I still feel responsible."

Michael didn't respond though he did continue to pace. Sadie wanted to ease his fear, but she didn't know how. He had called Fester his brother, and Chloe was his sister. It seemed that Michael had more to lose than any of them. He was protective of Chloe and now Sadie could see that he was protective of Fester as well. How the man couldn't blame her for all that had happened was baffling. *'It's worth it to protect the girls.'* Why did Fester include her in that? Michael won't want to protect her when he already had two others to worry about. He didn't owe her any amount of kindness. Her debt was to them, not the other way around.

Fester hadn't been in his room for long, yet the wait had been insufferable. It was difficult not to go to the door, press her ear upon it, and try to listen. Several times she reminded herself that he went in there for privacy. Whatever he had to say to Sal, he obviously didn't want them to overhear it. All that was left for her to do was listen to Michael pace and try to calm her own torrent of emotions. Chloe had been silent in her room and Sadie was worried about her fear hurting the girl again. When Fester's door finally opened, she sat up straight.

"So?" Michael asked.

"She said she'll help as payment for the job." Fester said sadly.

"What she gonna get from ya?" Michael sounded worried, which was to be expected.

"It's another hacking job."

"Is that bad?" Sadie asked.

"Yes and no. It's not dangerous, but who knows what the info I get her will be used for."

Michael walked loudly towards Fester. "Get ta listenin, kid, ya ables ta get backin out," he said. "We gonna fucking picture a thing out. Ya ain't gotta get doin them shits."

"Yeah, I do, Michael. If it'll protect us – even a little bit – then I have to do it. Sal said she'll keep an ear out for any moves towards us. She even said she'll help us out if it comes down to a fight or flight situation. There's just...well there's a thing more she wants, too."

Michael groaned. "I gotta clue it ain't never gonna be fucking easy. The hell she wantin?"

Fester sighed and walked over to the couch. "Sal wants you to come, Sadie," he said.

"Me?" Sadie couldn't fathom why Sal would want her to go.

"Abso-fucking-lutly not! No!" Michael said furiously.

"Yeah, that's what I said! But, she insisted," Fester said.

"The fuck story ya tellin the cunt?"

"I told her I would ask Sadie. The choice is hers, Michael. Not ours."

Sadie's head swam and her chest felt like it would burst from the pressure that had built up within her body. Her lungs felt constricted as well. It was difficult not to hyperventilate and she had to focus to steady her breathing. What could this Sal woman possibly want with her? She didn't have any skills that someone like Sal could use. Then again, there was no way to know what she would look for. Earlier Michael told her, *'I be gettin fucking 'fraid from Sal. She ain't good ta get 'round.'* Once again she felt that anyone who could scare Michael like that must be avoided whenever possible.

"What does she want from me?" Sadie asked with a voice that betrayed the fear she felt.

"Oh, Sadie, I don't have a clue. She said she just wants to share words with you. I don't know what her plans are," Fester said gently.

"Plans?"

"Yeah. Sal's not the type to do anything without a good reason. Or...rather...a good for her reason. People like her always have some sort of plan."

"I'm scared, Fester. What will she do if I say no?"

Fester sighed and Sadie felt the cushion move as he sat back down. "Honestly, I don't know," he said. "She might just leave you alone."

Michael swore. "Ya got morer smarts, Fester. Fuck! It ain't right I letin ya get ta callin the fucking bitch. We just maybe gonna get runin or a thing same instead."

He began to pace again.

If Sadie didn't go with Fester would Sal be angry? Would she hurt him? The thought of something bad happening to him filled her with an overwhelming sense of dread. The last thing she wanted was to put them in further peril. Then they would have more than the government to worry about. Her cowardice could cost Fester his life if Sal was furious enough. Like him, she felt as though there wasn't an actual choice in the matter. To protect her friends she would do whatever was necessary.

"I'll go," she said finally.

Words she hadn't heard before mingled with Michael's usual swearing. He had become especially loud, and his speech more difficult to understand. Sadie cringed and sank into the cushion behind her. She almost recanted to stifle his tirade, but she couldn't. These people were the only ones to ever try and help her. They continued to keep her safe when she clearly didn't deserve such kindness. They fed her and gave her a warm place to sleep. Her debt was so high by this point that cleaning the apartment wasn't going to be enough. Nothing less than helping them survive this in any way she could would suffice.

Michael's ranting died down and Sadie listened for any movement from Fester. He seemed to have gone utterly still. "Sadie," he said softly, "are you sure about this? You don't have to do it y'know. It's OK to say no."

"I'm sure."

"Get ta listenin, Sadie–" Michael began.

"Michael?" Chloe said tearfully. Sadie hadn't noticed the child's soft footsteps enter the room.

"Hey, Chloe! Ya K?" he asked.

"I havin troubles with my homework. Ya guys been too 'fraid and I ain't able ta finish up."

"Sorry 'bout them shits, kiddo. We ain't gonna be 'fraid no more. C'mon. I gonna get helpin with ya homework."

"Why ya so 'fraid?" The tearful quality to Chloe's voice worried Sadie. The men were having trouble controlling their fear and that wasn't a good sign at all.

"Ya ain't gotta sweat it. C'mon, ya gonna get ta ya room now," Michael said extra gently.

Michael's loud footsteps overshadowed Chloe's as he led her away. Sadie leaned against the back of the couch and sighed. She felt more than a little overwhelmed. At first she had been so sure that the men would be furious with her. Instead they only seemed to be afraid of what may happen as a result of her mistake. Now, she was terrified about what Sal could want from her. Michael seemed to think that the woman didn't have any good within her. What if Sal asked her to do something horrible? Saying 'no' to someone that scary could be unwise.

Sadie felt Fester shift his position. "Are you really truly sure?" he asked.

"Yes. I mean...I don't want to see her, but I will. I have to if it'll help," she said honestly.

Fester sighed and didn't press the issue. For the rest of the evening no one spoke about Sal or the government. That was fine with Sadie. Terrified of what was expected of her, she felt that talking about it would make her feel worse. The possibilities of what might happen the next day were too much for her to bear. Her anxiety steadily increased despite her efforts.

There was more to worry Sadie than the fact that Sal was scary. The only people she had interacted with regularly, other than her parents, were the men and Chloe. She wasn't ready to have a full conversation with someone new. Would Sal see how wrong she was and then hurt her or Fester? If Fester didn't know, then she wouldn't be able to figure it out.

What she couldn't put out of her mind was the thought that Sal might be as bad as her parents had been, or worse. Sadie knew that if the woman wanted to hurt her or her friends, then she would have to use her wind again. Each time she controlled the air, she found that she was stronger with it. No matter what Sal may have to protect herself with, or to hurt Sadie and Fester, the wind would be able to save them. If she went with Fester, then she could at least protect him from the horrifying woman.

There were no alternatives. The people she had come to care about could not be harmed. No matter what, that would never be an option.

Chapter 16

That night Sadie had an uneasy feeling in the pit of her stomach. The next day was going to be a long one and she didn't feel ready for it. Her mind filled with endless possibilities as to the future they may all face. The government could come and kill her friends. This PSI Team would be the ones the government sent to do this. Sal was another danger to consider. The woman seemed as though she would help them for a heavy price, and Sadie didn't want to be in debt with someone like her.

If only she had left in the beginning, then her friends would still be safe. If she left now, however, then they would be left to fend off these dangers without her. The unending cold outside was another threat, if she were to leave. Plus, it wasn't hard to guess that no matter how strong her wind became, she probably wouldn't be able to defend herself against the government or their PSI. Her safety, and her friend's lives, depended on what transpired the next day. If only she knew what would be expected of her. Neither Fester nor Michael could say much, which left her with a cold and empty feeling inside.

She lay on the couch for what felt like hours. Sleep wanted to avoid her, as though her dreams knew of how wrong she had become. That hadn't happened in a long time. Had her sleeping mind been frightened away by the uncertainty of her future and the possibility that it may end soon? Perhaps not. Usually an upset mind and an uneasy time falling asleep were clear signs that it was going to be a bad night for dreaming. The thought of having bad dreams again was almost as distressing as their current situation.

Finally sleep claimed her and allowed Fear to take control. Sadie soon found herself lost in a sea of nightmares. In the darkness of her mind, she heard her parents' laughter. The sound alone was tormenting, as it told of the horror that would follow. Her body jerked violently as it was riddled with pain while her parents gleefully tore at her flesh. She screamed through the agony and begged for an end to the torment. From somewhere nearby Sal also laughed at her, urging her parents on. She yelled at them all to stop, but they didn't listen. Over and over again she screamed from the pain she was forced to endure. Off in the distance a baby cried. Fester's voice cried out from the darkness as well, begging her parents to leave her alone. Sadie urged him to take care of the baby. Her life didn't matter so long as the baby was saved. She would endure the pain if it meant that he would live.

Strong hands grabbed her shoulders, shaking her as she screamed in terror. Instinctively, she struggled against whomever held her. It took a few seconds for Sadie to realize that she was awake and in the apartment. Her body trembled violently while she tried to clear her mind of the dream.

From the other room she heard Chloe's fearful cries, and Michael yelled at Fester with a panicked tone. "Damnit, Fester! Get on a thing wakin that chick, an calmin her fucking ass down now!"

"I'm tryin!" Fester yelled. He sounded like he too was panicking. "Sadie...Sadie, wake up! Can you hear me? It's OK. You're clear. It was just a dream. Only a dream. Can you hear me, Sadie?"

Sadie couldn't answer him at first. His words barely registered, though she knew that the pain of the nightmares was finally over. Someone sat on the couch behind her, causing her to sway with the movement of the cushions. Unable to resist, she allowed herself to be pulled back. An arm gently reached across her body, from her shoulder down to her stomach where a large hand was placed. At the same time another hand stroked her hair.

"Shhhh. You're OK, Sadie. I got ya. No one's gonna hurt ya. You're clear and you're OK. I got ya an won't let no one get to ya," Fester whispered in her ear.

Trembling, Sadie touched the large hand on her stomach. "Fester?" she asked uncertainly.

"Yeah, it's me. You're OK. It was just a dream."

Sadie cried softly as a wave of relief washed over her. She wrapped her arms around Fester's and held onto him tightly. There was no flinching this time, only a strong sense that everything truly was alright. Her body shook with emotion and fresh tears flowed freely down her cheeks. Fester continued to whisper in her ear and her fears were washed away with his words. In his arms she felt whole, safe, and secure.

"It's OK, Sadie. You're clear. Safe. You don't need to be 'fraid. I have you. You're clear."

Michael's heavy footsteps came into the room. "Good works, man. Chloe sayin she feelin relief an shit. She done got heavy freaked the fuck out, but good." He left the room quickly.

A shudder passed through Fester's body. His head rested on hers as she held his arm tighter. Silently he cried with her as his breathing became uneven. An intense sense of guilt began to rise within her when she realized that she was the source of his tears. Slowly and gently, Sadie released Fester's arm and adjusted herself so that she could face him.

"Fester, don't cry. Please? You don't need to cry," she said softly with the hope that her tone was soothing for him.

"I'm...I'm not. Don't sweat it." His breathing was uneven and she knew he lied.

"Yes, you are."

Sadie surprised herself when her hand reached out to touch Fester. Never before had she been so bold with another person. Her fingers brushed his arm and she resisted the urge to flinch or jerk her hand away. Instead she used his arm as a guide while she slowly ran her hand up towards his face. When she felt his wet cheek she cupped it with her hand and brought her other hand up to do the same. Gently she wiped his tears with her thumbs.

"There's no need to cry, Fester. Please don't. You really don't need to cry," she whispered. "Crying is only for when things are really bad. Nightmares aren't that bad. Please, don't cry."

"Sadie...I..."

"It's OK, Fester. Even you said so. It's OK."

Beneath her palms she felt him smile. As her fingers brushed his lips, she found herself smiling in return. Slowly her fingertips moved along his other features as her curiosity grabbed hold. While she had felt him with the air before, this was the first time she was able to notice any real detail. Her smile widened the more she explored his face.

Having only felt her own face before, Sadie didn't have much to compare his features to. She noticed that his eyes were wider and rounder than hers, as was his nose. What felt like jewelry pierced his skin on his eyebrow and nostril. It seemed like an odd and painful way to wear jewelry, but she didn't comment. Instead, she continued to feel around his face and head, wanting to know more of how he looked with every stroke of her fingertips.

His hair was short and soft. His ears had more jewelry on them, including ones that made a hole in his earlobes big enough for her pinky finger to fit through. Again she didn't comment on the oddness of the jewelry. For all she knew, it was perfectly normal for people to do such things to themselves. Instead, she focused on the shape that his head and features made. Her smile widened and she liked the way he felt. Eventually and reluctantly she brought her hands down and placed them in her lap.

"Sorry," she said.

"Nothin to be sorry 'bout," he said. "Are you OK?"

"Yes. Are you?"

"Perfect."

Sadie smiled again, her nightmares and impending danger forgotten. In this moment, her world consisted of Fester and the contentment which only he could bring. For a few minutes neither of them spoke. There was much she needed to say, but the right words were too elusive. Michael's voice traveled softly from Chloe's room as he sang to the child. Sadie thought it was strange but didn't inquire about it. His normally harsh voice sounded soothing and she figured that was the point.

"You should go back to sleep," Fester whispered.

"OK."

The cushion moved again as Fester slid off of the couch, and Sadie lay back down. She felt content and safe. A restful sleep was bound to come easily. Fester laid the blanket back over her and she rolled onto her side, snuggling into the cushions. She listened as he moved away and sat on one of the chairs. Even though she wondered why he hadn't gone back to bed himself, she resisted the urge to question him. This was Fester's home and he was welcome to do whatever he wished. She, on the other hand, was only going to be here temporarily. As a result, she had no right to question where he went or what he did.

Sleep didn't come as soon as she had hoped. Sadie's mind was full of thoughts about Fester. The way she felt when he had his arms around her was completely different from anything she could ever have conceived. She wished he would hold her again so she could feel that good inside once more. Knowing that this probably would never happen, she held onto the memory. It was one of the few that would have the power to make her smile. Remembering the past was worth it when the memories were this pleasant.

It took Sadie a while to notice that Fester hadn't moved. She heard him when he shifted slightly. He never said a word and she wondered what he was doing. Did he watch her sleep? Why would he do that? Once again she pondered at Fester's motives. Knowing she would never understand him, she silently waited for sleep to claim her. It wasn't long before she heard Michael's heavy footsteps as he entered the room.

"How she be?" Michael asked.

"Sleeping," Fester said. "How's Chloe?"

"Same. Them shits got fucking heavy, man."

"Yeah."

Sadie considered opening her eyes and rolling over to let them know she wasn't yet asleep. Feeling far too tired to bother; she lay still and listened to the two men whisper. She wished they would go whisper somewhere else so she could sleep in peace. Didn't they know they were being rude?

"Ya gotta clue how them shits got goin?" Michael asked.

"I did," Fester said sadly.

"How ya sayin?"

"I tried to get her to share her story 'bout her past a few times. It truly freaked her out."

Michael sighed. "K, well, get ta listenin, ya gotta get ta bed. Ya both gonna be gettin a long day t'morrow."

"Yeah, in a one-two."

"Ya ain't gonna fucking keep eyes on her all night?"

"Maybe."

"The fuck, Fester! Ya fallin' for them chick?"

"Think I already have." Michael swore softly and Fester said, "I can't help it, man. I love her."

Love was a confusing emotion for Sadie. Throughout her life, no one had ever said that they loved her. She couldn't understand why Fester would. An uncomfortable feeling began to build as she realized that she didn't want to listen in on such a private conversation. Again she considered letting them know that she was still awake but felt that would be a bad idea. She didn't know how they would react if they found out how much she had overheard already.

"Fester, get ta usin them brains ya got up in ya head, an gettin a picture 'bout them shits. K? That girl o'er there done been putin through a ton o' crazy fucked up shits."

"I get it."

"Man, I fucking serious," Michael said, "she done gots every flavor of abuse tossin on her ass. I gonna guess she got a shit ton o' brainwashin to go with them shits. I ain't able ta picture how she survivin so's fucking long, surer in hell."

"Yeah, I get it," Fester said.

"Fester, I serious an true, man. The girl there done got morer damage than any 'nother. Get ta lookin how 'fraid an skittish she gettin o'er easy shits. Ya ain't never gonna be *with her*, man."

"I don't have a care about that. I just want to help her, Michael. I have to."

"Helpin her ass or helpin ya own self? Ain't ya gettin ta lookin ta me them ways, Fester. Ya gotta get a clue what I sayin 'bout them shits. Ya done gettin fucking pound on abusin by ya pops. I get it. But ya ain't never gonna get none them shits gone from playin shrink with her."

"That's not why I want to help her, dick."

"Yeah, ya so's fucking in-lovins with her."

"Yeah, I am."

Love? That was the reason why Fester always wanted to help her? Sadie wasn't sure she understood. Why would he love her? No one ever had before. In her book the girl loved her family. There wasn't enough mention of it for her to fully understand the emotion. She had heard of love but didn't know what it would feel like. Just as no one had ever loved her, she had never loved anyone either. At least she didn't think she had. She definitely didn't deserve something like that from Fester or anyone else.

"The fuck ya gonna be picturin 'bout lovins, Fester?" Michael asked. "Ya be fucking sixteen!"

"I know what I feel, Michael," Fester said defensively.

"Look, even if ya be lovin her...ya ain't gonna be able ta get ta helpin her none, man. She gotta get her serious pro help. Ya gotta know ya ain't gonna be able ta get givin her them same shits"

"I can try. I read seven psychology books today, most of 'em on childhood trauma and abuse. I can try."

"Books ain't never gonna get ya experience, kid. Keep it in ya mind. Ya ables ta get all them book smarts, but when ya ain't got no experience then ya ain't got nothin."

"I don't want to share words about this no more," Fester said. He sounded tired.

"Fine," Michael said with a sigh. "Just...get ya ass a bit o' sleep. K?"

"Yeah."

"I fucking serious, Fester. Get ta bed."

"In a one-two."

Michael sighed again and his heavy footsteps told Sadie that he went to his room. In the following silence,

Sadie heard Fester breath unevenly. She knew that he was crying again. Why did he always cry? Did she really make him that sad? Resisting the urge to get up and comfort him, she could only lay still and listen. She didn't think it would be a good idea to let him know that she heard what he and Michael talked about. He might not take kindly to knowing that she invaded his privacy.

Her head swam with unsettling thoughts. She wished she knew more about love. Sadie had become used to asking Fester what something was or meant. This, however, she wouldn't be able to ask him about. Perhaps if she paid attention then she might come to understand what love was all about. It seemed unlikely. She wished her mother's nicer lessons had taught her more useful things.

Michael had said that both she and Fester had been abused. She knew now that what her parents had done was abuse. That meant that Fester's past held terrible pain as well. She didn't know. He never said or did anything that made her think that he'd had a childhood like hers. Knowing that his past held the same pain caused Sadie to want to comfort him even more. Perhaps he was sad because, in his own way, he understood what it was that made her feel so wrong.

Sadie knew that she cared for Fester, but she doubted what she felt was love. Didn't love need trust? She swore that she had heard that somewhere. Even now, she couldn't bring herself to trust the man. He was far too different from anything she had ever known. All her life, be it with her parents or on the street, she never met anyone willing to help her for free. It was confusing that this man would go against everything she knew to be true and then expect her trust. Now he claimed to love her.

Listening to Fester as he sobbed a few feet away caused a deep sadness to fill Sadie. She knew that even if she couldn't trust him, she still didn't want to hear him cry. If she could, she would wash away his sadness and pain the same way he had washed away her fears tonight. He said he wanted to help her and she now knew that she wanted to help him too. The concept was new to her and she didn't know what to make of it.

With her thoughts on Fester, Sadie began to drift off to sleep. Her dreams were once again peaceful and calm.

Chapter 17

Sadie awoke to the sound of someone knocking on the front door with more force than was needed. Slowly she sat up as she waited for one of the men to answer. No one else seemed to be around. The only other sound she heard was a light snoring from somewhere nearby. Feeling groggy, Sadie stood up and stretched. She carefully felt her way around the coffee table and towards the sound of the snoring. Someone was asleep in one of the chairs across from the couch.

"Fester?" She asked, hoping that it was him.

"Huh? What?" He sounded like Fester at least.

"Someone's at the door."

Fester swore and he groaned as he got up. She stood and waited while he shuffled towards the door. The person on the other side began to bang incessantly.

"OK! I'm comin!" Fester called.

The door opened and a man with a low deep angry sounding voice said, "Ms. Vinnachelli doesn't like to be kept waiting."

Fester swore. "We must've slept through the alarm. Give us a one-two. We'll be out as soon as we can."

"Hurry up."

The door closed and Fester called to Sadie in a panicked tone. "Hurry up and get ready. We have to go now!"

"What's wrong?" she asked as her fear rose up inside.

"We overslept. We have to go see Sal right now! Fuck! Why the fuck didn't Michael wake us up?"

Fester loudly ran into his room and roughly opened some drawers. Curses flew from his mouth in a way that Sadie had begun to associate with Michael. Sensing the obvious urgency, she quickly moved to her bag and readied herself. She scrambled to make herself presentable the way her mother had taught her, and then rushed to get her shoes. In her haste she hadn't noticed Chloe's soft footsteps as the child entered the room.

"Sadie? Fester? Why ya guys so 'fraid?" Chloe asked sleepily.

Fester swore. "Chloe, what are you still doing here? Why ain't ya at school?" He ran towards Michael's room and banged on the door. "Michael! Wake the fuck up! We all o'erslept!"

Sadie didn't like the panicked tone Fester used. It meant that he was scared and that caused Sadie to be scared as well. Up until now she thought that Fester wasn't afraid of Sal. Now she knew that he had hid his fear more than she thought. In truth he was terrified of the woman, or at least at making her wait. She quickly finished with her shoes and ran her brush through her hair, putting it up in her usual pony tail. Fumbling around the coffee table, she tried to find her cane. She was beyond nervous and that made locating it more difficult.

"Here," Fester said as her cane was pressed into her hand. "I have your coat. Let's get gone."

Anxious to go, Sadie grabbed her coat and struggled into it as they rushed out the door. Michael called out a warning to be careful before the door shut behind them. She held tightly onto Fester's arm for balance as they ran down the hallway and out into the cold. The icy ground made it difficult for her to keep her footing. Fester's arm proved to be more useful than before.

A car door opened and Fester guided Sadie inside. Placing her still folded up cane in her lap, she let out a nervous sigh. Fester's hip touched hers when he slid in after her. Doors were opened and closed some more before the car jerked and began to move. Her heart beat wildly, as though it wanted to break free of her chest and flee in terror. She focused on her breathing with the hope that it would calm her heart and perhaps ease some of her fear. Vehicles never seemed to bring her to nice places. The only time she had ever been in one before was when her mother dropped her off Downtown. The memory was bittersweet.

No one spoke during the entire ride. Sadie had

never minded silence before. There was a certain level of comfort that came with the knowledge that she wasn't expected to speak. This time, however, the silence was unnerving. Desperately she wanted to hold onto Fester for comfort, but resisted. One disadvantage to her blindness was that she didn't know if anyone was watching. The last thing she wanted was to show one of Sal's friends was how weak she could be. She didn't know these people and they didn't know her. At the very least she could follow Fester's lead and try to appear to be strong and unafraid. There was no way to know if she was successful or not.

It felt like an eternity had passed before they reached their destination. Sadie had spent the ride focusing on her breathing the way Fester taught her. It would be a good idea to keep a level head around these dangerous people. Her parents had taught her that fear was a weakness. Regardless of how many times her mother's lessons had to be repeated, she always had difficulty controlling any emotion. Fester had taught her that she could control them with practice. Yet, nothing she had tried in the car eased the flurry of fear that writhed within. When the car stopped and the door on her side opened, it took everything she had not to ask to go back.

"May I take your hand, beautiful?" Sal asked from outside the car.

Sadie turned her head in Sal's direction. "Me?"

Sal let out a small laugh. "Yes, you," she said sweetly.

Fester swore softly beside her as she carefully reached out. Sadie noticed that Sal's hand was barely larger than her own. The woman held her hand up as she climbed out of the car. Even though she shook uncontrollably, she was proud to find she could still open her cane with one hand. If Sal noticed her trembling, she didn't comment. Gently she pulled Sadie away from the car. Their feet made crunching sounds as they walked on packed snow. The snow made it easy for her to hear when Fester was also out of the car. It also allowed her to hear that there were three other people nearby, and only one had arrived with them.

Thankfully, Fester's footsteps moved quickly towards her. "I'll lead her in, Sal," he said.

"No need to worry yourself, Fester," Sal said in her friendly tone. "I can lead our dear Sadie in. Shall we?"

Sal's hand moved to Sadie's elbow and she flinched. Gently the woman's small hand guided her forward. She wished that it were Fester who helped her. While she didn't feel she needed help from either of them, he was far more preferable than Sal. If she could hold onto Fester then she would at least feel safer. Offending Sal, however, could prove dangerous. Without being given a choice, she remained silent about her preferences and discomfort.

"There's no need to be so nervous, sweetheart. I don't bite," Sal whispered in her ear.

"Biting isn't what makes me nervous," Sadie said softly.

Sal let out a pleasant laugh that brought anxiety to mix with Sadie's fear. That Sal would find biting someone funny didn't sit right with her. What other forms of pain did she find enjoyable? Sadie shivered and hoped she would never find out.

They paused for a moment and were greeted with a loud sound of metal scraping on metal. Sadie resisted the urge to cover her ears. It was tempting to ask about the noise but she didn't want to show her wrongness in such a way. Thankfully the painful sound was over soon and a current of warmth greeted them as they moved into the building. Their echoing footsteps told her that the room was large and mostly empty. Having never been in such a place, Sadie's unasked questions grew.

"Fester," Sal said, "there's a program I have that is highly encrypted. I need you to get us past the encryption so I can access the program uninhibited. Think you can do that?"

"I don't have much of a clue, Sal. It all depends on how sophisticated the encryption coding is. I can try, though."

Sal's voice took on an unfriendly and authoritative tone. "Trying is only worth something when followed by success. Remember that, Fester. You know how I feel about failure."

"Yeah, Sal, I do," he said.

Fester seemed to speak with confidence. Knowing how frightened he was this morning, Sadie wondered where he found the strength. She could only hope that she too showed strength when dealing with Sal. Chances were she wouldn't, but there was always hope. Sometimes she had surprised herself in the past. Perhaps in the present she would be as lucky.

They stopped walking abruptly. "Here is your station. If you need anything, Cliff here will assist you. Don't disappoint me, Fester," Sal said in that same hard tone.

"I'll do my best."

"Come, Sadie," Sal said in her friendly voice, "let's go and sit where it's more comfortable."

As Sadie was gently pulled away from Fester, he swore. "Um, Sal? Don't ya think Sadie would be more comfortable over here by me?" he asked.

"Don't be silly, Fester. You have work to do. You don't need us girls distracting you and getting in the way. Don't worry, your pretty friend and I won't be far."

Again Sadie felt a gentle pull on her arm. It took all of her own strength to allow Sal to take her away from Fester. She was terrified by this point, and wanted nothing more than to run away from this place and never stop. Trying not to shake and let her fear show, she kept her stride even with Sal's. Neither of them spoke as they walked into another room. Knowing that Fester couldn't see her anymore was worrisome.

Sal led her over to a couch and let go of her arm. She urged her to take off her coat and sit. Sadie instantly obeyed. The cushions of the couch were far more comfortable than the one at the apartment. The material felt soft under her fingers as well. Unsure of where to put her things, she folded up her cane and placed it in her lap along with her coat. Her mother had taught her many times how to be presentable and she followed those instructions now. She sat with a straight back and kept her head level with her eyes downcast.

Her legs crossed at the ankles and her hands were folded on top of her coat. Hopefully her good posture would please Sal, and thus she would be safe from the threat of an angry lesson. Sadie knew that someone like Sal probably had lessons of her own that were just as painful, or worse, than her mother's.

The door closed and Sal's footsteps moved about the room. Their sound was softer in here, suggesting that the room was carpeted. Holding her breath, she wondered what the woman was going to do. The anxiety of anticipation still grew inside of her and she couldn't stand it. She listened closely, though, hoping to catch what was in store for her before it happened. Off to the side she heard the sound of liquid being poured into glasses. Sal then came and sat down beside her.

"Here," Sal said softly. "Have some wine."

"No, thank you." Sadie was glad to hear that her voice was steady.

"There's no need to worry, Sadie. It's just a little wine. No one's going to be angry at you for having some."

Sadie hesitated before finally holding out a hand for the glass. The cool glass was placed in her hand and she gently closed her fingers around it. It was an odd little container, with a wide round opening and a thin stem on the bottom. Sadie had no idea what wine was and wondered if it was always served in such an unusual glass. Slowly she lowered her hand and held the wine glass in her lap.

"Relax, Sadie. It's just the two of us in here. I want you to be comfortable."

"I'm fine, thank you," Sadie said.

Sal let out a soft sigh. "If you're sure. Sadie, do you know who I am?"

"Not really."

"My name is 'Salvina Vinnachelli' and I come from a very powerful and influential family."

"OK."

"There are certain...obligations that I have to society, Sadie. You see, I have to continuously make an appearance for the public. I have to attend various functions around the world, and go to some amazing places. What I need is someone whom I can share this life with. Someone beautiful and special. Someone like you."

"I…I don't understand," Sadie said with a frown.

"If you're worried about the whole age thing, don't be," Sal said. "I may run my late father's businesses, but I'm not much older than you are. Even so, my businesses are flourishing, and I've even been able to expand. Some would say that what I've done is nothing short of remarkable for being so young. Don't you agree?"

"I wouldn't know."

Sal let out a short laugh. "I see."

Sadie heard Sal place her glass on top of a nearby table. The sound came from Sal's side of the couch. Sitting more in the center, Sadie had nowhere to place her own glass. A gentle movement of her legs told her that there was no coffee table. Without knowing what to do with it, she held onto the wine nervously, careful not to break the delicate feeling stem. The cushion behind her moved then, and she felt Sal lean in close. She must have leaned against the back of the couch for support.

Sadie flinched when she felt Sal's hot breath on her neck. The woman whispered in her ear, "You know, I only tell you all of this because I want you to know exactly what I'm offering you. Your life could be so much better, Sadie, if you allow me to be a part of it. I can make sure you live a very comfortable lifestyle."

The more Sal spoke the more confused Sadie became. She didn't know how to respond. Instead she sat, frozen in her confusion and fear. There was no hope of understanding what Sal had offered. How could she make her life better? Her life was fine as it was. There was nothing that Sal, or anyone else, could do to improve things.

Deep within, she knew that coming here was a bad idea. She wanted desperately to leave this place. Sal's hand slipped under Sadie's coat and squeezed her thigh and confirmed Sadie's suspicions of how wrong this all was. It was obvious that she had missed something important and she feared that she may soon pay a dreadful price for her ignorance.

"I can make you very, very happy, you know," Sal said. "I love to spoil my girlfriends. I love to pleasure them too."

Sadie scooted away from Sal to the other side of the couch. While she didn't understand what words such as 'spoil' and 'girlfriends' meant, she did know the word 'pleasure' and what it implied. *'Pleasure'* was what her father sometimes referred to his lessons as. She didn't know how it would be possible for a woman to do that to another woman, but she knew that she wanted no part of it. Pleasure lessons brought with them a different kind of pain, and she didn't want to live that way again.

"No, thank you," she said as her voice shook with fear.

"What's wrong, Sadie? Are you straight?" Sal asked. Her fingertips brushed Sadie's cheek, causing her to flinch harshly. The woman sighed and said, "If you are, then we can forget about the pleasure part. I'm fine with having straight arm candy to spoil, too. You just have a certain...look I'm going for."

"No, thank you. Can I go back to Fester please?"

"Ah, so that's the issue. You and Fester are a pair? That's OK. I can share. Though, I have to admit, I would prefer to have you all to myself." The cushion moved as Sal came closer, once again whispering in her ear. "Just remember, I can give you more than that boy will ever be able to. Gutter boys like him are generally hopeless. But I could take very, very good care of you. I can give you anything you desire, you know. I'm Highborn and have that ability."

Sadie swallowed hard and tried in vain not to tremble with fear. Not wanting to look too weak, she closed her eyes to hold back her tears. She inhaled deeply in an effort to control her emotions as well. Memories of the apartment and how safe she felt there filled her mind. She thought about how she felt when Fester held her. That safe and secure feeling which she had never known before began to find its way in. Holding onto that feeling, Sadie felt her fear begin to subside.

"Relax, Sadie," Sal said. "I don't know what Mickey and Fester have told you, but I'm not really all that bad. I can be very, very good to my friends. Don't you want to be my friend, Sadie?" When Sadie didn't respond Sal said, "I tell you what, you can take all the time you need to consider my offer. In the meantime, why don't we sit here as friends and drink our wine? What do you say?"

The cushion moved as Sal slid back towards the other side of the couch and away from Sadie. Sadie didn't move, however. She continued to sit still and hold her wine glass. In her mind she wished for the day to be over. Sal's voice had been friendly throughout the entire discussion, but that couldn't be trusted. It was no secret how easily the woman switched her tone. There would never be trust with Sal no matter what she offered. Sadie didn't want to be her friend. She didn't want to be anywhere near her.

"Drink, Sadie. This wine is expensive and I would hate for any of it to go to waste."

Understanding the value of something expensive, Sadie obeyed and had a sip of the wine. The taste of the dry fruity liquid was unpleasant. She wondered why Sal would insist they drink something like that. Without having an answer to her question, and not wanting to upset Sal, she drank what was in her glass. The last thing she needed now was for Sal to cease being friendly towards her.

"Would you like some more?" Sal asked when Sadie finished.

"No thank you," Sadie said softly.

The other woman sighed. For several minutes the two of them sat in silence before Sadie heard an unusual tune. When Sal answered her phone, she had lost the friendly tone to her voice. Even so, the woman sounded pleased. Sadie heard the phone close and Sal let out a content sigh.

"Well, it looks like our boy Fester was able to crack that code sooner than I expected. Why don't we go and have a look?"

Sal gently took the empty glass from Sadie. Standing up, she felt a little lightheaded. Unsure as to why, she put her coat back on and opened her cane. If she still felt dizzy when they were away from Sal, then she would tell Fester and he could figure out what was wrong. For now, she tried not to flinch when Sal took her elbow and led her back into the large room. The closer she was to Fester, the more relaxed she became. If he was done, and Sal was pleased, then they could soon leave and forget about this frightful place.

"Sal." Fester sounded relieved as they approached. "I managed to crack the encryption code. It wasn't easy. You should be able to access the program now."

"Excellent work, Fester," Sal said, sounding pleased. "As we agreed, I'll keep an eye out for any PSI activity aimed at you all. Also, my Boys and I will be available should they turn their sights onto you."

"Thanks, Sal." The relief in Fester's voice was unmistakable.

"Well, we're all done here. Cliff, make sure they both get home safely. I hope to see you again, Sadie."

Sadie couldn't help but flinch when the other woman gave her a kiss on the cheek. The gesture reminded her briefly of her father, though, he pressed his lips to... other places. Again she began to tremble and was relieved when she heard Sal walk away. Her arm was soon taken again by Fester who swiftly led her out of the building. It was difficult not to run for the awaiting car. She was happy to be leaving that place, and Sal, firmly behind her.

The sound of the car door closing after them caused Sadie to jump, even though she had expected it. Fester leaned over and asked her if she was alright. Not trusting her voice, she simply nodded her head. She wanted to tell him how scared she was, and how confusing her talk with Sal had been. Once more she held her tongue, afraid that it wasn't safe to talk openly inside the vehicle. Thankfully Fester didn't ask her anything else for the rest of the ride.

Sadie's mind was full of everything Sal had said. She wasn't sure if she fully understood what the conversation was truly about. All she could tell was that Sal wanted something from her and she doubted it was to simply be friends. Fester said people like Sal always have a plan and it's not always good for others. She intended to ask him about it once they were in the comfort of the apartment.

It was amazing how quickly the apartment had become someplace she looked to as a safe haven against the horrors of the world. With how much Sal frightened her, Sadie wanted nothing more than to be within its secure walls.

Chapter 18

As they entered the apartment Sadie let out a sigh of relief. They were both unscathed from their ordeal and it was finally over. The fear and anxiety that had built up inside of her had finally begun to ease. When Fester offered to hang up her coat for her, she gratefully handed it to him. She was unsteady and would be embarrassed if she had trouble placing it on its peg. Her body felt weak and her mind swam with a host of emotions. She quickly sat at the kitchen table. There was no guarantee that she would make it to the couch. The experience had affected her more than she initially thought.

Fester moved to her side and placed his large hand over hers. Thankfully she didn't flinch at his touch. It had become easier to keep herself steady around him. There was no doubt that he was worried about her. He seemed to worry nearly as much as he tried to help. Wishing to reassure him, she turned her head in his direction and smiled. It was over and they were safe. Her fear had already eased considerably since they walked through the door. Perhaps the longer they were home the more it would loosen its grip.

"Are you OK, Sadie? She didn't hurt you, did she?" he asked.

"No, I'm fine, Fester. Just a little shaken."

"Are you sure?"

"Yes."

Fester gave her hand a gentle squeeze before he moved away. "We didn't have a chance to eat breakfast or lunch. I'll make us something. You just sit there and relax."

With no desire to move, and feeling quite hungry, Sadie was content to listen as Fester moved about the kitchen. It wasn't long, however, before she became the one who was worried. He sounded rushed and she wondered if something bad had happened. The dishes were placed harshly on the counter, and the fridge was closed with the same force. When something fell to the floor and shattered, Fester swore heavily and her concern deepened.

"Fester, what's wrong? Are you OK?" she asked.

"Yeah…yeah…nothing's wrong. It's just…I wish we didn't go there today is all." The sound of glass being swept by a broom accompanied his frustrated tone.

"Why? What happened?"

"Oh, it's just the program Sal had me unlock for her. It was full of schematics. I only saw a few of them and I'm pissed that I can't picture exactly what they're for. It looked like a weapon of some kind…but I didn't see enough to be entirely sure."

"What kind of weapon?"

"The kind that kills a lot of people at once," he said sadly as he put a plate in front of her.

"Oh."

Sadie didn't want to know why someone would need a weapon like that. The idea that one single person could easily cause so much death was frightening on a level she had never experienced. Her wind could cause people to be hurt, as could Michael's lightning. But, Michael would only use his lightning to protect himself or someone else, like with the man from the alley. Sadie was the same way. Having a weapon such as the one Fester described wouldn't be for protection. Why would Sal want to hurt a lot of people at once? The knowledge of this weapon only served to increase her fear of the woman.

Neither of them spoke as they ate. While Sadie wanted to talk to Fester about what she and Sal spoke about, she also didn't want to interrupt his thoughts. He seemed upset with the work he had done. She knew that it was her fault, and her guilt cut through her like a knife in her gut. If only they hadn't gone down that street, then none of this would've happened. Fester wouldn't have had to help someone like Sal, and in turn Sal wouldn't have such a dangerous weapon. Her mistake seemed to be more costly than she could have ever imagined. Why did she have to be so wrong!

They hadn't finished lunch yet when she heard the door to the apartment unlock. Fearful that Sal might have decided that she wanted more from them, Sadie quickly told Fester what she had heard. He stood to investigate and patted her arm reassuringly as he passed her. His touch was anything but comforting. If Sal had come back, what could he do? What would she do? Sadie held her breath in anticipation. When the door opened, Fester let out a sigh of relief.

"Michael? What are you doing home so early?"

Sadie could breathe again once she realized that it was Michael at the door and not Sal.

"I ain't gone fucking workin, man. When I gone callin an sayin my sorries for bein lates, Dan sayin Chris takin my shift an shit. I fucking be gettin bored waitin on ya asses so's I gettin me s'more smokes. Fucking goin through two packs cause ya all gone an shits."

"Sorry, man. We just got in ourselves."

"Good, ya taked more time an I gettiin ready ta stroke. Damn! I fucking worrin surer in hell! I even got ta callin ya cell, but ya up an left them shits home!"

"We're fine. We met Sal at some abandoned warehouse that was way outside of the city. I knew that she wouldn't let me have my phone, so I didn't bother bringing it."

Fester walked back to the table and sat down. Michael had been afraid for them, though seeing they were safe seemed to do anything but ease his concern. He started to pace after he took off his coat and that made Sadie nervous. Whatever reason he had for still being upset, she hoped it wasn't something she had done. The last thing she needed was to have done something wrong yet again and not know it. He was probably more upset about Sal than he was with her. All of this was clearly Sadie's fault, but neither of the men saw it that way.

"So? Ya kids gonna get ta fucking tellin a story on what she gone an got from ya asses, or I gotta get words from the bitch my own selfs?"

"Sorry," Fester said. It sounded like his mouth was full of food. "We're just hungry from skipping breakfast and lunch."

"Right. Well I ain't gonna let no fucking anxiety an shit keep ya from shovelin food down ya fucking traps or nothin. I gonna just get ta sitin on my mother fucking hands till ya done."

"Michael, don't be like that. Fine. We'll tell our story while we eat. OK?"

"Yeah, whatever. So what the bitch gone an got from ya two?"

Fester sighed. "She wanted me to unlock an encrypted program. I actually wasn't sure if I could do it at first. The codes were way more complex than what I'm used to. But I managed." Was that pride in his voice?

"Good for ya ass, dick. What fucking program she gone an got ya hackin?"

"Not sure. I only got a glimpse of it before one of her goons swept in and kicked me off of the computer. It looked like schematics for some kind o' high powered weapon of mass destruction. Couldn't tell a thing more 'bout it, though. I'm not even sure it truly was a weapon, that's just what I'm guessin."

"Fucking shits ain't good, Fester. Ya 'guesses' been gettin all kind o' fucking true. Them shits gettin crazy scary, man!"

"Yeah, I get that."

Both men were silent for a while. This weapon sounded worse than anything she had ever known. Once again she realized that she didn't want to know what a woman like Sal would want with such a thing. She had said that she ran her father's businesses. What sort of business needed something like what Fester worked on?

"What 'bout ya ass, Sadie girl? The fuck them bitch gone an got from ya?" Michael asked.

"I'm not sure," she said.

"Didn't she say?" Fester asked.

"Well, yes. But I'm not sure I understand what she was talking about."

"Maybe we can help. What did she say?"

"Fester, she said a lot of things that didn't make

sense. First she gave me something called 'wine' and talked about her businesses…and money I think. Something about making my life comfortable. She…" Sadie hesitated and then told them the rest quickly, her tone matching her own anxiety. "She whispered in my ear and touched my leg and said something about girlfriends and…other things that I…I didn't like."

"Fuck me!" Michael pounded his fist onto the table.

Sadie flinched at Michael's outburst before continuing. "She told me that if I didn't want that then I could be something called 'straight eye candy' or something. She said she could give me things that you can't, Fester. She told me you were hopeless, though I don't know how. At the end she said she could make a very good friend. I don't know…it was all so confusing. I'm still not sure what exactly it was that she wanted." Sadie held back the tears that threatened once again to fall.

Fester stood up from his chair and moved to her side. While she had begun to flinch less and less around Fester, her anxiety and fear made it hard to not do so now. "Sadie, what did you say to her?"

"No, thank you."

"Good," Fester said as he squeezed her hand. "You did real good, Sadie."

"I did?" she asked.

"Yeah," he said gently as he moved away.

Sadie smiled. Deep down she knew that whatever it was that Sal had offered, she shouldn't accept. It was good to see that her instincts were right this time. If only she hadn't been as confused as usual, then perhaps she would have understood what Sal wanted. At the moment, all she could do was make herself sick with worry. Having finished her lunch, she decided to head into the living room. She didn't want to think about this anymore. When she reached out to grab her plate, she found that it was missing.

"Don't sweat it, I've got it." Fester said.

Sadie sighed and yet again wished that he would let her do things for herself. Resisting the urge to scold him, she turned towards the living room. Michael followed her, his footsteps betraying his proximity with every step. When she sat in one of the chairs, he sat in the other one. She listened as he adjusted himself and wondered what it was that he wanted.

"Sadie, how many wine Sal givin ya?" he finally asked.

"A glass."

"Ya swallow them shits?"

"Yes. Was that wrong?"

"It ain't 'bout bein right or wrong. It just...that bitch pass ya a thing for eatin or drinkin 'gain, ya sayin her 'fuck off'. K?"

"OK," she said.

"I fucking serious as fuck, Sadie. Sal done been bad news an a side o' fucked up. I ain't never gonna put it past her not ta slip a thing in what she givin ya. It gonna be riskless if ya just curb her pass next time."

"I...OK."

It was frightening to think that Sal could have put something in the wine. Would it make her sick if she did? Sadie couldn't understand why anyone would want to make her sick. Even her parents had never done such a thing. Michael obviously knew more than she did when it came to people like Sal. He knew more than she did when it came to anyone. Even though refusing Sal was a scary thought, if she met the woman again she would refuse the wine. If Michael said that it's dangerous, then she was going to heed his warnings.

Fester asked nervously from nearby, "Do you really think Sal would've drugged her?"

"I done been knowin them fucked up Vinnachelli family near all my livin life, kid. I ain't never gonna put nothin past her," Michael said firmly.

"Michael, you never said how you know Sal. Did you work for her or a thing?"

"Fuck, man. Them a crazy uber lil story." He sighed heavily. "K, I fucking tellin ya the shorter kind. My 'rents done been doin some works for Sal pops. Them done startin back 'fore Chloe been birthed. Lil shit, same as ya gone an done, Fester. Thing is, them got true an tight with Sal family. So, I been knowin the lil cunt from when we was kids. Kinda gone an growed up with her an shit."

"'Rents?" Sadie asked. She had heard the word before, but it was one of the few that she didn't fully understand.

"Parents," Fester said.

"Oh. Where are they now?" she asked.

"Them dis'peared two year gone now. See, Sal pops done got from her runnin a lil his business back when she done been fucking thirteen. When the fucker up an got dead, she done takin the thing o'er. Even gettin her hands in them shits ain't true legit. One day she done got my 'rents doin a thing for her, an thems ain't never fucking come home. Bitch done been sayin she gonna get me an Chloe dead, cause I gotta go get ta learnin where the fuck she sendin my 'rents! Crazy shits be, I gotta clue she gonna be makin good on them threatin too. I gotta backs off so's the cunt ain't gonna get ta hurtin my sis. I ain't never gonna be lettin her get dead. No!"

Fester swore heavily. "Why didn't you tell me?"

"Because I ain't never likin picturin 'bout them shits! K? Fucking pissin me off surer in hell! But in the one-two, ya gotta clue for why I ain't never gonna get ta likin ya gettin works from her. Bitch been bad news an I ain't fit for ya gettin all gone an shit same."

"Sorry, man. I didn't have a clue about that shit."

"Yeah, well, now ya get it."

Sadie hadn't heard Michael sound sad like this before. Fester's voice was always the one to hold sadness. Michael usually sounded too harsh and angry. Knowing how protective he was over Chloe, Sadie now understood why Sal scared him so much. He was afraid of losing both their lives. He seemed like he was afraid of losing Fester's as well. The reality of how bad this woman really was set in, and Sadie found herself trembling.

"Hey, I gotta get Chloe. Get ta listenin, she ain't got no damn clue the fuck went down with us own 'rents. I ain't havin her gettin no clue just yet neither."

"What does she picture happened anyway?"

Michael swore. "Fester, I ain't got no clue what story I gonna fucking sayin her. So I done sayin her thems got gone, an gonna get ta commin home when thems able. Just...just I ain't gonna have ya tellin her nothin. K?"

Sadie wondered why Michael didn't tell Chloe the truth. Lying to the girl made no logical sense. She may be young, but she also deserved to know what happened to her parents. If they were anything like the parents in Sadie's book, then Chloe and Michael must miss them very much. The harsh man must be more afraid than she thought, if he didn't want his sister to know what had happened. By the time she heard the front door close, tears ran down her cheeks. Anyone who could scare a man like Michael...

"Sadie?" Fester sounded worried as he came closer. "What's wrong?"

"What does someone like her want from me?" Sadie asked at a whisper. She didn't trust her voice.

"Oh, Sadie," Fester said in a soothing tone. She heard his clothes rustle as he shifted position and lowered himself. "I don't think she wants to hurt you or a thing. From what you said, it sounded like she likes you."

"I don't understand, Fester. What does she want?"

Fester didn't answer her at first, and Sadie wondered if he was going to speak at all. His hesitation was frightening. Was it really something so terrible that he couldn't even bring himself to say it?

"What is it?" she asked.

"I...I don't think she wants to hurt you, Sadie. I picture she wants to...well...how do I say this? It sounds like she wants to date you."

"Date me?" Sadie didn't even try to hide her confusion.

"Yeah, y'know...date. Sal is a...well...she likes being with girls. Basically she wants to take you places and do things with you."

"Do things? Like pleasure things?"

Fester let out a short laugh. "Yeah, probably."

"I don't want that!" Sadie shouted and cringed

against the back of the chair, terrified that Sal would do to her what her father had done so many times before. The thought put her at a near panic. "Please, Fester! Don't let her do that to me!"

"Hey...hey. It's OK. You don't have to do nothing you don't want to do. You don't even have to see her again. There's nothing to be 'fraid about, Sadie. I won't let her hurt you. OK?"

Slowly Sadie nodded. A strange realization washed over her. Fester had only recently come into her life and now she found herself trusting him. She still feared that he would hurt her with the past, but she also believed him when he said that he would protect her. Time and again he made her feel safe when no one else could. Strong emotions wrapped themselves around that new found trust, fragile as it was, and filled her entire body with an odd sense of warmth. She wondered if it was wise to feel so strongly for this man.

Unsure as to what she should do, Sadie relaxed a bit and closed her eyes. She felt rather exhausted from the high emotions of the day. Fester stood up and moved over to the chair beside her. He sighed, and then came the familiar sounds associated with the unpleasant smoke. It was the first time Fester had done that in her presence since she came to live with them. She wondered if that was significant, especially since Michael seemed to do it a lot.

Looking back on the events of the past few days, she realized how much had happened in such a short amount of time. Sadie not only learned more than she had expected, but she also found people who were honestly willing to help her. No one else had even tried to help her before. It was odd and more than a little frightening. She still didn't understand how they could give their kindness away for free.

Then there was Sal. That woman frightened Sadie more than her parents. With her mother, she knew what would get her hurt and what would keep her at least a little safer. Her father had a routine that helped her to know when he wanted pleasure and pain. With Sal, however, there was no way for her to know. The more she learned of the woman, the less she knew what to expect. She could only hope that they never had to meet with her again. Now that Fester knew why Michael hated Sal, maybe he would refuse to work for her in the future. Sadie knew that she would refuse to see her again, if given the choice.

There was no need to dwell on it further. Sal was scary and that was all Sadie needed to know. Holding back new tears, she closed her eyes and wished that woman would only become an unpleasant memory; a part of her past to never think on again.

Chapter 19

When Chloe and Michael returned home, the usual bursts of excitement from the girl were strangely absent. Sadie heard her tiny feet shuffle along the floor towards her room. She barely managed an audible "hi" before closing her bedroom door. Neither Fester nor Michael gave notice to the change. Chloe had behaved similarly when they went to the park as well. This new behavior was too stark of a contrast with how she usually was. It made Sadie nervous. She never did have the chance to ask Fester about it, and the urge to know was even stronger now.

"Fester? Why is Chloe quiet?" Sadie asked.

"What do you mean?" Fester asked.

"The other day when we went to the park and just now...she's so quiet. She's not talking and excited like she usually is."

"It been her empathy," Michael said as he walked over. "She been gettin all kinda fucking o'erwhelm some a one-two. It been makin her all tame an shit."

"School is really hard on her too," Fester said.

"Yeah. We done homeschoolin her a one-two ago. But, she be fucking wantin ta get 'round 'nother kids. She ain't never gonna get them shits gone."

Sadie wasn't sure she understood why Chloe would want to go to school if the emotions she felt there were too overwhelming. Without having experienced school before, she couldn't fully comprehend what it was. She had tried to listen to Chloe when she talked about it the day before but found herself more and more confused. Obviously it was important enough to the girl that she would willingly be hurt by the emotions of others. What was so special about that place? Perhaps it was somewhere for her to play with other children. Remembering how much fun she had playing with Chloe the other day, Sadie was able to understand the attraction. Even the pain of emotions would most likely be worth how it felt to play. The next time school was mentioned, she would listen more closely and brave a question or two. For now, she wanted to make sure that the child was OK.

"Is there anything that can be done for her?" Sadie asked.

"Not really," Fester said. "She just needs some time alone. She'll be back to her usual self before you know it."

"Yeah, them gooder shits for the girl in the one-two gonna be lettin her deal her own fucking ways. A thing more an it gonna get fucking worser," Michael said.

Sadie heard a click and the TV turned on. Realizing that there wasn't anything else the men had to say about the subject, she returned to her book. The story had captured her attention while Michael was gone. Now her thoughts were on Chloe and she had difficulty focusing on her reading. What must it be like to constantly feel what everyone else felt? It was not a life to be envied. Deep inside, she was thankful that she didn't have empathy. Her own emotions were difficult enough to cope with.

Sadie put down the novel and listened to the TV. There was no hope of reading with her mind so occupied. To her delight, the program that the men watched was actually informative. Instead of jokes or odd noises, the people talked about events from around the world. There was no way for her to understand what much of it meant, or where the locations mentioned existed. However, this seemed to be another good way to learn. She had just begun to enjoy herself when both of the men swore. Before she could ask what was wrong, the woman on the television allowed her to understand their reaction.

"In local news, three men are dead and another is in critical condition after an attack by a small group of Supernaturals in the Gutter District of the Downtown area yesterday afternoon. There has been no word as to whether or not a Paranormal and Supernatural Investigation Team, also known as 'PSI', has been called in to investigate. Police are asking that anyone with information come forward so these dangerous people may be apprehended and turned over to the proper authorities."

Sadie jumped as Michael yelled, "God Fucking dammit! Shit!"

He continued to swear as he turned off the TV and paced about the room. Fester made no sound, he didn't even swear. The combination of Michael pacing and Fester's silence worried Sadie. Obviously the woman on the television had talked about them. Sal had mentioned something about PSI earlier. Sadie had already figured out that whatever this PSI Team was, they probably worked for the government. The implications filled her with an intense fear.

Chloe's crying wafted in from her bedroom. Immediately, Sadie attempted to control her emotions and hoped that the men had done the same. Michael's footsteps moved quickly towards the girl's room while he muttered something under his breath. Shortly after his voice could be heard as he comforted his sister. His calm and reassuring voice was strong and soothing. She wondered how he was able to master his emotions with such ease.

"What do we do now?" Sadie asked, terrified of the answer.

"We lay low," Fester said in a low and fearful voice. "We don't do a thing that'll let people know we're Supernatural. We stay inside unless we absolutely have to go out. Hopefully no one will be able to ID us."

"What if they do? You made it sound like they can."

"I don't have a clue, Sadie. If they had any mind what we looked like they would probably have posted it on the news. It wasn't there so I just don't know. What I do have a mind for is that I won't let them take you or Chloe. I'll do whatever it takes so that won't happen. Michael, too."

The sentiment gave Sadie little comfort. While she didn't know anything about this PSI Team or the government, logic dictated that they would have powerful weapons. If they always went after Supernaturals, then they would definitely be prepared for what Sadie and

Michael could do. How could Fester think he would be able to protect them against that? Once again Sadie worked on controlling the familiar fear as it strongly rose up within her. She didn't want Chloe to have to feel such a strong emotion.

"I'm trying not to be scared, Fester. I don't want Chloe to hurt because of me. But, I don't think I can stop being scared this time," Sadie said while blinking back tears.

"I know," he said softly, "I'm 'fraid just the same. This is crazy big. I think we'll be OK though. Sal said she would help us if we had to run."

The thought of Sal being involved worried Sadie immensely. "I don't want to see her again, Fester. I hope we don't need her help."

"Yeah, me too."

The couch cushion moved as though Fester had leaned back. Sadie leaned back too and turned her head in his direction. She yearned for him to hold her and make her feel safe like he had during the night. Resisting the urge to lean into him, she held her arms to her chest. While the thought of being held by Fester was pleasant, it still made her nervous. She still wasn't used to the touch of another.

Chloe had experienced the emotions of many people while at school. She had definitely been through enough for one day. The thought of what the girl must be experiencing caused Sadie to work even harder at controlling her fear. It was frustrating to have to constantly watch what she felt.

Reflecting on how often she almost left this place and these people, she wondered again if she had done the right thing by staying. Because of her blunder, her friends were now in mortal danger. Yes, they said that it wasn't her fault, but she didn't feel that was entirely true. They were being nice so she wouldn't worry and Sadie didn't deserve such special treatment. Her safety from the cold wasn't worth this threat their well being too.

What would happen if she decided to leave now? It wouldn't make the others any safer. The government would still be after Michael because of his lightning. If she left, then she would be out in the cold and alone once more. It was tempting to return to a solitary existence. Sadie knew, however, that she would never survive the winter. Nor would she be able to protect herself against this PSI Team without help. The reality of the situation was that she was stuck. She had been imprisoned once more, except this time by her situation rather than any specific person. She knew that she brought this on herself. The realization sat uneasy in the pit of her stomach.

Resisting the urge to dwell on it further, she decided to distract herself in the only way she knew how. She would clean. Without saying a word, she got up from the couch and opened her cane. As she walked into the kitchen, Fester audibly stood and followed her.

"Everything OK, Sadie?" he asked with concern.

"I'm fine. I'm just going to clean."

"Now? Really? Uh...OK. Want any help?"

Sadie sighed and shook her head. She now knew that he wanted to help her because of love, and not because he thought she was helpless. That didn't change the fact that this was her job. It was as if he didn't understand how important it was for her to pay her debt; one that grew every day she allowed them to help her. She would never be able to pay them back if they didn't let her do it on her own.

"I can help, Sadie. Just tell me what you want me to do. I can do the dishes or wipe down the counters or..."

"No, Fester," Sadie said as she turned towards him. "I can do it myself. I need to do it myself."

"You don't have to do everything your own self y'know." Sadie couldn't understand why he sounded so sullen.

"Yes, I do."

Not wanting to talk about it any further, Sadie turned and walked over to the sink. Fester's footsteps were close behind. It was difficult to ignore his hovering. She reached the sink without tripping and placed her cane on the counter beside it. When she heard the dishes in the drain board being put away she was furious.

"Fester, stop. Let me do that," she said firmly.

"It's no trouble. I don't mind," he said.

"I do!" she shouted. Sadie took a deep breath to steady herself before continuing. "I do mind, Fester. Stop. Please just....just stop."

"What is this, Sadie? Why won't you ever let me help you? You won't let me help you with nothing! I want to help you with your past and you try to get gone. I want to help you with the chores and you yell at me. What is so wrong with it all?"

Sadie took another deep breath. "My past is fine where it is and I can do the chores on my own. You don't have to try and help me all the time, Fester. I don't want it or need it."

"But I want to help you, Sadie. I know you can do things on your own and I have a ton of respect for that. But, I like helping you and I like doin things for you. Why won't you let me?"

Sadie closed her eyes and took yet another deep breath. She was steadily losing her patience. "Why can't you understand? If there is something for me to do then I have to do it on my own. I can't ask for help and I can't accept it. This is *my* debt, Fester! I won't be able to repay you for anything if you keep on doing things for me. I can't accept your help. I don't want it."

"Sadie..." he whispered.

Fester only said her name yet his voice spoke of a deep sadness caused by her rejection. The tone made Sadie wish that she could accept his help. She didn't like causing him such pain. It was obvious that he wanted to help her as much as she didn't want him to. Neither of them spoke while Sadie moved over to the drain board and began to put the rest of the dishes away.

"Shouldn't it be up to me to decide if you owe me a debt?" he asked angrily when she reached out to turn on the water. When Sadie didn't respond he said, "You don't owe me a thing, Sadie."

"I know you keep on saying that. I just can't accept free kindness, Fester. I can't."

Tears welled up in her eyes as Sadie turned on the water and started the dishes. Blinking them away, she was determined not to cry in front of Fester. It would only serve to make him press harder. Instead she focused on the dishes. She couldn't understand why he wouldn't accept that his help wasn't needed nor wanted. He always insisted, over and over, that she didn't owe him anything. The truth was that she did owe him. She owed him more than she would ever be able to repay, especially now.

"The hell did they do to you that you steadily curb my pass?" he asked.

"*Kindness is never free. There is always a price,*" she quoted her mother with perfect inflection, just as she had been taught so often before.

"Sadie, I already told you–"

"No," she said. "You're wrong, Fester. You should be smart enough to realize that you are wrong. There is always a price and I owe you more than you seem to realize. I don't know why you can't understand that kindness is never free. Never. It's never free..."

Tears began to flow from Sadie's eyes, as though they neglected to acknowledge her desire to hold them back. She put the cup she had been washing down and leaned on the edge of the sink. Needing to calm herself for Chloe's sake, Sadie began to breathe deeply. Her emotions were running higher than usual. Michael and Chloe had both been so quiet that Sadie almost forgot that they were home. Now she needed to focus on controlling herself. She didn't want to hurt Chloe again.

When she felt Fester's hand on her shoulder she jumped. "C'mere," he said as he pulled her into an embrace.

Sadie had dreamed that Fester would once again hold her, but never thought that it would happen. Even though she felt uncomfortable with physical contact, she noticed that it didn't bother her as much when it came from him. Carefully she wrapped her arms around him and buried her face into his chest. The tension that had built up over the past two days released its grip over her. She allowed her tears to wash it all away.

Fester's scent filled her awareness and she breathed deeply. His hold on her was tight yet it made her feel secure. Tears flowed uninhibited down her cheeks and mingled with strong overwhelming emotions. For a moment she forgot about Chloe and her empathy. All that existed was Fester's arms and the unusual comfort they provided. Sadie had cried so deeply that she didn't hear when Michael came into the room.

"The fuck goin on up in here?" Michael yelled.

Sadie felt Fester jump and turn slightly. "We were just...um...well..."

"Whatever, man. Ya both gotta fucking get controlin ya damn minds! I just done gettin Chloe all calm, an she cryin 'gain 'cause ya two!"

"Sorry," both Fester and Sadie said in unison.

Michael's heavy footsteps headed back towards Chloe's room. Fester sighed and released Sadie. Disappointed at the end to their embrace, she relaxed her arms and allowed him to step back. A terrible weight had been lifted from her chest, and it made it easier for her to breathe. Sniffling, she wiped her face with her hands and returned to the sink. The fact that she felt better after crying was confusing. Usually she felt either the same or worse. Shaking her head at the peculiarity of it all, she returned to the dishes.

"You OK?" Fester asked gently.

Sadie nodded her head. "Yes. Are you?"

"Yeah."

Neither of them spoke while she continued with her chores. Though she could tell that Fester was still nearby, he didn't offer to help. Sadie was glad for that. She wasn't sure what she would do or say if he offered his aid once more. Inside she felt a whirlwind of strong emotions she didn't quite understand. Wanting to prevent causing Chloe any further harm, she kept her mind on the tasks before her. Thinking about certain things always seemed to lead towards the child crying. Unfortunately, she didn't know how to control her own mind. It was even more difficult than controlling her emotions. She held mastery over neither.

Sadie was elated that Fester had held her again. Knowing that such a joyous feeling wouldn't hurt Chloe, she focused on it. In his arms she had felt safe and that fact continued to amaze her. Twice now, he had been able to comfort her simply by holding her. For Sadie this was more than remarkable. In a world that terrified and confused her, there was something truly beautiful for her to experience. The emotions she felt when he held her were far different from anything she had previously known. They swelled within her body, and gave her a sense of peace and...something else she couldn't identify.

Within her very being she knew that she would be safe so long as Fester was near. With him she didn't need to fear. She felt in her heart that he truly wouldn't hurt her, and in turn she wouldn't hurt him, either. Even though he didn't have a power as fierce as hers or Michael's, she also believed him when he said that he would protect her. His brain was powerful and would find a way. All she had to do was trust.

For the first time in her life, this was truly possible. It would take a while longer before she could feel safe enough with Fester to trust him completely. With time, however, such things may become easier.

Even though her world threatened to turn upside down, Fester was there to keep her steady.

Chapter 20

Sadie had finished cleaning most of the kitchen when she heard Michael's heavy footsteps exit Chloe's room. She listened as he moved into the living room. Only his boots were heard, and no sounds came from the child's room. Content that he wouldn't be in her way, and that Chloe was no longer hurting, she grabbed the broom from the corner by the fridge. When she began to sweep, Fester's footsteps moved away from her and into the living room as well. Though she didn't actually mind him being in the room with her anymore, she still wished he wouldn't hover about as much as he did. It was good that he went to sit with Michael.

"How's Chloe?" Fester asked.

"Good...she takin a nap." He paused for a moment before he called out from where he sat, "Sadie, ya ain't gotta do all fucking cleanins ya own self, y'know."

"Yes, I do," she said without stopping.

"We just had this talk," Fester said.

"The fucking deal?" Michael asked.

"She insists that she has to pay us back for our help. She wouldn't even let me put the dishes away. Curbs my pass every time."

Michael's unmistakable footsteps brought him into the kitchen and stopped in front of her. Sadie continued to sweep, moving around him as she went. Determined to continue as though he weren't there, she used the broom as a guide for where his boots were. It was frustrating but not difficult to clean around him.

"The fuck, Sadie! Get ta stoppin them bullshist. Ya ain't owin us no damn thing."

"Kindness is never free. There is always a price," she quoted softly as she continued to sweep.

"Fuck them shits!" Sadie flinched at Michael's harsh tone. "I gotta clue ya ain't been payin no people back for helpin ya!"

With that, Sadie stopped sweeping. She was furious

at the accusation. "I always pay my debts, Michael. Always!" she said through clenched teeth.

"Bullshit! Fester sayin he seein ya fucking beggin for scraps out on the block. So I ain't wanna hear no bullshit words 'bout kindness ain't never bein fucking free!"

Sadie turned towards Michael. "I wasn't begging, Michael. Sitting with the sign was my task. The money I was given was my payment for that. They just didn't pay me enough in the winter."

Fester's footsteps came in, and from the sound of it he moved to stand near Michael. "Sadie," he asked gently, "what do you mean that it was your task?"

Sadie sighed. She didn't want to talk about work but didn't see a way around the topic. "When my mother brought me Downtown, she told me that holding the sign would be my task – my job – and that by doing it, I would be paid. She told me to use the money for food and water. That's exactly what I did and I'm going back to my job once the weather is warmer and I can get paid for it again."

"Wait! Ya true tellin story there 'bout ya mother fucking shithole moms done droppin ya ass in the fucking Gutter, an tellin ya gotta job holdin a fucking sign?" Michael's tone was disbelieving.

"Yes."

"An ya picturin she true?"

"Of course." The idea that her mother would lie was preposterous.

"The fuck she done tellin ya gonna sleeps?"

"On the ground."

Michael swore. "Ain't ya never fightin her 'bout them shits?"

Sadie was shocked at the suggestion. "Why would I do that? I always obey my mother. It's not safe to go against her wishes."

"Ya moms done been one fucked up bitch."

"Sadie, do you know what your sign says?" Fester asked.

When Sadie shook her head, Fester asked her to bring it to him. Frustrated that the men weren't letting her finish her cleaning, she carefully made her way to her backpack. She hadn't touched the sign since she came to stay at the apartment. It felt odd taking it out of her bag now. She brought it over to where she had last heard Fester and held it out.

Michael let out a short laugh. "That rich!"

"What?" Sadie asked.

"It's your sign, Sadie," Fester said. "It says, 'Blind. Need food. Please help.'"

"It doesn't say that. You're making that up!" Sadie felt her face grow hot with anger.

"No, I'm not. That's really what it says," Fester said.

"It can't say that," Sadie said. Her voice rose with every word she spoke. "My mother gave me that sign. She was very clear all my life that I should never ask for help and any kindness must be paid with a price! It's impossible for her to have given me a sign asking for the very help she forbade me to ask for! You have to be lying! You have to be!"

Fester's footsteps moved towards her and she backed away. "Sadie," he said softly, "it does say that. Your moms lied to you. She set you up to beg so you could eat."

Sadie felt lightheaded and her breathing became labored. Between breaths she exclaimed, "It can't say that, Fester! Kindness is never free. Always pay your debts. Never ask for help. Don't show your weaknesses. Disobedience brings the most pain. Those are the fundamental lessons they taught me constantly! She wouldn't send me to beg! She wouldn't send me to ask for help! She wouldn't! She wouldn't!"

Collapsing from the weight of her own emotions, she was caught by Fester. "Sadie, shhhhh. It's OK," he said as his arms wrapped around her and they both knelt down on the floor. "It's OK. Calm down. It's OK."

Sadie leaned into Fester and cried. She had nearly hyperventilated and had trouble catching her breath as she sobbed. Fester held her close to him and whispered softly in her ear. Michael swore when Chloe began to cry as well. Once again Sadie felt guilty for hurting the child and waking her up with her own painful emotions. Even so, she had a more difficult time than usual controlling herself.

All her life, the harsh fundamental lessons were a constant reminder of how she was to behave. The pain brought through them had been intense and was the source of most of her scars. Both of her parents had taught her these lessons. Her mother did so through pain as she hit her across the back with various objects. Her father did it by forcing her to do things with him in bed, acts which brought about their own pain as well. The thought that her mother had told her to do something that went against those lessons was inconceivable.

Chloe's cries began to turn into screams as Sadie's internal torment escalated. Try as she might, she had no hope of calming down this time. It felt as though something inside of her had broken and she would drown from the tears. Fester continued to talk softly as he tried in vain to calm her. Eventually she felt a hand that wasn't Fester's touch her shoulder. In her current state she couldn't even flinch.

"Sadie," Michael said gently, "ya gotta get ta calmin ya mind, girl. Please, Sadie. My sis ain't gonna be able ta take it...it strainin her ass. Please, get ta calmin the fuck down!"

There was no hope of replying. Between the crying and the shortness of breath, it was all Sadie could do to keep from passing out. She wanted to calm down. She didn't want to hurt Chloe. The child's screams were as terrifying as the emotions running through her own heart. A vicious cycle began as Chloe's screams fueled Sadie's angst and vice versa.

Michael's footsteps sounded louder than usual as he ran towards the bathroom. He came out as quickly and Sadie could barely hear the sound of something rattling inside a bottle. She had no idea as to what he was doing. His footsteps moved about the kitchen but both she and Chloe were far too loud for anything else to be heard. It wasn't long before she heard him near her again.

"Sadie, listen, ya gotta take them poppers. K? It gonna get ya mind calmin down. Please, for my sis, just get ta takin em."

Her hand was taken and two pills were placed in her palm. Folding her fingers around the medicine, she slowly leaned away from Fester so she was upright. A glass was pushed into her other hand. Trembling, Sadie tried to stop crying. She was able to do so long enough to take the medicine. The pills felt rough as they went down her sore throat. Immediately she began to cry again.

"Go see to Chloe," Fester said, "I have her. She should calm down soon."

The glass was taken from her hand and Sadie was once again pulled back into an embrace with Fester. She felt him shift so that he sat on the floor. Gently he pulled her into his lap. With her head on his shoulder she continued to sob. His hands stroked her hair and back in a way that was unexpectedly soothing. After a few minutes her sobs decreased, and her breathing became a little easier. She began to feel sleepy and calm. Chloe continued to cry in the other room.

"I'm sorry," she whispered hoarsely.

"It's OK. I'm sorry too."

"I'm going to have to go back out into the cold again. Aren't I?"

"Shhhh. No."

A few tears spilled down Sadie's cheek. She wanted to believe that she could stay. The reality was that she kept hurting Chloe. Surely, after tonight Michael would insist that she had to leave. He even said it himself, her emotions had become too much for the child to handle. It wasn't fair to make Chloe suffer so she could be warm. She had to accept whatever her punishment for this may be.

Her eyelids felt heavy and she snuggled into Fester, enjoying the feeling that came with his arms wrapped securely around her. It was difficult to accept that she may never again be held by him. Sadie wanted him to hold her for as long as possible. Taking a deep breath, she breathed in his scent. She wanted to memorize everything about him. The memory was sure to keep her sane once she was on the streets again.

Chloe's cries died down and Sadie heard Michael talking softly to her. Feeling that she must apologize to the child, she reluctantly pulled away from Fester. She felt unsteady as she stood up and swayed. Gingerly, she moved towards the counter and felt for her cane.

"Sadie? What are you doing?" Fester asked nervously.

"I need to tell Chloe I'm sorry before I leave."

"Leave? I told you, we're not going to kick you out."

Sadie turned towards him. "You might say that, but what about Michael? After last night and just now, there's no way he's going to let me stay, Fester. I'll say I'm sorry and then I'll say good-bye."

"Sadie...please, no..." The pain in his voice tore at her heart.

"I'm sorry, Fester," she said sadly. "This is how it is."

Shaking, Sadie walked slowly past Fester. She fought the sleepiness that overcame her as she headed towards Chloe's room. Fester's footsteps followed close behind. She wanted to stop walking and ask to be held by him again. She didn't want to say good-bye. In the apartment she was safe and warm. On the streets she would surely die. She didn't want to die and she didn't want to leave her friends. Her fate had been decided by her own actions. Chloe couldn't be hurt anymore.

Sadie walked slowly into Chloe's room and stopped in the doorway. "Chloe?"

"Sadie, ya K?" Chloe asked. Her voice held a higher pitch than usual.

"I'm fine. I'm sorry, Chloe. I keep hurting you without wanting to and I'm sorry."

"It K. Why ya feelin them ways, Sadie? Why ya feelins hurtin so bad?"

Remembering how Michael had asked her not to talk about her past, Sadie couldn't answer the girl. "I have to leave now, Chloe. I'll miss you."

Chloe began to cry again. "No! Sadie, please no! I feelin ya. Ya ain't wanna get gone none. Ya 'fraid ta go. I ain't never likin ya ta get gone neither! Please!"

"I have to. Good-bye, Chloe. Good-bye, Michael."

Sadie said as she turned to walk out of the room.

"No!" The sound of old springs creaking told her that the child had jumped off the bed. A second later she grabbed Sadie's free hand. "Ya ain't goin, Sadie! Ya ain't! I gotta true picture what ya feelin, Sadie! I gotta true picture what Fester feelin! Please, say ya ain't never gettin gone!"

"Chloe," Michael said gently as he moved closer, "get ta lettin Sadie go. We gonna get ta helpin her find a riskless joint ta keep at. But, she true. She ain't gonna keep here no more."

"Michael! How the fuck can you say that?" Fester asked.

With Fester blocking her way out of the room and Chloe holding onto her hand, Sadie was trapped. The sound of Chloe crying, begging her to stay, tore at her from the inside. The girl was right, she didn't want to go. She was afraid of what would happen. However, Michael had also been right. She couldn't stay here anymore. It wasn't right that Chloe had to feel her pain.

"I sorry, Fester," Michael said gently. "Them shits gettin heavy strainin. She gotta get her a shit ton o' fucking help, an we ain't never gonna be able ta give it. I gotta mind callin CPS in the mornin. Foster care might–"

"Foster care? Fuck that shit, Michael!"

"Them ables ta be gettin her care she fucking needin, Fester."

"No! That's bullshit! You know what they'll do if they find she's Supernatural?"

Michael sighed. "Sadie, I sorry 'bout them shits," he said softly.

Sadie turned her head in his direction. "It's OK," she said, "I know I can't stay here." She turned back towards Fester. "Please move, Fester. I have to gather my things."

"No. You can't do this. You can't leave."

Fester's voice cracked when he spoke and Sadie knew he was close to crying. Chloe still gripped her hand and was already crying uncontrollably. Not only was Fester willing to put Chloe in danger, but Chloe was willing to take on the risk as well. Normally this would cause Sadie to reconsider. Instead she asked Fester once more to move. Being caught between the two of them was making her head swim.

"Fine," he said, his voice wavering. "If you're gone, then I'm gone the same. I won't let you go out there alone."

Michael swore heavily and Sadie gently pulled her hand from Chloe's grasp. She reached up for Fester's face and cupped his cheek in her palm. "You don't have to go, Fester. It's safe here, and warm. You've done so much for me. You've shown me so much more. You saved my life even. You don't have to leave your home for me as well. I don't deserve that, not from you or anyone. I don't deserve any of it."

Surprisingly, she didn't flinch when Fester touched her cheek as well. "Sadie, you do deserve it. You deserve so much more. I won't let you go out there alone." She felt a tear touch her fingertips.

Chloe wrapped her arms around Sadie's waist. "Ya ain't both goin! No! Michael, ya ain't gonna let them! Please!"

Michael swore again. Chloe's mattress squeaked and she assumed that he had sat down. "Fester... Chloe...ya both done got ya minds gone. Fester, ya ain't gonna go sleepin on no fucking block. Chloe, I gotta do a thing gonna be bester for ya. Get picturin 'bout the feelins ya got from tonight. Ya wanna get them shits 'gain?"

"Yeah," Chloe said while burying her head in Sadie's back.

Sadie brought her hand down and placed it on Chloe's arm. "Chloe," she said gently, "I don't want to hurt you anymore. Michael's right, I have to go."

"I ain't mindin! I ain't for true! Ya gonna get better, Sadie! I able feelin ya. I feelin ya ain't 'fraid here no more. I feelin hows ya feelin 'bout us. I able feelin what ya feelin 'bout Fester. I feelin what he feelin 'bout ya same. I likin them feelins, Sadie! I likin them true!"

Sadie was in shock. Never before did she consider that Chloe would actually enjoy some of her emotions.

She had been too concerned with how her fear and sadness affected the girl. It never occurred to her that the child would also feel the good emotions as well. *'Ya gonna get better.'* Did she mean that her emotions made her sick somehow? The thought was unsettling.

Chloe released Sadie and ran in Michael's direction. "Michael! Says ya ain't never lettin 'em get gone! Please, be makin 'em keep here!"

For a while no one spoke nor moved. Sadie knew that Michael tried to decide if she should stay or not. It didn't matter what he thought, she had to leave. A part of her wanted Fester to come with her, but she couldn't bear the thought of him suffering alongside her. She knew she had to leave and she had to do it alone.

"It's OK, Chloe," Sadie said finally, "This is what needs to happen. Fester, you can't come with me. You need to stay here. Just...just let me pass you so I can go...alone."

"No." Fester's voice shook with emotion. "Either you keep here or I'm gone with ya. I won't let you go out there alone. I can't."

"Michael, them both so sad! Please, ya ain't gonna let 'em get gone!"

"Ain't nobody gonna get nowheres." Michael's voice was forceful. "Ya both be stickin here. Fucking shit, man! Ya kids gonna get me damn near strokin with them shits. Just get ta them fucking livin room. an I gonna get to makin dinner in a one-two."

Chloe cheered and Fester thanked Michael. Sadie wouldn't accept it. "Michael, I have to go."

"No," he said, "ya ain't gettin gone. I ain't gonna take no more fucking words 'bout them shits. Now, get ta the livin room. Get ta movin ya asses now."

Fester took Sadie's hand. "C'mon. Let's go sit."

Sadie was in a daze. What just happened? All she knew was that now no one wanted her to leave. It felt like every time she tried to go her plans were thwarted by the others. Fester had even threatened to leave with her. Why would he go out into the cold when he didn't have to? That was going beyond helping her. He would've put his life at risk unnecessarily. Shaking her head, Sadie couldn't understand any of it.

She allowed herself to be pulled gently into the living room. Her head swam and she had trouble thinking clearly. Why was it that whenever she tried to leave these people were so adamant that she stay? It made no logical sense and she wondered why they had to be so strange. Since the adrenaline had worn off, she was left feeling exhausted. She felt sleepier than she should. Sitting on the couch, she leaned back into the cushions with a heavy sigh and closed her eyes. She didn't deserve what they were doing for her. There truly was no way she could ever fully pay them back for their help.

Knowing she should leave but with no energy to argue the matter, Sadie began to formulate a plan for how she could stop hurting Chloe. The girl made it clear that she liked feeling the good and happy emotions. Perhaps she could focus on those feelings and keep the bad ones at bay. The problem will be when it's time for bed. With how the day had gone, there was no doubt that she would have nightmares again. It was important to figure out how to keep that from happening as well.

Listening to the sounds of Michael cooking and Chloe dancing around the room caused Sadie to feel content. She was aware of Fester sitting next to her and wondered if he felt the same way. He was willing to put himself in mortal danger for her. Now Chloe was willing to feel such horrible emotions so that she could stay. Once again, she knew she didn't deserve anything they did for her. It was unfathomable that they didn't know it, too.

As her debt increased, Sadie realized that sometimes you had to accept what's happening around you. She didn't want more debt with these people. At the same time, however, she truly didn't want to leave them. Ever.

Chapter 21

While Michael cooked, Sadie fought to stay awake. She couldn't understand why she felt this sleepy. Yes, a lot had happened that day. However, she didn't think it was enough to cause such a high level of exhaustion. A nap was tempting but she didn't want that. If she slept then she would have a nightmare, and she was desperate to keep that from happening for as long as possible. If she hurt Chloe again, then Michael might not let anyone stop him from sending her away.

Finally they were all called to sit at the table. From the smells that permeated the apartment, Sadie could only assume that he cooked some sort of beef. She stood up and didn't complain when Fester offered to lead her into the kitchen. It wasn't difficult to find the table and never had been. However, she was too tired to argue with him. She was still in a daze from what had just happened, and wasn't sure she would win such an argument anyway. It was better to just go along with him...this time.

Michael told them they were having burgers as they sat. Sadie didn't care. She wasn't even sure she would be able to eat. Their late lunch hadn't been all that long ago. As Fester had said, her stomach shrunk from not eating enough while on the street. She wondered how long it would take for it to reach a normal size so this wouldn't be an issue anymore. Not wanting to anger the men, she dutifully picked up her burger and forced herself to take a bite. The burger was greasy yet it tasted good. Regardless, she doubted that she would be able to finish even half of it. Her stomach twisted around the food, causing her to feel nauseous with each bite.

No one spoke and the silence was oddly unsettling. Everyone, it seemed, had something weighing on their minds. With a guilty heart, Sadie could only assume that she was the cause of their silence. Before her thoughts could wander about the matter, there was an odd mechanical sound which came from Fester's direction. Putting down her hardly touched burger, Sadie turned her head in his direction and flinched when she heard him swear.

"It's Sal," he said nervously before answering the phone. "Yeah, hey, Sal. What's up? ... Yeah, the news was talking about us. ... Well, it's not like we meant ta – y'know! ... Are you true an sure? Should we be worried? ... Alright, keep us posted. And, Sal, thanks."

After a soft click there was silence. It was hard to tell what Fester felt throughout the call. His voice was calm, even though she suspected that he felt differently on the inside. Patiently she waited for him to tell them what was said. She didn't want to ask in case there was a reason for the silence. The possible answers were also terrifying and she didn't want to feel those emotions just now. Chloe was calm and needed to stay that way. Not knowing what else to do, she folded her hands in her lap with her cane and waited.

"Chloe," Michael said finally, "get in ya room."

"What I done?" Chloe sounded upset.

"Nothin. Just fucking get in ya room. Ya eatin ya burger there. Get."

No one spoke as Chloe's chair was harshly pushed back. Sadie listened to the child's footsteps as she stomped towards her bedroom. The fact that Michael had sent her away made Sadie nervous. It obviously upset the child, who had no idea what was happening. She could only assume that he had done it so she wouldn't overhear whatever it was that Fester had to say. Perhaps Michael knew something Sadie didn't. Her stomach was twisted in more knots by the time the men began to talk.

"So, what the bitch done sayin?" Michael sounded frightened, and that made Sadie's pulse quicken.

"First she yelled at me for our being on the news. She said that if we were gonna kill someone then we should've done it 'cleanly and quietly'."

Michael swore. "Yeah, them words soundin same bitch true. She tellin a story 'bout PSI?"

"She said she didn't hear a thing about a team being called in. She said we're not clear riskless though. They might still send someone."

Sadie was scared. "Do you think they will?" she asked softly.

"I don't have a clue."

"Fuck them shits, Fester. Ya gotta picture them gonna get ta sendin a team. It just a matters o' when."

"Michael..."

"No! Ya gotta clue same as me that them shits ain't fucking never lettin us alone. Ya punk ass an Chloe got some chances. But Sadie an me gonna get fucked!" Michael's words held a lot of emotion and Sadie worried about Chloe.

"Why us?" she asked.

"'Cause, Sadie, we both been havin what them sick fucktards callin 'offensive power'; we able ta get doin crazy assed shit. It be makin us a favored target."

"We're not really safe here. Are we? We're not safe anywhere," she whispered fearfully.

"Sadie," Fester said softly, "I won't let them get you. You're safe."

"I don't think you can stop them, Fester. You don't have an offensive power." She had trouble keeping her voice steady.

"No, I don't. But Michael does. You do. As for me, I have my brain. It's good for more than reading. I'll picture a plan for us. OK?"

Not wanting to talk about it further, Sadie stood and opened her cane. Even though she had told herself she would eat, there was no hope for her to do so now. Her stomach hurt from her anxiety and her head swam with the danger of their situation. Eating at this point was not only impossible, but it would also make her sick. She needed to sit somewhere comfortable. Slowly she headed into the living room.

"Hey, Sadie! Get ta sittin the fuck down an eatin ya fucking dinner."

Sadie flinched at the annoyance in Michael's voice. She wasn't going to worry about his anger now, there was absolutely no way she was going to eat. Turning her head slightly in his direction she said, "I'll eat it later."

Fester swore softly and she ignored him. Not wanting to hurt Chloe, she felt that it would be a good idea to ignore everything the men had to say for now. Unfortunately, that was difficult to do. Even as she sat on the couch, she could hear their attempt to formulate a plan. It was difficult not to overhear what they said with how close the rooms were together. They both sounded calmer than Sadie would've expected. Again she wondered how they managed that.

"So, ya got a plan growin up in ya uber brain, kid?" Michael asked.

"Don't have one yet. Right now we have only two options. Stick here or get gone."

Michael swore. "I ain't runnin with Chloe. She gotta be gettin fucking clear true stability, man."

"Yeah, I get it. But, there aren't enough variables for me to have a plan, Michael! I don't have a clue what they would bring with them. It's not like I know the ins and outs of a freak fucking PSI Team!"

"Yeah, kid, I get it. I ain't got no clue the fuck them gonna carry neither. Them shits fucking suckin on monkey balls."

Sadie flinched at the sound of someone punching the kitchen table. Neither of the men knew what they should do. This only served to confirm her suspicions that they weren't safe anymore. It was difficult to fully understand the scope of their problem, and she tried desperately. She understood that the government, whatever that was, wanted Supernaturals. This PSI Team obviously worked for them. They were probably experts at capturing people who had an offensive power. Without knowing what exactly they would do, it was understandable how Fester couldn't have a plan. She really didn't expect him to have one, no matter how much she wished he did.

Leaning into the couch cushions, she sighed and closed her eyes. It surprised her how little fear she felt. Usually she would be terrified right now. Instead she was only slightly afraid and very sleepy. Whatever it was that had been keeping her from losing control, it worked well. Hopefully she would figure out what that was before she needed it again.

The men had both been quiet for a while and Sadie was too lost in her thoughts to pay attention to where they might be. Eventually she heard one of the chairs move and a dish was placed in the sink. Not long after, Fester's footsteps moved towards her. He sighed and she felt the cushion shift as he sat down beside her.

"You OK?" Fester asked. "You didn't finish dinner."

"I'm sorry. I tried to but I'm not hungry enough."

Michael's footsteps also came into the living room and Sadie heard him sit on the chair opposite them. "Ya gotta get eatin, Sadie. Ya been too fucking bony."

"I'm sorry."

"Ya ain't gotta be fucking sorry, dammit! We just gotta get a bit o' meat on them bones is all."

"I'm...I'll try to eat later."

"Whatever."

Sadie hated the guilt she felt for not eating. It seemed as though there wasn't anything she could do correctly. Her wrongness hung about her like a shroud and fueled her guilt. If she ate right now then she would be sick. If she didn't then the men would be angry with her. There was no way to win. She couldn't dwell on it, though. There were larger concerns to ponder.

The click of the TV turning on was clearly heard in the silence that had fallen. Soon after, Chloe came out of her room and Michael said she could stay out. Sadie was glad for that. It didn't seem fair that the child had no idea what was happening. The girl knew what they felt. One could only assume that she was confused by it all. To leave her to wonder didn't feel right. When Chloe finally went back to her room, Sadie decided to broach the subject.

"Shouldn't Chloe know what's going on?" she asked.

Michael swore. "No, ain't time yet. Ain't no reason for her knowin a damn thing in the one-two."

"I don't understand. Why?"

"'Cause she gotta be a fucking kid! Ain't no kid gotta get worryin 'bout them shits. Ain't no good scarin her if I ain't gotta."

"Michael, if she can feel our emotions then won't she already be scared?"

"Fuck, Sadie! Ya ain't gettin it. Chloe been a kid. Yeah she gotta clue we gettin fucking 'fraid 'bout a thing. But we get ta sayin the fuck we got goin in us minds, then she gonna feel morer fear from her own God damn self. I ain't puttin a same thing on my lil sis if ain't no need. No more words."

There was obviously no point in arguing. Sadie was too tired to try anyway. Michael was more protective of his sister than she initially realized. He didn't want her to feel any amount of discomfort. For a moment she wondered what it must have been like for them to grow up without the lessons and constant fear. She may not envy Chloe's empathy, but she did envy her childhood.

For the rest of the evening Sadie didn't speak much. Listening to the TV had become enjoyable in a way. It wasn't difficult to keep her mind occupied with whatever she heard. Everyone else was just as quiet. If they talked at all then it was about simple subjects, which helped her to have a better understanding about what was happening in the shows. It was as though the men avoided talking about their situation, and she thought she understood why. It didn't make much sense but a lot of things were like that.

Feeling incredibly bored, Sadie decided that perhaps it would be a good idea to do a little laundry. It was beginning to feel as though the only way to keep herself occupied was through cleaning. Back home, with her parents, it had been the same way. They didn't try to stop her from cleaning though, and they never tried to help. Considering she enjoyed doing her chores, this wasn't much of an issue either back home or here. Besides, laundry was simple to do and didn't take a lot of time or effort to complete. Her clothes could also do with a bit of washing.

"Does anyone have clothes that need to be washed?" she asked.

"No. We fine," Michael said.

"Can I–"

"Ya ain't gonna fucking do our fucking launderin,

Sadie! No more words. Jesus!"

"That's not what I was going to ask," she said sullenly.

"Then the fuck ya gonna ask?"

"I wanted to know if I could wash my own clothes. I don't have anything clean to wear."

Michael swore. "Sorry. Yeah get ta washin ya shits."

"I'll go with you."

"You don't have to, Fester. I can do it."

Fester sighed, "I get you can. I was just going to carry the detergent and quarters for you is all."

Sadie felt silly and mumbled her thanks.

As Fester headed into the kitchen to grab what was needed, Sadie moved over towards her belongings. She pulled out her dirty clothes from her backpack and wrinkled her nose. While her clothing didn't smell too horrible by itself the bag had a definite odor. Not knowing how to clean it, she decided to leave it for now. Perhaps one of the men could tell her how to get the stink out later.

Fester was ready and waiting when Sadie approached the door, her laundry in her hands. She held her cane awkwardly as she carefully walked out into the hallway. There were a few objects that could trip her, and she wanted to avoid them without asking Fester for any guidance. The last thing she needed at this point was to ask him for the same help which she overwhelmingly refused earlier in the evening.

It was difficult maneuvering down the hallway with her clothes piled in her arms. She realized all too late that she should have carried the laundry in her backpack. Next time she would have to do that to save herself the hassle of juggling the laundry and her cane.

"Hey, Sadie. Do you want me to carry some of that?" Fester asked.

His offer was tempting but she refused. If she let him help her now, then he may never stop. That was a scenario she wanted to avoid. The sooner he accepted that she didn't want his help the better off she would be. It wasn't as though this task was impossible. Perhaps she would accept his offers if she had no other choice.

For now she had a choice, however, and she chose to do it herself. Fester would have to accept that and move on.

In the laundry room, Sadie continued to be adamant that she do the laundry herself. "I'll do it, Fester. Please, just let me do it myself," she said when he tried to take the clothes from her.

Fester sighed. "Even after learning that your mother set you up to ask for help, you still curb my pass?"

"I'm sorry," she said as she filled the machine. "It's just the way I am. Hand me the detergent please."

"No, I won't. Not until you admit that it's alright for me to help you."

Sadie turned towards him and frowned. "You can't be serious."

"Oh, girl, I'm more serious than you realize."

"Fester, I'm not in the mood for games."

"Good. I ain't playin."

"Hand me the detergent."

"No."

Sadie reached out to try and take it from his hands but only grasped at air. She barely heard him move away from her over the sounds of another machine going through its cycles. Frustrated beyond measure, she manipulated the air in the room. Carefully she moved the air around her so she could feel where he was. It had been a long time since she played with the air indoors, and she wasn't sure what would happen in such a small room. Thankfully it didn't seem to be a problem. The air moved about her in gentle yet unnatural patterns. The hair that had come loose from her pony tail brushed her cheeks as it was pulled by the light breeze. Gradually the shapes of the machines and Fester were clearly felt. Sadie smiled. She walked purposefully over to him and held out her hand.

"The detergent, Fester. Now," she said firmly.

"Using your power, I see. That doesn't change a thing, Sadie. All I want is for you to admit that it's OK for you to take my pass."

Refusing to answer, she reached out and tried to grab the laundry detergent out of his hand. He was too quick for her, and once again moved it out of her way. Holding it above his head where she had no hope of reaching, he slowly walked away from her and towards the machines.

"I'm not joking, Fester."

"Neither am I," he said softly.

Refusing to cry she asked, "Why do you keep doing this to me? It's unfair and cruel."

"How is it cruel, Sadie? Ya just have to say it."

"I...I can't! OK? I can't!" Tears began to fill her eyes and she wanted to swear like the men. This insistence of his had become too much for her to bear. "Please, Fester, don't make me do that."

Fester let out a heavy sigh. "Fine, here. Whatever. You don't need to cry about it. Jeez."

Thankful that he was finally easing off of her, Sadie took the bottle from him and walked over towards the machines. Once more she was blind as she released the air and returned to her task. Neither of them spoke while the detergent was poured and the machine started. Having won her little battle, she allowed Fester to put the coins in their slot. Her point was made and there was no reason to fight with him again.

For the rest of the evening both Fester and Sadie were quiet. She couldn't understand why he was so adamant about helping her. Why did he constantly insist that she ask for it? He didn't want the debt; that much seemed certain. She knew that he loved her, but it still didn't make sense. It wasn't as though his help with the laundry would've made that much of a difference. The task was not a complicated one. There was no reason to request any form of assistance. If it was impossible for her to do what was needed, then she would consider asking him for help.

Once again she realized that these people were far too strange. While it was more likely that she was the odd one, she still wished they would at least try to understand her views. Constantly she tried to understand them and why they did certain things. Yet, they appeared to be content in their ignorance of her.

The realization was both infuriating and insulting.

Chapter 22

After the laundry was done and Chloe went to bed, Sadie realized that she wasn't as sleepy as she had been. This was a good thing in her mind. It meant that she could do what was needed so Chloe wouldn't be woken by her nightmares. The decision was made and she would stay awake all night. She could sleep after Chloe and Michael left for the day. This way her nightmares wouldn't hurt the girl anymore, and Michael wouldn't send her out into the cold. He said she could stay, but she didn't want to push her luck. Soon, not even Fester and Chloe would be able to convince him to keep her around.

Knowing that the men would never approve of her staying up, she pretended that she was going to sleep when they did. There was a small argument between her and Fester about who would make up the couch. Readying the bedding was another overly simple task that she obviously didn't need help with. Eventually and reluctantly, Fester dropped the issue. Sadie was proud of herself for winning an argument twice in the same night. It wasn't as though she wanted to fight with the man, however, she had enough of his fussing. He needed to learn to stop.

Sleep pulled at her when she lay down and patiently waited for the men to go into their rooms. They had been up late and she feared that she would fall asleep. Shortly after she heard both of their doors close, she sat up and felt for her novel. Someone had moved it without telling her, so finding it took a little longer than usual. Once she did, she delved into the story.

It had been an odd story for her, and she realized that she would need to read more books if she was to understand the world. At least she had begun to understand what Christmas was, although it had only been mentioned once by Fester and a few times on the television. While the idea of the holiday sounded wonderful, Sadie wasn't so sure such pure happiness could exist. By the end of the book she felt that the story had to be unrealistic. No family could ever be that happy. It simply wasn't possible.

Now there was nothing to occupy her mind. If she sat on the couch and let her thoughts wander then she would surely fall asleep. Figuring she would need something to do, she decided to clean. There wasn't much of the usual cleaning left so Sadie felt that perhaps some deep cleaning was in order. Although she didn't actually feel like doing that, or anything else, she was desperate to keep herself awake. There was no way for her to know how much longer it would be until morning. The more she could do to stay awake, the better off Chloe would be.

Carefully and quietly she went into the kitchen and dug out some of the cleaners. The familiar strong smells from them were unpleasant and made Sadie's stomach turn. Thankfully, she never ate the rest of her dinner. With almost nothing inside of her belly to come back up, the nausea settled down and she set about her task. She wondered why their cleaners were so different from the ones her parents made her use. Her parents' cleaners were almost pleasant to the nose.

Ignoring the odor as usual, Sadie cleaned the cabinets and walls in the kitchen. She scrubbed the front and sides of the refrigerator. If it had a surface of any kind, then it was cleaned at least twice before she moved on. When she finished with the kitchen she felt exhausted. Deciding to take a much needed break, she sat down at the table with a heavy sigh. Unfortunately, not long after she sat, Sadie found herself nodding off. Quickly she jerked her head up and realized she needed to keep moving. If she fell asleep now, then Chloe would be hurt and Michael would be angry. No, she needed to clean some more.

Quiet as ever, she scrubbed the walls and floorboards in the living room and entry way. She scraped the grime out from the corners of the floor and even cleaned under the couch and behind the television. When she finished, she decided to continue in the bathroom.

Earlier she had felt the handle of a thick bristled brush under the sink. She decided to use that to scrub the bathroom floor. Knowing that the men hadn't cleaned much before she came to stay there, she assumed that the floor was probably as gross as the public bathrooms she used when she was homeless. It was time that it had a little extra attention. She had been so engrossed with her cleaning that she didn't hear Fester's footsteps when he approached.

"Sadie," he said groggily, "its 2 am. The hell ya doin?"

Without pausing she simply said, "I'm cleaning the bathroom."

"Yeah, I can see that. So...why?"

"Because I don't want to sleep."

"What? Are you going to stay up all night?"

"I plan to."

Fester sighed. "Can I at least pee?"

Reluctantly Sadie stood and left the bathroom. While Fester did what he needed to, she sat at the kitchen table and yawned repeatedly. She was more exhausted than she had expected and her eyelids were heavy. When she heard the door open she stood, anxious to get back to her cleaning. As she headed back into the bathroom, she felt Fester's hand on her arm. Thankfully she didn't flinch. Perhaps she was too tired.

"Sadie, hold on a one-two. I want to share words with you," he said.

Sadie sighed. "What is it?"

"C'mere, let's sit."

Fester led her back towards the kitchen table and pulled out chairs for both of them. Sadie hesitated before she sat, afraid that he was going to yell at her for not sleeping. It was more important that she stay awake then whether or not Fester was angry. His anger could wake up Chloe and then she would be in more trouble. Readying herself for a lecture about the importance of sleep, she sat and waited.

"Sadie, what's going on?" Fester asked.

"What do you mean?"

Fester sighed. "Why don't you want to sleep? I can't believe that this is also because of your nonexistent debt."

Now it was Sadie's turn to sigh. "Fester, I keep on hurting Chloe. Yesterday was the worst. I just can't give her nightmares tonight. I can't do that to her again."

"What are you going to do? Try to stay awake every night so Chloe's OK?"

"If I have to."

"And when did you plan to sleep you're own self?"

"When she's at school."

"And on the weekends when she doesn't have school?"

"I...I haven't figured that out yet."

At first neither of them spoke. Sadie didn't have anything more to say so she waited patiently for Fester to ask her more questions. Normally she would be annoyed that he kept her from a task. Anything that helped her stay awake was more than welcome this time. He could talk to her all night long if he wanted. She was pleased that he didn't yell at her and hoped that he wouldn't start.

"Is there a thing I could do to get you to sleep?"

"No."

"Would you feel better about sleeping if...if...if I slept with you?"

Sadie paused. He sounded nervous when he asked that question. While she didn't understand why he would feel that way, she did consider his offer. She felt safer and less afraid when she was with him. Perhaps sleeping together would help keep her nightmares away. The thought was a little frightening because she didn't know if he would try to touch her where she didn't want. She reasoned that if he hadn't done so yet then he might not now. The idea of it still made her wary.

"I don't know," she finally said slowly. "I feel safer with you and less afraid. It might be OK."

"C'mon. Let's go over to the couch. We can sleep there if you're comfortable with it."

Sadie stood and didn't argue when he led her over to the couch. By this point her exhaustion was winning the battle. There was no doubt that she would fall asleep peacefully. Whether or not that sleep would continue to be peaceful was another matter. Still, she knew that she had been fooling herself. There was no way that she would be able to last the rest of the night. At least with Fester beside her, there was hope that Chloe would continue to be safe.

Unsure how they would be able to sleep together on the couch, she stood and waited for him to tell her what to do. It made more sense to sleep on the bed where there was more room. Knowing Fester, there probably was a reason behind the suggestion. What that was, however, she couldn't fathom. Still, he knew far more than she did and she was willing to trust that he knew what he was doing. He didn't seem the sort to suggest something without a somewhat rational motive.

Fester was heard sitting on the couch and he urged her to sit beside him. She felt him shift his position as he lay down with his legs hanging off the side. Gently he pulled her back and she found herself resting her head on his chest. His right arm wrapped around her. She felt a little squished as he sat up slightly to pull the blanket over the both of them. When he lay back down she relaxed into him and sighed.

"Comfortable?" he asked.

"Yes."

As she lay there she became extremely aware of Fester. She easily smelled his scent and, not for the first time, realized that she liked it. His arm that wrapped around her felt strong and secure. His other hand rested on hers and once again she was amazed by how large it was. As sleep began to creep up on her, she thought that perhaps sometime she should ask him about his hands. They were such a curiosity.

Sadie did indeed feel safe and peaceful lying this way. Even so, she nearly resisted sleep, fearful that she would hurt Chloe with her dreams. Sleep, however, was stronger and she eventually succumbed to it. As she began to drift off, any wariness she had previously felt melted away. Perhaps in Fester's arms she could keep away the nightmares for good.

Unfortunately, Fester had been wrong. Even in the safety and security of his arms, Sadie found herself once more surrounded by horror. Memories of the pain her father would inflict on her swam through her mind. For what felt like an eternity, she was trapped in a whirlwind of torture and rape. The noises he used to make, snarling and laughing at her torment, filled her ears. Off in the distance, she heard a baby screaming. Someone was hurting the baby! Immediately she began to fight her father so she could save the baby. She didn't care about the punishment for disobeying him. The baby must be saved!

Sadie woke to Fester shaking her gently. It took a few seconds for her to realize that it was he who held her and not her father. She nearly asked him where the baby was but caught herself. That would spark a conversation that she felt she would never be able to have. Tears ran down her cheeks as she realized that not even Fester could keep her bad dreams at bay. Poor Chloe!

"Hey, hey, it's OK. You're clear, Sadie. It was only a dream."

A shudder ran through her body as her tears flowed. Silently she cried and held onto Fester with all her strength. If he couldn't keep her nightmares away then perhaps he could at least be a comfort in their aftermath. She listened for Chloe's cries, wondering how badly she had hurt the child. Only her own sobs and Fester's soft voice were heard. Slowly she lifted her head.

"I don't hear Chloe," she whispered fearfully.

"She's still sleeping," he whispered. "I woke you up before your nightmare could affect her."

Sadie let out a sigh of relief. "So, I didn't hurt her then?"

"No. Not at all."

Sadie smiled as she lay her head back down onto Fester's chest. It was a comfort to know that Chloe was still safe. While Fester wasn't able to keep her from having nightmares, he was at least able to keep them from hurting the girl. Such dreams had been a part of her sleeping life for as long as she could remember. She didn't mind having them so long as the child didn't have to suffer, too. As she slowly drifted off to sleep, she felt at peace. This time her dreams were calm.

Sadie awoke again when she felt Fester stir. Gently he slid out from under her and off the couch. Instantly she snuggled into the cushions, ready to once again drift off to sleep. Sleep didn't take her, however. Michael had woken up Fester and now the two of them were whispering furiously in the kitchen. Unfortunately, she could easily hear them from the couch. Trying to ignore them, Sadie turned her back to the kitchen and attempted to fall back asleep.

"Fester, the fuck ya doin?"

"What? I'm not doing anything!"

"Ya gotta clue God damn well what. Ya takin' advantage o' them girl there?"

"No! Michael, it's not like that at all."

"Get ta lookin, all I gotta clue of: yest'day ya both got all nice an cozy an shit up in the kitchen, an now I gettin out here an fucking find ya sleepin all cuddles an shit up on the couch! The fuck ya got goin in ya head?"

It had never occurred to Sadie that Michael might be angry that they slept together. There was no reason that she could think of for that to happen. Was it wrong? Once again she was reminded at how much she didn't know. Apparently, there were rules about sleeping that no one had bothered to tell her. She and Fester must have broken one of them. Nervously, she tried to figure out what other rules she didn't know about. She would have to ask later.

"No, Michael, you have it all wrong! Look, last night I got up to piss and I found her scrubbing the bathroom floor."

"Ya gotta be fucking kiddin!"

"She was sweatin she'll have another nightmare and 'hurt' Chloe. Man, she was tryin to keep herself awake. So, I lay down with her to try and make her feel riskless enough to sleep. That's all! I swear it!"

Michael swore. "And? She done fucking get one?"

"Yeah. Seemed like a big one but I woke her up

before it could affect Chloe."

Both men were silent at first. Finally Michael said, "Shit, man. Get ta listenin, ya gotta fucking get ta lookin out for ya ass. I serious an true, Fester! That chick done got more damage than I coulda lived from. Ya fuck up, ya gonna get ta makin her worser."

"I'm not going to hurt her. I told you the other night..."

"Yeah. Fucking lovins. Whatever, man. Just be mindful riskless." Sadie thought she heard him sigh. "Get ta listenin, I ain't got no time to deal with them shits in the one-two. Dan callin 'bout an hour passed. I gotta fucking get ta workin early. Ya good takin Chloe ta school?"

"Yeah, don't sweat it."

"K. I gonna need ya pickin her up same. Doin double shift today an truly gotta get them overtime. Ya good with them shits?"

"Yeah, yeah, I got it."

"Good. See ya laters. Keep it in ya brain, Fester. Be fucking mindful! Them girl been 'bout ta fall o'er the fucking edge as is."

"Yeah, trust me, I get it true."

Michael's heavy footsteps moved about the kitchen. A minute later, Sadie heard the front door open and then close softly. She listened for whatever Fester was doing and didn't hear anything at first. Finally she heard him sigh and move in her direction. Not knowing if she should open her eyes or pretend to sleep, it seemed best to stay as she was. Once again she was nervous about letting him know that she overheard their private conversation.

Fester let out a grunt and Sadie heard a distinct pop. The sound reminded her of when she would crack her back. He sighed again and she heard him sit in the chair across from her. Although she wanted him to lay with her again, Michael would probably be upset if he did. Instead he seemed to have gone silent in the chair and she wondered if he was sleeping or watching her like he had once before. Did he watch her often? The thought made her feel slightly uneasy.

He swore, and once again she wondered if they

had broken a rule by sleeping together. Michael told Fester to be careful and warned that he could make her worse. The comment reminded Sadie what Chloe had said the day before. *'Ya gonna get better, Sadie!'* Did they think that her fears or nightmares made her sick? Other than feeling rather out of it yesterday evening, she didn't think that she was ill. Right now she felt fine. Why did Fester have to be careful? What had Michael meant by her being damaged and *'bout ta fall o'er the fucking edge'?* Realizing that she wasn't going to get any answers in her own head, or be able to go back to sleep anytime soon, Sadie rolled onto her back and opened her eyes.

"Hey," Fester said softly, "you're awake pretty early. I thought you would've slept longer."

"I just...I woke up."

"You should try and get more sleep. It's still pretty early and you were up late."

"You're up."

"Yeah, well, Michael woke me before he left for work."

It was a while before either of them spoke. Finally Sadie gathered up her courage and asked, "Fester? Was it wrong for us to sleep on the couch together?"

"What do you mean?"

She turned her head in his direction. "It's just that I don't know what the rules are here. No one told me yet. I'm afraid that I'm going to do something wrong and make Michael angry again."

"Oh. No, it wasn't wrong. As for the rules...there truly aren't any."

Fester's words confused Sadie. If it wasn't wrong then why was Michael so upset? What sort of place didn't have rules? As far as she knew, rules existed everywhere. These people had to have some as well. Perhaps Fester thought that she was talking about rules other than obvious ones. Not knowing what those might be worried Sadie.

"There have to be some rules, Fester. I really need to know what they are," she said.

Fester sighed. "Listen, Sadie, this isn't your parent's

joint. We don't have a ton of rules that need to be strictly followed. It's simple really. Don't hurt anyone, and Michael gets the final say."

Sadie waited for him to continue. When he didn't she sighed heavily. "Fester, what else? That can't be all there is!"

"Nope, that's it for true."

Sadie became extraordinarily anxious. There was no way that could be all. Something was missing and she hated that she didn't know what it could possibly be. Why would Fester keep this from her? It's not as though there was something he could achieve if she broke the rules. He said on many occasions that he didn't want her hurt. If that was true, then why was he keeping important information from her? The idea that he had told her the truth made her head swim. A place that had only two rules? That was totally inconceivable. She didn't have much time to consider it further before Fester began to speak once more.

"Do you trust me, Sadie?"

The question caught her off guard. "No, not really." She wasn't ready to let him know what she had been thinking.

"Why not?" He sounded hurt.

"I'm not ready, I don't think. My whole life I could really only trust myself, Fester."

"I see," he said sadly.

"I'm sorry. I want to trust you. Out of everyone I've ever met, you're the only one I think I *could* learn to trust. I just don't know how. Not really."

Sadie heard him get up and walk over towards her. His knee popped and his clothes rustled as he shifted his position. She didn't flinch as he moved some of her hair from in front of her face. Carefully he caressed her cheek with his fingertips. The gesture was strange, yet comforting.

"I wish you could trust me, Sadie," he said softly. "I trust you."

"You do?" she asked. "Why would you trust me?"

"I know in my heart that you would never hurt me. And, Sadie, I wish you could believe that, no matter what, I would never hurt you, either. I couldn't bear the thought of causing you any amount of pain or grief. I would give up my life if it meant yours would be happy and peaceful."

"I don't understand. Why would you do that?"

"Because...Sadie, I...I..."

"Michael?" Chloe's sleepy voice came from the direction of her bedroom door.

Fester swore softly before he stood up and moved towards the child. "Hey, Chloe, Michael had to go to work early. I'm going to take you to school today. OK?"

"K!" Sadie heard Chloe run in her direction. "Guess what, Sadie! I ain't gettin no nightmares last night!"

Smiling she said, "Good. I'm glad."

Chloe ran off towards the bathroom and Fester moved about the kitchen. The growl from her stomach reminded her that she hadn't finished dinner the day before. Stretching, she proceeded to rise from the couch. She hoped Fester would be happy that she was going to eat. The thought brought a small smile to her face. She realized that she too would do anything to make him happy. She wasn't sure if that included dying, however. She couldn't imagine giving her life up for anyone except...

Shaking her head, Sadie tried not to let her mind wander in that direction. Her nightmares were getting to her and she needed to try to keep all unpleasant thoughts out of her mind. The anguish that such thoughts were known to cause were already about to tear at her heart. She couldn't handle anymore and didn't want to hurt Chloe with such a powerful emotion either.

Yawning from too little sleep, she felt around the coffee table for her cane. It was found easily and she headed into the kitchen. Desperate for something to distract her from her distressing thoughts, she sat down at the table and asked Fester if he would make her something to eat.

"Really? Yeah, just give me a one-two." He sounded happy and that helped to ease her internal pain.

Chloe came out of the bathroom and Sadie could

hear her walk slowly towards the kitchen. "Sadie? Ya K there?"

"Yes," she lied. "I'm OK, Chloe. I'll try not to be so sad."

"What's wrong?" Fester asked as he placed a bowl in front of her.

"Nothing," she said softly. There was no way she was going to have this conversation.

No one spoke as they ate their cereal. Sadie desperately wished that someone would say something. She wasn't adept at starting conversations and for once she truly didn't want to be alone with her thoughts. Without knowing what to say, she instead tried to keep her mind blank. Her pain had only eased a little. There was nothing she wanted more in that moment than to feel numb. Thankfully Chloe broke the silence.

"Fester, when it snowin 'gain? Them snows outside gettin hard ta plays in."

"I don't know. Let me think...it'll probably snow in the next day or two."

Chloe let out a squeal of delight and Sadie found herself smiling. "How do you know that?" she asked.

"I just thought about the weather patterns over the past few weeks and calculated what the probability of snow would be. I can't predict it accurately without instruments, but its close enough."

Sadie was amazed. "You were only thinking about it for a few seconds!"

"Well, yeah. That's how long it took me to picture it," he said.

Once again Sadie was amazed at the extent of Fester's power. Perhaps he was right. With a brain that can figure things out that quickly, they should be able to avoid PSI and anyone else who tried to come after them. Finally she began to relax about their situation. For the first time in a while she had actual hope, and for once she truly believed that perhaps Fester could save her after all.

There wasn't much in this world which could give her that level of peace. Given how serious their situation had become, it was amazing that she could feel safe at all. Deep within her very being she knew that if she were to ever fully trust anyone, then it would be him. The thought left an uneasy sensation in her belly. Would such a thing truly be possible? Would it be wise?

Conflicting thoughts swarmed Sadie's mind. Her greatest fear came from the idea that if she allowed herself to trust Fester, to really trust him, then she would have put herself in serious danger. *'Sadie, I'm never, ever, ever, never gonna do nothing like that to ya. Not ever. Never.' 'I trust you.' 'I wish you could believe that I would never hurt you.'* Although he constantly said such things, and he hadn't done anything to actually hurt her, she still wasn't sure how true his words were.

Kindness is never free. Her mother may have set her up to freely accept kindness with her sign, but she couldn't shake the notion of that primary lesson. So ingrained into her psyche, there was no way for her to let it go. Fester had to want something from her. It was impossible for Sadie to believe he didn't. Possibilities fluttered in her mind like wasps. If he didn't want to hurt her, and he didn't fully accept her offers for payment, then what could he possibly want? Everyone wanted something.

Sadie reflected on what Michael had asked Fester earlier. *'Ya takin' advantage o' them girl there?'* She wasn't sure what he had meant but it did make her worry. What was it that he thought Fester had done? While she didn't have an answer to that question, there was a distressing thought which entered her mind. Until she knew what Fester truly wanted, then her trust could never be placed with him. Once again she wondered if she was truly safe and considered leaving.

Whatever pain he might one day inflict on her, it wouldn't hurt as much as the betrayal that would accompany it. For Sadie, such a thing would cause her more agony than her parents could have inflicted. It wasn't a chance she wanted to take. There was no way she would allow herself to endure such torment. She knew that to protect herself she would have to leave. PSI Teams or not, it would be safer to go quietly.

Better to save herself the agony of betrayal by avoiding it completely.

After eating, she moved to the couch and listened to Fester and Chloe as they got ready. Chloe had been exceptionally quiet. Sadie could only assume that it was a result of her own dark mood. Preferring her own company to those around her, she sat in silence. She had been especially distant with Fester. On more than one occasion, he had tried to talk to her about what was on her mind. Each and every time she ignored him. Her only response to his frequent inquiries was to hold up her hand and shake her head violently.

Having already made up her mind about his future betrayal, Fester was the last person she wanted to speak with. When it was time for Chloe to leave for school, Sadie refused to go with them. She gave the simple excuse that she was still tired from the previous night. Sitting rigid on the couch, she silently listened as both of them left the apartment.

The door closed and the place was suddenly blissfully quiet. Sadie waited a few minutes to gather her courage. It was time. She could no longer deny that staying with these people any longer would be a grave mistake. She had nearly given her precious trust to one of them, she constantly hurt Chloe with her emotions, and she brought danger upon them. The reality was that she couldn't allow herself to stay. It wasn't safe for her or for them. To deny that now would be foolish.

A great sadness came over her as she began to pack her things. She sobbed as she moved about, gathering what little she had. Checking her tin, she found that she only had a few coins. It wasn't enough to buy even the smallest amount of food. She considered taking some from the jar in the kitchen. Shaking her head at the thought, she knew that it would be better to go hungry than steal from these people. They had only tried to help her. To take what was theirs would be worse than not repaying them, even if Fester would betray her eventually. No, starvation was better.

Her heart was heavy as she forced herself to move towards the door. Part of her screamed and begged to go back inside. Ignoring such thoughts and the pain in her core, she stepped out into the hallway with her belongings strapped to her back. She truly didn't want to go and for a moment she almost reconsidered.

Fresh tears streamed down her face as she pulled the door closed and opened up her cane. The only thing she had left behind was her library book on the kitchen table. She wanted to take it with her as a reminder of the time she had spent there, but she knew it wouldn't be right. After all, it wasn't hers to take.

Once more Sadie hesitated before heading out into the cold. Why was it that the most difficult decision in her life had to be so terribly painful? Putting the apartment behind her, she carefully stepped out of the building and onto the sidewalk. The pain in her heart made her wish Fester had left her to die in the first place. It would've been better to die on the street that day than to return to such an existence with the knowledge she now held. Before, she hadn't known that a home could make her feel safe. Now, she wished she didn't know about such things at all. It would have left her with less to miss while the freezing cold stole her life.

Fester...why couldn't he have stayed 'the food-man' and never let her know him?

Chapter 23

Once Sadie was back on the street, she had no idea what she should do. In her haste to leave, she hadn't thought of a plan. Anxiety filled her once more as she realized that if any of them saw her, they would try to stop her from doing what she knew was right. She hadn't asked where Chloe's school was and that meant there was practically no way for her to avoid Fester. If he saw her then her plans would be lost. He couldn't be allowed to force her to stay.

Realizing that he would find her easily if she continued to stand in front of his building, Sadie decided to head towards the park. At least she might be able to hide there for a while. Quickly she walked down the street, trying to remember its exact location. In her mind was a grid-like map of the city. When she reached the corner, she had a good idea of the direction she should take. The park, if she remembered it correctly, wasn't far.

As she walked she began to feel around her immediate area with the air. She kept the details to a minimum with the hope that no one would notice. At this point, however, she wasn't sure if she cared. She knew how rare those three people had been. There wasn't anywhere she could go where someone would show her the kindness which they had offered so freely. If the government found her now, there wasn't anything it could do to make her life worse than it was at this point.

Tears streamed down her face as she entered the park. Carefully she tried to make sure she stayed on the path and didn't step in the deep snow. Her feet felt frozen already and she didn't want to make it worse. While searching for a place to rest, Sadie almost considered going back. Those people were strange and she had trouble understanding them. However, they were also the only friends she had ever known.

Sitting on a bench, she realized all that was wrong with returning. Although she liked them, those men were terrifying in their own way. Constantly they frightened her, even when that wasn't their intention. In turn, her fears hurt Chloe. The cycle was unbreakable. Yes, it was warm, but she barely felt safe there. The knowledge that soon one of them would surely cause her pain was the best reason not to return. She had vowed she would not allow herself to be harmed again. She was going to stick to that vow, even if she hurt herself in the process. Better she be the cause of her own final torment.

Sadie shivered as the cold bit at her ears and face. It hadn't taken long for her to feel unbearably frozen. Quickly she untied her sleeping bag and wrapped it around her body and head. Fear swelled in her chest when she realized that she was going to die here on this bench. Desperate for warmth, she stopped reaching out with the air and once more focused on warming the air under the sleeping bag. It was a futile attempt and the cold crept in unhindered.

Fearful of the death that was sure to take her, Sadie began to weep uncontrollably. It was fitting that her life should end this way. This park was the first place she had ever felt pure joy. She tried to comfort herself with the memory of playing in the snow with Chloe. Instead of making her feel better, the memory fueled the depression that had washed over her. Never again would she feel that happy or hear Chloe's beautiful laugh. In her heart was a terrifying pain as she mourned those experiences that were never to be had again.

Harder she cried as she slipped into true despair. It became difficult to breathe as the cold air seared the inside of her lungs, yet she was unable to stop crying. So deep was her grief that she didn't hear the crunch of footsteps as someone walked towards her in the snow. The bench shifted when whoever it was sat down. The motion barely registered in her mind. Her lack of awareness at this time made her truly blind.

"Did you really picture I wouldn't have my eyes favorin ya?" Sadie's heart stopped at the sound of

Fester's voice. "Sadie, if you don't want to keep with us, then that's fine. But, there's no way I'm gonna let you freeze to death."

"Just let Death take me, Fester!" she said through her tears.

"I can't let you die, Sadie. I just can't." Fester paused before he asked, "Why do you want to die?"

"I don't. But, I can't stay with you all, and I can't live any other way. So, just leave me and allow me to die alone, like I'm meant to."

"Sadie, you're not meant to die and certainly not alone. I couldn't bear it if you died. It would be too painful." Sadie couldn't respond. When he spoke again his breath was uneven, his voice cracked, and his words were shaky. "I...I love you, Sadie. I'm terribly, madly, deeply, in-love with you. I will not let you die!"

Sadie felt as though she were a raging river of emotions, full and overflowing. Her very being was flooded with them. She brought her cold hand up to her mouth and closed her eyes. Hearing the sadness and fear that his voice contained, she knew that Fester ached on the inside as well. Unable to contain herself, she leaned into him and grabbed his coat with her hand. He wrapped his arms around her and rested his cheek upon her head.

"I really don't want to leave!" she said. "I'm scared, Fester. I'm scared of being helped. I don't know what else to do."

"It's OK, Sadie," he said as he held her tightly, "It's OK and ya don't have nothing to be 'fraid of. Listen, my prediction was off. Based on the weather this mornin it's gonna snow soon. Let's go back to the apartment where it's warm. I'm true here, Sadie. I won't force you to keep there if you don't want to. But, you're freezing and we need to get you warm."

Sadie hesitated before agreeing. Regardless of what he said, she felt that once more he was trying to force her to stay. Shivering in the cold, her desire to be warm won out over her desire to be alone. Slow and unsure of herself, she nodded. For once she didn't complain when he helped her to stand and offered to carry her things. She was far too frozen to care about debt now.

Swiftly Fester guided her out of the park and towards his building. There was little thought as to what she would do once they were back in the apartment. Sadie felt deep down that it was futile to go there. It wouldn't be long before she was freezing once more. She couldn't imagine staying, and was doubtful that Fester would want her to after this incident. Going back was cruel.

When they were in the apartment Sadie began to cry as the warm air touched her nearly frozen face. It was mean for Fester to bring her here, knowing that soon she would be in the cold once more. Again she wished that he had simply let her die and be done with it. Her fears ran through her being, filling her to the brink as the world spun around her. As her anxiety rose, she began to feel incredibly dizzy. Fester grabbed her arms as she almost lost her balance.

"You OK, Sadie?" he asked. Concern filled his voice and caused her heart to ache.

"I don't know," she said honestly. "I don't think I ever will be. You should've just let me die."

"I don't want to hear any more words like that. Please. No matter what happens I will never let you die. C'mon, let's take off your coat and get you by the heater."

Once more she didn't protest as he helped her with her coat and hung it up. With his hand firmly on her elbow he guided her in the direction of the heat. He asked her to wait a moment as he moved a chair closer to the heater. When he was ready for her, she gratefully sat. Tears continued to flow down her cheeks as she silently cried. She heard the wood on the coffee table creak as he sat upon it.

"What's goin on, Sadie?" he asked after a moment.

"Nothing."

"A thing had to happen to make you get riskful with your life like that. Was it me? Did I do something wrong 'gain?" His voice sounded pained.

"No, Fester. You didn't do anything wrong."

"Then help me to get why you were about to kill yourself! It doesn't make any logical sense!"

Sadie brought her hand to her mouth. "It's not safe here."

"Why do you always think that? Did something new happen to make you feel unsafe?"

Sadie thought about what to tell him. In her mind swam all the possible ways she might be hurt by him or Michael. "I don't know what you want," she eventually said. "I don't understand any of you. There has to be something you want. The things you all do and say make no sense, Fester. They just don't make sense. How can I stay somewhere that's so unpredictable? It makes me miss my parents' home. There I knew what to expect."

Fester sighed. "So, that's the issue. You're so used to the abuse that you feel riskful danger without it. You're just waitin for us to hurt you. Is that it?"

"Yes," she said as relief briefly flowed over her. Finally he was beginning to understand.

Fester moved so he was in front of her. Gently he took her hands in his. "Sadie, tell me what I can do so you feel clear here. I don't know how else to show you that Michael and I won't hurt you. I don't want to ever hurt you. I love you, Sadie. It hurts me so much to see you like this. I only want you happy. That's all I ever wanted."

Sadie nearly jumped when she felt Fester's forehead touch the top of her hands. He trembled and his breath was uneven. She knew that somehow she had hurt him. It felt as though she had done that a lot lately. The reminder of how she seemed to always do the wrong thing only fueled her insecurity and made her want to leave again. If she stayed, then he and Chloe would continue to feel pain and sadness because of her. If she stayed, then she was in danger of being hurt more than ever before. It wasn't safe. It just wasn't safe.

"I know I said I wouldn't ask you about your past," Fester said softly. "But, Sadie, I have to know... Who else, other than your 'rents, hurt you?"

With thoughts of betrayal fresh in her mind, she

hesitated before answering him. "My parents were the only people I knew before coming Downtown. There wasn't anyone else in my life to hurt me."

He lifted his head off of her hands. "Are you sure?"

"Fester, I didn't know anyone else. I never left the home and no one ever visited."

"You weren't around no one else? You weren't hurt by no one else true?"

"No."

"Then...then who's Nathan?"

Sadie went completely still. Her heart beat wildly in her chest and there was an intense pressure inside of her head. Her breath caught in her throat and her body shook violently. She stood and tripped over the chair as she frantically tried to get away from Fester. As quick as she could, she got up again and continued to back away from him.

"Sadie? Sadie, what's wrong? Who is he?"

"How...how do you know that name?"

"I'm sorry. I didn't have a mind that you would react like this. I shoulda been mindful and not asked. I just need to know."

"How do you know that name, Fester?" she asked through clenched teeth.

"You yelled it both times you had a nightmare. I need to know who he was, Sadie. Please, tell me, what did he do to you that's making you react this way?"

Sadie collapsed to her knees. Her breath came out in short, uneven spurts. Her chest hurt and her head swam with the intense grief that filled her. She was barely aware of Fester when he came over and sat on the floor beside her. His tone was soft and gentle as he urged her to tell him who Nathan was. It was difficult to find her voice at first.

"He's my son," she whispered.

"You...you have a son?" Fester sounded completely shocked and Sadie could only nod in reply. "When? How?"

"He was born a few months before my mother sent me away."

Fester swore worse than Michael. Sadie flinched

hard, unsure if he would go back on his word and hurt her now. He sounded angry and stood to pace about the room in a way that was also like Michael. Hugging herself, she stayed where she was on the floor. It felt as though the tears would never end. The entire time she had been Downtown she refused to think about Nathan. It had been too painful, and now she was experiencing all of that missed torment. Her heart felt like it was breaking and she yearned to be with him once more. Her son; her tiny baby.

Fester stopped pacing and sat back down beside her. Pulling her close to him, he wrapped his arms around her and held her tightly. Sadie, in turn, held onto him with all of her strength. An intense sorrow coursed through her body and tore at her from the inside. There was no awareness of the passage of time. All she knew was her own immense pain, and the suffering she was destined to endure forever.

"Sadie," Fester said after a while. "Where is he? Where is Nathan now?"

"My parents have him."

Once again Fester swore heavily. "We have to get him back. We can't let him stick with them. We need to get your son back, Sadie."

"How? I don't know where they are!"

"I ain't got no clue. We'll picture it out though. We have to. There has to be a way to find him. I won't stop trying until we do."

Without knowing where she was from, there was no way that Sadie could fathom for them to find her baby. She had accepted that he was gone from her life forever. Even Fester's powerful brain couldn't pull information out of nothing. Her son was lost and there wasn't anything she nor Fester could do to save him. All she could do was mourn.

Hope no longer existed, only despair remained.

Chapter 24

It took longer than usual for Sadie's crying to die down. In the end Fester had to give her the pills from the day before. Between the medicine and the emotional turmoil the morning had provided, she felt utterly exhausted. Fester tried to get her to go to sleep but she refused. The thought of dreaming was enough to keep her wide awake. Thinking about Nathan had taken its toll on her psyche. There was no doubt that any sleep now would bring about the worst nightmares imaginable.

Fester left her on the couch while he moved about the kitchen. She hoped that he wasn't making more food. Her stomach wouldn't be able to handle it at this point. The last thing she needed to do was vomit all over everything. Her belly already felt queasy as it was. Taking her mind off such unpleasantness, she listened to the sounds he made. It was near impossible to determine his actions. Unsure of what he was planning, she stiffened as he approached her.

"Here," he said. "Be mindful, it's hot."

"I can't eat right now," she said. Her voice was hoarse and her throat was sore from crying.

"It's not food, Sadie. It's hot coco. It'll make you feel better and help warm you s'more."

Nervously she held out her hands. She had never had hot coco before and wasn't sure what to expect. When she felt the warm mug touch her hand, she gently took it and held it in her lap. Not only did she not want to eat, she also didn't want to drink. What Sadie really wanted to do was cease to exist. Since that wasn't a possibility, she settled for sitting and holding the mug. Inside she felt numb and any movement took far too much effort.

"You OK, Sadie?"

"Yes," she lied.

"You don't look OK. I don't blame you. I can't picture in my mind what you've been through." He paused a few seconds. "Please don't be mad at me but I still think you should share your story 'bout all this."

"There is no point in talking about the past, Fester. No good will come of it. It won't bring me Nathan and it won't bring me peace. It'll only hurt." The hollow tone to her voice frightened her.

"Sadie," he said softly, "I want you to just listen to me for a one-two. OK? Don't say nothing until I've finished. Can you do that for me?"

"I don't see why not."

"Good. I know that you think telling your story won't help but it can. I speak from experience. My pops... he used to...he used to hurt me too. Shortly after my moms died he started pounding on me and sometimes would do...other things. By the time I finally runway from home my mind was really messed up by it all. Then Michael took me in, and after a one-two I started to share my story 'bout what had happened to me. I'm not completely over what my dick pops did, and I'm not sure if I ever will be. What I do know is that when I share words...talk about it...well...it starts to be less painful. Y'know?"

Sadie had listened to his words carefully. He said he had been hurt, too, but she didn't think he understood. "Fester, if I talk about the lessons...it'll hurt. A lot. I'll remember it like it was happening again. I'll feel it like it was real. My nightmares are like that too. They feel so real." Tears rolled down her face. "I can't. I just can't do that. I...I really don't want to feel the lessons again. Please, Fester. Please don't make me. Please?"

"I've had memories like that, too. They're called 'flashbacks' and will also lessen. Please believe me. If we talk, it might help."

"No," she whispered. "It won't help. Please stop asking me to talk about these things. Please, Fester. I can't handle it. I can't....I can't...I..."

Her body began to tremble violently. The conversation had brought some of the memories close to the surface and they brought an intense feeling of terror with them. Swallowing hard, she worked at forcing them back into the darkest reaches of her mind.

Something must have shown in the way she looked. Fester's mug made a loud sound as it was placed harshly on the coffee table. Nearly immediately after, her own mug was swiftly taken from her hands.

"Sadie? Sadie, what's wrong?" Fester asked. His tone was of pure concern.

"I...I'm trying not to remember," she whispered, her body and voice shook uncontrollably.

"It's OK. Shhhhh. It's OK, Sadie. Keep in mind, you're clear and riskless here. OK? You're safe and I won't let that happen to you ever again..."

Fester continued to speak to her in soft, soothing tones. His words sounded reassuring but did little to ease her fears. When his fingers brushed her hand she jerked violently. The fierce motion caused her to accidentally hit the coffee table with her leg. Liquid was heard sloshing out of the mugs and onto the surface of the table. Her shin ached from the impact.

Fester swore and quickly removed his hand. He apologized many times before falling silent. The problem wasn't that he had touched her. The memories had been so close to the surface that she was beginning to forget where she was. His touch had been so startling that she couldn't help but react the way she had. Needing an anchor to hold onto, she reached out and grabbed his arm and held it tightly. Reality had slowly begun to fall away and it wasn't long before holding Fester wasn't enough.

Turning towards him, she grabbed at him with both hands and whispered, "Help me..."

Fester gently wrapped his arms around her and pulled her into a sweet embrace. She in turn wrapped her arms around his body and buried her face in his chest. Breathing in his scent, she cried as her memories washed over her. She felt as though she would drown in them. It wasn't long before his scent and security were pushed away by the past. Slowly he fell from her existence and she was back home again, being taught the lessons once more. Screams tore from her lips and her body burst into spasms. The pain she warned him about had begun.

The torture ravaged from within and all she could hear were her parents as they repeated their lessons. She felt as though she would die while enveloped in the excruciating pain they wrought. Every lesson she had ever been taught were all combined into one immense and unending sensation. This time when she screamed, there was no sound to be heard from her lips. So great was her agony, that even her voice had fled.

Sadie's fingers dug into Fester as she tried to bear all that had been done to her. For as long as she could remember, there were always lessons to be endured. To attempt to count the number of times she had been beaten or forced to pleasure was impossible at best. Her suffering had been her payment thousands of times. Even now, far from her heinous parents, the lessons raged on. She knew that no matter where she went or what she did, there was no hope of escape. The lessons would always be there, waiting for her to have them over and over again.

There was no way to tell how long this continued. Sadie felt as though she would be tormented for an eternity before the pain eventually died down and the memories gradually retreated to where they had come from. They tucked themselves away to wait for her to fall asleep or be reminded of them once more, whispering through her mind that she would never be free. Her entire body ached as she trembled in Fester's arms. She felt lightheaded and dizzy from the energy that had recently coursed through her. She noticed that Fester was also trembling and he had an unusually tight grip on her. Sadie tried to pull away but he was too strong.

"Fester," she whispered, her voice hadn't fully come back. "I'm OK. The memories are gone. Please, let me sit straight. You're hurting me."

Fester slowly released her. "Sadie," he said in disbelief, "the fuck was that shit?"

"I...I don't usually get them that bad. This time... they hurt too much. I couldn't handle it. I told you, the past needs to stay where it is. No good will ever come of it. Please, please don't ask me again. It hurt way more than before. Please..."

"My God, ya ain't got no clue, do ya?"

"What?"

"Ya power, Sadie. The joint's a mess. It was like we were in the center of a twister! Ya near destroyed everything." The fear in his voice worried her.

"I...I did?" The idea that her wind reacted to her memories and destroyed the apartment was terrifying.

"We have to clean this joint true. Michael's gonna get pissed!"

Sadie had no idea that her wind could be released in such a way. During the flashback she had no awareness of her surroundings. The cascade of memories had been too severe. Now she was afraid but for a different reason. Fester could have been seriously hurt because of her. Michael would surely force her to leave now. He had said she was damaged, and now that damage had spilled over into his home. The danger that she had become made her feel extremely guilty. Unfortunately, guilt was beginning to be as common a feeling as fear.

Sadie felt weak as she stood. She was determined to fix this. Even if he did make her leave, she still needed to return the apartment to the way it was. Fester said that she had nearly destroyed everything. She wondered how severe the damage actually was. Her head swam and she felt unsteady. Fester grabbed her arm as she began to sway on her feet.

"Sadie, you need to sit. You look way too pale."

"I'm fine. I need to fix this. I can't let Michael see what I did."

Sadie jumped as she heard a knock at the front door. There was a sense of urgency to the sound, as though the person on the other side was in a rush. Fester swore as he released her and moved away. She stood there, not knowing what else to do, and listened while he carefully made his way across the apartment. Even blind she could tell that he had to step over several objects to keep from falling. It was tempting to use air to see but at this point she was terrified of what that might do. If she caused any more damage...

From where she stood she couldn't hear what was said after Fester opened the door. Gingerly Sadie took a step and nearly collapsed. Her body was far too weak and her exhaustion was worse than she had ever experienced. With a heavy heart, she sat back down and waited. There was nothing else she could do for now. Thankfully it wasn't long before Fester invited the visitor into the apartment.

"Holy Mother Mary! It looks like a tornado blew through here." Sadie went still at the sound of Sal's voice.

"Yeah. We're...uh...redecorating. Thought we would start by tearin everything ta bits. Out with the old, in with the new, yadda yadda yadda."

"Bullshit, Fester. I don't need to know what happened but I don't appreciate sarcasm either."

"I get it. Sorry."

Sal's footsteps moved in Sadie's direction. "Sadie, Fester, we need to get the both of you out of here right now."

"What's going on?" Fester asked. He sounded alarmed and that put Sadie on edge.

"A PSI Team has been called in. They're due to arrive within the hour. I've already sent someone to fetch Michael and Chloe. I wanted to come for you both myself."

Fester swore. "OK, let me just get some things together."

"There's no time. They're bringing in a Tracker."

Fester swore again and Sadie asked, "What's a Tracker?" Her voice squeaked. It still hadn't fully returned.

"It's a Supernatural whose power allows them to track down anyone. There are only a few that are known to exist and one works for PSI. Fucking traitor! Come on, we don't have time to talk about this. We need to move now! I'll send someone for your things once it's safe."

Sadie was terrified. She began to frantically feel around for her cane. The broken coffee table was covered in hot coco and debris. Trying not to panic, she continued to search though it felt nearly impossible to find in the mess. It wasn't long before someone pressed the cane into her hand and then grabbed her elbow to help her stand. The hand was too small to be Fester's.

Sal pulled her up harshly. "Come on, sweetheart. We need to hurry. The more distance we put between ourselves and the Tracker the better it will be."

Sal continued to pull Sadie away from the couch. She didn't even have a chance to open her cane. Her head felt uneasy and she had trouble keeping her balance. Her feet kept on kicking random objects and she tripped more than a few times. Not only did she fight not to fall, she also struggled to stay conscious. She didn't think she would make it out the door.

"Shit, Sal, wait! Sadie? Are you OK? You don't look so good."

Unable to speak, she decided to be honest and shook her head. The motion hurt and she completely lost her balance. Both Fester and Sal caught her as her legs gave out. She tried with everything she had to stand again. They needed to leave. Sal was adamant and the urgency was obvious. There was no hope. Her legs had lost their strength and her mind slipped away.

Both Sal and Fester swore as Sadie passed out.

Chapter 25

At first there was nothing. Sadie floated in the darkness of her mind, unable to tell what was happening around her. From somewhere nearby she heard painful and torturous screams. There were others begging for freedom. What was happening? Slowly she sat up, only to find that she had been bound to the floor by chains on her wrists and ankles. A terrible fear ran through her when she recognized where she was. *Home.*

As her head cleared she came to the realization that the terrified screams were from Chloe. Fester and Michael were both screaming too, begging for Chloe to be released. Together they offered themselves to be put in her place. She wondered what could possibly have happened that brought them here of all places. They hadn't been anywhere near her parents. Did Sal bring them here? Was this her idea of keeping them safe?

"Ah, you're finally awake," Sadie's mother said joyfully. "I was afraid you would miss your next lesson."

"Mother," Sadie said, "please don't do this. Let my friends go!"

"Friends? Who gave you permission to have friends? You disappoint me, Sadie. You haven't paid your debt and now your 'friends' will pay it for you."

"Please, Mother! I beg you! Please don't hurt them!"

"Oh my sweet child, you know that if a lesson isn't taught properly, then it needs to be repeated. This Chloe hasn't had any lessons. She has some catching up to do. But don't worry, your father is teaching her right now."

Sadie began to scream. She cried and begged for them to let Chloe go. "She doesn't deserve the lessons! It's my debt, Mother, let me pay it! I beg you: let me pay the debt and not Chloe!"

"Oh, she's going to do more than pay with pain and pleasure. All your friends are going to die. You are meant to be alone. Didn't I teach you that already? You knew this and yet you were selfish. Because of your greed these worthless people will suffer and then die! *That* is your payment!"

Despair tore through Sadie's core as she screamed. This was an agony like none she had endured before. Her mind broke from the torment and all she could do was scream Chloe's name. She felt like her screams would go on forever as anguish raged through her mind. The child didn't deserve the lessons. Only Sadie deserved them. Cause her grief, cause her agony, torture her until the pain itself destroyed her mind and body, but let her friends be free!

Suddenly her mother grabbed her shoulders and she instantly fought her with all the strength she could muster. She refused to allow any of them to suffer anymore. Neither Chloe, nor anyone else was meant to pay her debts. As her desperation rose, she forced the full magnitude of her wind to burst forth in a wide spread sweep across the room. Finally her parents would learn of the strength of her wind and her revenge. She wasn't going to allow them to teach another lesson ever again!

That was when she heard people yelling her name. The shackles no longer held her to the floor and her mother's voice had vanished. Everyone called for her to wake up and stop the wind. Upon realizing that it had only been a terrible nightmare, and that she used the full force of her wind on her friends, Sadie caused the air to instantly become still. There was a loud thud as something fell to the floor some distance away.

"What did I do? What did I do?" she asked anxiously.

No one answered her at first. Chloe was screaming in terror and Michael tried his best to calm her down. He then asked, "Sal! He fucking K?"

"I don't know. His head is bleeding and he's not moving. He is breathing and has a pulse, so that's good," Sal said from across the room.

Michael swore and went back to soothing the terrified child.

"What did I do?" Sadie asked again. "Someone tell

me!"

"Ya done got ta fucking screamin at Chloe 'fore ya fucking flyin Fester the fuck o'er the room, bashin his ass in the mother fucking walls! Shit, Sadie! The fuck?"

"Fester? Where is he? Someone tell me where he is!"

"He's over here," Sal said.

Terrified that she had seriously hurt the one man she swore to never harm, Sadie carefully moved off the couch and felt for the coffee table. She had no idea where her cane was and needed to make sure she didn't hit her shin again. Surprisingly the table wasn't there and she wondered if it too had been blown away by her wind.

Carefully she moved through the room towards Sal's voice. Bumping into furniture she didn't recognize, she wondered where they were. This was not the apartment. Stumbling amongst the unfamiliar objects in her path served only to increase her panic. Tears stung her eyes when the obstacles caused her to finally stop.

"Sal," she said, "I need you to tell me where to go. Please, I need to get to him!"

Sal's footsteps came quickly to her and the woman took a hold of her elbow. As she guided Sadie over towards Fester, Chloe's cries began to turn into a painful whimper. She felt bad that she had frightened the girl, but at that moment her main concern was for Fester. After she learned if he was alright, then she would worry about the child.

Sal stopped and told Sadie that he was on the floor in front of her. Instantly she fell to her knees and felt for him. Her hand touched his head and she felt something wet. Fear coursed strongly through her veins when she realized that it was the blood which Sal had mentioned. As tears streamed down her face, she placed both of her hands on Fester's cheeks.

"Please, Fester. I'm so sorry! Please, wake up! I'm sorry! Please oh please..." she said.

Sadie's voice trailed off as she cried in near hysterics. Her throat hurt, but it was nothing compared to the agony in her heart. If she had seriously hurt Fester, then there would be no way she could forgive herself. Already her guilt was far too heavy a burden to bear. She knew her heart wouldn't be able to take any more.

When Sadie felt Fester begin to stir, she released the breath she had held. Relief poured out of her when she felt his familiar large hand on hers. Gingerly she removed her hands from his face and grasped his hand firmly.

"Sadie?" His voice sounded strained.

"I'm sorry, Fester. I'm so sorry! I didn't know it was you! I never wanted to hurt you! Please, I'm so very sorry!"

Sadie continued to apologize as he struggled to sit up. A thousand apologies couldn't express the grief and guilt that she felt.

"Easy, Fester. We don't know how severe your injuries are. Try not to move," Sal said.

"I guessin I'm OK. Sore but OK." He placed his hand on Sadie's and spoke gently. "It's alright, Sadie. I'm OK and I know you didn't do that on purpose. Don't sweat it, it's OK."

Michael's loud footsteps moved swiftly across the room. "Them some heavy bullshit, Fester. Ya lil girlfriend near got ya dead, an damn near got us hurtin ta boot! Fuck man! Shit gettin heavy deep an ya gotta wake the fuck up. I sorry I gotta get sayin them shits but: Sadie, ya got morer riskful fucking danger in ya than good."

"The fuck words you saying, Michael?" Even angry, Fester's voice sounded strained.

"It's OK, Fester," Sadie said. "Michael's right. This never happened before. But, now I'm losing control. My nightmares and the memories feel too real. Sometimes I don't even know what is real or not, like just now. Because of me you're hurt and that's not OK."

"Where are you going with this, Sadie?" He sounded scared.

"You need to let me go, Fester. I'm meant to be alone. I'm not supposed to have friends. I've been selfish and greedy. I'm not allowed to...to love you."

Tears flowed down her face. She realized for the first time that it had been love which she felt for Fester. Now, for all of their protection, she had to leave. Fate, it seemed, was as cruel as her parents. Regardless of her attempts to keep it from doing so, the past continued to creep into her present. As she had once feared, the lines between reality and memory were fading. Michael was right, she had become dangerous. She loved Fester and didn't want to ever hurt him again. Nor did she want to hurt the others. The only course of action, the only way to protect them all, would be to leave.

"Sadie," Sal said as she moved to sit beside them on the floor. "I understand what you're saying and Mickey is right, you definitely are dangerous. But, I need to remind you that if you leave, then PSI will find you. Trackers are able to find other Supernaturals with great ease. I can't protect you if they capture you."

"That's OK," Sadie said with that hollow tone added to her already strained voice. "Let them come. I don't care anymore, Sal. I don't care and I'm not afraid. For the first time in my life, I'm not afraid." The realization had hit her hard and now she knew what she needed to do. "I'll distract them. The four of you can escape, and I'll fight them and keep them away."

"Sadie, have you lost your mind? If you fight them then they'll kill you!" Fester said. His voice cracked sharply.

"Fester, it's OK."

Sadie stood and used the air to see. The air currents that moved about her body felt comforting in a way they never had before. As the room became known to her she noticed that much of the furniture was overturned. Chloe was curled into a ball on another couch and Sadie's heart broke at the fear the girl must have been feeling. She turned towards her and smiled.

"I'm going to need you to take care of them, Chloe."

"Sadie," Michael said as he walked over and grabbed her arm, "Them words gotta be fucking mad assed crazy bullshit. I ain't gonna fucking care on the danger ya got in ya. I ain't even gonna care on what ya makin my sis feel. 'Cause I ain't never gonna let ya get ta fucking sacrificin ya ass an gettin dead. Ain't nobody gonna neither."

She turned her head in his direction and removed his hand from her arm. "I'm not going to sacrifice myself, Michael. I'm going to save my friends and I'm going to be OK. I can't run from my past and I won't run from PSI either. I have to do this."

"Sadie," Fester said, "I already told you...Shit, someone help me up!" Both Sadie and Michael helped him to stand. He grunted, obviously in pain. "Listen, I'm not going to let you die. I love you. I can't let you do this."

Sadie smiled. "I love you too, Fester, and I don't plan to die."

"I hate to interrupt this little love fest you have going on here," Sal said. "We need to go. Enough time has been wasted and we don't have much more of it if we're going to get you all to safety. The Tracker is already on our trail and we need to move out."

"Then go," Sadie said. "I'll be fine, I swear."

"No such luck, beautiful. You're coming with us whether you like it or not," Sal said.

Sadie laughed. "I don't understand any of you. It's as though what I say means nothing to you."

"Sadie, fucking get ya ass listenin ta them words, God dammit, an get ta listenin good," Michael said. "It ain't true we ain't listenin ta them bullshit words ya spoutin all 'round. It just...half the one-two what been spillin out ya trap gotta be fucking uber mad crazy bullshit! Now get ta shuttin ya trap the fuck up an tamein them words, an get ta doin what we tells ya!"

Sadie didn't know what to think. Michael's anger was terrifying but for some unknown reason she wasn't afraid. She accepted her future, yet these people were more than willing to be at risk so she wouldn't have to experience it. Deep within herself she knew that she wasn't worth the effort. She was meant to live and die alone. This fact was undeniably obvious. Better to die protecting the one she loved, than for him to perish beside her. Why none of them could comprehend this was beyond her level of understanding.

Sadie sighed and said, "Michael, please listen to reason..."

"No! Ya get ta fucking listenin ta fucking reason, Sadie! Ya gonna close ya trap shut, or I swearin to God right high, I gonna fucking shock ya ass! We gonna get easy draggin ya body all knocked out an shit. Them how we got ya here first. Ya bony ass ain't real hard ta sling on a shoulder, Sadie. I be hatin ta say it here, but Sal got them words true. We ain't got no fucking time for no fucking bullshit! Ya gonna get, an ya ain't gettin no mother fucking choice. Get it?"

"OK. I think you're insane but fine. I won't hold them off and when this Tracker person finds us, you'll wish you listened."

"Oh just shut the fuck up!"

"Enough!" Sal said. "I've never seen a sorrier group of people in my life! Considering what I do for a living, that's saying a hell of a lot. Right now I don't care what you people do! But if you want to live you'll come with me now. The van is ready and waiting and we need to get the four of you out of here."

"Where's my cane?" Sadie asked.

"I got it," Chloe said meekly.

The child had been so quiet throughout everything that Sadie had nearly forgotten her entirely. Suddenly, she felt lightheaded as she carefully walked towards Chloe. The sheer force that she used to blow the wind earlier had weakened her considerably. Using the air again so she could see was draining her at a constant rate as well. Soon she wouldn't be able to stand on her own. When she neared the girl, she saw her cringe. That Chloe was so fearful of her made Sadie's heart sink.

"What's wrong, Chloe?" Sadie was glad to hear her voice return to normal.

"I 'fraid ya, Sadie. Ya hurtin Fester an fightin with Michael. Ya ain't feelin true. Ya so scary."

Sadie released the air. Exhausted and sad, she knelt beside the girl. Chloe had been right. She wasn't behaving like herself. She's never forceful, and usually too afraid of Michael to argue like she had. As the realization of her actions and words struck, she suddenly became afraid. Trembling on the floor, tears filled her eyes and her chest felt tight.

"I'm sorry. I'm sorry to all of you. I don't know what came over me."

Fester's hand rested on her shoulder. She hadn't heard him move. "It's OK, Sadie. We're all stressed and 'fraid. Let's just get gone."

Chloe handed Sadie the cane and Fester handed her a coat. He helped her get up and began to lead her towards the door. There was a loud bang as the door was violently thrust open. Her heart nearly stopped when she heard several heavy footsteps move into the room. She couldn't tell how many entered or why. Did the Tracker find them already? Fearfully she gripped Fester's arm and froze as the door was slammed shut.

"You Boys had better have a damn good reason for this!" Sal said.

"Yeah, Boss!" A man with an unusually deep voice said. He sounded familiar. "We've got trouble. All main roads leading outta the area are blockaded. Looks like PSI's agents are keeping everyone put so the traitor can do his sweeps."

Sal swore and spat. "How many of our safe-houses are available to us?"

"Eyes reported that here is our only one. It's stocked, I saw to that yesterday. Problem is they locked this area down tight. Eyes said we're cut off. Even alternate routes are down. We're fucked, Boss."

Sal swore again. Chloe whimpered and Sadie knew it was from everyone's fear. She didn't know what was happening, but she did understand that they were trapped. If they couldn't leave, then they couldn't run. They were helpless and this traitor Tracker person would be able to find them with no problem.

"Actually, this could be a good thing," Sal said after a moment.

"The fuck it good, Sal?" Michael asked. He was understandably terrified.

Sal continued to think out loud as she paced. "A

poverty-stricken and thrown-together family trying to protect one another from wrongful persecution. Trapped with nowhere to go and an oppressive government sure to capture them..."

"What are you thinking, Boss?" A second man asked. He sounded both curious and excited.

"I'm thinking it's time to ignite the underground."

"Sal, the hell are you talking about?" Fester sounded as frightened as Michael and Sadie gripped his arm tighter.

"Boss," the first man said, "Do you think the others will agree? Kronos seemed to think--"

"Forget Kronos. You don't know the human psyche, Cliff. Think about what we have here. Jack and Maria Coldman: Heroes of the cause. How many have they helped? Now, their son is trying to protect his little sister, and he also has two traumatized street urchins he has taken under his wing. That's just the sort of thing his parents would do. Oh yes, they'll agree and they'll come. Sound the horn."

"Yes, ma'am!"

Cliff, the second man, and one other moved away from them and spoke in strong yet hushed tones. They were too far away for Sadie to hear what they said. She desperately wanted to know what was going on, and she wasn't the only one.

Michael swore. "Sal, the fuck! My 'rents? What shit ya droppin us selves in?"

Sal's footsteps moved slowly towards Michael. "When your parents worked for my father and I, they actually worked for an underground movement that has been secretly fighting for our rights as Supernaturals. We just paid the bill. They did a lot of good; helped a lot of people."

"What are you saying?" Fester asked.

"It's time that the movement wasn't a secret anymore," Sal said.

"Sal," Fester said, "I thought you were a criminal."

"Oh, I am. Doesn't mean I can't have a cause. Right?"

Michael let out a laugh. "Them shits too fucking

rich!"

"So, those schematics..." Fester asked.

"Are for something completely unrelated," Sal said.

Oh." Fester sounded disappointed.

Michael let out a series of swears before he asked, "The fuck we gonna do? I ain't lettin Chloe be part o' them shits! She a lil kid, Sal!"

"Mickey, grow the hell up. Have the fumes in the garage you work at damaged your Gutter brain? Think. She's already a part of this. We all are. I'm not going down without a fight, it's our only option. Unless, of course, you want her to wind up in PSI's hands. In that case I'll leave and you can just give her to them like a present. I'll even give you a cute bow to put on her forehead. I think I saw a gift shop nearby that would have a nice sparkly one she'll enjoy."

"Fuck off, Sal!"

Sal laughed. "That's what I thought."

While Michael's anger had increased considerably, Sal had sounded calm and collected throughout the entire conversation. It seemed as though she wasn't even afraid of what was happening. Sadie thought about all the times Michael had called Sal *bad news*. He said she was a bad person, and that she had once threatened to kill him and Chloe. Now Sadie wondered if what he told her had been an understatement.

It was obvious that whatever was going on, it wasn't going to have a good outcome. Fester and Chloe had to be protected. They didn't have an offensive power that could help them now. Sadie decided that she would defend them with her life if needed. Feeling like she had before, she accepted her future. She was even comfortable with the idea that she most likely would perish in the process. It would be worth it if the man she loved could live.

"You're starting a war," Fester said as Sal began to walk away.

"BINGO!" She called back and didn't miss a step.

"Bitch created a willing army of Supernaturals, and is making sure they'll all be loyal to her," he said with disbelief.

"Yeah, an why I gettin a feelin she gonna throw our lot under a bus?" Michael asked with his voice trembling slightly.

"Because she has heavy hopes that this'll also give her some political gain. You basically told us that she's some sort of prodigy. I don't doubt that she truly does have a plan for everything. A sad story can be used to sell votes and gain influence. Who knows what she'll do with us after she's done."

Michael swore. Chloe continued to cry and it sounded as though she was also trying to be quiet. This was not a good place for someone as sensitive as her. Sadie wanted to comfort the child but wasn't sure Michael would want her near his sister after the damage she had already caused. The hopelessness of their situation was as infuriating as it was frightening. All her fault...

Her chest hurt when she remembered how Chloe had cringed when she came near. It was understandable that she felt that way. Sadie was scared of herself as well. She had no idea what she was capable of, nor did she know exactly what they were up against. It seemed as though they were guaranteed not to make it. Her guilt rose up within her once again. This truly was all her fault. There was no hope of denying that now.

Sadie let go of Fester's arm and moved towards the couch. She heard him follow. *'He's going to be a problem,'* she mused. When PSI finally came for them, he would most likely try and protect her. She couldn't understand why he didn't accept her fate as easily as she had. Then again, he never made sense that way. If her wind could help him to live, then she was going to make sure that he survived no matter what. He and Chloe, they both needed to live through this. If they were hurt and she could have stopped it...she wouldn't be able to live with the added guilt. Her heart was simply too heavy with the feeling already.

Sitting down, she let out a nervous sigh. It would be a good idea to rest. Sadie needed all of her strength to get them through this and she was already tired. When Fester sat beside her, she leaned into him. He wrapped his arm around her and she closed her eyes. Even with the chaos that surrounded them, and the certainty of death that awaited them, she felt better in his arms. It was tempting to believe the illusion of safety they provided.

Sadie didn't deserve him, especially after what she had done and the danger she brought down upon them. Still, Sadie knew she was lucky and vowed to make herself worthy of Fester's love. Out of everyone there, he was the one who mattered the most.

Chapter 26

The four of them sat helplessly as Sal and her men moved about on the other side of the room. They were too far away for Sadie to overhear their plans. Terribly she wanted to walk over to them and demand answers. Those feelings of bravery from before seemed to come and go at random. Now, she didn't have the courage to confront Sal and her men, though that could change at any moment. The constant flux she had been experiencing was both frightening and confusing. Their situation wasn't the only thing that had gone terribly wrong. Sadie feared that she was losing her sanity as well.

She no longer trusted herself and wanted to get as far away from everyone as she could. Solitude would be far better than this. If she lost control again then someone she cared about could be seriously hurt. If it were anyone other than her friends then she wouldn't worry as much. She didn't care about Sal's safety or that of her men. However, there was no way she wanted to hurt Fester or Chloe. She didn't even want to hurt Michael, though she wasn't sure she could say the same about him.

Sadie snuggled against Fester. "I'm scared," she said.

"I get it," he said, "me too."

Michael's clothes rustled as he shifted himself closer to them. "Hey, Fester. Ya got a plan growin, man? We fucking needin one 'bout now."

"I've been watching Sal and her guys. I'm trying to picture out what sort of power, if any, they might have. Sal made it sound like she's Supernatural and I suspect the big guy – Cliff – is as well. I'm not sure about the other two. One thing is true, those guys are definitely ex-military or mercenaries or a thing same. Look at how they carry themselves. I think we have a chance if none of them have an offensive power, and you two can take them by surprise."

"Sal got power," Michael said. "She able ta get invisible an shit. Her pops was same. I ain't got no clue 'bout them militia men there. I only ever got ta seein her fucking family, ain't never seein the God damn people gettin works from 'em."

Sadie's fear built upon itself and threatened to smother her as she listened to the men. The knowledge the conversation gave her made it difficult to keep her emotions about their situation, and Sal, under control. Chloe needed her to stay calm, though. The girl wouldn't be able to handle an attack of fear right now. Michael was right, she shouldn't be caught up in this. She was too young. Anything to make it easier for her needed to be considered. Unfortunately, Sadie didn't know what that would be.

"Invisibility...I think they consider that to be an offensive power and it can be deceptively dangerous. If she were to disappear then we wouldn't be able to defend 'gainst her. She could also slip out of here unnoticed when PSI attacks." Fester said.

"I might be able to see her," Sadie whispered, fearful that Sal would know.

"Yeah? The fuck ya seein her ass?" Michael asked.

"The air: when I feel with the air I sense where it touches something and where it doesn't. It's almost like seeing. I don't think she can be invisible that way as well. So long as she's still in the room then I can feel her and what she's doing."

"Really? Ya got it goin in the one-two?"

"No, Michael. I used a lot of wind today. I'm saving my energy for when we need it."

"Smart moves."

"OK," Fester said, "So, what we need to do is to find what they're planning and who they've called in to help them."

"I able ta find out." Chloe's small voice sounded frightened yet she bravely offered.

"No, Chloe. I ain't lettin ya get no more involved."

"Michael, Sal sayin I involved 'fore. Them ain't gonna be seein me ifs I hidin good an listenin quiets."

"It heavy mother fucking riskful. No."

"Then I'll do it," Sadie said. "I don't have to get as close to hear them. My ears are pretty good compared to most people."

"Wait," Fester said, "just how good is your hearing?"

"I can hear them talking now, but I can't make out the words."

"Sadie, them shits be holed up on 'nother side the fucking room, an it ain't no lil room neither." Michael sounded surprised.

"I know," she said.

Everyone was silent for a few minutes. Sadie carefully considered how she might be able to get closer. Based on where they sounded like they were, there wasn't much furniture to use as cover. It was difficult to determine how much closer she would have to get since she wasn't skilled at measuring distance. Then again, there might be another way to protect her friends. After all, she was willing to do anything to keep them safe, especially Fester and Chloe.

"I have an idea," she said as her fear began to retreat once more. When she stood, Fester and Michael stood as well. "No, I need to talk to Sal, but you two can't come."

"Sadie, what are you planning?" Fester asked.

"Don't worry, Fester. I'm just going to talk to her. There can't be any harm in that. Right?"

"I ain't likin it, girl," Michael said. "Ya got them fucked-up an crazy looks on ya face same 'fore."

Sadie smiled. "That's only because I'm not afraid right now. It's a good plan. I'll be right back."

She began to walk towards where she heard Sal talking when Fester grabbed her arm. "Sadie, I want to know what you be picturing 'fore you go over there."

"Do you trust me?" she asked.

"Yeah," he said slowly.

"Then don't worry."

Sadie gently removed Fester's hand from her arm and once again headed in Sal's direction. Her cane constantly showed her where furniture or debris from her wind blocked her path. If she had been thinking about it earlier, she would've mapped the room in her head when she was using the air to see. The hindsight didn't help and she put it out of her mind. She needed to focus on the now. The closer she was to Sal, the more nervous she became. Her bravery wasn't lasting as long this time.

"Hey, Boss, the blind one's coming over here," the one called 'Cliff' said.

"Sadie," Sal said as she walked towards her, "go sit with the others."

Sadie took a deep breath to steady her wildly beating heart. "I want to talk to you, Sal. It'll only take a minute."

"Alright. Talk."

Sadie hesitated. "Can we talk alone?"

Sal let out a frustrated sigh. "We don't have time for games."

"I know."

Sal agreed, though she sounded reluctant. She led Sadie to a nearby room and Cliff followed. When Sadie again requested that they talk alone, Sal insisted that Cliff stay. It almost seemed as though they were afraid of Sadie. It was understandable after what she had done earlier. However, there was no intent to harm Sal or anyone else at this point. She only wanted to talk.

They entered the room and the door was closed behind them. Sadie licked her lips. "I want to know what you plan to do with us."

"I actually don't have a plan for any of you yet. It all depends on how today goes."

"I don't believe you, Sal. I...I want to make a deal. I want to give you something for my friend's to be let free."

"Oh, really?" Sal giggled as though amused. It wasn't a friendly sound. "And what could you possibly offer me?"

"I don't have anything other than myself to give you. So, that's my offer. I'll be yours and you can do whatever you wish with me. Just let them go free."

Sal was silent at first, and Sadie hoped she was seriously considering her offer. It had taken every ounce of bravery she had left just to say those words. If

Sal refused now, then she didn't know what she would do. She didn't want her to accept either, but her friends' safety was more important than her freedom.

Finally Sal said, "Cliff, leave us for a moment."

"Permission to speak freely?"

"Denied. Go. Take her cane with you."

After he took the cane and left, Sadie heard Sal lock the door. Forcing her body not to tremble, she readied herself for whatever was coming. Memories of her father threatened to come to the surface. She swallowed hard and forced them back. It wouldn't be a good idea to allow her past to creep forward at this point. Losing control now would be far too dangerous.

Sal's footsteps slowly came towards her. "What exactly is it you're offering, Sadie?" she asked. "I want to make sure we understand each other."

"I already told you: I'll be yours. You can do whatever you wish with me and I'll always obey."

"Really? And for how long do you plan on allowing me to have you?"

Sadie swallowed hard once more. "Until you're tired of me and don't want me anymore."

Sal's fingertips stroked Sadie's cheek and she tried her best not to flinch. She didn't want to make Sal upset with her. Flinching used to anger her father and Sadie suspected that Sal would be exactly like him. After all, she was a bad person who liked pleasure. Ready for what was to come, she only flinched slightly when Sal grabbed a fistful of hair from the back of her head.

Slowly Sal bent her head back, exposing her neck. Sadie closed her eyes and held her breath as the woman began to kiss her along the neck. Her kisses were gentle but that didn't fool Sadie. She knew that such kindness would come with a price, like it had in the past. Forcing herself not to tremble, she accepted that she was no longer free. She no longer owned herself. Once more the lessons would rule her life.

With her hand still in Sadie's hair, Sal led her across the room. She didn't pull or yank, instead it was as though she simply guided. When they stopped, Sal removed her hand and said, "There's a bed in front of you. Sit on it."

Obediently Sadie sat on the bed. Sal placed both of her hands on either side of her face and made her tilt her head up. When she let go, Sadie kept her head in the same position. She knew this game. Once more she had to force herself not to flinch when she felt Sal's lips upon hers. Reluctantly she returned the kiss, precisely as she had been taught. She knew that the more obedient she was, then the better off she would be. Despite her efforts to hold back her tears, one escaped and rolled slowly from the corner of her eye to wet her ear.

When Sal stopped kissing her, Sadie kept her head in the same position. "You truly would do whatever I told you, wouldn't you?" Sal asked and Sadie nodded. "Lie down, Sadie."

As obedient as ever, she did as she was told. Sal crawled on the bed and straddled her. Sadie's head was pulled to one side and Sal licked her neck and continued up the side of her face. It was obvious where this was going and she closed her eyes. Sal reached her hand up inside Sadie's shirt and there was no protest. She hadn't lied; she truly gave herself over to the woman. When Sal's cold fingers cupped her breast another tear fell.

"Amazing," Sal said softly. "You obviously don't want me to touch you. You don't truly want me to own you. Yet, you're completely complacent. Who taught you how to be like this? I can see you've had training."

"My father," Sadie whispered, refusing to trust that her voice would be steady if she spoke any louder.

Sal's swearing was nearly inaudible. Slowly she removed her hand from Sadie's breast and crawled off of her. "Sadie," she said gently, "I won't enjoy anything we do unless you enjoy it as well. I don't force women to have sex with me and I sure as hell won't start with you. Your offer is declined."

Sadie felt her eyes sting as they filled with more tears. "Please, Sal. I can learn to like it. Please, I just don't want them hurt. I'll do whatever you want, be however you want, and for as long as you desire, if you'll just let them live."

In an attempt to prove her words, Sadie sat up and reached for Sal. Carefully she moved her hair and began to kiss the side of her neck. Seductively she ran a hand down the front of Sal's body, caressing her breasts and stroking her stomach. Yes, her father had taught her well and she would prove it. She leaned in and whispered in Sal's ear, telling her how she would be a good girl and what she could do to make sure Sal was always pleased. Abruptly the criminal stood up and moved away. Sadie nearly fell off the bed from the sudden motion.

"Your father was a sick man," Sal said. "I don't know what you think of me, but I'm not like that. There isn't much I won't do, Sadie. My line of work demands that I do a lot of horrible things. To be honest, I even enjoy some of them. But this...I won't do this. I know it's not what you want. I'm not going to rape some girl for the fantasy she offers, even one as tempting as you."

Sadie sat in stunned silence. Tears spilled uninhibited down her cheeks and onto the mattress. Her intention was to save her friends, to save the man she loved, and she failed. She realized she should have pretended harder. If Sal thought it was what she wanted, then she would've accepted her offer. The others would be safe and secure as a result. She failed them because she didn't know how to hide her emotions. Now they were all going to die.

"I don't know what sort of monster you think I am, Sadie," Sal said, "I know you all think the worst of me. I'm not really that bad, you know."

"You're starting a war."

"Well...yes, but that's because I think it's time for one. This is something I believe in, Sadie. Sure, I'll also make money. Conflict, even one such as this, tends to be very profitable. But that's not my only reason. I told you all before: I may be a criminal, but that doesn't mean I can't have a cause."

"What do you plan for me and my friends then?"

"At the moment, I don't have any plans for you. I told Fester I would help you all run or fight, whichever was needed. That's exactly what I'm doing. It just so happens that it's also going to help me get what I want. Why? What did you think was going to happen?"

Sadie shrugged. "Michael and Fester think you're going to kill us for your war."

Sal laughed. "Oh please, Sadie! I don't want any of you dead. I promised Mickey's parents that I would protect him and his sister from PSI, if needed. I have a plan for Fester that doesn't include hurting him. His brain is highly valuable to me, actually. As for you... well, I like you. I would like for us to be lovers, but I can see now that will never happen. I still don't want to see you harmed."

"If...if you're not planning to hurt us, then what are you planning to do?"

"It's simple. We Supernaturals aren't as rare as the government wants everyone to believe. My father spent a great deal of his life organizing the network. His businesses, both criminal and legitimate, helped to fund the whole thing. After he was assassinated, I picked up where he left off. This war was planned before we were born, Sadie. It's the only way we can all be free. All I'm doing is ensuring that my father's life work comes to fruition. Don't worry your pretty head about the details."

Sadie was stunned once more. Would Sal have accepted her offer if she thought she was willing, even though she had never planned to hurt them? While Sal had said that she wouldn't force her to do things in the bed against her will, she had still considered the offer. Regardless of what Sal said, she was a bad person.

It was a great relief that she refused. To live like that again would've killed Sadie on the inside. She had been willing to break her vow to save Fester. Her heart wanted to sing that she could still be with him and not be forced to pleasure this criminal. This was not the time to rejoice, however. Their lives were still in mortal danger.

"Come, Sadie. There's work I have to do before the Tracker finds us. A lot of things need to be put in place if we're to survive this. Go back out and sit with your boyfriend. We'll take care of everything else. OK?"

Slowly Sadie nodded her head. She knew that one day she would have to repay the kindness Sal just showed her. "I owe you a great deal for this," she said with her heart gripped in fear.

"We can talk about that later. For now, I want you to go and join your friends."

Sal gently grasped Sadie's elbow and led her out of the room. By the time Cliff handed her the cane, she was trembling uncontrollably. The encounter in the bedroom could have easily gone in a terrifying direction. Instead, she was given back her freedom and assured that her friends still had theirs. Feeling grateful, she carefully made her way across the room. It was a little difficult walking back to the couch and she tripped at one point over a broken lamp. When she was about halfway, she heard Fester move swiftly towards her. Gently he took her elbow and helped her to avoid further obstacles. The feel of his large hand was more than welcome and she didn't flinch despite the emotions swirling within her.

"What went down in there? She didn't hurt you did she? I'll kill her if she..."

Sadie gave him a weak smile. "Don't worry, Fester. Sal's not going to hurt us. She's actually trying to help."

"How ya picturin them shits be true?" Michael asked as they came closer.

"I think that she's made too many promises and won't go against her word. She told Fester she would help us, and I think that's exactly what she's going to do."

"She's trying to start a war," Fester said.

"I know. I also know that she doesn't want any of us hurt."

Sadie continued to tremble despite the confidence in her words. While she believed that Sal didn't mean them any harm, she wasn't so sure about her men. Likewise, she knew the government wouldn't let them go without a deadly fight. If whatever help Sal was trying to get didn't arrive in time, then they could find themselves in an impossible situation. She didn't want to find out what the government would do to any of them if they were captured. From the way Sal and her men made it sound, they were definitely going to be found soon.

Sadie leaned into Fester and wrapped her arms around him. No matter what happened, she would get him through this. He was always trying to help her and now it was her turn. She had only just realized what it was that she felt for him. There was no way she could let him die now. While she didn't want to die either, oddly enough she didn't care about her own safety. She was, as Michael said, too dangerous. Regardless of what happened that day, she knew her future.

Her life would have to eventually end so no one else would be hurt by her lack of control. Better it be to save the others than for no reason at all.

Chapter 27

Fester held Sadie tighter as time wore on. He didn't seem to hide his fear anymore. Unfortunately, although she worried for him, there wasn't anything she could do to comfort him at the moment. She also worried about Chloe. The child had to be feeling their fear yet she hardly made a sound. Sadie couldn't imagine how difficult all of this had become for the young Empath. If only she knew how to ease the minds and hearts of her friends!

When her stomach growled, she realized that none of them had eaten anything since breakfast. She was used to going without food for long periods of time, so her hunger wasn't a bother. The others were used to eating regularly, however. It must be difficult for them to be so hungry and not have anything to eat. Perhaps if she made them something...

"Fester? Didn't that man say that this place was fully stocked? Did he mean food?" she asked.

"I hope so," Fester said. "I'm starving."

"Should one of us go and ask?"

"No," Michael said, "We ain't gonna get ta fucking pissin the bitch off. We sitin an waitin. Them shits ain't been eatin nothin neither."

"I'm tempted to go over there just to find out what the hell they're doing," Fester said.

"No, Fester. It worser me lettin Sadie go o'er. Ya done seein Chloe freaked till Sadie commin outta them rooms, an Sadie face done lookin same. I ain't lettin nobody fucking share words with them shits 'less we ain't gettin a mother fucking choice. Stick ya ass in ya seat. Same goin for all three ya."

Sadie rested her head on Fester's chest and closed her eyes. Even though she was afraid, she had an eerie calm about her. Soon, there wouldn't be a need to worry about anything. When it was time for her to do what was needed, her fear would melt away as it had earlier. She knew that with her fear suppressed, even if only for a little while, then she would be able to whatever was needed.

"Michael?" Chloe asked, "What wrong with Sadie?"

"Nothin," he said, "she fine."

"No she ain't. She ain't feelin true. This mornin she ain't true neither."

"Chloe, ya got ya head fucking picturein a bullshit thing. We four gettin freaked the fuck out same, is all."

Despite Michael's words, Sadie was worried. Knowing her own fear that she was going insane, she wondered if that was what Chloe sensed. All that was needed was for her to hold onto her sanity for a little while longer. She needed enough time to make sure Fester was safe. After that…she wasn't sure. It was a difficult decision to be made. Death, insanity, or perfect solitude? None of those options were appealing at the moment, and death seemed most likely. If only…

"Hey," Fester whispered, "you OK?"

"Yeah," she said.

"I need to know, Sadie. What words did you and Sal share in there?"

"I wanted to make sure she wasn't going to hurt any of you."

"How were you going to do that?"

Sal's footsteps were fast approaching and Sadie stiffened. "It looks like PSI won't reach our area until tomorrow," she said when she was near. "Turns out you aren't the only ones they're looking for this time. The entire county is in lock-down."

"The fuck them shits sayin 'bout us?" Michael asked.

"Unfortunately, our reinforcements are having trouble reaching us. Are you prepared to shed a little lightning tomorrow?"

"Only if I ain't gettin no choice, Sal. I ain't likin fucking killin nobody dead."

"A little late for that isn't it? What about you sex-pot? How precise can you be with your wind?"

"I…I don't know," Sadie said. She was confused with how Sal had addressed her.

"Listen up folks, you're all going to have to fight.

Even little Chloe here will have to hold her own. For both she and Fester we have weapons. But we need anyone with an offensive power to use it as fully as possible. And yes, Mickey sweetie, you're probably going to have to kill some people. Get over it."

"God fucking dammit, Sal!"

"Hey, listen up and listen well. Your actions brought us here. You and Sadie here killed three men using your power. If you didn't want this to happen, then you shouldn't have done it in the open like that. As I told Fester, if you're going to kill someone, do it cleanly and quietly. You don't get caught. What you did was a child's mistake!"

"He gone pullin a mother fucking piece on us three, Sal! What ya gonna get me doin? Huh? Ya gonna get me fucking lettin the prick killin Sadie an Fester?"

"No, you should have made sure that if any of them died, they did so without any implications that would lead back to you. I'm not angry that you killed them, Mickey. I'm angry that you were found out."

"Hey, Sal. Lay off him and let me ask you a thing." Fester said.

Sal sighed. "What is it, Fester?"

"What went down in that other room?"

The criminal let out a short laugh. "Ah, so your girlfriend didn't tell you? Let's just say that she's a keeper, Fester. Such loyalty as hers is rare. I'm serious. I wouldn't let her go if I were you." There was a scraping noise as she turned on her heel and began to walk away.

"Hey, Sal, the fuck do you mean?" When she didn't respond, Fester asked, "Sadie, what did Sal mean?"

"It's nothing. Don't worry about it."

"Sadie," Michael said slowly, "what ya gone an done?"

"We talked. That's all. I wanted to make sure she wouldn't hurt any of you."

"And what did you talk about?" Fester asked.

"Don't worry about it. It doesn't matter."

Sadie didn't want Fester to know what she had almost done. If he knew that she almost gave herself to

Sal, then he might become furious with her. He might even decide he wanted nothing to do with her. The criminal almost owned her and may never have allowed Fester to see her again. Perhaps later they could talk about it, but first he needed to be safe. If her actions disgusted him as much as they did herself, then she didn't want to know it yet.

"Sadie, talk to me."

"Fester," she said as she leaned away from him and put her hands in her lap, "I wanted to make sure she wouldn't hurt you. I wanted to make sure that you'll be able to leave here and be free. That's all. I really don't want to talk about it anymore."

"Sadie," Michael asked, "ya holdin a fucking deal with Sal?"

"No."

"Say them fucking words true!"

"Michael, I...I don't want to talk about it."

"If nothing happened and you didn't hold a deal, then why won't you tell us about it? The look on your face says it's a thing," Fester said as he placed his hand over Sadie's.

Sadie felt trapped. The men were only trying to keep her safe, though what they were trying to protect her from eluded her. She reasoned that they most likely wanted to keep her from Sal. If Sal had accepted her offer then there would've been nothing they could do. So why try to protect her now? What happened in the bedroom was now part of the past. Nothing more needed to be said. Not knowing what else to say, she ignored the question.

"Where's the kitchen?" she asked instead.

"What? The fuck the kitchen gotta do with a thing in the one-two?" Michael sounded angry and Sadie didn't care.

"I'm hungry and want to find something to eat."

Michael swore. "Fuck me, now ya wanna get fucking eatin?"

"Yes, now I wanna get fucking eatin," she said as she stood up and began to see with the air.

As Sadie felt around the room she noticed that the

kitchen wasn't far away. Without the aid of her cane, she walked purposefully towards the small room. She could tell that the men were watching her, their heads turned purposefully in her direction. Sal and her men paid no notice at all while they huddled around a table at the far side of the room. Sadie was happy for that. The last thing she wanted was for the criminal to take an interest in her now. Michael shook his head and Fester stood but made no move towards her.

As she entered the kitchen, all thoughts of the men and their reactions quickly melted away. An overly pungent smell emanated from one of the cabinets and clogged her lungs. Immediately she backed away and coughed. She released her control over the air to save energy.

Fester was instantly at her side. "What's wrong?" he asked.

"Something's not right. There's a weird smell in there. I can't breathe!" Sadie said as she continued to back away.

"I don't smell nothing," he said.

"Trust me, Fester. Something's wrong in that kitchen. I feel like I'm choking on it. I need to get some fresh air!"

Fester brought her over towards a window and called for Sal. The further she was from the kitchen the better she felt. The blast of freezing air on her face was a relief and she inhaled deeply. Her lungs hurt from the deep breath and she coughed again. Sal's footsteps were heard as her boots clicked along the hard floor. Sadie wished Fester had gone to her instead of bringing her over to them.

"You shouldn't open the window, Fester. We don't know if anyone's watching the house."

"There's a thing wrong. Sadie smelled a thing in the kitchen. She said she couldn't breathe and needed air." Fester sounded as though he was about to panic.

"What did you smell, Sadie?" Sal asked as she came to stand beside Sadie and Fester.

"I don't know what it was. It was strong and a little sweet, but not in a pleasant way. It seemed like it was coming from one of the cabinets near the stove."

Sal's footsteps moved swiftly towards the kitchen. Not long after she was coughing as well. "Cliff! We have gas!"

Sal's men instantly jumped into action as they moved towards the kitchen. Sadie heard them talk about measuring the air quality. There were a few loud beeps, though from what she couldn't fathom, before two of the men swore heavily.

"Boss, we gotta get out of here. Looks like they're using that chloro we heard about." Sadie didn't recognize the man's voice.

"If they're gassing us then they know we're here. Forget about fighting tomorrow Boys, looks like it's going to be now. Jeff, get a weapon for the kid and this one over here. Make sure everyone has enough ammo. Jordan, open the windows and get us some fresh air. I owe you one, Sadie. Looks like you caught this before it could hit the rest of us. If that chloro were to fill this room, we would all be helpless within an hour."

With that she walked off, barking orders to her men and demanding that someone hand her a phone. Fester's hand squeezed Sadie's shoulder reassuringly. The gesture gave her anything but comfort, unfortunately. If ever there was a time for her fear to melt away, now would be preferable. Instead she felt it rise stronger than ever, heating her body from navel to neck.

Sadie tried not to tremble as everyone exploded into motion. Fester grabbed her arm and brought her over towards the door. He quickly handed over her coat and told her to put it on. Sal had suggested they find a way out of the house to escape the gas that was being pumped into the space. Chloe cried softly from somewhere nearby. Michael tried to soothe her and told her to stay close to him. With all of the chaos around her, Sadie felt disoriented.

Immediately she reminded herself that she needed to protect her friends. This situation was entirely her fault and she would do anything to make it right. Logically she knew that she would never be able to protect them all. Perhaps if Michael took care of Chloe, then Sadie could do the same with Fester. At least Michael had an offensive power as well as bravery. Together they might actually survive this.

"Eyes!" Sal said as her footsteps belied her pacing, "I told you to call me if there was any PSI movement! ... Then get on that damn satellite and tell me what's around. Someone's pumping chloro into the house and we need to evacuate now! ... Shit!" When Sal swore Sadie flinched. This wasn't good. "We're making our stand here then. How far away are the others? ... Good."

There was a sharp click before Sal started calling for more weapons. For a while Sadie wasn't sure what was happening. There were too many sounds and Fester had gone with Michael to help. She and Chloe stood out of the way and held onto each other. Both girls trembled as they hugged one another, and Sadie desperately wished she knew how to comfort the child. When Sal came over, Sadie found herself more than a little nervous. The men hadn't returned and she didn't want to be alone with the criminal. Her hands shook and when Sal handed Sadie a knife she almost dropped it.

"Careful with that, sweetheart," Sal said. "It's one of my sharpest blades. I can't give a blind girl a gun but at least you can use this if they get too close. With your power that shouldn't be a problem, but it's always best to be prepared for anything."

"Thank you," Sadie said softly.

Fester was soon at her side and Sal walked away. "Girls, stick to me and Michael. We'll protect you. OK?"

"No, Fester. I'm going to protect you. You don't have an offensive power."

"I don't have that but I do have a cool gun. Let's not argue. We can protect each other."

"OK."

"Keep in mind, Sadie. I love you. I won't let them take you gone."

"I know. I love you too. I just wish I'd known it before today."

Fester wrapped an arm around her and pulled her close. Even though the knife had a sheath, she was still careful not to hit him with it. Everything seemed so out of control and she tried to understand the commotion. It was impossible to identify most of the sounds which swirled around her. Feeling the need for added security, Sadie went to wrap her arms around Fester and felt the large weapon hanging off of his other shoulder. Never having touched a weapon before, she gently ran her hand over it. There were too many bumps and grooves for her to tell much.

"Sadie," Fester said softly, "don't touch the piece. I really don't want it to go off in the one-two."

Immediately she pulled her hand away. Michael explained to Chloe how to use the gun she had been given. He didn't sound like he was alright with her having one. More than once he told her to only use it if she had no choice. Sadie hoped the child wouldn't have to kill anyone. While she didn't want to kill anyone either, she felt that Chloe would have a more difficult time with it than the rest of them. The girl was calm at the moment, but this whole situation had to be more than she could bear. Sadie felt sure that she was going to have to protect her as well as Fester. Taking a deep breath she told herself that she could do this. It was her mess and she was going to make sure her friends wouldn't be hurt by it.

The pressure was on and suddenly Sadie felt amazingly calm. Every thought and sound rang true in perfect clarity. She was ready to make her stand.

Chapter 28

Everyone waited patiently for Sal to tell them what to do. Not being prepared or trained for this sort of situation, Sadie was more than willing to obey any orders that were given to her. Although she felt perfectly calm, she was also annoyed at how nervous Fester and Michael seemed. Even with the protection Sal gave them to wear, the men acted as though they were terrified. Why the men, who have had plenty of time developing the skill to master their emotions, couldn't get a handle on their fear now, was baffling.

"Alright, listen up. PSI is aware we are here and they know that we are prepared. Eyes reports two teams surrounding the property. Our back-up is 10 minutes away but they're taking longer due to the blockades. They're going to have to barrel through them and we don't have that long to wait."

"What do you need us to do?" Fester asked.

"Stay close. We have our van out front but there's practically no cover on the way to it. I want you four to get yourselves inside as quickly as possible. Sadie and Mickey, if you see us fighting, I want you to use your power as much as you can. It'll make things easier if you do."

Sadie held tightly onto her knife and folded cane. Both would be used against anyone who got too close. She anxiously hoped that they would leave soon. The smell of the chloro had finally reached them, even though they were far from the kitchen and all of the windows were open. There was no way that she wanted to find out how the gas would render them helpless.

"Sal, I can smell that stuff again," she said.

"I love that nose of yours. Unfortunately that means we're out of time. Let's move people."

Quickly they all moved in unison towards the door. Sadie used the air so she could see what was happening around them. Once outside she would have to reach out as far out as she could. Her only hope was that she didn't pass out from the effort before they were all safe. She wasn't entirely sure how much longer she could continue utilizing the air and wind before it became too much.

Sal and her men stood in front. All but the largest of them had huge weapons. Fester's was just as big and Chloe's was much smaller. Michael didn't have one which made sense if he were to use his lightning instead. He and Fester stood with Chloe and Sadie between them. Fester brought up the rear. In a sudden burst they all ran out the door.

Before she was outside, the sound of gunfire blasted in her ears. She had never imagined the weapon would be so loud. It was disorienting, but the adrenaline coursing through her veins kept her steady. Once outside she was able to see everything that was happening. Sal and her men shot their weapons at a group that had started to advance on the left side of the house. There was nothing between them and the waiting van to hide behind, just as Sal had warned. The large man, whom Sadie assumed was Cliff, sent out strong waves of heat in the direction of the PSI Team and caused many of them to scream in terror and pain. The smell of burned flesh filled her nose and turned her stomach.

Sensing others coming from the right, Sadie blew a gust of wind that swept them into the neighbor's house. Immediately she did the same with the attackers that Sal had been fighting. Bursts of electricity shot from Michael and hit a few of the PSI Team who managed not to be affected by the wind. Neither Fester nor Chloe used their guns.

As they neared the van, Fester let out a painful yell. Sadie's heart stopped when she saw him collapse behind her. Immediately she helped him to his feet. He leaned on her the rest of the way, with his right arm hanging limply at his side. Fear gripped her heart with the knowledge that he had been injured. He was still able to walk, and that helped to ease her worry.

A few vehicles blocked their escape on the road.

Sadie paused before getting into the van and focused all of her wind on the blockade. Sal and her men surrounded her as she tried to blow the vehicles away. There was a loud roar as the wind increased with incredible speed and force. Sadie had to hold onto the van to keep herself from being knocked over. Cliff, Sal, and another man all leaned into the van to protect themselves as well. Many of the men fighting them were thrust into the air and slammed into the blockade in the road. Their limp bodies told her that they died from the impact. She didn't have time to dwell on that fact. Focusing her wind as much as she could, she narrowed the gale force winds and pushed with everything she had. Unfortunately the wind wasn't strong enough to move the larger of the vehicles more than a few feet.

Sal yelled at her, though she couldn't hear her words. Ignoring the woman, she continued to push against the vehicles blocking the road. Her concentration broke suddenly when she was thrust into the van from behind. Immediately the wind died down and Sadie felt her energy do the same. Michael pulled her fully in and the door was shut behind her. Exhaustion warned her to stop using the air and conserve what was left of her energy. The air in the van went still and she became blind once more.

Sal climbed over Sadie and someone moved to the front of the van. Loud bangs and pings on the sides of the van caused Sadie to wonder if the weapons had continued to rain bullets down on them. They didn't seem to cause any harm, but she didn't have a way to know for sure. Controlling the air outside of the van wasn't possible since she would have to be partially outside to connect with it.

"Anyone hit?" Sal asked frantically.

"Them fucking shits got my shoulder." The pain Fester felt was evident in his voice.

"Grazed my leg but I'll be fine," Cliff said as he also moved towards the front.

"Cliff, use fire on those cars and Jeff I want you to ram them. We didn't outfit this thing for nothing. Fester, hold this against your arm."

Both of Sal's men let out an enthusiastic "Yes Ma'am!" before doing as they were told.

Shaking from the effort of calling so much wind, Sadie sat helplessly on the floor. Her head hurt and she heard the whooshing sound of her pulse echo in her ears. Dizziness washed over her, causing a fight for consciousness. Passing out now wouldn't be wise.

Cold air cascaded through the van as a front window opened wide. Soon a blast of intense heat followed. There were sounds of explosions and people screaming in pain as Cliff shot heat out through the open window. The engine started and the van jerked as they began their getaway. Unsure of what to do, Sadie sat on the floor and tried to hold on. There was a loud bang and glass shattered from somewhere outside, causing the van to jerk violently some more. She was thrown about roughly and desperately tried not to panic.

"Dammit, Sadie! Get ya ass in a seat!" Michael yelled over the commotion.

"I don't know where they are!"

Someone lifted her from under her shoulders and thrust her into an empty seat. She let out a grunt as her left hip hit the cushion first. At some point she must have bruised her side. Instinctively, she reached down to touch the injury and found that her pants were wet. Dizziness washed over her and once more she felt like she was going to pass out.

"Can anyone tell me what this is?" she asked, indicating her side.

"It's too dark, Sadie. We can't see anything right now," Sal said.

"I think I'm bleeding!"

Sal swore and nearly fell on top of Sadie when the van swerved. "Fuck, you really are bleeding! Let me get a closer look." Sadie moved so that Sal could see her hip better. She flinched from the pain when Sal pressed her fingers against the wound. "It looks like the bullet only grazed you but you're bleeding pretty bad. Here, press this against it and try to stay still."

A wad of cloth was pushed into Sadie's hand and she did as Sal instructed. She felt her body vibrate as more explosions shook the van. With one hand pressed against her hip, she desperately tried to hold onto her seat with her other one. She had no idea what had happened to her cane and knife and wasn't sure why that mattered now. Slowly that familiar feeling of fear overcame her and she began to tremble. Her mind was in turmoil and it was difficult to think clearly. The sounds and vibrations were highly disorienting as well.

"Hey Boss, looks like the cavalry was able to make it after all!" called Jeff from the driver's seat.

"Good. Jordan, get on the phone and let them know what's happened. Once we all regroup then we'll turn this fiasco into something we can actually win."

By that point, Sadie stopped listening. She was too busy fighting her own battle to stay conscious. Gradually she began to sway in her seat. It took a great deal of effort to keep from falling onto the floor again. She jumped when she felt a large hand on her shoulder. At first she didn't register the hand as Fester's.

"You OK?" he asked her.

"I'm fine," she lied.

There was no need to worry the others. They had enough to deal with as it was. So long as she could stay awake then she knew she would be alright. It was just a small matter of not passing out. Sadie couldn't tell if she was still bleeding and her arm ached from pushing the cloth against her wound. Her entire hip felt like it was on fire and bursts of pain shot down her leg and up her side. Tears rolled down her cheeks from the intensity of it all. When the van took a sharp turn her hip banged into whomever sat beside her. It took all of her effort not to scream in pain. The best she could do was to keep it to a whimper.

Fester wrapped his good arm around her shoulders and she leaned into him, happy that he sat next to her on the other side. Even through the commotion and danger, she felt safe and secure in his arms. It wasn't enough to completely calm her increasing fear, but it did help to ease much of it. Slowly she noticed that her body had grown cold despite the heat emanating from Cliff's attacks. Shivering she tried to snuggle closer into

Fester.

"Hey, you sure you're OK?" She hardly understood what he asked and couldn't figure out how to respond. Her mind had become muddled and she lost her ability to focus. "Hey, Sal. A thing's wrong. Let me see that light ya got."

Sadie wanted to protest when Fester moved. He was comfortable and made her feel good. Thankfully, the motion didn't bring her more pain. Her side had started to become rather numb. She didn't even flinch when Fester's fingers poked at the wound. Thanks to the lack of pain, she almost didn't register that he had touched it at all.

"Fuck, Sal! She's lost too much blood! The bullet did more than graze her! Sadie! Sadie, can you hear me? Open your eyes. Please, just open your eyes."

Sadie hadn't realized that she closed them. His voice sounded as though he were far away. She frowned in confusion. If he was far away, then how was he touching her? He asked her to do something, didn't he? Oh, right, she needed to open her eyes. It took some effort to open them for him. She didn't like the sound of panic in his far off voice.

"Good, now I need you to keep awake. Can you do that for me?" Sadie shook her head. She didn't think she could stay awake for much longer. "C'mon, Sadie. I need you to stay awake! You have to keep your eyes open! Open them, damnit!"

Sadie sat up and forced her eyes as open as they would go. Unsure as to why Fester was so scared, all she could think about was keeping that tone from his voice. Until he was safe, then she would obey and do what needed to be done. If that meant forcing her eyes open, then there was no reason why she should resist. Perhaps later they could take a nap on the couch.

"That's it, Sadie. Just keep them open. You'll be OK if you just keep them open and don't fall asleep. Please, just stay with me!"

Fester pressed the cloth harshly against Sadie's hip which brought a small cry from her lips. Across from her Chloe cried softly. Immediately she knew that she needed to control her fear so the child wouldn't suffer. She also needed to do as Fester instructed and stay awake as much as possible. If she fell asleep now, then her nightmares would surely hurt Chloe and she couldn't let that happen. The child had been through too much as it was.

"I'm sorry, Chloe. I'll try not to dream," Sadie said softly.

"Fuck me, she goin inta shock!" Sadie wondered why Fester sounded so upset. Did she do something wrong again?

"Hey, Boss! They're closing in on us. The rendezvous is about three more miles but I don't know if we'll make it."

"Then drive faster," Sal said, "Mickey, think you can shoot your lightning at the vehicles following us? We need some room to breathe!"

"If we gettin dead tonight ya gotta know...I been hatin when ya callin me 'Mickey' since we was kids, *Sally*!"

Although Sal laughed in response, it wasn't a happy sound. Sadie shivered as she was blasted with cold wind from the back of the van. Crackling sounds filled the air as Michael began to shoot at whatever was behind them. The strange aroma of ozone filled her nose and made her sneeze. Soon after, there was a loud burst of sound as metal impacted with metal and glass shattered. Fester let out a cheer for Michael and she wondered what had gone right.

It wasn't long before the van came skidding to a stop. Sadie fell out of her seat and Fester let out a yell when he used his injured arm to catch her. The van doors were pushed open and she heard yelling and gunfire. Explosions caused her body to vibrate though the sounds they caused were muffled, and she couldn't hear Fester's voice well either. Without the strength to stand, she sat on the floor of the van. She wanted to stay awake. Fester told her she needed to and she wanted to make him happy. Furious about her mind and body not obeying, she felt her heavy eyelids close. The man she loved was in danger, she needed to wake up. She needed to save him...

As her mind slipped into unconsciousness, Sadie's only thought was of Fester's safety. She couldn't go yet, he still needed her.

Chapter 29

Sadie awoke from a dreamless sleep with only a vague memory of recent events. Lying still upon the bed, she tried to clear her groggy mind. It was important to figure out where she was and what had happened to the others. At the moment there was no way to tell. Other than a faint beeping sound to her left, the room was quiet. As her mind began to clear, she remembered being shot and slowly brought her hand down to her hip. Surprisingly there was no pain from her touch. The wound seemed to have healed completely. How long had she been unconscious?

Fear began to rise swiftly within her as she realized that she had no idea what happened after they reached the van. Under the heavy blanket that covered her, Sadie found her body was clad in a thin cloth. She wondered for a moment who would have dressed her. The bed and blankets were unfamiliar, and the beeping sound had become frustratingly annoying.

"Hello? Is anyone there?" Her meek voice shook with fear. "Fester?"

No one answered; she was all alone in the room. Slowly she struggled to sit, wincing at the stiff tightness of her muscles. The room smelled like it had been cleaned with an unfamiliar cleanser. It was an entirely unpleasant scent that tickled her nose until she sneezed. It was unusual to her that a bedroom would smell this way. Sadie wondered if the government had her, or did Sal bring her to this strange place? For a moment, she wasn't sure which scenario frightened her more.

One thing was for sure, she couldn't stay in this bed. It was important that she find Fester and make sure he was alright. There was no way for her to relax until then. Slowly she scooted to her right and away from whatever caused the constant beeping. Before she could move very far, there was an unmistakable pull on her left arm. With her mind still clouded from sleep, she didn't notice that something had been attached to her until now.

Gingerly she touched her forearm and found a tube taped to it. Carefully she peeled off the tape surrounding the tube and felt a pinch where it went inside her arm. It was difficult not to panic. She had no idea why anything would be stuck to her arm in such a manner. With her heart beating wildly in her chest, and impatient to get away from this strange new place, Sadie quickly yanked at the tube. A small whimper escaped her lips, despite her efforts to be silent, as her arm was scraped from the sharp piece that had been under her skin. There was no way for her to know the reasons for such a strange thing and she hoped it wasn't something bad.

Where was Fester? She needed to find him and learn what had happened. Flashes of memories threatened to overwhelm her mind. It had become increasingly difficult to keep her fear from turning into a severe panic attack. Fester was hurt and she needed to find out if he was safe. Sadie wouldn't be able to forgive herself if something horrible had happened. She was supposed to protect him. It didn't matter that she had also been injured. Fester's well being was far more important than a bloody hip. Silently she berated herself for her weakness.

Granted, he had Michael there to help him as well. But, Michael would've been busy protecting Chloe and shooting electricity. There would've been no way for him to also keep Fester safe. Sal could have, but Sadie didn't believe that the criminal would have saved anyone other than herself. She was just another cruel and selfish person of which the world seemed to have an overabundant supply.

Tossing the tube aside, Sadie reasoned that now wasn't the time to focus on the past. She almost let out a small laugh at the thought. Fester had constantly tried to get her to talk about the past back at the apartment. Now, when she needed most to stay in the present, she found herself doing what he had wanted. Unfortunately focusing on what had happened, or what might have happened, wasn't going to help with her current situation. First she needed to find out where she was. Then she could learn about what had happened to the others.

Before she could get off of the bed and explore, Sadie heard an alarm come from the same place as the annoying beep. The sound made her heart jump into her throat and she froze in place. Was this sound to warn someone that she was getting off the bed? She couldn't imagine what sort of place would have such an alarm. Before she could dwell on it, she heard a door open. Ready to use her wind at whomever entered were they to attack her, she waited for them to announce themselves.

"Ah, you're awake." Sadie didn't recognize the woman's voice.

Not knowing what else to do, she continued to sit on the side of the bed. The woman's footsteps indicated that she walked around to the opposite side. Soon after, the alarm stopped.

"We were all worried about you, Sadie. It seemed for a moment like we might lose you. Thankfully one of our Healers was able to save your life. You're a lucky girl." Sadie flinched violently when the woman touched her wrist. "Don't worry, dear. I'm just checking your vitals. I'm Nurse Jen, Ms. Vinnachelli hired me to take good care of you."

"Sal?"

"That's right, dear. Do you want me to fetch her for you?"

"No!" Sadie's fear threatened to overwhelm her. She did not want to talk to Sal.

"OK. Calm down. I won't get her if you don't want me to."

"Where's Fester? Where is he?"

"The others you came with are all downstairs. It looks like you cut your arm when you took out the IV. Let me clean it and then I'll bring you to your friends."

"Take me to Fester now, please."

"I really should put a bandage on your arm first."

"No, please! Just take me to him! Please!" Sadie was on the verge of panicking again. Why wouldn't this woman take her to Fester?

"Shhh. It's OK, dear. Come on, I'll take you to the people you came with. I guess your arm can wait till later."

Sadie paused before standing up. Sal had them, not the government. She wasn't sure how she felt about that. It would've been preferable if neither had them and they were all free. This new woman worked for Sal and that meant that she couldn't be trusted at all. Logically Sadie knew she wouldn't be able to find the others without her assistance. Perhaps it would be a good idea to let her help...for now. If she was hired by Sal, then that meant Sadie's debt would be with the criminal and not this nurse woman. The prospect of owing Sal was almost more than she could take.

"Where's my cane?" Sadie asked as she stood.

"Your what? Oh, I don't know, dear. Here, I'll lead you."

Once again Sadie flinched when the woman took her elbow. Not having her cane caused her to suddenly feel vulnerable. She always had it with her. Yes, she could see without it if she used the air. However, after everything that had happened, such actions probably wouldn't be wise. This Nurse Jen woman didn't mention anything about being a Supernatural, and Sadie wasn't sure how much she knew. Having her cane would definitely help ease some of her anxiety though. After all, it could be used for more than showing her when something was in her path. She didn't want to rely on this woman to show her where to go and needed some form of protection besides the wind.

Neither of them spoke as the woman led her down an unfamiliar hallway. Sadie tried to determine where they were by the sounds she heard. All that was evident were the sounds of the woman's footsteps clicking strangely on a hard floor. Without shoes on, Sadie could tell that the floor was made of a hard cold stone. The sounds they both made echoed slightly, telling Sadie that they were somewhere with a high ceiling and a wide open space. Were they at the warehouse place again? The sound wasn't quite right for that, but she had no way to be sure.

It wasn't long before they reached a set of stairs. The woman, her voice as kind and soft as before, gently guided her down the steps. Here Sadie's bare feet touched a soft carpet. She was encouraged to hold onto the railing beside her, and did so without hesitation. The hand rail was cool to the touch and obviously made of some sort of metal. If only she had learned more about the world, then she would be able to piece these clues together. For now she needed to be patient, and again try not to panic.

As they reached the bottom of the stairway Sadie heard a familiar squeal. "Sadie! Ya woked up!" The sound of small feet running towards her helped to prepare for the arms that were thrown around her waist. Automatically, she placed her hand on the child's back, relieved that she was safe as well. The exuberance of the girl helped to ease some of her fear. If Chloe was happy and excited, then they were probably safer than she had originally figured.

As Chloe held tightly onto Sadie, she also heard the familiar sound of heavy footsteps coming towards her. "God damn, girl! Ya got us fucking worryin surer in hell!"

"Sorry, Michael."

"Ain't lettin ya sweat it none. Just lovin ya be K. Fester gone ta 'nother room with them bitch, an his ass maybe gettin back soon."

"He's OK then?" Sadie's heart beat fast at the sound of his name.

"Fuck yeah! That boy done got way morer fucking smarts than ta get his goose cookin."

Sadie frowned at the expression. She had no idea what cooking geese had to do with anything. Did they actually do that? She didn't have a chance to ask about it before Chloe grabbed her hand and began to pull her forward. The motion made her a little unsteady. Without her cane to show what was in front of her, she had no idea if the child would accidentally steer her into something.

"C'mon, Sadie! We watchin cartoons!"

Sadie followed Chloe, though the child gave her little

choice. Behind her, Nurse Jen whispered something to Michael about Sadie's arm. Soon after, the sound of clicking footsteps told her that the woman had turned to leave. She was glad. The last thing she wanted was someone who worked for Sal nearby. As she sat down with Chloe, she asked where they were.

"We been takin ta one them joints Sal got," Michael said as he took her arm. Sadie couldn't help but flinch from the unexpected contact. "Shit, girl, I just puttin them here band aid on ya." Sadie didn't respond and let him do as he wished. She waited patiently for him to say more. Finally he asked, "Ya ain't got no clue the hell been goin down, huh?"

Sadie shook her head.

"Well, ya got a rememory or two 'bout the fuck happen ta ya ass?" he asked

"The government was after us. I don't remember much after getting into the van. I know I was shot," she said.

"True, well, a uber fucking firefight done gone down. Supernaturals 'gainst PSI. A shit ton o' fucking people done got themselves hurtin or dead. Sal lil fucking war gettin it starts with a big bang I s'pose. The news done been all filled up with words 'bout splinter cells o' Supernaturals fightin heavy 'gainst PSI o'er the damn continent true. Shit! It gettin be mad crazy fucking mess out there. True civil war, surer in hell. I ain't gettin Chloe all mixed up in no more them shits. I hopin we gonna find us selves a way ta lay low, til them fucked up war gettin ta blowin o'er an we gettin home."

"Where's Fester?"

"I sayin 'fore, Sadie, he with Sal. She done got from his ass hackin some gov'ment computers or whatever. Fucking bullshit she gettin him doin that 'gain just so's we gettin the fuck outta here. One works for her helps, my ass! Whore bester not be gettin him in no more troubles."

Not knowing what else to say, Sadie leaned back into the soft couch cushions. If Fester was working for Sal than that meant he was alright. It also meant that they had somehow increased their debt to the criminal.

The idea of owing more debt caused her heart to race. Chloe had an unusually tight grip on her hand. She reasoned that the child must be as frightened as she was. Remembering Chloe's empathy, Sadie worked on controlling her own fear. Deep breathing seemed to be helpful but she wasn't sure she would be able to relax completely until Fester was beside her as well.

They sat in silence as Chloe watched her cartoons. The familiar sounds coming from the TV reminded Sadie of the apartment. While she was going to miss it there, she felt relieved that Michael wouldn't know about the destruction that she had caused to his home. Not wanting a repeat of that day, she pushed the memory of how overwhelmed she had been out of her mind. If she were lost in a sea of memories now then she may never regain control again. Her sanity still felt threatened by everything that had happened.

"Michael? How long was I asleep?" she asked.

"Hmmm? Oh, ya ass out for two days. The Healer Ms. Bitch got ta findin done fixin ya up good an true, but he ain't been able ta woked ya ass up. Ya done lossin a ton o' fucking blood, Sadie. Near morer than ya could."

"What's a 'Healer'?"

Michael let out a short laugh. "A fucking Supernatural that gots power healin peoples an shit. What else?"

"Nothing else. Sorry."

Michael let out another short laugh. Sadie didn't understand what she had said to get such a reaction. There wasn't anything funny that she could tell. It seemed like perhaps it was yet another thing she would never understand; something new to show her wrongness. At least she learned that there were Supernaturals who could heal injuries as serious as the one she had sustained. It wasn't a comforting thought when she realized that Fester was probably working off her debt for this Healer person as well as his own. She had no doubt that he would insist on paying her share anyway. That is, of course, if she had been given the chance to argue with him about it first.

While she waited for Sal to be through with Fester, Sadie tried to piece together all that had happened.

Sal had started a war between Supernaturals and this government thing. Were they all in more danger now than before? Michael had said that a lot of people had been hurt or killed. Deep from within she knew that many more would die because of all of this. It was all her fault and there was nothing she could do to change things. How did this situation get so out of control?

Truthfully, she didn't care about those she didn't know. Most of the world seemed full of horrible people who were no better than her parents. If anything happened to them, she wouldn't be bothered by it in the slightest. She only cared about four people at this point: her friends and her son. What would happen to Nathan if the war spilled into her parents' home? The memory of Nathan, coupled with what she imagined his fate to be, filled her with a great sadness. Her eyes stung with unshed tears and she shut them tight.

"Sadie?" Chloe's voice sounded worried.

"Sorry, Chloe. I'll try not to be sad."

Not being sad or afraid felt like an impossible task. Remembering about how she had those strong bursts of courage back at the other house, Sadie wondered if there was a way to bring such bravery back. She enjoyed not feeling afraid and the confidence that it had given her. For now, she was stuck with her emotions. Since Chloe continued to hold her hand, she had to keep herself extra calm. Fester had mentioned once that touch made the child's empathy stronger.

With Fester, Nathan, and this war so strong in her mind, she had no idea what she was going to do. The immediate danger had passed and they survived. There was no time to relax, though; they were far from safe. Her son also wasn't safe. Sadie remembered what Fester had said about saving her baby. *'We need to get your son back.' 'There has to be a way to find him. I won't stop trying until we do.'* Saving Nathan seemed more impossible than controlling her emotions; an impossible task to add to their complicated predicament.

Before Fester had said anything, Sadie wouldn't have imagined that she would have ever been able to save Nathan. Now that he had put the idea into her head, she couldn't stop wondering if she would be able to do what was needed. Sadie considered for a moment telling Michael about the baby. Perhaps he would know what they could do. After all, Michael knew far more about the world than she ever would. Even though he spoke strangely sometimes, he seemed to be intelligent about things she couldn't possibly fathom. Ultimately, she decided to wait. Michael had his concerns firmly on Chloe and keeping her safe. Just as Sadie didn't want to feel any fear right now, she was also sure that Michael didn't want yet another child to worry about. The man was under enough stress, they all were.

No good would come from wondering about such matters now. It would be best to put it all out of her mind. Nothing could be accomplished by dwelling on things which she had no hope to change. Doing so would only serve to increase her fears and that would hurt Chloe. Better to just keep her mind, and her voice, silent. Once more she wished Fester were beside her, holding her, and comforting her with his words and his embrace. No matter how hard she tried to focus, she continued to feel unsteady without him.

Listening to the TV didn't ease her mind, even though she tried to pay attention to the cartoons. Chloe kept a firm grip on Sadie's hand and Michael loudly paced about. Chloe had never held onto her like this and Sadie wondered at the girl's change in behavior. Usually cartoons would bring about little bursts of laughter from the child. Instead, she didn't laugh or giggle or make any sound whatsoever. Michael's pacing also worried Sadie. While he had done that a lot at the apartment, there was a different quality to it here. The sounds of his heavy footsteps made it sound like the patterns he walked in were erratic and fast paced. That wasn't like him at all. Usually he would walk in an oval and his pace would be steady. She shivered as she realized that things weren't going well at all. What hadn't they told her?

Sadie knew that Chloe would become very quiet around other people. It made her wonder if there were others about. She couldn't hear anyone and had assumed that they were alone. Even when a person attempted to stay silent, they would eventually make some sort of noise to betray their presence. A cough, a sniffle, a shift in weight, a sigh...there were many ways for a person to make any number of sounds. Surely if anyone else had been in the room then she would have heard them by now.

"Michael? Is anyone else here?" Sadie asked. She needed to know for sure.

"In the joint or in here room?"

"Both."

"Well, we only ones in here room. Fuck, I ain't got no clue how many walkin 'bout the joint. It be a huge fucking joint, Sadie, an Sal done got ton o' foolish shits gettin works from her here. I gotta picture in mind, them here be one the bitch's true homes an ain't some damn hideout. Why?"

"You two aren't acting normal."

"The fuck ya sayin, Sadie?"

"I...I just...nothing. I'm sorry, Michael."

"Whatever." He returned to his erratic pacing.

"Michael worryin heavy, Sadie," Chloe said.

"He is?"

"Yeah, he 'fraid same. Thems all 'fraid. Thems all freakin out!"

"Oh."

It made sense. Chloe would be silent if there were other people in the same place and they were worried or scared. Michael had said, *'I ain't gettin Chloe all mixed up in no more them shits. I hopin we gonna find us selves a way ta lay low.'* It seemed that Michael didn't know how he was going to keep Chloe safe. Sadie suspected that extended to herself and Fester as well. Unfortunately, she didn't know enough about the world, or wars, to be able to do anything about their safety either.

"Michael, do you know where my cane is?"

"The fuck I gonna get a clue 'bout them shits? The fuck ya needin it for in the one-two?"

"I just...I...I want to explore. I want to know where

I am."

Michael swore. "Yeah, K, um just get ta lettin me seein if I gonna be able ta find the fucking thing. I gonna get back in a one-two. Ya girls stickin there, an I ain't gonna be happy if ya fucking gettin somewheres else."

"Why can't we go anywhere?"

Michael swore. "Damn it, Sadie. I ain't got no trustin or lovin up in here. Ya gotta clue 'bout them shits. It fucking weirdin me out! On a two, Sal done got some others up in here. I ain't got no clue where them fucks at or nothin same, an I ain't got no trust for a damn one 'em. Just be stickin there with Chloe an I gonna get ta fucking lookin for ya stupid cane."

Sadie didn't respond. Michael sounded angrier and harsher than usual. His tone suggested that he was just as worried and afraid as Chloe had said. It was frightening to think that someone as strong and powerful as Michael would behave this way. By now it was obvious how he felt about Sal. He always seemed terrified of her. Knowing his past with her, it was easy to see why. Yet, Sadie couldn't help but feel that Michael was far more frightened than he had ever been before. The idea of it sat uneasy in her mind. He had seemed a master at controlling his emotions back at the apartment.

What bothered her most was Chloe. The child would usually have been crying from an outburst like that; the emotions would've been too much for her. However, all she did was hold onto Sadie's hand as though she was going to suddenly disappear. As far as Sadie knew, only Sal had that power. What had happened in the past two days that made Michael so unbelievably afraid and Chloe so uncharacteristically clingy? What changed them?

Then there was the fact that Fester still hadn't shown up. Where could he be? Michael had said that he was working on something for Sal. The last time he did work for her, it didn't take nearly this long. Shouldn't he be back by now? Sadie's fears began to swim in her mind, caused by the horrors she imagined the criminal had forced Fester to endure in payment for her healing.

She was anxious to hear his voice, and know with her own ears that he was alright.

"Sadie?"

"Sorry, Chloe."

"Ya morer 'fraid than 'fore."

"I know."

"Why?"

Sadie sighed. "Because, Chloe, I want to know where Fester is. He should be back by now."

"He with Sal tons. Then, when he ain't with her he be with ya. I ain't seein him no more." The sad tone to the girl's voice worried Sadie even further. Whose sadness did her tone portray? Her own or Sadie's?

Fester wasn't around, Michael was more upset than usual, strange people all over, plus the start of a war...it was no wonder that Chloe held onto Sadie so fiercely. She remembered what it had been like her first few nights on the streets. Her entire world had drastically changed and everything happened too fast. She was surrounded by people she didn't know and danger lurked everywhere. Now she was OK with those changes. But, for Chloe it was still new and terrifying. Sadie wished she knew how to help the girl. She didn't want her to become afraid of everything, too.

With all that had happened, Sadie couldn't help but wonder if she would ever hear Chloe laugh again. It was odd that she should think of it now. Once in her mind, the urge became stronger. There was no way that she could let Chloe's laughter die from this war. Especially since this was all her own fault anyhow. She had to make it right in some way. If only they hadn't gone down that street...

Now Sadie had three objectives. Keep Fester safe, free her son, and find a way to make Chloe happy once more. The problem was that she didn't know how to do any of those things.

Chapter 30

It wasn't long before Michael returned. When Sadie heard his heavy footsteps sooner than expected, excitement rose up within her. With her cane she could explore and actually know her surroundings. Perhaps she could also find the room where Sal had been keeping Fester. Oh to hear his voice again!

"I sorry, Sadie. Ya fucking cane ain't fucking nowhere. It morer true done got lefted 'hind," he said as he neared them.

"Are you sure?" she asked.

"Sure an true. Them here joint been spotless, an I ain't seein the fucking thing nowhere. Ain't nobody I askin gone seein it neither."

"Oh." Sadie's heart caught in her throat. She swallowed hard and tried to hold back her tears. Chloe's grip tightened around her hand.

"I showin Sadie 'round?" Chloe asked softly.

Michael swore. "Chloe, I ain't lettin ya fucking get ta wanderin off an shit. Just both ya get ta stickin right there. Here, Sadie. I got ta bringin ya some socks. Ya feets gonna get fucking freezed with none. Ya hungered?"

Sadie shook her head. She wasn't hungry and she didn't feel cold but she held her free hand out for the socks anyway. She ignored how harshly they were placed there. Her mind was on her cane. What was she going to do without it? Chloe let go of her so she could put the socks on. As she brought up her foot, however, Michael swore heavily.

"Sweet Jesus! Get ya fucking leg down, girl! Ya ain't got morer a God damn nightgown on ya ass, for fuck's sake!"

"Sorry."

Sadie put her foot down and leaned over her lap to put on the socks. She didn't understand Michael's reaction. What did she do wrong? It seemed that no matter what she did, it was somehow the wrong thing to do. She always managed to upset those around her, especially Michael. It was baffling that after all of her mistakes, Fester and Chloe still wanted her around. Once again she knew that she shouldn't be with these people. She deserved only to be alone. The difference was, now she couldn't leave regardless of whether or not she wanted to. This time she really was trapped.

After putting on her socks, Sadie leaned back against the cushions and closed her eyes. She had only been awake a short while and already she was physically and emotionally drained. It was tempting to take a nap but she refused to ask if she could. Fester might be done with Sal soon and she wanted to see him immediately after.

"Sadie, ya 'K?" Chloe asked.

"I'm just tired, Chloe," Sadie said.

"I gonna get ya ass ta ya fucking room?" Michael asked.

"No, I want to wait for Fester."

"Ya ain't gotta fucking get ya mind gone, Sadie. If ya tirin then get ta takin a nap. When Fester gettin back an shit, I be sayin ta him ya woked up, an he gonna get ta ya ass. K?"

Reluctantly, Sadie nodded her head. Michael's voice held a concerned tone. She didn't want to argue with him or make him mad at her. She had done enough to upset him already. He was worried about her as well and she didn't want to make it worse. Remembering his reactions whenever she apologized, she resisted the urge to do so now. After all, he had never accepted it before.

"C'mon," he said as he took her elbow. "I gonna get ya bony ass ta bed. Chloe, ya stickin here."

"No! Michael, ya ain't leavin me alone!" Chloe's panicked tone alarmed Sadie.

Michael let out a heavy sigh. "Still? K, c'mon! Fuck! Ya girls gotta get a thing all damn heavy an shit!"

"Sorry," Sadie and Chloe said simultaneously.

"Whatever. Just get goin."

Michael guided Sadie back towards the stairs and up

to her room. It was the first time she could remember him touching her for more than a few seconds. Strangely, his hand didn't feel as large as Festers. It was still very large though. Perhaps it was common for a man to have large hands. Her father didn't have them. But, with having only felt the hands of a few different men, Sadie didn't have any way of knowing what was normal and what wasn't. She shook her head. Hands? Michael was right, she must be tired.

The brief moment where she thought about her father's hands had caused her to think about her son as well. Pushing the thought of her father as far away as she could, she focused on her memories of Nathan. How was she going to find him? With how little she knew about her parents' identities, or where they lived, she felt blinder than usual. She needed to figure something out. More mobility would help.

"Michael, what am I going to do without my cane?"

"Fuck, Sadie. I ain't got no clue. Maybe a way we gonna find ta get ya one all new."

Sadie knew better than to ask Michael or anyone else to buy her a new cane. The amount of pain her mother had given her as payment for the one she had was almost more than she could bear. While she doubted that Fester would take such a payment, she wasn't so sure about Michael or Sal. This was especially true with Sal, since she was already cruel and would probably enjoy it. After all, she almost took her as a possession. Beating her wouldn't be far out of the woman's reach.

"Well, we got here fine," Michael said as they stopped. "Lookin like them shits got ta makin the fucking bed all ready. Ya gotta clue where it at?"

Sadie nodded her head and walked into the room unassisted. She carefully closed the door behind her and walked slowly in the direction of the bed. Without the use of a cane, finding her way around was a bit more difficult. To ensure that she didn't bump into something and hurt herself, she needed to walk slowly with her hands out in front of her. It took a few minutes for her to find the bed.

It was disturbing how accustomed she had become to the object. Her mother had only presented her with the cane a few weeks before taking her Downtown. Since then it had always been in her possession. At her parent's house she didn't need it because she knew where everything was. It had become the same way at Michael and Fester's home. There she had only used it in case something had been left on the floor. Now that she was somewhere new, however, she felt completely lost without it. Especially since she didn't know if Sal would allow her to see with the air. She didn't want to be punished by the criminal, nor owe her another debt, by using her power without permission.

Not feeling cold enough to use the blankets, Sadie climbed onto the bed and lay down. She curled up into a ball facing the door and tried unsuccessfully not to cry. Her heart felt heavy and her breathing became increasingly uneven and labored. Tears spilled from her eyes and wet the pillow beneath her head. Sniffling, she tried not to make a sound. She didn't want anyone outside of the room to know she was crying. It was bad enough that Chloe would be able to feel her sadness, and that couldn't be helped. The last thing she needed was for everyone else to be made aware of it as well.

What pulled at her heart the most was how guilty she felt for everything that had happened. If she had known more about the world, then she could have avoided most of the issues presented to her. Everything she did caused severe problems for herself and her friends. Now there was this war, people were dying, Chloe wouldn't laugh, and Fester was forced to work for that horrible criminal. It was all her fault, every last bit.

If only she hadn't gone down that street. If only she had paid more attention. Everything could be tied to that singular incident. It didn't matter that the men had said it was that other men's fault. All she had to do was continue avoiding that alley. Then she and Michael wouldn't have had to use their power, and they would all be back at the apartment. The apartment, that is, which she destroyed.

Sadie truly was a danger to these people. They

had all said so before. Even Sal admitted that she was dangerous. If they found a way out of this mess then she would have to leave. Already Fester had been hurt when she lost control of her wind after a nightmare. If she were to hurt him again – or worse, if she were to hurt Chloe – then she would die right then and there.

Sadie turned her head and screamed into the pillow. There was no way she would be able to leave Fester! She couldn't leave him, she couldn't stay with him, and there was no other alternative that she could find. To leave him would kill her. The thought of being without the only person she'd ever truly loved was unbearable. Add to that the fact that without Fester she would never be able to find and take care of her son, and it was more than she could handle.

Over and over Sadie screamed into the pillow. Her situation was dire and it wasn't the first time that she wished Fester had never saved her that day. She wished he had never brought her into the warmth of his home and his heart. A few times now she had come close to death. Perhaps that was what was supposed to happen. Perhaps she truly needed to die. After all, each day she lived, someone else was harmed. It would be only right to ensure that those whom she loved would actually be safe from her.

Having come to the decision to find a way to end her life, an intense sense of relief washed over Sadie. She wasn't able to savor the feeling before someone threw the door open, burst into the room, and rushed to her bed. Alarmed, she bolted upright and resisted the urge to shove whoever it was away with her wind.

"Sadie? Sadie, are you OK?"

"Fester!"

Sadie reached out in the direction of his voice and felt his shoulders. Kneeling on the bed, she threw her arms around his neck and held him tight. Likewise, he hugged her with the same intensity. The sound of his voice eased her anxiety and she relaxed in his arms. Her heart felt as though it would burst with joy where there was only despair moments ago. Sadie tried not to think about her sadness or the decision she had made.

If this was to be one of the last times Fester held her, then she wanted to enjoy it for as long as possible.

It wasn't long before Fester pulled away and placed his large hands on her shoulders. "Sadie, what's wrong?"

"Nothing," she lied.

The mattress shifted as he sat down. "Don't bullshit me, Sadie. I have a clue that a thing's been wrong. Chloe's been screamin bloody murder downstairs. She was feeling your sadness, wasn't she?" he asked as he brushed her tear stained face with his fingers.

"It's OK, Fester. Really."

Fester sighed as he pulled her into another embrace. This one was far more gentle. "Sadie, I've never seen Chloe act that way. It was really scary. You sure you're K?"

For a moment Sadie considered telling him the truth. "Yes," she lied, "everything's fine." She even managed to smile for him.

"Ok," he said as he gave her a small squeeze.

"We're done for the day, Fester. You and your girlfriend can spend some alone time if you want," Sal said from the doorway. The sound of her voice made Sadie stiffen. She didn't know anyone else was there.

"Thanks, Sal," Fester said as his body turned slightly.

"Yeah, no problem."

Sadie couldn't relax again until the door closed and she was sure they were truly alone. Closing her eyes, she buried her face in Fester's chest. Inhaling deeply, she reveled in the scent of him. The smile on her face this time was genuine, and a feeling of contentment washed over her. She let out a small sigh as the anxiety and sadness from earlier washed away completely. Perhaps all she needed was to be held forever.

"Hey," Fester said softly, "are you hungry?" Sadie shook her head. "Are you tired? Do you want to sleep?"

"I did before, but not now."

"Do you mind if I sleep then? I've been up for twenty hours now."

Sadie held onto Fester tightly and began to panic. "I don't want you to go!"

"Shhhh. It's OK. I'll keep here with you. It'll be like when we slept on the couch except...well...comfortable. I won't go nowhere. I promise."

"OK."

Fester suggested that they should get under the covers. While she wasn't particularly cold, she didn't want to argue either. If he wanted to be warm then they would be warm. It was the least she could do after the mess she had made of things. Hearing his voice and feeling his arms around her helped Sadie to feel better than before. Fester really was OK, and his arm seemed as healed as her hip. At least for now something had gone right.

Since they had never slept together in a bed, it was difficult to find a comfortable position. Sadie couldn't lean her head on his chest like she had on the couch. His body was too high for her and his chest was too hard. The cushions on the couch must have held her higher next to him than the soft mattress they were now on. He had suggested that she face outwards and he lay behind her with his arm wrapped around her waist. Sadie didn't like that idea either. She wanted to face him. They finally settled on facing each other with his arms wrapped around her. This way, she was able to be in his embrace, and have her face against his chest where she could both feel and smell him.

It wasn't long after they were settled and comfortable before Fester began to snore softly. Careful not to wake him, Sadie took a fistful of his shirt in her hands and snuggled in as close as their bodies would allow. Silently, she wept. Her body shook as the emotions from earlier threatened to overwhelm her once more. She didn't want that to happen. Fester said Chloe had been screaming from her internal torment earlier. That couldn't happen again. Knowing that she had caused the child such intense pain increased her guilt.

Sadie found it difficult not to cry. Even in the safety of Fester's arms, and with her heart overflowing with love and affection for him, she knew that it wasn't going to last. That is what made her sad in this moment. Someday soon she was going to have to sacrifice herself so that no one else would be hurt by her constant blunders. This was something that had to happen regardless of how happy Fester could make her. Her joy was not worth the price of their safety.

For a moment she wondered what would happen to this wonderful man when she was gone. He loved her, of this she had no doubt. If his love felt anything like hers did, then she knew he would be devastated if she were to leave. He had even said it himself, *'I couldn't bear it if you died. It would be too painful.'* If that were true, than even in death she would cause him to suffer. Sadie's tears flowed freely as her crying increased. She realized that no matter what she did, there was always someone she would hurt.

Sadie considered sneaking out of bed and finding her way outside. She couldn't handle the pain her emotions gave her and the danger she brought to the others. If she went outside then at least the freezing weather would help her to end it all before anyone woke up.

Her heart felt like it would explode and her body heat rose. So strong was her internal agony that she couldn't get out of bed. She was far too weak to complete even the simple task of taking her own life.

Chapter 31

"Sadie? Sadie, wake up. You're having another bad dream. Wake up!" Gently Fester began to shake Sadie in an attempt to wake her from a nonexistent slumber.

"I'm awake, Fester," she said between sobs.

The mattress moved as he pulled away from her. He placed his fingers under her chin and gently turned her face up towards his. Sadie closed her eyes, allowing him to move her head with ease. She tried to stop her tears and was unsuccessful. Despair tore at her heart, and her sorrow was expressed without hindrance. There was no way for her to pretend that everything was alright this time.

"Sadie," Fester said softly as he wiped her tears, "hey, what's wrong?"

She couldn't answer him. If she told him what she had been thinking, and why she was so terribly sad, then he would be sad as well. There was no way she would be able to allow herself to hurt him. Instead of trying to explain or lie, she lowered her head and continued to cry. Her hands clutched his shirt tight enough to bruise her fingers and her body shook violently with the strength of her emotions.

"Shhhh." Fester wrapped his arms securely around her and pulled her in close. He laid his head upon hers and talked in soothing tones. "It's OK, Sadie. Whatever it is, it's OK. You're alright. You're clear riskless. Please, Sadie, please don't cry. What has you so upset? Please don't cry."

With every ounce of strength she had within her, Sadie did her best to obey. Back at the apartment there were many things she had learned to do to help control her feelings. Fester had once told her to think about something that made her happy or something she loved. Both of those had the same source in her mind. He was what made her happy. He was whom she loved. Unfortunately, he was also, in part, the reason for her tears.

"I'm sorry, Fester. I'm so sorry," she whispered.

"Why are you sorry?" he asked with an overly concerned tone to his voice.

"I made such a mess of things. I'm so wrong!"

"What? What are you talking about?"

"Nothing. Go back to sleep. It's nothing."

Fester swore with enough force to cause Sadie to flinch harshly, a movement she hadn't used with him in a while. "That's bullshit, Sadie! No one, not even you, cries like this for no good reason. Please tell me what's wrong. Damn it! Trust me! Let me help you! What's wrong?"

Sadie froze and her despair quickly turned into terror. Never had Fester spoken to her with such force. While she had heard him swear like this with Michael or Sal, he had never used such harsh words in this manner with her. In her attempt to spare him from the anguish of her own torment, she had somehow angered him.

"I...I'm sorry, Fester. I'm sorry. Please don't be mad. I'm sorry, I'll try not to cry. Please don't be mad at me!"

"Oh, hey, no...that's not it. Shit! Sadie, I'm not mad at you. OK? I just...I can't stand to see you in pain. I love you. If I had the power to do so, then I would make it so you were always happy. I just...I can't even begin to help you if you won't share words with me!"

"I...I can't tell you, Fester! Please, just let it go. I won't cry. I'll be good. I swear it!"

Fester brushed her hair with his fingers as he held her. "Sadie, are you 'fraid of me?"

"No," she said in a small voice.

He moved away from her slightly, and lifted her face towards him again. "You look terrified. What's going on?"

Before Sadie could hope to answer him, she heard her door burst open. "The fuck ya two got goin up in here!"

"Michael, a thing's wrong. She won't tell me what it is."

Michael's heavy footsteps moved swiftly towards the bed. Sadie continued to lay as still as possible. Her tears had stopped but fear still had its grip on her heart. She held her breath as she waited for Michael to yell at her. Perhaps he would even hit her if her emotions had caused Chloe too much pain. At this point there was so much uncertainty in her life that she didn't know what to expect. Sadie closed her eyes tight and waited for whatever was to come. She nearly jumped when she felt him sit on the mattress.

"Sadie," Michael said softly, "ya gotta get ta calmin ya mind the fuck down. I picturin ya got a clue Chloe feelin ya. She gettin all freaked out, an I ain't able to get her ass calmin down none. 'Fore an now...I get how ya been gettin all 'fraid an shit, but Chloe got ta sayin this shit worser than ever 'fore. So...the fuck, girl? What goin in ya mind?"

Sadie didn't answer him. She couldn't find her voice and didn't know what she would say anyway. Off in the distance she heard Chloe crying. Her breath caught in her throat. Once again...

"What do you mean 'worse than ever before'?" Fester asked.

"She sayin she ain't never fucking feelin no morer pain feelins from nobody, Fester. Never. What be goin on in Sadie mind...it be fucking bad, man. Crazy assed bad."

"Sadie, you have to talk to us."

"No," she whispered. "Just forget it. I'm fine."

"Fuck, Sadie, ya ain't fine!" Michael said, "Ya ain't never been fine but now ya be less fine than ever. We done been through a shit ton them last few days, an we ain't ables to be havin ya fucking fallin ta bits all o'er the joint!"

When Sadie didn't respond, Michael said, "Look, it done been real clear what Fester got in him for ya. Chloe...she...she got uber stickin ta ya ass. Hell, even I likin ya. There ain't no doctor here to be helpin ya – not that ya gonna let 'em – an so it gettin put on us: the peoples who be carin for ya. I hatin on them shits but them words be true. So get done bein a God damn babe, an get ta lettin thems who got ta carins 'bout ya ables ta fucking helpin ya ass!"

For the first time since Fester woke up, Sadie changed her position. She rolled over onto her back and sighed. Her eyes were still burning from her tears and her breathing was unsteady. She had no idea what to say to them. The fact that Michael was there with her, and not with Chloe, meant that he really was worried. She had never expected that. It had always seemed like he tolerated her for Fester and Chloe's sakes. He liked her too, and also wanted to help. Why?

How could she tell these people what she had been feeling? It would only make them upset with her if she told them that she was planning on killing herself. Perhaps...perhaps she could just tell them why she wanted to die. They don't have to know why she had been crying right now, but they can know what led to those feelings. Maybe then they'd be satisfied and let her be.

Sadie took a deep breath and let it out slowly. "You don't understand," she said, "you don't even try to understand sometimes. I'm not right, Michael. I keep on causing so much trouble. I don't mean to but I do. Now there's this war and we're running from this government thing. I know that we'll never be safe. I know that I can't take care of myself by myself, and that means that even if Fester helped me find Nathan, I couldn't take care of him either. I'm wrong and hopeless and there's no making it right and..."

Her words trailed off and she began to cry once more. She rolled back towards Fester and curled up into a ball. Softly Fester swore and wrapped his arms around her.

"Who 'Nathan'?" Michael asked.

Sadie didn't respond and Fester said, "He's her son. Her 'rents have him."

Michael swore just as softly as Fester had. "The fuck ya kids ain't never sayin nothin 'fore?"

"I found out just before Sal got us. So much has happened that I..."

"It gonna be K, kid. Shit. Get ta listenin, Sadie, I ain't got no fucking clue how, but the faster we ables, we gonna get ya boy gone from them sick fucks. Ya hearin my words?" Sadie didn't respond but her crying did cease. "We ain't never gonna let them shits get ta hurtin him like they done on ya. Hell, I gonna get works from Sal if them shits gonna get it fucking done."

"You hate Sal," Sadie whispered.

"Yeah, well, I been hatin on ya mother fucking piece o' shit 'rents morer. Ya kids get ta sleepin, I gonna get ta Chloe." The mattress shifted as Michael stood up. Sadie heard him walk towards the door. "I fucking serious. Sleep. Now."

"OK," Fester said as the door shut.

For a moment neither of them moved. Sadie curled up on her side, facing Fester, and with her arms crossed over her heart. She could tell that he was propped up on one elbow but other than that she didn't know how he was positioned. In order to know, she would have to touch him. She felt too weak and numb to even bother. Her mind was as blank as her face.

"Sadie?" Fester whispered.

Although she was aware of him, she didn't acknowledge him at all. Everything felt as though it had been drained out of her. No movement, not even the slightest flinch, came from her when she felt his large hand on her shoulder.

"Hey, you OK?"

Again she gave no indication that she had heard him. She didn't have the energy or drive to do or feel anything. Her body lay still upon the bed and her breath was even. She rolled slightly when Fester shifted his weight on the mattress. There was a distinct click before he moved back.

"Sadie!" He sounded like he was panicking. This time he grabbed her shoulder roughly. Even with the force of it, she didn't flinch. "Sadie look at me!"

In a monotone voice she said, "I can't look at you."

"Yeah...right. I know. It's just...you just had me 'fraid half to death."

She considered for a moment telling him that she was sorry but the words wouldn't leave her throat.

"What's going on?" Fester asked. "You look so...I don't know. You look like you're catatonic!"

"I don't know what that means."

"Yeah well, you're talkin so it don't matter. Ya feelin K? Is it 'bout Nathan?"

At the sound of her son's name, Sadie felt a flutter deep in her abdomen. The sensation faded as soon as it appeared and she returned to feeling numb. "I don't feel anything."

Fester sighed and then swore. "I...I...Sadie, I don't have a damn clue what to do."

"Sleep," she said and then closed her eyes.

"Yeah," he said, "Yeah, let's sleep. We're both freaked out and maybe we should just sleep."

Again the mattress moved and she rolled slightly just before hearing a click-click. As Fester turned back he paused and gently touched the side of her face before lying down. He then lifted her head slightly and slid his arm underneath as though it were a pillow. His other arm draped over her side and he drew her close to him.

Sadie allowed herself to be pulled into the embrace, but she didn't return the gesture. The only movement she made was to turn her head to the side so she could breathe. Against her cheek she could feel Fester's chest shudder with each breath he took. His heart beat strongly, and the sound filled her ears. Again she felt a flutter from inside.

"I love you, Sadie," he said and she felt yet another flutter. "God help me, I love you so much."

"I love you too," she said.

There was something in the way he held her, or perhaps it was the quality of the tone in his voice. Sadie couldn't identify what it was, but she did notice it call to her heart. At that moment, she was able to feel again, and what she felt was Love. There was no more sadness or fear or guilt. There was only the purity of love within her. She didn't know what had just happened and she didn't want to.

The future was still uncertain and so was her sanity. Yet she held no worries about it. Her mind calm and her body heavy, it wasn't long before she entered a deep and dreamless sleep.

Chapter 32

When Sadie woke there was a loud commotion from somewhere outside their room. The walls and door were thicker than those at the apartment and she couldn't tell what was actually happening. Her heart raced and every nerve in her body came alive. Did the government find them? In her fear, she grabbed at Fester.

"It's OK," he said groggily, "I hear it, too. Lemme see what's goin down."

Reluctantly she let him go. As the mattress shifted from Fester getting out of bed, Sadie sat upright. She wanted to go to the door, open it, and use the air to see what was happening. It was no use though, her fear kept her glued to where she sat. How do you fight a PSI Team? They'd be ready for her wind this time!

When Fester opened the door, Sadie heard a lot of yelling and people running about. Something fell with a loud bang and someone she didn't recognize swore furiously. The intensity of alarm in the actions and voices of those outside was unmistakable.

"Fester," Sal said from the other side of the doorway, "give these to Sadie. They should fit."

"What's going on?"

"Long story. Basically, our position's been compromised."

"What? How? You said–"

"Not now! Just get dressed and then downstairs. Hurry!"

Fester swore heavily as the door quickly closed. His footsteps brought him swiftly to her side. Immediately after, something was placed in her lap. When she touched it she found some folded clothing and sneakers.

"Here...I'll wait outside while you get dressed."

"No! Please don't leave me, Fester!" Sadie said as she reached for him.

"Hey, it's OK," he said soothingly and took her hands

in his. "I'll just be right outside the door."

"Please don't!"

"Do you...do you want me...to...to...uh...keep here?"

Sadie nodded her head.

"Uh, OK. Um...I'll just be...ah...I'll be over by the door then," he said nervously. "I promise I won't look!"

Sadie didn't understand what made him so nervous. Perhaps it was because of whatever *compromised their position.* Even Sal had sounded a little afraid about that. Sadie didn't know what it meant, but she didn't want to find out either. He was being strange like everyone else and she didn't know why. Pushing the confusion out of her mind, she dressed as fast as she could. Now wasn't the time for figuring out Fester's oddities.

After dressing she turned to face where she thought he was standing. The clothes and shoes were big on her, but not by much. At least this time she won't have to hold up the pants. If only she had her cane!

"I'm ready," she said.

"Good," he said, "let's go!" Fester grabbed her hand and pulled her towards him. "Can you use your power to see?"

"Yes, but what if—"

"Good, do it. No one will care."

Sadie began feeling with the air and Fester thrust open the door. Standing just outside were two figures, one tall and the other short. Beyond them two more figures ran by, leaving a trail of disturbed air in their wake. Before she could question anything, the tall one spoke.

"Ya done takin long enough! Get the fuck goin. Now!" Michael sounded like he was more afraid than Sadie. This fact frightened her further.

Fester pulled Sadie as they ran through the hallway and towards the stairs. She had but a moment to realize that the upstairs portion wasn't as large as she had initially thought. There was a wall missing on the same side as the stairs, and the ceiling matched the one for the room below. Thankful that the air allowed her to see where the steps were, they ran down and joined the group at the bottom. From what Sadie could tell, there were about ten people, some holding large weapons, crowded about. Someone handed Fester and Chloe weapons as well.

"I ain't fucking likin them shits," Michael muttered.

"Ya know what's happening?" someone unfamiliar asked.

Utilizing the air, Sadie saw Michael shake his head. "Wish I did."

A figure not much taller than Sadie moved to the front of the group. "OK, listen up people!" Sal's voice rang out strong in the foyer, "We need to evacuate now. Eyes reports PSI activity in the area and they're headed our way. Everyone without an offensive power has been given a gun. Let's hope you don't need to use it. There are vans out front that will take us to more secure locations. Move out! Go!"

Somewhere Sadie heard a baby wailing. It sounded like Nathan! She shook her head. It couldn't be him! Before she could say or do anything about the sound of her son, Fester pulled on her hand and she was dragged in the direction everyone else had begun to move. Pushing out with the air, Sadie could tell that there were no children other than Chloe about. Yet she distinctly heard the baby – her baby – as though he were nearby.

As they burst through the front doors of Sal's home, which was larger than Sadie had imagined a house could be, the sound of the baby disappeared. It was difficult to put Nathan out of her mind, but Sadie knew that there was nothing she could do about him now. If he was nearby then surely he would be in one of the vans and taken to the same place as she. Wouldn't he?

Unlike the safe-house they had been in before, the vans were parked directly outside of the door. Sadie was thankful that they didn't have to run down a walkway with PSI shooting at them. At least this way Fester wouldn't be hurt again. Sadie didn't think she would be able to handle it if he were. The air she used to see shifted harshly with the thought.

Fester guided her to a van at the head of the group

and they got in. This time she could tell that the seats were lined up along the wall inside. Immediately she chose one beside Fester and watched as Michael and Chloe climbed in after them. Small whimpers came from Chloe and she clutched her gun awkwardly. Sadie knew that the girl was far more terrified than any of them. Once more, she didn't envy the Empath's power.

A few more people climbed into the van and it began to move. Sadie released her control over the air and was once again blind. With nothing left to do but sit and wait, she couldn't help but think about her son. Could that really have been him? Why would Nathan be in Sal's house? Did Sal even know that Sadie had a son? Did Fester tell her?

The questions swam in Sadie's mind and she grabbed onto Fester's arm to anchor herself. She didn't want to be lost in her thoughts right now. There was too much at stake.

"Are you OK?" Fester asked in a whisper.

"I don't know," she said.

Fester put his arm around her shoulders. "Don't worry. We'll be clear soon."

Sadie didn't respond. Instead she leaned in towards him and held onto his shirt. In their haste, no one had thought to grab any coats. Although warm inside the van, it was very cold outside and Sadie wondered what they were going to do about that. Fester and Michael had both made it very clear that a person could die from the cold. Were they in more danger without their coats on? Did Nathan have one?

Sadie realized that she needed to let Fester know what she had heard. "Did you see a baby there?"

"What? No. Why?"

"I heard him, Fester. I heard Nathan while we were leaving."

"Ya sure?" When Sadie nodded he called out, "Hey, Sal, were there any babies at your joint?"

Sadie stiffened. She hadn't realized that Sal was one of the people who entered their van. She wished she could tell who people were when she saw them. Other than the differences in their general shapes, she had no way of telling one person from the next.

"No. Chloe was the youngest person there. Why?"

"It's nothing." To Sadie he whispered, "Are you sure you heard him?"

Sadie nodded solemnly, knowing without a doubt as to what she had heard. Nathan's cry was nearly exact to how she had heard him before in her dreams. While this was the first time that she had heard him while awake, she couldn't help but wonder why. Was her desire to see her son so strong that she heard him when he wasn't there? No, that couldn't be true. He sounded far too real to have been her imagination. Had she finally lost her sanity? She shivered at the thought.

Sadie felt Fester move forward in his seat as he removed his arm from her shoulders. "Hey, Sal. Where are we goin anyway?"

"There's a compound about 100 miles from here that is run by the Supernatural Underground Movement that I lead. I wasn't planning on making it a base of operations, but it'll have to do for now."

"Ain't the government gonna fucking be findin them shits same?" Michael asked.

"No. It's well hidden, Mickey. Plus, we've taken every precaution to keep it from being found."

"Yeah, bullshit. Ya done got all full o' words on how we ain't gonna be found at ya joint neither!"

The compound is more secure than my home. One of the people there has the ability to make any place he doesn't want found so well concealed that even a Tracker couldn't find it."

"Then, how are we going to get there?"

"You can find it if you've been there before, Fester."

Sadie wondered why they weren't taken to this compound sooner. It sounded like it was the perfect place for them to 'lay low' while Sal had her war. Deciding she'd had enough of being afraid and silent, Sadie told Sal what she had been thinking.

"The compound wasn't originally designed to house people other than those who work for the movement," Sal said, "It seems that until we can take care of the traitor we'll need someplace where he can't track us.

The compound is the only place on Earth that I know of with such security. So, that's where we're headed."

"How many people know about it?" Fester asked.

"A few. Your parents visited there more than once, Mickey. I received word yesterday that some families have been brought there recently. Mostly it's people who are too old or too young to fight and are in danger because of PSI. I didn't authorize it and was tempted to boot them. But, so long as they don't get in the way, then I guess I'll let them stay."

"Ya gotta be one cold assed bitch, Sal," Michael said.

"Yeah, well, maybe that's why you hate me so much, Mickey dear," Sal said as she let out her familiar unpleasant laugh.

Fester leaned back in his seat and put his arm around Sadie again. She leaned into him and a shiver went down her spine. It had nothing to do with the cold and everything to do with the thought that this woman held their very lives in her grasp. Sal made light of everything that had happened, as though she enjoyed their situation. At any moment she could easily turn on them and hand them over to the government...or worse.

Sadie knew that wouldn't happen, of course. Sal had made it very clear that it was because of their plight that she was able to rally the other Supernaturals and get them to fight. With so much at stake, there was no way she would hurt them now. It seemed to Sadie that they were safe until Sal no longer needed them. People were fighting now; the war had started. Would her army turn on her if she hurt them? She wanted Fester's brain for something, but what of the rest of them?

Tears threatened to spill from her eyes and she shut them tight. Sadie was not going to give Sal the satisfaction of seeing her cry. *'To be weak is to be a failure,'* her father used to always say. *'To show weakness is to admit that you are less.'* Sadie was never good at appearing to be strong. Her weakness always showed and her father continuously punished her for that flaw. *'When you are strong you can have anything you want, just like I have you.'*

Sadie leaned into Fester and held onto him. Now was not a good time for her to start recalling the lessons her father had taught her. Neither of her parents were here. They couldn't touch her anymore. The past was in the past and she desperately wanted it to stay that way. The last time her memories came to the surface, she destroyed Michael's apartment. She wasn't sure what would happen if her wind were unleashed in a space as small as the van.

The van swerved and Sadie nearly fell off of her seat. Forcing her mind away from her father, she tried to focus on what was happening around her. She didn't know how long it would take to get to this compound place and she hoped it would be quick. The van swerved again and she grabbed onto Fester's arm. Whoever was controlling the van seemed to be having trouble keeping it straight.

There was another swerve and this time Sadie and Fester both fell out of their seats. "The fuck, man!" Michael called out.

"Sorry," said a man's voice from the front. "Just trying to avoid debris left from some of the fighting."

Michael swore. "Get ta seein, Sal, what ya war gone an done."

"Please, Mickey. I've seen what wars can do to places. This is nothing."

Michael swore again and Sadie Chloe whimpered. She wanted to ask if the girl was alright but felt she knew the answer. Chloe was able to see the destruction while Sadie was blind to it. But, she wasn't blind to the knowledge that the Empath also received the emotions of the others while they looked upon the same scene.

Hopefully this would all be over soon, though she knew that was unlikely. There was no way for her to know how long a war usually lasted. *'Conflict, even one such as this, tends to be very profitable.'* Sal was probably going to make sure it continued for as long as possible.

Again she heard a baby cry. The sound came out of nowhere and caused the hair on the back of Sadie's neck to stand on end. Snuggled against Fester, her body went stiff. She knew beyond any doubt that there was no baby in the van with them. It was impossible for her to hear her son. Yet hear him she did.

Was she going mad? Did her mind finally break? Or perhaps she was actually dreaming...

"Fester?"

"Yeah, what's up?"

"I'm not dreaming, am I?" she asked

Michael let out a short laugh and Fester said, "'Course not. Why would you think that?"

"It's nothing," she said, suddenly embarrassed.

The others had obviously not heard Nathan. If they had, then one of them would've said something by now. She wasn't dreaming, and she was ashamed to have asked. If she was losing her mind, then she really didn't want the others to know. She couldn't leave this time to spare them the agony of witnessing her descent into insanity. If they were still Downtown, perhaps she could have tried harder to leave and find a way to survive. If she were stronger then maybe she would've been alright. If she were stronger, then Fester wouldn't have had to help her, and this war would not be happening.

Sadie refused to let herself cry at her predicament. She instead listened to her son cry for her. Nathan sounded so lonely and sad. It was as though he cried for his mother who was so far away. Her heart ached and she yearned to hold him in her arms. Fester and Michael were right, her parents couldn't keep him. Now that she knew happiness could exist, even if only for short and fleeting moments, she also knew that her son didn't have to suffer the same fate as she. Even if she wasn't strong and couldn't take care of him without help, he would still be better with her than with them.

Sadie knew she needed to find a way to become strong in the same way Sal was strong. It was the only way to save her son and her own life.

Chapter 33

Sadie's eyelids were heavy and her body fatigued by the time they neared the compound. For the duration of the ride, her head had rested on Fester's arm and she pretended to sleep. Thankfully Nathan hadn't cried for long. It was torture to hear him and not be able to comfort him. Since no one else could hear the desperate cries of her son, there was nothing that she could possibly do. She was as helpless as her baby.

When she heard Sal say that they were close she sat up. Her neck hurt from leaning in the same position, though she didn't complain. Instead, she silently allowed her body to sway with the movement of the vehicle. The road here was rougher than earlier, and the tires sounded different as they moved over the uneven ground.

"Hey, look at that. The sun's coming up." Fester sounded as though he had just awoken.

"Oooh! It so pretty!" It felt good to hear Chloe sound happy.

"Ya ain't never gonna see shit same way in them fucking city," Michael said. "Crazy uber smog."

Not able to see what they saw, Sadie ignored them. The sun's rising meant only that it was dawn. For Sadie, unless she was paying attention to where the warmth of the sun touched her body, then it didn't matter. Nothing more and nothing less was to be gained. Why everyone seemed so intent on watching the phenomenon eluded her. She knew they saw something that she couldn't, even with the air. As a result, it held little interest.

"Ah, Sadie," Fester said sadly.

"What?"

"I just...I wish you could see this."

"Oh."

That was the second time that Fester mentioned wanting her to be able to see. Did her blindness make him sad? She couldn't fathom why it would. Being blind didn't make her sad, so why should it affect anyone else? Why did Fester have to be so strange?

"Y' know," he said, "when the Healer came to help us, I asked him if he could cure your blindness too."

Sadie didn't know what to say to such a statement.

"Why ain't he done them shits?" Michael asked.

"He couldn't. He said her eyes weren't damaged. The problem is that there's a nerve missing that connects her eyes to her brain. He didn't know what it was called but I was able to figure out what he meant. I've never read about that happening, but I guess anything is possible."

"What's wrong with being blind?" she asked.

Fester sighed again. "Nothing. I just wish you could see things like this."

"If it doesn't bother me, Fester, then it shouldn't bother you."

Fester didn't reply and Michael let out a short laugh. "Chick got a point, bro."

For a moment no one spoke. Sadie wanted to drop the issue but something kept on nagging at her. She leaned away from Fester and turned to face his direction. "Is my being blind the reason why you're always trying to help me? Do you think I can't do things right because of it?"

"No, Sadie," Fester said softly, "I've told you already, I want to help you because I love you. Is that so bad?"

"I don't know," she said honestly and turned so she was sitting properly.

Fester's arm slid around her shoulders and he rested his head on top of her own. Sadie didn't know what to do or say at first. He said that he wanted to help her because he loved her. Yet, if that were true, then it wouldn't feel as though he thought she couldn't do things on her own. Now he seemed to think that her being blind was a bad thing because she couldn't see the sun. She desperately wanted her blindness to never be another point of discussion with him. She needed to get him to stop.

"You know, Fester, I can't see the sun or whatever it is you're finding so pretty," Sadie said, "But, I can experience beauty. I can smell things, touch them, and hear sounds...all of which can be beautiful too."

"Sadie, I didn't mean—"

"Yes, Fester, you did. You said once that I should use my power to see so that I wasn't blind all the time. You seemed surprised when I could do something as simple as chores. I know there are some ways that I need help, but I don't need help because I'm blind. When I actually need help it's because I don't understand the world yet. I like doing things by myself. I just...I just wasn't taught everything I needed to know. My parents' lessons...they didn't teach me everything."

"I get that. I'm sorry."

"Being blind doesn't make me helpless. It's not bad."

"I get that same. Again, that's not what I meant. I'm sorry."

Accepting the genuine sound to Fester's apology, Sadie once again fell silent. She didn't want to think on it anymore. Part of her felt proud for standing up to Fester and letting him know what she thought. It was a small part and a small victory. She wasn't blind to the fact that not being able to see did put her at a disadvantage. It didn't mean that she couldn't do things for herself; it only made it more difficult to know what was happening around her in some ways. That wasn't such a bad thing. Right?

It wasn't much longer before the van stopped. Michael let out a harsh laugh. "Sal, the fuck them shits ya got goin on up here? There ain't nothin here but fucking nature shit."

"I told you it was well hidden. Hold on boys and girls," Sal said with more than a hint of amusement in her voice.

"You sure about this, Boss?" asked the man who had been driving.

"Trust me, it's there. See those trees over there?... No, the ones that look half dead...Yeah, those. Head straight for them."

"I ain't fucking likin them shits." Michael's voice shook with fear and that worried Sadie.

The van lurched forward and then moved about violently as they drove off the road. Sadie was terrified and held onto Fester as tightly as possible. Chloe let out some uneasy whimpers and Michael spoke to her softly. Beneath her fingers, Sadie felt Fester stiffen. He was scared too, though he didn't make a sound.

"Uh...Boss?" The man driving sounded as though he wasn't sure of Sal's plan.

"Trust me, Jordan. The entrance is where those trees are."

Sadie wondered at why Sal sounded annoyed at Jordan. From what she had said, they were headed towards trees. Sal had told them all before that no one could find the compound if they didn't know where they were going. Even if this Jordan person trusted her, Sal couldn't possibly expect someone to head straight for something solid like a tree, and not feel nervous. Then again, she couldn't understand how this was all supposed to work anyway.

Suddenly Chloe began to cry wildly while both Fester and Michael swore repeatedly as the van sped up. The combination caused Sadie's heart to race and she broke out into a cold sweat. She clutched Fester's arm as tightly as she could and held her breath. It was obvious from everyone's reactions that they were almost at the trees. It didn't matter if the driver trusted Sal. Sadie didn't trust her, and after hearing everyone's reactions that lack of trust helped to fuel her own terror.

Fester grabbed Sadie and wrapped his arms tightly around her. His body trembled and he too held his breath. Not a second later and Chloe began to scream. Sadie's blindness was probably a blessing at this point since she couldn't see what had terrified everyone else. Her imagination let her guess instead.

There was a vicious shake that nearly knocked her out of her seat, and then the van began to ride smoothly. Everyone except Sadie let out a collective sigh of relief. While she could tell that they were now safe, not knowing more than that allowed her fear to continue its hold on her mind and body. Fester's arms relaxed around her but her own muscles were still tense.

"It's OK, Sadie. We're clear," he said.

"Where are we now?"

"I'm not sure. It's some kind of tunnel."

"The compound is subterranean," Sal said from the front. "This is one of three tunnels that lead into it."

"So, the Supernatural underground is literally *underground?*" Fester shifted his weight and chuckled

"Fester..." Sal sounded annoyed again. "Don't try and be cute. You're not very good at it."

"I thought it was funny," he said sullenly.

They had made it and were safe. Once more Sadie was in a place with which she had no familiarity. There was no way for her to know what to expect in a complex that was under the ground. The idea sounded insane. Apparently she was the only one who thought it was odd, especially considering Fester had tried to make some sort of joke about their situation. All Sadie knew for sure was that they weren't in danger of PSI for now. That is, of course, assuming Sal had told them the truth about the tracker not being able to find them here.

As her fear slowly melted away, she leaned in against Fester and closed her eyes. Chloe still cried, though her sobs were softer now. Sadie felt her heart go out to the girl. It was only a moment ago that everyone, except for Sal, was terrified. Now they were all relieved, but some residual fear was bound to be left over. Someone like Chloe would most likely feel that as well. It couldn't be easy. Would the child ever know peace?

Now that they had made it to the compound, and were safe, Sadie wanted nothing more than to sleep. She was also insanely hungry. The combination caused her to decide that as soon as she could, she was going to have a meal and then go to bed. It didn't matter to her that the sun had already risen. She felt that if they were underground, then the sun would have no bearing on their lives anyway. Even if the others felt differently, she was still going to sleep for as long and hard as she could.

Without knowing how far the tunnel would be, Sadie leaned her head against Fester's chest and sighed.

She doubted there would be enough time for her to have a nap at this point, but at the very least she could relax. It had been an exhausting end to an exhausting journey.

She didn't want to even think about what could happen next.

Chapter 34

"Sadie, wake up. We're here."

Fester gently nudged her awake. Sadie hadn't realized that she'd fallen asleep. Reaching up as high as she could with her hands, she stretched and felt her back pop. A sigh of contentment came from her lips. While her nap may have only lasted a few minutes, she felt as though she'd had nearly a full night's rest.

Sadie listened as everyone left the van and then carefully followed suit. Surprisingly, the air outside of the vehicle was pleasant. Thankful that she didn't need to worry about a coat after all, Sadie allowed herself to smile. It seemed odd, but she felt a general sense of well-being that she couldn't quite place. It wasn't a state she was accustomed to.

In an attempt to understand her surroundings, Sadie listened to the sounds they all made as they walked. There was a slight echo to their footsteps but it was light enough that she didn't think they were in a large room. With Fester guiding her, and the empty feel the sounds gave the room they walked through, she wasn't worried about not having her cane.

"Fester…Michael," Sal said as they walked, "you're both tall so watch your heads. There are some pipes running along these corridors and I don't think you want to bump into them. The main part of the complex has higher ceilings."

"Yeah…sure…whatever." Michael said.

Fester remained silent and Sadie desperately wanted to know what he thought. After their conversation in the van, she didn't want to ask him to tell her what he saw even though she was curious. From the way things had sounded, they might be at this place for a while. That would give her plenty of time to explore and get to know her new environment. Perhaps since she was surrounded by Supernaturals now, she might be able to use the air to see, and not have to worry about her cane anymore.

Sadie jumped and covered her ears when she heard a loud metallic screech. Having highly sensitive ears caused her near unbearable pain from the prolonged sound. It was difficult not to collapse from relief when it stopped. Even though her ears didn't hurt anymore, she still felt shaky as they continued to walk.

"What was that?" she asked.

"Just a really big and heavy door," Fester said.

He sounded distracted so she didn't ask anything else. Everyone was silent, even Chloe. While she was more curious than before about their surroundings, she felt that there was probably a reason why everyone was quiet. Perhaps it was like the library where you were expected not to talk. She sighed when she realized that this place most likely had more rules to it than even her parents' home. Especially since Sal called this her *'new base of operations'*.

Sadie realized then that she wasn't entirely sure what a war was. It was obvious that it involved fighting, and people could get hurt or die. The others made it sound like roads and perhaps buildings were damaged as a result as well. They weren't the only ones displaced from their homes. Other than that, however, she was clueless. Sal had said that Michael and Chloe's parents worked for *'an underground movement that has been secretly fighting for our rights as Supernaturals.'* How fighting and death would help the Supernaturals gain rights was beyond her. Not only that, it brought the realization that she truly didn't want to know anything more about war. Perhaps some things about the world could remain a mystery a little while longer.

There was a sound of another door as it was opened. Thankfully this one sounded like an ordinary door and didn't hurt her ears. If the one from earlier was the only one that made such a sound then she would be delighted. Her ears seemed more bothered by such sounds than the others, and she hoped that there would be no more. After they walked through the door, Fester stopped and she felt him shift as he closed it behind them. Apparently they were the last in line.

It wasn't long until another pair of footsteps could be heard. These had a sort of shuffle and were accompanied by a metallic click on the ground. Sadie wondered at the sound while Sal greeted the new person.

"Kronos," she said in the same friendly tone she had originally used with Sadie, "it's so good to see you again."

"Salvina," a gruff voice said joyfully, "you grow more radiant every day. They told me you were coming in this mornin with some refugees."

"Sorry to get you out of bed so early."

Kronos laughed. "Eh, these old bones can still get up with the sun, young lady. Now, let's see here, are these young people who I think they are?"

"Yes, actually they are. May I introduce Michael and Chloe Coldman. Behind them are Fester and Sadie, both of whom Michael takes care of."

The man chuckled. "Ah yes. Young man, you are the spitting image of your father."

"Ya done been knowin my pops?" Michael's voice still held a wary tone.

"Sure did. Knew your mother too. Jack and Maria were some of the best people the movement ever had on its side. But, you don't want to hear an old man go on about what's past. You all look so exhausted. Let's get you settled in. There's plenty of time to chat later. Salvina, will you and your Boy be staying as well?"

"No, we actually have to leave soon. There are some unrelated matters I need to attend to first. I just wanted to get these people someplace safe."

Michael snorted. Sadie wondered if Sal's friendly tone worked with this Kronos man. When she had first met the woman, she nearly believed that she was a good person by her tone. It was because of how Fester reacted to Sal, and the things which Michael had said later on, that allowed Sadie to know for sure that she wasn't a good person at all. Kronos, however, seemed to respect the criminal. Perhaps he didn't know about the bad things she was capable of doing. Then again, he could also be a criminal as well. The thought of being handed from one bad person to another made Sadie uneasy.

"Yep, young lady, you did the right thing. Your father would've been so proud of you. Well," he grunted, "let's see what we can do for you kids. Do you have much to bring in?"

Michael sighed. "All our shit done been lefted 'hind, Mr. Kronos. In the one-two, we ain't got nothin we ain't wearin."

"It's a damn shame. We'll figure something out for y'all. C'mon, I'll show you around."

Michael and Fester both thanked the man and they all began to move forward. Sal and Jordan didn't sound as though they were following. At first Sadie hesitated. The calm which she felt earlier had been replaced with a great unease. There was a moment where she considered trying to find her way back up the tunnel and out of the compound. Before she could think more on it Fester grabbed her elbow and urged her to come with them.

It wasn't long before she turned and grabbed Fester's arm instead, preferring to hold onto him rather than be led by the elbow. Her heart beat more and more wildly as they entered what sounded like a very small room. Everyone stood close to one another. There was a brief sound of a bell and then the sound of gears grinding softly.

Even though the floor stayed beneath her feet, Sadie felt as though she were falling. Her stomach lurched within her body and she tried not to panic. Having never experienced this before, she grabbed onto Fester as tight as her small hands would allow. A scream was stuck in her throat, and she refused to allow it to move passed her lips. It became increasingly difficult to hold it back.

"Michael?" Chloe sounded upset. "Why Sadie so 'fraid?"

As Michael spoke softly to Chloe, Fester leaned in to whisper in Sadie's ear. "Hey, what's wrong?"

"It feels like we're falling!"

Fester pulled her into his arms and held her. "It's

just the elevator taking us down. Don't sweat it, we're clear an riskless."

Kronos whispered, "That girl ain't quite right, is she?"

Michael whispered, "Sadie just been...ah... sheltered. She ain't really got no clue the fuck goin on 'round her in the one-two."

Sadie buried her face into Fester's chest and fought the tears that threatened to pour from her eyes. Even Kronos could tell that there was something wrong with her. *'That girl ain't quite right.'* Such words rang true as they stung her ears. *'She ain't really got no clue the fuck goin on 'round her.'* Memories of other things Michael had once said flooded her mind. *'The girl ya got in there ain't keepin here.' 'I ain't believin, she true gettin all fucking not sure by them words.' 'She gotta get her a shit ton o' serious fucking help.' 'The girl there done got morer damage than any 'nother.' 'Chloe gettin heavy curious 'bout ya...Ya gotta be fucking mindful what ya sayin ta her... I ain't letin her get ta fucking picturin ya past yet.' 'Ya ain't seein what we be seein whens we got eyes on ya.' 'I ain't got no clue she been heavy bad.' 'Half the one-two what been spillin out ya trap gotta be fucking uber mad crazy bullshit!' ' I ain't able ta picture how she survivin so's fucking long surer in hell.' 'Them girl been 'bout ta fall o'er the fucking edge as is.' 'Ya got morer riskful fucking danger in ya than good.'*

Sadie felt as though she were becoming consumed by the memories of how often she showed her inability to understand the world. Michael had been right each of those times. Her parents damaged her; she was broken and wrong. There was no place for her in the world, and she knew deep down that no matter what Fester said, she would never be right either. She had known this, but to hear a stranger and Michael talk about it freely – such validation of her fears was harder to accept than she would've thought.

Tears escaped from her tightly shut eyelids. As the elevator took them deeper underground she felt her ears begin to pop. The sensation was painful and she grabbed the sides of her head. Unable to handle anymore, she couldn't help but cry. The entire elevator ride took only a minute, but for Sadie it had been an eternity. She was grateful when it was over.

With one arm still around her shoulders, Fester steered her away from the falling room as soon as it stopped moving. Sadie kept her hands over her ears and allowed herself to be maneuvered. Her hearing after her ears popped was more sensitive than ever before. The increased volume of everything around her was unsettling and caused her to feel slightly disoriented.

When Fester asked her if she was alright she nodded her head slowly. Although she had stopped crying, some tears still ran down her face. Perhaps this would always happen when she entered that falling elevator room. Hopefully she wouldn't have to use it again until they were ready to leave this place forever. The others didn't seem bothered by it and so she didn't mention her discomforts. There was no need to show to this Kronos man how much more wrongness she had within her. Eventually she relaxed and was able to remove her hands from her head. Gratefully she returned to holding onto Fester's arm.

The sounds of the corridor they walked through were odd. She heard people walk passed them as they talked about one project or another. That wasn't so strange, but there were several other noises that she couldn't place the cause of. She heard water dripping and some sort of machinery moved on the other side of the wall to their right. Occasionally she felt a slight burst of air as they passed some sort of vent. The air left a metallic taste in her mouth and the smells were indescribable. It was terribly disorienting and confusing. For a while it seemed as though this place would be far harder to get used to than the streets were a few months prior. What sort of place was an underground compound anyway? This seemed to do more than 'house people'.

Soon they stopped and Sadie heard the sounds of keys jingling. They were all ushered inside a room shortly after the door was opened for them. From the feel and sound of the ground, it appeared that the room was carpeted. It was also quieter and the air wasn't as metallic and damp. From somewhere nearby she heard a clicking sound that reminded her of the computer Fester used at the library.

"Diana, these young people were just brought in. They're going to be staying with the other refugees for a while," Kronos said and the typing stopped. He then introduced them all.

The woman – Diana – sighed heavily. "You poor kids," she said softly, "let's get you four settled. OK?"

"Diana will take you all from here. I have some... uh...work to do."

Kronos's footsteps, and the strange click that accompanied them, retreated the way they had come. More delicate footsteps were heard on the carpet in the quiet room as Diana came to stand before them.

"You know, dear, you look awfully familiar. Have we met?" the new woman asked.

For a moment no one replied until Fester leaned over and said, "She's talking to you, Sadie."

"Me?" Why would she think they had met? "No, I don't know you."

"What's the matter? Why won't she look at me?"

"Um..." Michael said, "Sadie done been blind, Ma'am. She ain't never gonna be able ta lookin at ya."

"Oh! OK...right...um...well let's...um...let's get you all to your rooms."

The woman sounded flustered and Sadie wasn't sure why. Did she feel wrong for asking Sadie to look at her when she was blind? It dawned on her that some people in the world were probably wrong like she was, only in their own way. Perhaps this Diana person was wrong, too. The idea that Sadie wasn't alone in that aspect was welcoming.

As they walked, Diana pointed out various areas that they all should know. She showed them where they could go to eat, watch TV, the computers and other common areas, and where the rooms and bathrooms were. Sadie tried to map out the spaces in her head but found it too complex and difficult to memorize. It would take at least a few days before she knew the area well enough not to need to ask for directions. It wasn't long before she began to miss her cane and the grid like pattern of the city streets.

"We don't have single rooms here," Diana said as they walked down a residential hallway, "so we'll have to figure out where to put you all. Most of our rooms hold two to four beds. Some hold more but we reserve those for single adults or larger families. Should we have the girls in one room and you boys in another?"

Sadie didn't like the idea of sleeping without Fester. With only Chloe in the room, there would be no way to stop herself from giving the child nightmares. At least with Fester there she would feel safe enough to sleep and also know that she wouldn't hurt the delicate Empath. Thankfully Chloe felt similarly.

"No!" Chloe yelled. "Please, Michael! I gonna stick with ya! Please? I gonna stick with ya an Sadie an Fester gonna stick ta one 'nother same! Please?"

"Yeah," he said. "Get ta lookin, Ma'am. I gotta clue how it ain't usual protocol or some shits, but my sis sayin it true. We four gonna get ta stickin with one 'nother, or we gonna do same she sayin. Get trustin, it gonna be fucking bester them ways."

"Well," she said with a small chuckle, "we don't mind family staying together so you and your sister could definitely share a room. But these two teens are obviously not related. We can't let them stay together. It wouldn't be right. Perhaps we can have them both stay with others in the same hallway."

Sadie stiffened. She didn't need to see to know that the woman was talking about her and Fester. The idea that she would be forced to stay with a stranger instead of her friends was terrifying. Fearfully, she held onto Fester's arm. There was no way she would allow these people to take him from her. He was the only one here with whom she felt safe!

"Yeah, get ta lookin good," Michael said, "ya ain't gotta sweat no shits ya got picturin in ya head 'bout them two. Them been true good fucking kids. All us four got now be one 'nother. Get it?"

"Y-yes but–"

"No buts. Them kids been under my care an I gonna be makin all fucking choices for 'em. In the one-two, that meanin no fucking takin us 'part. I ain't gonna care one bit how the damn rules tellin 'bout them shits."

"Fine," She said as though she were speaking through clenched teeth. "Since you're their guardian then we can put you all in a room with four beds. I'm not giving a teenage couple their own private room."

"Them shits been all I askin."

"There's one more thing, Mr. Coldman. I don't care if your parents were heroes. You will clean up that Gutter mouth of yours and not overstep yourself."

"Yeah...sure."

Sadie felt nervous with the exchange and was glad when they began to walk once more. There were rules here that didn't allow Fester and her to sleep in the same room. Now, Michael was forcing Diana to allow them to break that rule. She hoped that Diana or Kronos or anyone else wasn't going to try to hurt them because of this. If someone down here tried to hurt her or her friends, then Sadie would fight them with all the wind she could possibly call.

Michael had said they only had each other. It was her fault that her friends now had nothing. She wasn't about to let them be hurt because of her as well. A plan was needed.

Chapter 35

When they were finally given a room, Diana said she would try and see if someone could get them all a change of clothing. The woman had to guess Sadie's size since she didn't know. Diana didn't seem surprised with Sadie's lack of knowledge about such things, and that helped her to relax. Perhaps this woman knew that Sadie was wrong, and was so helpful because she was wrong, too. In a strange way, it made a lot of sense. Thinking about the existence of others who might also be wrong continued to be a small comfort.

When the door to their room closed Fester asked, "Are you going to get mad at me if I make up one of the beds up for you?"

Sadie shook her head. She didn't know where the beds or the bedding were. It only made sense that Fester did it for now. After everything that had happened, there was no way to calculate what sort of debt she had with him up to this point. Perhaps his powerful brain could figure it out, but he most likely would refuse to try. Fester was very strange in that way.

While the men made the beds, Sadie felt around the room. With so much newness to her environment, the very least she could do was understand one room in this place. With her feet and hands to guide her, she felt the dressers, door, closet, and beds. Due to the compact nature of the room, she was able to map it in her mind with ease. There was one thing about it that bothered her however.

"Why are the beds so strange?" she asked

"Them bunk beds," Chloe said joyfully. "I done been wantin one!"

"Yeah, ya gonna get ta takin an under bunk, Sadie," Michael said. "It gonna get easy for ya fucking climbin in an out."

"OK."

She couldn't imagine climbing in and out of the top

portion, so she was more than happy to use the bottom
one. Gingerly she sat on one of the beds, careful not
to bump her head. The mattress felt stiff and wasn't
very comfortable. She didn't mind, however, when she
considered that at one point she had slept on cement.
After that, any sort of mattress was welcome.

"OK, get ta listenin, kids," Michael said once the
beds were made. "I ain't fucking likin it up in them joint,
surer in hell. I ain't crazy 'bout them fuckers gettin
works from Sal, an sure as hell I ain't gonna trust a
single one o' them."

"Do you think we're in any riskful danger?" Fester
asked as he sat down next to Sadie.

"True be, I ain't got no clue, man. I picture if we
gonna get ta keepin us own noses clean an shiny, then
we gonna be fucking clear."

Sadie gingerly touched her nose. "How will that
help?"

Michael swore. "It done been a fucking sayin,
Sadie. Damn!"

"Lay the fuck off, Michael!" Fester said before
addressing Sadie, "It just means we need to keep out
of trouble."

"Oh."

"Yeah, well, I done gettin all kind o' serious with the
lady back there. We four be all us got lefts an we be
family. Ya three gotta get ta lookin out for one 'nother
backs. Fester, I gonna be needin ya helpin keepin the
girls clear up in here, man."

"No need ta sweat it. I won't let no one get to Chloe
or Sadie. You get that."

"Yeah."

The men had sounded sullen while they spoke.
Again Sadie felt a twinge of guilt, knowing that it was
her mistake that led to their current situation. Having
both of them there to protect Chloe and herself was
comforting, however. Fester was highly intelligent and
Michael had an amazing offensive power. Sadie knew
her own wind would help as well. They could be safe
here. Still, the others most likely missed their home
and were sad that they lost their possessions as well.

She wished she knew how to comfort them.

Instead she asked, "Michael, do you think it…would it be OK for me to use my power here?"

"The fuck for?"

"So I can see," Sadie said meekly.

Michael swore. "True. I ain't fucking rememberin ya gotta power ta be doin them shits. Truthful, I ain't got no clue. I be picturin every 'nother fucker down here been Supernatural same as we four. I gonna ask. I ain't sayin it ain't gonna be no problem, but I gonna ask."

"Thank you," she said.

It was understandable why Michael was so nervous. She didn't want to ask about using the air to see with either. The problem was that she could tell this place was huge. If she had her cane then it wouldn't be as much of a problem. The object consistently kept her from bumping into things, and let her know where the walls were. Without it she would have to always rely on others to help her to avoid objects, even after she got her bearings. Being able to use air instead just seemed like a simpler solution.

In the silence someone yawned.

"Get ta listenin, kids. We four gotta get us selves some sleeps. I ain't got no damn clue when breakfast fucking happenin 'round here, but we gonna get ta findin some shit laters if we missin it."

"I saw a sign by the cafeteria. It said breakfast is at 8," Fester said.

"K so's them shits gettin us an hour. Damn wishin it been more like four. C'mon Chloe, ya gotta fucking get sleepin more than rest us here."

Chloe let out a squeal in protest. "I ain't sleepin!"

Michael sighed. "We done been o'er them shits, Chloe."

"No."

Michael swore softly and Fester moved from Sadie's side. "Still gettin bad dreams?" he asked.

Sadie didn't hear Chloe say anything before Fester continued to talk. Both of the men spoke to the child softly, encouraging her to try to sleep. Sadie tuned them out and lay down on the bed. Chloe had become afraid of her nightmares. She wondered if she had given her so many of them that now the girl wouldn't sleep. The thought was highly unsettling.

Both of the men had so much to worry about. This place was probably just as unnerving for them as it was for her. They were both responsible for Chloe and needed to take care of her. Because of her own issues, they now had to take care of Sadie was well. She wished that she hadn't become such a hindrance on the family.

Family. Michael had told Diana, *'Them kids been under my care, an I gonna be makin all fucking choices for 'em.'* and when the woman was gone he said, *'We four be all us got lefts an we be family.'* The night before, when they were at Sal's home, he had told Sadie, *'Hell, even I likin ya...get ta lettin thems who got ta carin 'bout ya ables ta fucking helpin ya ass!'*

Family. Sadie was a part of their family. The thought weighed heavily in her mind. She rolled over so her back was to the others. All this time she had seen herself as an outsider who had destroyed a family with her own ineptitude. It never occurred to her that they would want her to be one of them. Fester loved her, she knew this. But, other than knowing how it made her feel, and the things he had said, she was still learning about love. Chloe liked her, which was obvious. Michael liked her, which was surprising. Now...

We're all family.

All this time and such a thing had never crossed her mind. She was trouble. She was dangerous. She destroyed their home and ruined their lives. She made everything crazy in their world. All this time she had never thought that they would be alright with her being around much longer. She was constantly debating about when she should leave. She even tried a few times! All this time they wanted her to stay.

Family.

Tears spilled out of her eyes and rolled down the side of her face to wet her hair. She didn't deserve these people. If they were to have someone new join their family, then it shouldn't be the one who made so much trouble for them. Why would they want her? What was wrong with them that they should want her? She needed to find a way to be worthy of their affection.

As it was, right now she wasn't much help. She didn't know what use she could be here. In a home she knew what to do. It was her fault that they didn't have a home to go to anymore. Chloe was afraid to sleep because of the nightmares she had given her. Both of the men were stressed because of the situation she put them in. How could she find a way to be worthy when everything she had done served to confirm her lack of worth?

More tears fell to the pillow. So lost had she been in her own thoughts that she was startled when the mattress moved from someone sitting on it. She hadn't realized that the men had stopped talking to Chloe, who was crying.

"Sadie? What's wrong?" Fester asked.

When she didn't respond Michael swore. "Get ta listenin, girl, an listenin good. Ya gotta get ta calmin ya mind. I gettin them shits done got heavy mad assed crazy, an we gonna be stressin, sleepy, an 'fraid ta hell an back. I ain't gonna blame ya for them tears. Hell, I wanna get ta cryin 'bout now, same as ya been doin. But them shits ain't gonna help nobody in the one-two."

"I'm sorry, Michael," Sadie said. She rolled over so she could turn her face towards him. "I'll try not to cry. I'll be good."

She flinched when a small hand touched her cheek unexpectedly. She hadn't heard Chloe cross the small space. "Ya 'fraid from them nightmares same, Sadie?" the child asked.

Sadie smiled weakly at the girl's small voice. "Chloe, I've had nightmares all my life. I'm more scared of everything else."

"Why?"

Michael spoke before Sadie could respond. "No need ta sweat 'bout them shits now, Chloe. It fucking near ta fucking 8 am. We gonna get eatin."

"I'm not hungry," Sadie lied. She didn't want to

leave the room.

"Bullshit! Ya ain't takin one bite 'fore fucking shit went ta hell. Get ya bony ass outta bed! Ya gonna get fucking eatin same as us! No more fucking words 'bout them shits!"

Michael's voice rang about the room, and his anger ran through Sadie's core like lightning. Immediately she sat up. Her body trembled and she desperately fought her tears. Forgetting about Chloe's empathy, her fear rose up through her body like wildfire. Michael sounded like he was on the verge of losing his temper. He said he liked her, but Sadie couldn't trust him not to hurt her. His anger sounded far too much like her mother's when the pain was the most severe. At those times the lessons could last for hours. To avoid any added torment, she had learned to be as obedient as possible and not fight back.

Without any warning, Sadie felt as though she were home again. Logically she knew where she was. But, the sound of Michael's tone, coupled with the memory of her mother, caused Sadie to react in a way she hadn't for months.

Silently and with grace, she slid off of the bed and onto the floor. Her hands rested peacefully in her lap and her eyes were gently closed. Without a word she lowered her head and then went still. It was a position she had assumed at least once a day for her mother for as long as she could remember. She was ready for the lesson that was to follow.

Chloe screamed and Sadie knew it was in reaction to her own terror. If she couldn't find a way to calm herself, then the lesson would be far worse. In an effort to keep Michael pleased, she fought her fear. Swallowing hard, she forced the familiar heat down into the pit of her stomach. She took in a deep breath and forced herself to be numb.

Fully aware of the commotion that swirled around her, Sadie didn't move or flinch. Within her was a calm that contrasted harshly with Chloe's panicked screams.

"There nothin, Michael! There nothin there! What got wrong with Sadie? Why nothin there? Michael!"

Michael tried in vain to calm Chloe down. Finally he yelled, "Fester, God fucking dammit, get on a thing!"

Both Michael and Chloe sounded as though they were on the other side of the room, near the door. Fester's voice, however, came from right in front of her. "I ain't got no clue what ta do!" Gently his hand touched her shoulder. She gave him no reaction. Flinching usually made the lessons worse. "Sadie? Sadie, what's going on? What are you doing?"

Sadie could hardly hear her own monotone voice over Chloe's cries. "I'm waiting for my lesson." She couldn't understand how he didn't know that. Fester was so strange.

"Sadie...what...oh no! Dear God! No, Sadie, no! There's no lesson." Gently she was pulled into his arms. Chloe began to quiet down. "Sadie, there will never be another lesson. Please believe me. No one is going to hurt you. I wish I had a clue how to get you to understand that." He kissed the top of her head and held her to his chest.

"Fester, man, the fuck she sayin?"

Sadie felt Fester's body turn towards Michael. "She's talkin 'bout what her 'rents used to do to her. I picturin ya yellin triggered a thing. I ain't got no clue what to do, Michael! I'm fucking 'fraid, man..." His voice cracked with the last sentence and his breathing became uneven.

There were a few heavy footsteps and the rustling of clothes before Michael's voice came from somewhere near her face. She could smell his breath. His teeth needed to be brushed. "Sadie, dear fucking God, ya gotta fucking get ta picturin in ya mind, girl: I ain't never gonna pound on ya same as them 'rents done. Shit just ain't fucking in me, hurtin a chick. Shit, girl! Ya gotta get a clue in here, we ain't never gonna get ta hurtin ya. Ya fucking gotta!"

Sadie didn't speak for a moment. She knew she should say something. "I know," she finally said and swallowed hard. "Michael, I know you don't want to hurt me. I know you and Fester think the lessons were wrong. I don't know why I keep on feeling like you're going to give me one. I'm always so scared!" She wrapped her arms around Fester as her feelings returned and she began to weep. "Everything I've experienced my whole life has told me that everyone was cruel and everyone would hurt me. You all are the only ones who don't seem bad and cruel and selfish. You don't do lessons, and you talk about love and family. I guess...I guess it's hard to believe that you're true."

"So used to the abuse that you expect it everywhere," Fester whispered hoarsely and Sadie nodded.

Michael's clothes rustled again and he grunted as he changed position. "Chloe," he said gently, "C'mere please. Get sittin same us o'er here."

Chloe's tiny footsteps padded softly over towards them. "Ya gonna be K, Sadie?" she asked.

Sadie nodded her head. "I'm sorry. I wish I wasn't so wrong."

"Get ta listenin, ya ain't wrong," Michael said softly. "Ya done been gettin a shit ton o' shit from birthed. Ya gonna get better in ya mind, an ya gonna heal up good. Maybe one day ya ain't gonna be gettin fucking 'fraid all o'er. Here in the one-two, we gotta get morer fucking riskless surer in hell. K?"

Sadie nodded.

"Now, we gonna be needin ya girls ta be gettin way not freaked. I sayin 'fore and I sayin now: I ain't got no trust for none them mother fuckers in here fucked up joint. The lil'er them shits get a picture on us, the easier time we gonna have here. So, Sadie, ya gotta get ya mind calmin. Ain't gonna do none good gettin all crazy, same as Sal's safe-house an here now. Just...if ya gonna go get heavy freaked the fuck out, get ya tellin Fester or me. We gonna get ya ass the fuck gone, so's ya gettin calm. Ya get it?"

Again, Sadie nodded.

"Chloe, I ain't knowin what emotion shit them here maybe bringin with 'em. Them gonna be caryin lots o' sad, angry, an 'fraid shit...an crazy shit put on top. Ya gotta be a bit growed-up, an get ta handlin it bestest ya ables for me. Get it same as Sadie: shit gettin heavy for ya, then get ta tellin us, an we gonna get ya gone. 'K?"

Chloe didn't say anything and Sadie hoped she had nodded her head. Michael was making a lot of sense.

"I tellin ya kids, we gonna get us all passed them shit we got hittin us, if we get ta sticking ta one 'nother. We done been fucking family, I ain't got no care two ya ain't my blood. All I gotta care for is: I got a bro an two lil sis I gotta fucking get ta keepin clear an riskless. Ya kids gotta get helpin one 'nother keepin clear same. Get it?" Again Sadie nodded. There was movement from Fester too. "Good. Now we gonna get ta eatin. I fucking starvin as fuck!"

Fester helped Sadie to stand. She swayed a little and heard a swooshing sound in her ears. When Fester asked her if she was alright, she nodded and held his arm. Although lightheaded, she felt better now than she had in a long time.

They all walked towards the cafeteria in silence and Sadie was happy for that. She was deep in her own thoughts and didn't want them interrupted. Fester led the way since Michael couldn't remember how to get there. He said that he was able to map out the entire complex, or what he saw of it, the first time they walked through. It was what had distracted him when they first arrived. His brain recorded everything he saw.

The night before she had seriously considered ending her life, and now she wanted to live. These people had shown her, over the short period of time that she had known them, something that she would never have learned on her own. They showed her love. Even though she didn't feel for Michael and Chloe what she felt for Fester, she knew the affection she had for them was love. There was no other explanation.

Sadie leaned into Fester and smiled. She had a family who would protect her and never harm her in any way. It didn't bother them how wrong she was. These people willingly put themselves in harm's way by having her around, all because they wanted her with them. They cared for her as much as she cared for them. This is what the girl in the book she read had experienced with her own family. Michael had said that she would heal. Perhaps this was a part of it. She was still afraid that she would hurt them, but maybe they could help her regain control of her sanity.

If she could heal, then her wrongness could be cured. Such a thing would allow her to finally be able to take care of herself and fit in with the world. It was strange to know that now she didn't have to worry about that as much. She had a family to help her. *Family.* It seemed too good to be true, but her history with them suggested that it was real.

It was strange for her to feel this good with all of the uncertainty that surrounded their situation. There was something about the way Michael had spoken in the room that convinced Sadie she wasn't in danger so long as he and Fester were around. She felt sure that neither man would ever hurt her. This was a new experience that her life had never prepared her for. She had been so sure that it was only a matter of time before someone gave her a lesson. Now she could trust that the two men would never allow that to happen.

Sadie never imagined she could feel this safe and secure and have it be real. She never imagined it would be possible for her to feel this much love in her life. The lessons truly were over.

Chapter 36

Sadie heard the murmur of voices before they reached the cafeteria. There was no way for her to be able to tell how many people were in there without using the air to see. Michael hadn't had a chance to ask anyone about it, and so she had no choice but continue to be blind. Although she ordinarily didn't mind her blindness, and sometimes it seemed to be a good thing, in that moment she wanted to know everything that was happening around her. If Michael didn't trust the people here, then she knew she definitely wouldn't.

Fester placed one of his hands over hers, completely covering it. She turned her face towards him and gave a weak smile. She would try to keep her fears in check. To survive, she would do whatever Fester and Michael asked. They knew far more than she about places such as this. She had learned to trust them and that helped her to feel very safe. The men knew what to do.

When they reached the cafeteria doorway the chattering stopped and so did they. Sadie stood next to Fester and waited. It wasn't long before the people began to make noise and talk once more. She didn't care how many were there. In that moment she wished she was far away with Fester, Michael, and Chloe as her only company. Hopefully, they would leave Sadie and her friends alone, and let them eat in peace.

"Chloe," Michael said softly, "ya gonna get Sadie an ya o'er ta plain table. We gonna get ya girls a bit o' eats. Get ya mindful, now. Ya ain't gonna bump her in nothin."

"Don't sweat it," Fester whispered in Sadie's ear, "we'll have eyes on ya."

She removed her hand from Fester's arm and it was soon taken by the child. They slowly made their way across the room. Sadie tried not to be afraid. The men could see her, and hopefully they would also be able to stop anyone if they tried to hurt her or Chloe.

The thought helped ease the fear that was threatening to rise. The feel of Chloe's hand squeezing her own helped as well.

When they stopped, Chloe told Sadie where her chair was. Wordlessly she sat. Neither of the girls spoke, and she instead listened to the people in the room. Some talked about the war and what they had lost. Others speculated on who Sadie and her friends were. A few were right when they mentioned Michael and Chloe. It bothered her a lot and it wasn't until the men returned with the food that she was able to relax again.

They ate without speaking, which felt unusual. Sadie had become accustomed to listening to her friends when they all sat together for a meal. It saddened her that no one spoke now. She understood the reasons behind their silence. Chloe was probably quiet because of all of the people, and Michael didn't want anyone to know anything about them. She didn't like it, but it made sense.

Trying not to think too hard on anything so her emotions would stay in check, she instead focused on her breakfast. Fester had brought her eggs and bacon. It tasted good enough, but she worried that he may have given her too much to eat. Although she felt her starvation like a knife twisting in her belly, she still didn't have much room in her stomach. He always insisted on giving her too much food.

Michael had been right. Sadie hadn't eaten anything since they were last at the apartment and she needed the food badly. It was difficult not to devour the eggs, and she had to force herself to eat at a normal pace. There was no way for her to know if the others were watching them. Michael didn't want the people here to know anything about them, and that made her want to hide her wrongness as much as possible. It was difficult not to be anxious while she tried to figure out how to keep from bringing undue attention to herself.

If she didn't eat slowly then someone might have noticed her hunger and begin to ask questions. She wasn't sure exactly what information Michael had wanted to keep from these strangers. What if she did something wrong? She realized that she would have to ask him later how she should behave around these new people. Her behaviors no longer affected only herself. There was no way she wanted to bring more danger to her friends...her family.

Sadie was half way done with her eggs when she heard a chair slide harshly across the floor nearby. "So, eh, what be ya story folks?" a man asked from her left.

"Ain't got no story, buddy. We got dumped here same ya cranky ass," Michael said.

The chair slid in Michael's direction. "Ya got a story. Get ta lookin at ya! It plain ya be strong for fightin, yet ya stuck up in here with we gimps."

Silently Sadie lowered her fork and began to focus on her breathing. This man was asking questions and she wasn't sure why. His mannerisms made her nervous, and she needed to work hard to keep herself from being afraid of him. They were far from their room and she didn't want to give Chloe her fear. If either of them lost control now, it would definitely bring the sort of attention Michael wished to avoid. The breathing helped a little, but it seemed impossible for her to keep calm.

"I gotta get ta takin care of them three. Ain't no way I gonna fucking get fightin an doin then shits same."

"Yeah right." The man laughed. "Thems ain't belongin ta ya ass."

"Ain't tryin ta say thems mine, dammit. Just tellin ya true, gotta take care of them be all. Now if ya ain't got no care, buddy, get the fuck gone so's we ables ta get eatin in fucking peace. We ain't lookin for no troubles an shits."

Sadie listened to Michael carefully as he spoke. His voice had been low but his tone sounded frustrated. With the stranger sitting near them and asking questions, she couldn't ask Fester what she should do. As she continued with her breathing, she hoped that the man would do as Michael told him and just leave. The chatter that had filled the space earlier ceased and Sadie wondered if they were watching her table. The quiet increased her worry. This all seemed wrong.

"Get ta seein, ya got a story. Ya got a lil girl 'fraid out her wits, 'nother girl I picturin be blind an 'fraid same, an a fucking punk ass kid with fucking holes all o'er him head. Lookin at ya here, I gotta get sayin: Gutter trash like ya ass ain't never been foster parent material. Thems gotta be juicy story tellin there, son. Now, why ya ain't just tellin me the hell it be? Huh?"

"Get ta listenin, mister," Michael began with a soft tone that steadily increased in volume "we got our business an it ain't none for ya. So fuck off an get gone, for fuck's sake!"

By this point Sadie had gone as still as possible. It was difficult to keep her fear in check and she wanted desperately to be back in their room. Anywhere but in this cafeteria would be perfect actually. Michael was obviously angry with this man, and she could understand his reasons for that. What she couldn't understand was why this stranger kept in insisting that Michael tell him anything. For a moment, she was afraid that the two men were going to fight. No one had told her what to do if that happened. Her wind couldn't help Michael in a space filled with so many people.

"Awe, man, ya ain't gotta be them ways none. All ya gotta do--"

"Gus!" a loud voice said from the entrance.

In the quiet room Sadie heard the other people gasp and turn in their seats. She had jumped herself when she heard the man yell and held her breath. Her heart beat wildly in her chest and unshed tears stung her eyes. All she could do was focus on her breathing in an effort to keep the terror she felt from hurting Chloe. Please let this be over soon!

Sadie easily recognized the sound of Kronos's footsteps, with the distinct click and shuffle that accompanied them, as he headed towards their table. "These folks just come in this mornin. I bet not a one of them slept all night. Leave them be."

Once again the chair slid across the floor, only this time it was done far more harshly. The man mumbled something that Sadie couldn't understand before his angry footsteps took him out of the room. She had begun to tremble, and in an effort not to cry she closed her eyes. The man was gone and his unending questions silenced. There was no need to bring more attention to them with her tears.

"Sorry about that, son," Kronos said when he was near. "Gus is a good man. I think he's just bored down here."

Fester let out a short laugh. "I can't picture why."

"Yeah, well, how you kids settling in? Do you need anything?"

"Nah, we good," Michael said, "thanks."

There was a pause before Kronos spoke again. This time his voice was low and his tone held a hint of concern. "Look, I know y'all are tired. But, when you're done eating I want you to come see me. There's…ah… something we need to discuss."

Kronos gave them directions to his office and Sadie listened carefully. She knew that Fester would have them memorized, but it seemed important for her to learn as much as possible as well. It could wind up being important that she should know where things were around here, too. Kronos was definitely the one in charge. There might be a reason for her to go to his office in the future. The sooner she knew where the important rooms were the better.

Michael sighed. "Yeah, sure. Ain't gonna be for morer a one-two. Ya been truthful with them there jackass, we ain't got ta fucking sleepin an be gettin ready ta drop."

"I know, son. Maybe you can send the kids on up to the room and we can talk privately. What do ya think?"

Michael didn't respond at first. Finally he said, "No. We four be stickin the fuck ta one 'nother."

"Sure. Just come and see me."

"Yeah…sure."

Sadie listened to the click that accompanied Kronos's walk as he left the cafeteria. Shortly after he was gone, the other people started talking again. Their hushed tones kept her from overhearing what they said, though it wasn't hard to guess. Despite their best efforts, they somehow managed to bring attention to themselves. Were they in trouble now? Ignoring the din of conversation, she continued to focus on her breathing. When Fester's large hand touched her arm she jumped.

"Hey," he whispered, "are you OK?"

Sadie considered lying but decided on the truth. "I'm sorry. I'm trying not to be scared."

"Listen, Sadie, we're going to keep you two clear and safe. OK? Michael and I won't let anyone hurt you."

"OK."

"I mean it."

"I know."

Sadie wanted more than anything to believe him. He meant what he said, she knew that. What she didn't know was if he would actually be able to protect her. It dawned on her that they were now surrounded by Supernaturals. Instead of feeling safe, she felt as though everyone they met presented a new danger to be wary of. She knew what she and Michael could do, and it stood to reason that others here would have an equally dangerous offensive power too. How would Fester be able to protect her against that?

Even though she hadn't finished her eggs, Sadie couldn't bring herself to eat the rest. Her stomach felt as though it were in knots. First this stranger tried to get information about them, and now Kronos wanted to talk to Michael in private. Something didn't feel right and she was sure trouble was near. It seemed as though she would be in almost constant fear so long as they were at the compound. Perhaps Kronos could tell them where else they could live until the war was over. She was doubtful about the possibility, but the thought did lighten her mood.

"Sadie, get ya damn eggs gone. We ain't got all fucking mornin."

To avoid upsetting Michael anymore than he already had been, she picked up her fork and dutifully began to eat. Sadie truly didn't want any more of the eggs. There wasn't enough room in her stomach for all of the food Fester had put on her plate. Michael was understandably stressed, however, and she wanted to please him by doing something right. With her eyes still closed, she forced herself to eat the rest of her breakfast. By the time she was done, her stomach ached as though it had been stretched to its limit.

"Good," Michael said after she ate her last bite, "We gonna get words from them ass Kronos, an then we gettin us ta bed."

"Where do I put my plate?" Sadie asked.

"Don't sweat it, I have it," Fester said.

Sadie stood and waited while Fester put her plate away. Perhaps once she could use the air to see, then she could also put away her own dishes. It wasn't fair to make Fester do everything for her. Although she felt that being a part of their family erased her debt with the men, it didn't change the fact that she had her own responsibilities. Having anyone do what you're supposed to do wasn't right. Fester wouldn't agree, but that didn't make it any less real.

It didn't take long to make their way to Kronos's office. Michael told them to let him do all of the talking. Sadie was more than happy with that. There wasn't anything she wanted to say and Michael knew how to talk to these people better than she would. Her stomach hurt and she wanted nothing more than to go back to their room and stay there until the war was over. She reminded herself that she needed to ask Fester how long wars lasted. It would help to know when they'll be allowed to leave the compound and find a home. A home would be far safer in Sadie's mind.

While the majority of the compound had an almost stale and musty odor, except the cafeteria which smelled like food, Kronos's office smelled strongly of old wood. The scent caused her nose to itch and she rubbed it nervously. The man had ushered them all in and offered them somewhere to sit. Fester showed her where her chair was, and she trembled as she sat. The material felt smooth and the cushion had far too much padding. Folding her hands in her lap, she waited patiently to hear what Kronos needed to say.

"I know you weren't too keen on sharing your story with Gus, but I was wonderin if you would share it with me?" he asked.

"I ain't got a mind ta be rude, Mr. Kronos, but we be keepin ta us own selves," Michael said politely.

"I understand that, son. Honestly I do. See, the problem is that while you are your sister's guardian, I highly doubt that these two are legally yours to keep."

Michael swore. "Ya gonna stand there true, an say a story 'bout how ya be givin two shits 'bout legal? We sittin in a secret fucking compound for a militia that got thems at war with the fucking gov'ment! The fuck bullshit them shits be?"

"Easy, son. I just want to make sure everything is legit. I'm responsible for this compound and other things regarding the movement. I need to know when something illegal is going on."

"Yeah, well, ya ain't got nothin ta sweat 'bout by we four. We gonna get ta stayin out ya way, an we ain't lookin for no risk. True ta tellin, we ain't got no choice but be stuck up in here, an wanna lay low."

Kronos let out a heavy sigh. "What's that one's name?"

"Sadie. Why?"

"Hey there, Sadie. Can you tell me how you came to stay with the Coldmans?"

Sadie's heart stopped. Michael had said that he didn't want them to talk, but Kronos asked her a direct question. It seemed like the only thing to do was to keep her mouth shut. If it was OK to talk, then surely Michael would tell her so. After a moment he told her to answer Kronos honestly.

"I…I was sick. Fester took me into his home to get warm and well."

"I see, and where were you living at the time?"

Sadie licked her lips. "Outside."

"Michael, why didn't you report Sadie as a runaway?"

Michael swore. "Look, it ain't gonna be easy as them shits. She…if ya been gettin a clue what them 'rents gone an done ta her…what they…well ya ain't never reportin her neither. 'Sides, she ain't no runway.

Her piece o' shit moms done droppin her ass in the Gutter ta get dead, with a sign ta get beggin for food."

"What did your parents do to you, Sadie?"

Sadie cringed and Fester touched her arm reassuringly. "She doesn't like to share her story, sir," he said to the man. "It was truly bad."

"The fuck ya be gettin so's damn wound up 'bout Sadie for?" Michael asked.

Kronos sighed. "The war started only a few days ago, and even in that first battle a lot of Supernaturals have either lost their homes or been forced to flee because of PSI. You kids know this personally."

"C'mon, man. Get ta makin a point!"

"I'm getting to that, son. Now, I hear y'all were in that first battle. My understanding is that it was the most destructive thus far. Now, here's why I was asking Miss Sadie here those questions. See, on that night, a man who has done some work for the movement came in with his wife and infant. Sadie looks very much like the man and his wife. So much so that I would bet she was theirs."

Fester and Michael swore. Chloe's whimper told Sadie that she felt their emotions. For once, Sadie didn't know what to feel. Was he talking about her parents? Did he really say that her parents and son were here?

"Now, here's the kicker. At about 3 am last night the baby started crying. He was screaming his little head off. He hasn't stopped since."

"That's what time we left Sal's," Fester said.

Sadie stood. Her baby had been crying since they left. She didn't know how, but she knew that she truly did hear him earlier. Her baby had been crying for her and now she was so close to him. She needed to find him. Nathan was here! Without worrying about the possible rules, she immediately began to feel with the air. If she was going to help her son then she needed to see everything around her.

"Where are they?" she asked with more force behind her words than she had ever used before.

"Hold on, young lady. We need to figure out–"

"Where are they?" She yelled as the air swirled about in reaction to her emotions.

"In the infirmary. The nurse here is trying to figure out what's wrong with your brother."

Sadie was furious. She couldn't understand why Kronos wouldn't tell her exactly how to find her son. She turned towards Fester. "Do you know where that is?"

"Of course. I mapped out the complex when we got here."

"Take me."

"Sadie, girl, we gotta get ta talkin 'bout this shit 'fore ya get ta runnin."

"No, Michael! My son is here. I need to go to him. I need to!" The air shifted around her again as the currents reacted to her anxiety.

Kronos sighed and said, "Young lady. Sadie, we have rules about the use of offensive powers here..."

"Someone take me to my son!"

"Let's go," Fester said. He took her arm and led her out of the room.

As they walked towards the door, both Michael and Kronos protested. Sadie ignored them and hurried out of the room. With the air to guide her, she saw the other two men and Chloe follow. She realized that the click sound Kronos had when he walked came from a small cane that he leaned on. It felt good to know what the sound had been, but she didn't think about it for long. Fester moved swiftly down the hallway and she made sure to keep up with his long strides. The air helped her avoid bumping into people as they raced by.

Suddenly she stopped. They were close to her son. Sadie knew this without any doubt, just as she also knew that Fester was headed in the wrong direction. By this point Fester's hand was no longer on her arm, but he stopped running when she did.

"What's wrong?" Fester asked.

"That's not the right way," she said before heading down a different hallway.

There was no way for Sadie to be able to explain how she knew where her son was. She ran down the hallway at full speed now that she didn't need to follow Fester. The others followed and was glad for that. She was headed towards her baby, and she knew that she'd need help dealing with her parents. There was no worry in her mind about confronting them as they no longer held any meaning for her. She just wanted Nathan back.

"Sadie, where the hell are you going?" Fester asked as he kept his stride with hers.

"I can feel him, Fester," she said, turning her head towards him as she ran. "He's down this hallway."

"How can you feel him?"

"I don't know!"

Sadie broke out into a full sprint. Nathan was all that she could think about. He was near and she didn't even try to understand how she knew where to find him. They had always shared a special bond when she had lived at her parents' home. It had never affected her like this before, but she didn't question the phenomenon. She was simply happy that soon she would be reunited with him.

Her baby was only a short distance from her now. Joy and anxiety swirled together within her chest. Without warning, she stopped short and turned to her left. He was on the other side of the door before her.

It was time.

Chapter 37

"He's in there," Sadie said. Her side hurt from the sprint and she fought to catch her breath.

Fester's tall body bent over and his hands rested on his thighs as he panted heavily. "Are you...sure an... true...'bout that?" he asked between breaths.

"Yes."

Sadie's heart was stuck in her throat and her pulse beat wildly in her neck. It had been over two months since she held her baby. Would he remember her as fondly as she remembered him? Would he even remember her at all? It didn't truly matter. Even if he didn't remember her, he was still hers and she was finally going to have him back. Without a moment's hesitation, she opened the door when the others finally caught up. The only reason she waited was because she knew that she may need their help if her parents tried to fight her. Mother, Sadie suspected, was going to be the more prominent problem for them.

Inside the room were several small beds and cribs. The room itself was rather large in contrast to the tiny furniture. From the other side, she saw four figures stand around what seemed to be a small crib. While she didn't hear Nathan crying, she could feel that he knew she was there. He began to laugh and the joyous sound filled her ears. The figures hadn't turned in her direction, and she carefully made her way towards them.

"I don't understand it. Your son seems to be rather fine now. I was sure we would need to go to a hospital," a stranger said.

"I'm just glad he stopped. He cries like that often but never for this long."

Sadie paused when she heard her mother's voice. The familiar heat her fear usually brought began to rise. Remembering how she had rid herself of it the last time, she forced the heat into her belly. For her son's protection, she refused to allow fear to take hold now. He needed her to be strong. Unfortunately, she couldn't tell the difference between the people standing around her son. Without being allowed to use the air to see when she was with her parents, Sadie had no idea what shape they took. Fester and the others stood by the doorway. Kronos wasn't with them and she didn't care. Nathan was all that mattered.

Deciding that the best thing to do would be to get those people away from him first, Sadie used her wind in a new fashion. With her fear pushed down, she found she had an amazing amount of control. The air shifted violently and all four figures were swiftly pushed away from her son by the wind she wielded. She held them against the wall by continuously pushing the air at them. They screamed in fear and someone yelled at her, begging her to please stop. She ignored them all and rushed to her baby's side.

There he was. Her sweet baby boy lay in the crib. He was larger than she remembered. It had never occurred to her that he would have grown so much in such a short amount of time. Even so, there were no doubts in her mind that this was Nathan. It had to be.

Gently she reached into the crib and picked up her baby. The continuous use of her wind began to tire her, and so she released some of her hold over the air. She had her baby now. There was nothing anyone could do to change that. The knowledge that her parents were in the room kept her from relinquishing complete control over the air so she would not be blind. She needed to see them and make sure they didn't try to take Nathan from her again.

Her sweet little baby let out a series of giggles and her heart echoed his joy. In her mind she felt him, as though he spoke to her through her thoughts. He simply said, *'My real mother, you are back!'*

"Yes," she said softly, "I'm never going to leave you again."

While she held her baby and spoke softly to him, she felt everyone move about at once. The four people she threw against the wall slowly stood. They seemed hurt but not enough that it concerned her. Fester and Michael had already moved to her side. Chloe stood near the door. Kronos was now visible in the doorway as well. She wasn't sure where he had been, but he leaned against the frame of the door as though fatigued.

"Sadie, how do you know this is your son?" Fester asked.

"He can talk to me, Fester. He talks in my head. I know it's him."

Fester seemed to accept the answer better than she thought he would. The people she threw all stood now and one of them walked slowly in their direction.

"Who are you people? Put that baby down!" She didn't recognize the voice.

"He's her son," Fester said sternly.

"Sadie!"

Her mother's sharp tone cut through the air and caused Sadie's heart to go still. She refused to allow her fear to rise, and her belly felt tight from the effort. It was difficult to keep it away and some anxiety began to spill through. She desperately wanted to be away from her mother, and her son agreed. They needed to get as far away from her as they could. Ignoring everyone around her, she turned and began to leave.

"Do not walk away from me!" Mother said.

Sadie continued to ignore her. Fester and Michael stayed where they were and she didn't know why. They needed to leave now. The urgency she felt ran through her core. Her son knew it, too, his thoughts mixing with her own. Before she could reach the door, however, a bed slid sharply in front of her. Mother always could move things without touching them.

"Sadie, I said, 'do not walk away from me!' Obey me now!"

Sadie turned her head in the direction of her mother's voice. The figure she thought it came from stood next to another whom she assumed was also her father. "I won't obey you again, Mother. There's no place in my life for your lessons any more. I have a new family now, and so does Nathan."

The bed that had slid in front of her began to move

in her direction. Not wanting to fall with the baby in her arms, she backed away slowly. Her fear threatened to rise when she realized that the bed was gradually pushing her towards her parents. The smell of ozone and the feel of electricity told her that Michael had called on his lightning. He didn't seem to direct it anywhere which was odd. The crackling energy flowed instead around his hands and arms, waiting to be discharged. Where the ongoing static touched the air, Sadie saw small sparks. She winced at the slightly painful disturbance.

"Get ta listenin, lady. I got a true clue picture 'bout all ya fucking done ta them girl there. Ya ain't stopin her leavin with her kid. Ya get ta tryin, an I gonna drop ya ass hard an dead." Michael raised his arm, still surrounded by the crackling electricity, in the direction of Sadie's parents. "Ya ain't never gonna–"

"STOP!" Kronos yelled as his cane hit the floor sharply.

Everyone paused and Michael's electricity ceased to exist. Sadie found she couldn't move or speak. Even the air refused to obey her; she was blind once more. Nathan's 'voice' left her mind as well, and her fear began to rise steadily. How could she protect her son if she couldn't even move? Helpless and afraid, all she could do was listen as Kronos crossed the room.

"We have rules here. Rules which three of you have broken in this very room! Offensive powers are forbidden to be used within the compound unless under an emergency. This doesn't count." Sadie heard his footsteps and click stop beside her after moving around the bed. "By all rights I should lock you all in a neutralizing cell I designed. But, I'm not unreasonable. Now, Sadie, tell me why you are taking that baby."

Sadie found that she couldn't control her own voice and unwillingly told Kronos about everything. She told him in detail about the lessons her parents had forced upon her. She told him of the birth of her son. She told him about being left Downtown and how Fester had saved her life. Everything pertinent that had happened to her in her life, including and up to how she came to be holding her son once more, spilled out of her mouth. She didn't want to tell him any of it but couldn't stop herself. She was terrified, yet her voice never wavered as her tale unfolded.

When she finished, she felt whatever hold had been placed upon her suddenly release its grip. She and Nathan could move once more. Trembling with fear, she held him protectively against her chest. Kronos's shuffle and click headed towards where she remembered her parents had stood. For a moment she thought of Fester and how he had always wanted to know about her past. The strange man finally got his wish.

"You two make me sick! You are disgusting beyond belief! What you did to that child of yours is beyond evil. Now that I know the situation, I will forgive these two for using their power. But you can never be forgiven for what you have done. Take them away."

Sadie heard the heavy footsteps of three people move swiftly through the room. Both of her parents pleaded with Kronos and insisted that she had been lying. Their shouts preceded the sounds of a struggle, and she jumped when she felt someone touch her.

"It's just me," Fester said. "Let's get out of here."

He took her arm and instantly led her away from the commotion and out the door. With all of the noise in the room, she couldn't hear if Michael and Chloe were with them. She hoped they were. Holding her son securely against her chest, she trusted Fester not to steer her into anything. He would make sure she and her son were safe, there were no doubts about that. He and Michael would know what to do.

Once they were in the hallway, Fester stopped. Michael's voice was unsteady when he said, "Fester, get 'em on up the room. I keepin here an sharin words with Kronos. Maybe findin shit for the babe same. Just...just get 'em gone. Go."

Fester did as Michael asked and led her back the way they had come. She asked where Chloe was and he told her that the girl was on the other side of him. Nothing else needed to be said as they walked the hallway toward their room. The further they were from Kronos, the easier it was for Nathan to speak to her. It wasn't exactly words, but rather the understanding behind them which she received. She realized that her son had a power, too, and that it allowed for this to happen.

Nathan had been overjoyed to see her once more. He knew that her mother wasn't his mother as well. He knew from her mind what they had done to Sadie, and because of this he knew who his true mother was. She had been afraid that her parents would have given him lessons. Relief flooded her when he showed her his memories. From what she could tell, they had never touched him in a cruel way. Perhaps they felt that he was too young for lessons.

Sadie's blood turned cold when she realized that they might have planned on starting them when he was old enough to walk or talk with his voice. The fact that they had most likely made such plans gave Sadie a strong desire to tear her parents apart with her wind. While it was wrong to kill another, she would gladly kill anyone who harmed her baby. The love she felt for him was stronger than any emotion she had ever experienced before. She loved him more than she loved Fester. There was nothing that existed which could grab hold of her heart in such a way. She knew that she would never allow another to harm him; her son would never know the lessons.

Memories of the affectionate way Fester kissed the top of her head when he held her to him came to mind. With her son in her arms, she leaned down her head to kiss his in the same manner. It was the first time she had ever willingly kissed anyone and the gesture felt right. She kissed him once more when they entered the room.

The moment she crossed the threshold to their room, Sadie felt a tremendous relief flow through her. The smile on her face couldn't be wiped away by anything in that moment. Carefully and slowly she walked over towards her bed, using her foot to let her know where it was. Grateful to be safe and with her precious son, she sat with a contented sigh. Chloe and Fester sat down on either side of her.

"He ya babe true, Sadie?" Chloe asked.

"Yes. He is."

"I gonna holds him?"

"No. I don't want to let him go yet."

"Chloe," Fester said gently, "Sadie hasn't been able to hold her son for a long time. Let her do it."

"K."

"He's beautiful," he said.

"He is?" Sadie asked.

"Yep, as beautiful as his mother." Fester put an arm around Sadie's shoulders and she happily leaned into him. "I love you," he said.

"I love you too," she said.

A sigh of contentment escaped her lips. Chloe made cooing sounds at Nathan and he gave her little giggles in return. It felt wonderful to hear the child and baby both so happy. Sadie let out a wide yawn which her son echoed. She realized that neither of them had slept for most of the night. According to Kronos and Fester, Nathan had started screaming when they left Sal's home. She wondered why he had done that and how she had heard him. In response he told her that he had been trying to let her know where he was but didn't know how. He wanted her to come to him and knew that she would. He cried every night she was gone. When he realized that she was close, he cried for her until she finally came.

"Hey, how did you know where to find him?" Fester asked.

"I just did. I heard him crying when we left Sal's. He knew I was coming. He told me where to go I think."

"Sadie, you also said he talked to you in your head when we were in the children's infirmary. Is that what you mean?"

"I can hear him in my head, Fester. He knows my thoughts and I can hear his thoughts in my head too." She smiled as she remembered that they had such a bond since a few days after he was born.

"Telepath." Fester said softly.

His voice pulled Sadie from the pleasant memory. "What?" she asked.

"Your son is a Telepath. Telepathy is like empathy but with thoughts instead of emotions. He's like Chloe in a way."

Chloe let out a squeal. "He same as me? The babe same as me? It true?"

"Seems so," Fester said with a happy tone to his voice.

"Telepathy," Sadie whispered.

She worried that her son would experience his telepathy the same way Chloe's empathy affected her. Would he feel pain from bad thoughts like Chloe felt pain from bad emotions? She hoped that he wouldn't. Sadie never wanted her son to suffer. The thought of him being hurt or sad filled her with dread. She would do everything and anything possible to ensure that he was happy and safe. It dawned on her that these were things that Fester had said to her at one point or another.

"I understand now," she said softly.

"What do you understand, Sadie?" Fester asked.

"I understand why you want to help me all the time. I understand why you want me to be happy, and why you didn't want me to sleep on the street."

"Did Nathan tell you those words?"

"No, I just realized that I feel the same for him...and you."

Fester held her tightly and kissed her temple. The smile on her face widened. For the second time in her life, her heart was filled with pure joy. Sadie loved her son, she loved Fester, and she loved Chloe and Michael, all in different ways. It was strange to think that it wasn't so long ago that she didn't even know what love was. She had always loved her son; she just didn't understand what that meant before now.

'Ya gonna get better in ya mind, an ya gonna heal up good,' Michael had said before breakfast. Chloe had said once, *'Ya gonna get better, Sadie'* She wondered if this was what they meant. Was she beginning to heal her wrongness and fear with the love for her son and

their new family? She doubted it would be that simple. If the past was anything to judge by, she knew that she would feel fear again. There was far too much that she still had yet to learn. For the first time, however, she had real hope. *'Maybe one day ya ain't gonna go an get all fucking scared all o'er.'* That would be a wonderful thing.

Sadie realized that she hadn't heard Nathan in her mind for a while, and he was very still in her arms. "Fester, is Nathan alright?"

"Yeah, he's just sleeping. You both should sleep too. I'm going to wait up for Michael."

Chloe moaned in protest and Sadie felt her get off the bed. She listened as the girl's soft footsteps took her across the room and she fell into her own bunk. Chloe might be afraid of her nightmares, but she was obviously too tired to argue about sleep. When Fester moved off the bed as well, Sadie carefully put Nathan down on the mattress near the pillow. She then curled up next to him so her body blocked the open side of the bed. This, she knew, would keep him from rolling off. The last thing she wanted was for her son to be hurt from falling off the bed.

Sadie gently placed a hand upon her son's small body. She smiled as she felt his abdomen rise and fall with each breath. Somehow she managed to have everything she wanted. Fester was alive and well, with his injury fully healed. Nathan was safe beside her, far from her parents' terrifying and cruel lessons. Chloe had begun to laugh again. The sound of Chloe and Nathan giggling together earlier was quite possibly one of the most beautiful sounds Sadie had ever heard. She looked forward to hearing them both giggle again after they've all had a long peaceful sleep.

Gently she closed her eyelids, which had grown heavy as her fatigue fully caught up with her. Family. How did she become so lucky? She didn't deserve any of the wonderful things her life had recently brought. There was no doubt in Sadie's mind about her own lack of worth. Proving to herself, and anyone else who may be watching her, that she was worthy of these gifts was something she would spend the rest of her life attempting to accomplish. There was no need to die alone in the cold. Her son needed his mother and her family needed their sister.

With her mind and her heart at peace, Sadie gently drifted off to sleep. For the first time, her dreams were filled with laughter and joy. The nightmares didn't stand a chance. Perhaps her past would finally stay where it belonged.

Perhaps, she truly didn't need to suffer any longer.

Epilogue

To suggest that Fester was exhausted would be the understatement of the century. The past few days had definitely taken their toll. This war was insane and sometimes he worried that he wouldn't be able to protect the girls, and now the baby as well. If you had asked him a year ago if he would one day be sitting in a secret underground facility hiding from the government while a war raged up on the surface, he would've insisted you were nuts and get the hell away. Yet, here he was, facing the improbable and with more to lose than ever before.

Fester's internal clock told him that Michael had been gone for one hour, forty-two minutes, and eighteen seconds. He desperately needed to know what had happened to Sadie's parents. Were they going to be a problem? He doubted it. The old geezer seemed like he was going to lock them up and throw away the key. Even so, he hated not knowing the specifics. Regardless of what he would sometimes tell Michael, it was rare that he actually guessed anything. Most of the time, he knew exactly what was what. He only 'guessed' when he didn't want to admit the real answer. It was usually easier to pretend he didn't know something than it was to actually be ignorant.

With his back against the dresser, Fester could easily watch Sadie and the baby. It wasn't the first time he noticed how peaceful she looked when asleep. Her face was usually so animated and showed every emotion; the girl didn't know how to hide her feelings. When she slept, however, the crease in her forehead eased and the tension in her features relaxed. Her beauty showed best when it was unhindered by fear. Yet, her inability to hide what she felt was one of her more charming characteristics. It meant that she couldn't lie, or at least not lie very well.

He sighed as he looked at her. The clothes Sal gave

her were too big, but so was everything she wore. Her weight concerned him, too. He knew that she didn't eat enough calories, especially with how much an offensive power could raise one's metabolism. Thankfully she had begun to gain an appetite, though he still worried. They all needed their strength now more than ever, and she seemed so frail. *'Sadie's stronger than she seems,'* he reminded himself. She continuously defied the odds and surprised even him on more than one occasion. That wasn't something that happened often and he liked it.

Sadie was beautiful though. Her silky straight black hair was splayed over the pillow behind her. While she usually wore it up, he liked how it looked when it was down and around her shoulders. Her hand rested gently on Nathan's chest, rising and falling with his breath. The baby looked remarkably like his mother. He had the same black hair, the same delicate features, and the same impossibly blue eyes.

Thinking about their eyes reminded Fester how he and Sadie had first met near the beginning of October. He chuckled lightly when he realized that she probably never knew it was he. He had fought with Michael earlier that day, and stormed out of the apartment. Furious, he walked about the Gutter streets aimlessly until he bumped into this small blue-eyed blind homeless Chinese girl. She had looked so delicate and absolutely terrified. Before he could offer to help her, she had quickly moved away from him. That simple run-in cooled his anger in a way nothing else could.

There was something about her that he couldn't let go. Fester wasn't sure at first if it was the look of terror and mistrust she had on her face, or the statistics that flew through his mind at the probability of running into someone like her. He eventually realized that it was her eyes which he had the most difficulty getting out of his head. They had haunted him all day. Later that evening, when he saw that crabby bitch tell Sadie to move, he decided to buy her something to eat. What little money he had in his pocket was for his own dinner, but she needed the food more and he wanted to help.

It was endearing how she had tried to give him money. Having been homeless before, he knew how rare that simple act had been. So impressed was he, that he brought her breakfast the very next morning. He had hung around so no one would steal the food before she woke. It never occurred to him that she would be suspicious because he gave her eggs. After that morning, it seemed best to leave her alone for a while. That was until he saw her a few weeks later and saw that she had already begun to slowly starve.

On his way to the library he had noticed her begging on a street with little foot traffic. Thanks to his power, he could tell that she hadn't budged at all when he walked by again soon after the sun began to set. Curious, he watched her pack up her things and find a place to sleep, never going anywhere for dinner. It was baffling when she refused his food the next morning, especially since he knew for a fact that she hadn't eaten the day before.

When she had nearly frozen to death, he knew that he had to do something. There was no way he could have let her stay there to croak on the sidewalk. She deserved more than to become another nameless statistic who died in the Gutter streets that winter. Obviously no one else had bothered to show her that there were shelters to keep her warm. That she was so starved and malnourished meant that she also didn't know where to get free food. It didn't make any logical sense until he learned why she was so afraid to accept help. If anyone had tried to show her where she could go, she probably would've run away in terror.

The best decision he had ever made was to help her home. He nursed her back to health, and found himself falling in love in the process. He never thought that he would be able to feel a love like this. Usually he was too depressed to even hope that something so pure was possible. Yet, there she lay; the girl who effortlessly stole his heart.

Now Fester's internal clock told him that Michael had been gone for over two hours. He was starting to worry. The old guy obviously despised Sadie's parents too, but that didn't mean that he would allow her to keep the baby. He suspected that in this compound, the regulations weren't always going to work in their favor. It was rare when something did. As a kid who grew up in the Gutter, he should be used to such things by now. *'Michael won't let them take the baby,'* he reasoned. *'Not after all Sadie had been through.'* Fester knew that he would protect both mother and child with his life if it came down to it. No one was going to break up their family.

Finally the door opened and Michael came in. "Hey man, why ain't ya fucking sleepin?" he asked.

"I wanted to wait for ya. What happened to Sadie's 'rents?"

"Thems got takin ta some fucking jail room."

Fester glanced up at Michael and noticed his green eyes were bloodshot and glassy. The guy hadn't had a decent night's sleep since he had killed Sadie's would-be rapist. Fester could empathize since it had been the same for him, though for different reasons. Michael continued talking and Fester forced himself to stop analyzing the guy. It was a bad habit of his, analyzing based on observation, and he had learned how to stop himself before he really began. Instead he turned back to watching Sadie and listened to Michael talk.

"Kronos done sayin them rooms gonna stop them shits from gettin use o' them power till a thing bein done with 'em. He done sayin he gonna fucking share words with Sal, an seein what them bitch got in her mind. Sayin a thing 'bout 'policin we own'."

It had been difficult to be in the same room as the people who had done so much harm to Sadie and not react violently. After Kronos forced her to share her story, Fester wanted to kill them then and there. The only thing that kept him from doing so was the hold the old man's power had put on everyone. All he could do now was hope that those jerks would get the punishment they deserved.

"I never pictured I would say this, but I fucking hope they kill them slow," he said.

"Yeah, kid, I gotta get sayin, I feelin same." Michael

rubbed his eyes. "Fuck me. We got a fucking babe we fucking be takin carins for." He softly swore some more.

Michael took off his old and greasy cap from the garage and threw it onto the dresser. He roughly ran a hand through his blonde wavy hair, which looked like it hadn't seen a brush in a while. Fester noticed that his face also looked more worn than usual. His sad and tired eyes had begun to show wrinkles along the edges, and he had also developed deeper lines along his forehead. Michael might be almost 20, but he looked as though he had the stress and responsibilities of someone far older. Fester knew that he and the girls, and now the baby, were the cause of that. He knew that Michael loved taking care of them, even if he did always claim that they were going to give him a stroke any day now. Still, he tried not to feel guilty for his part in the man's added stress.

"You're gonna have to let me get workin now," Fester said with a smile.

Michael let out a snort. "Yeah, no shit."

Fester wanted to laugh. He was always trying to get Michael to let him work. If he had been staying with anyone else, and they told him what to do, then he would've left long ago. He liked being able to do his own thing and couldn't stand constricting rules. Yet, he would never forget how Michael had taken him in and treated him as an equal.

At the time, Fester had been on the streets for nearly a year, and Michael had caught him stealing money from the garage's register for food. By all rights he should have turned Fester in to the cops and let the state deal with him. Instead he took him home, and before Fester could blink, Michael and Chloe had become family. Letting him make the rules was just fine. After all, he still had more freedom than anyone else would've given him, and he was encouraged to read as well. It was a winning situation all around.

"Kronos done sayin them Diana chick gonna get ta bringin a thing o' clothes for we four, an shit for the babe," Michael said, breaking Fester from his thoughts.

"I gonna fucking bet she gettin ya wearin a thing with fucking colors!" He laughed softly, bringing a grease stained hand up to his mouth to muffle the sound.

"Fuck you. I like black," Fester said, though he let out a small chuckle as well.

For a moment neither of them spoke. Fester glanced over at Michael and knew the guy would be happy to get out of his work uniform. Sal had let them wash their clothes at her place, but didn't seem to care enough to give them all something new. Michael's coat had been ruined from shooting lightening during the battle. His sleeves also showed scorch marks from both that night and back in the nursery. For Fester it didn't matter much since he wore the same clothing often, but Michael could definitely use something less ruined. Although this place won't have something that Fester would like, it wasn't actually an issue. All that mattered now was keeping the girls and the baby safe. Who knew what else could happen here. He would worry about style when they had a home again.

"Get ta hearin," Michael said as he leaned against the dresser. "I been 'fraid them shits gonna fucking take ya ass, Sadie, an her babe." He looked down at Fester with a deeply sad look in his eyes.

Fester swore as his heart stopped from the implications. "What if they do?"

"Ya ain't gotta sweat it none. On a one, I ain't never gonna let them shits get ta takin ya. An on a two, Kronos gonna fucking 'overlook' that I ain't been ya legal fucking guardian an shit."

Fester didn't comment. They had done so well with avoiding this issue. Their luck was bound to run out eventually. While the geezer might have been fine with their arrangement, he knew that the law would be another story. Granted, laws didn't matter much since he was an enemy of the state now, just like every other Supernatural in existence. However, the war would end some day and when that day came they might have to face the legalities issue again.

The problem wasn't simply that Michael wasn't their legal guardian, with the exception of Chloe. Gutter

Trash weren't usually allowed to become foster parents. For that you had to be either Highborn or one of the few who somehow found themselves in the middle. Legally, Michael was only allowed to take care of his sister. Fester, Sadie, and Nathan should be in foster care, according to the state. For Fester, they might let him stay. He was from the Gutter and the rest of society didn't care about kids like him. Sadie, however, was obviously Highborn. Fester knew that by her accent, and it was confirmed when he saw the way her parent's dressed and spoke. If CPS ever stepped in, she and Nathan would be the ones most likely to be taken. He could only pray that would never happen.

Michael sighed and Fester glanced back up at him. He was looking over at Sadie and Nathan now with a thoughtful and concerned expression. "Ya gotta get a clue, man. She gotta need ta get a shit ton o' pro help."

"Yeah," Fester said reluctantly.

"She be fucking gettin worser an worser, man. Ain't she?"

"Shit, Michael, sometimes she seems to be deteriorating true and I don't fucking have a picture on what to do. After today...I have mind that it might get better. Standing up to her parents and getting Nathan back...it might be one of those breakthroughs the books go on about. Maybe..." Fester looked down as his voice trailed off.

"We gonna get a picture on them shits, kid." Michael reached down and patted Fester reassuringly on the shoulder. "Ya ain't gotta get worryin just yet. But for the one-two, I droppin, man. I gonna fucking get my ass ta bed, an be sleepin a God damn year! Ya ass gonna get sleepin same. Them girls ain't gettin no fucking nightmares, so's we maybe gonna get good fucking sleeps."

"I'll go to bed in a one-two."

"Jesus, Fester! Thems be good an fine. Them sleepin true. Get ya ass fucking sleepin, or ya ain't gonna be no good for nobody."

"Fuck man, I get that. I just want to have my eyes on them a little longer."

"I ain't gonna fucking bullshit: them shits gettin lil creepy. Well, whatever. I gonna crash."

Creepy. Yeah, Fester could see how Michael would think he was being creepy. It wasn't like that though. He couldn't help but worry about Sadie all the time. Sometimes, being able to see her sleep so peacefully was a welcome respite from all the fear her face usually wore. He loved her so much that it truly hurt him to see her suffer the way she did. Why was it so hard to help her? He had read enough books on psychology that he should know what to do. Yet, helping Sadie seemed to be one of those few things that books won't give a person. As Michael had said last week, he simply didn't have the experience needed.

Fester sighed and then glanced over at Chloe. The young girl slept peacefully and he was happy for that. It was adorable how her breath blew the curly blonde hair that had fallen in front of her small pale face. Michael didn't exaggerate. This looked like it was going to be the first time in a while that neither of the girls had nightmares. The poor kid couldn't handle any more of them. When they all heard what Sadie had said back in the nursery, Chloe's face had held a kind of horror that no child should know. It was exactly like it had been the night of the first battle. So much death and pain...Sadie wasn't the only one who had PTSD now. Sometimes he felt that he couldn't tell which was frailer: Chloe or Sadie. It didn't matter. Not truly.

A yawn he had been fighting broke free and he knew Michael had been right. He needed to sleep as well. If he didn't go to bed now, he would probably pass out on the floor. *Yeah...no thank you.* With a low grunt, he stood and leaned against the old dresser beside him. He bent down to get one last look at the girl he loved before climbing into his own bunk. As he crawled across the bed, he absently wondered why they had to give them sheets with a garish floral pattern splayed across the fabric. He didn't complain because while they were gross, they were also functional. The bright design made him miss his own plain black bedding though.

He wondered what would happen to all of his stuff now. Chances were the landlord would sell everything, or throw it all out. The prick would probably get a nice little bundle from the tech projects Fester had worked on when he had the money for parts. He didn't care so much about losing those, however. He could always make more when the war ended. Sadly, the only things he would miss were the few pictures of his mom that he had stolen from his pops when he ran away from home. She had mysteriously died when he was a toddler, and those pictures were all of her that he had left. At least his super computer of a brain allowed him to remember her in perfect detail. The pictures weren't important so long as he could do that. Other than Sadie, she was the only woman he ever really loved.

There were light switches near the head of each bed and he flicked his with a sigh. The room was plunged into complete darkness, and he thought about how this was what Sadie saw each and every day. She had been angry with him for mentioning that he wished she could see the sunrise. He honestly couldn't understand why she misunderstood him so easily. All he ever wanted was to make things easier on her. Weren't girls supposed to like that? He knew that her blindness didn't 'make her wrong' or any such nonsense. Obviously, she could do things on her own. He just wanted to help and ease the suffering she still felt from her past. He wanted her happy. Why had it taken her so long to understand that?

Fester lay down and rubbed his face, careful not to hit his nose ring. He had yanked it out once before and definitely didn't want to do that again. A chuckle escaped when he remembered the time Sadie had felt his face. She had an odd expression when her fingers touched any of his piercings. Most people didn't understand them and always seemed to think the worst. Yet it was Sadie who accepted them, and him, without needing to first tell him to be normal. Oddly enough, it had been the normal things he did which she found strange instead. He chuckled again at the irony.

Before he could sleep, he calculated the probability

that she would one day be his wife. Fester didn't care if she never wanted to sleep with him. He figured that her father had ruined any chance of her enjoying sex anyway. Still, he wanted to be with her forever. Unfortunately, the conclusion he came to was that she most likely wouldn't be ready, even when they were old enough to legally have a ceremony. Obviously, she had begun to trust him. But, yesterday Sal told him what Sadie had offered back in the safe-house. She had even told Sal that she owed her for refusing her offer. When he added that to all of the times she was afraid to stay with them, he knew that she wouldn't accept anything that might threaten her freedom if given a choice. That was fine; he didn't want to take that from her anyway.

It sucked big-time, though. He was sure that he could be a good husband for Sadie. He also wanted to be a good father for Nathan. Deep within he desired nothing more than to take care of them both. If he could always make her smile like she did today, then his life would be complete. She was the only one to ever chase his depression away long enough for him to feel any amount of joy. True, he did feel sad whenever he was reminded of the neglect and abuse that she received. But those moments were short lived. More often than not, she only needed to smile and his day was better. He didn't need her to be his wife for that.

Figuring out how to make sure that she would continue to smile, and how to heal her mind, was a daunting and overwhelming task. It was impossible to tell what the girl had running through her head sometimes. Her reactions tended to be unpredictable at best.

The fact that she seemed to be deteriorating was also a problem. When he told Michael that things might be better now, he didn't lie. There was definitely hope that he could help her. The problem was that it might get worse before it got better. When he and Sal had talked about Sadie, she offered him a job in return for decent pay and some of the best psychological help. With Sal's influence, that literally meant the best doctors.

Michael would probably never go for it, and Fester really didn't want to work for her. While Sal had her moments, he knew that she could easily turn on him one day. Sadie was worth it, but he didn't want to put her or the others in danger by working for the mob full time. Everyone else would tell him to simply refuse and walk away. Knowing this, he still told her that he would consider her offer.

It wasn't going to be an easy decision. Sadie's well being could depend on the work. The hacking job he had done at Sal's house earned him enough money for when they left the compound. He had wanted to make sure they would be able to afford a home, furniture, and anything else they needed once the war was over. It wasn't enough to get Sadie the help she needed though, and he wasn't entirely sure how he was going to manage that.

There was still a chance that he could learn what was needed to help the girl he loved, without having to work illegally. Sadie had continued to surprise him, and that wasn't necessarily a bad thing. She was obviously intelligent, even though she seemed to know so little information. There were things they all took for granted that caused a look of wonder and interest to spread across her face. Even when she was confused, he could tell that she worked hard to figure things out. If only he knew how her mind worked and what she was thinking. Then he would be able to reach her and know how to get her to understand why it's OK for him to help.

So often, he found himself actually guessing when it came to Sadie. Usually being so uncertain made him uncomfortable. With her, it was another thing he would always love. She was just so different and special in a way no other girl would ever be for him.

This wasn't the first time where he realized that Sadie would always be a mystery to solve. He could spend his entire life trying, and never fully figure her out. The thought caused him to grin widely.

Challenge accepted.

TARA'S ESCAPE: CHAPTER 1

"You can never go back," Vincent Vinachelli said as he leaned in to whisper across the table. His smooth voice threatened to lose itself in the disarray of the diner, and urged Adrienne to pay close attention. Despite the lazy summer heat, his stern gaze chilled her to the bone and her heart skipped a beat. "No matter what happens from here on out," he said once their eyes locked, "you will never again be Adrienne Jerrickson."

Adrienne licked her chapped lips and her eyes darted from the Italian Highborn to his young daughter beside him. Together, they regarded her with the same cold expression that refused to betray a person's thoughts. Narrowing her eyes, she tried another vain attempt to see their auras. It was useless. With nothing more than a stranger's words to guide her, how was she to know if this unique opportunity was a trap or salvation?

Desperation from a belly that had been empty for too long turned her hesitation into acceptance. Nodding her head she asked, "Who in hells I gonna gets ta be?"

"How about 'Tara'?" the daughter said with a sneer. Adrienne wanted to wipe the look off of the other girl's face. Like most Highborn preteens, Salvina Vinachelli held an air of arrogance that she was too young to have earned. Such behavior set Adrienne's nerves on fire. Why was this priss allowed to decide her new identity?

Before Adrienne protested the handle, Mr. Vinachelli slapped his hand on the table and smiled. "It's decided then. Welcome to SUM, Tara."

Tara's eyes flew open and she rubbed her face. Ten years had passed since her recruitment and it was odd to dream about it now. Serving the movement took a personal sacrifice: your past and your name. Life as a spy taught her that a name was little more than a word people used to call upon you, and her past had left her with no loved ones to miss or mourn. In many ways the sacrifice had been easy and never factored into her decision to serve. Where most people had seen little more than Trash to be discarded, the Vinachellis saw unique promise. It wasn't long before SUM had filled a hole within her that had been neglected for most of her life. A decade later and she held no regrets.

Yawning, Tara stretched and fought the familiar battle between getting up to use the restroom versus snuggling under the covers. Winter had brought its chill and the warm soft bed won the fight with little effort. Pulling the blanket over her head, she snuggled into her pillow and waited for sleep to reclaim her consciousness. As her mind began to drift away, something else pulled her back into reality.

Tara's body broke out into a cold sweat as she gasped for air and her heart felt as though it would explode in her chest. It was a struggle to control the terror that had shot its way through her core like lightning. Her muscles stiffened and protested as she sat up, rubbed her face, and blinked away the disorientation that brought bile to her throat. Fear energy had filled the room within seconds and called to her own emotions with a fury that refused to be ignored.

This was all wrong. Tara shook her head to clear her mind. The dream had been neither powerful enough nor significant enough to frighten her this way. Wherever this fear originated, it had altered the room's energy quicker than she had thought possible. Until she found the source, she needed to block out the energies that caused such a reaction. Anything less might have left her paralyzed and vulnerable.

As she focused on her own energy, an invisible shield began to spread around Tara's form like a protective bubble. Once cut off, her heart returned to a strong, steady beat and her breathing eased. This proof that the fear had not been her own sent her into a heightened state of awareness. A quick scan of the room for anything amiss revealed nothing unexpected in the metaphysical. Korwin, however, was absent from her bed. It was abnormal behavior for the PSI agent to leave in the middle of the night. If he had been called in for an emergency, he would have woken her first.

With the realization of the likelihood that it was his fear she had felt, Tara threw off the covers and ran for her dresser. As she knelt down, she felt along the bottom for the 9 mm hidden behind the decorative trim. Once the full weight of the loaded gun filled her hand, she turned off the safety, stood, and spun around to face the bedroom door. Adrenaline coursed through her veins, increasing her alertness and preparing her for a fight. Dropping the duct tape that had secured the weapon, her feet moved across the carpeted floor with a deftness that came from a decade of practice, while her attention remained on the energy from the hallway beyond.

Before she crossed the spacious room, the natural swirls of energy on the other side of the wall shifted, in a savage yet controlled fashion. Tara felt as though she had been blinded by charged energy as it nudged, tugged and then blasted the molecules that formed her bedroom door. Aware of the intense danger this presented, she leaped to the side and rolled over into a crouched position, her gun held steady with both hands.

Oakwood shattered and tore as though it had been made out of rice paper. Wooden shards erupted into the room, floated for a moment in mid air, and then fell to the floor in silence. Although her weapon remained poised and ready to shoot, something in the back of her mind compelled her to hold back. If the attack had been directed towards herself in particular, then there would've been a distinctive sensation indicating such intentions. The specific manner in which the wood dropped identified the intruder as a formidable Supernatural.

"We don't have time for this, Agent. We gotta move!"

Tara couldn't see the man's face well in the darkened room, but his voice she knew anywhere. Of course Boss would send one of her favorite Boys; mercenaries and former military who were loyal soldiers of the Supernatural Uprising Movement. Their blind obedience to SUM's leader was both infuriating and dangerous at the best of times.

With her gun lowered towards the floor, Tara rushed to the broken door frame and peered down the hallway. It was empty. With a cold glare she turned on the Boy. "The fuck are you doing here, Nate?" she asked through clenched teeth. "I've been working this cover for two fucking years!"

"Your mark is dead, Tara. Now let's move before we're found," Nate said.

Tara glared at him and he looked away. The Boys were known for their military bearing, which empowered them with the ability to hide their true emotions from unsuspecting eyes. Their background and the Vinachellis' training had proved useful to the mercenaries. Tara's training, coupled with her unique power, helped her to notice what others couldn't. Lowering her shield against fear, it became obvious that what she had felt earlier wasn't from Korwin's death. Beneath the pure determination set in Nate's features was a thick undercurrent of terror. To see his energy more clearly, she narrowed her eyes and drew her focus into his energy's unique patterns. Tension in the physical body had been accompanied by a tight knot between his shoulder blades. For a powerful mercenary to be this afraid meant that something unpredictable and disastrous had happened.

Tara returned to the dresser and set her gun on top. "You're afraid," she said flatly. He didn't respond -- not that he normally would have. With a snort she opened the top dresser drawer and pulled out a pair of underwear. "Fine, but, I'm not going anywhere until you give me an update," she said. Let him brood. Whatever on Earth had prompted the Boy to burst in and assassinate her mission along with her mark, it wasn't enough for her to leave without an explanation or clothing. If Nate was going to waste two years of gut-wrenching work, then the least he could do was share his story while she dressed.

"Short version? Boss started the war," Nate said

as he walked over to the window and pulled the curtain back a half-inch. "I'm your extraction," he continued as he peered outside. "It's no longer safe for you here."

Tara froze with her jeans in her hands and stared at Nate's back. Tension continued to spread throughout the Boy's broad shoulders as though he had been prepared for a full scale battle and was disappointed. Letting out a sigh of disgust, she pulled on her pants over her hips. "Now's way too far ahead of schedule," she said while pulling a sweater over her head. "I mean...even Kronos agreed that--"

"She knows what she's doing, Tara," he said with impatience.

Heat from his aura – the sort she recognized as withheld anger – found its way towards her and she forced herself not to flinch from the sensation as it hit her side. If he had faced her, then she would have seen a glare in his dark brown eyes as well. Instead he kept his silent watch by the window and she shook her head. There was no point in arguing with the Italian. The revolt had finally started and there was nothing she could say or do that would change things.

Anyone born with a power was now in more danger than at any other point in history. Although she hid it from those around her, Tara was a Paranormal and therefore a more favored target for The Paranormal and Supernatural Investigation Agency, also known as PSI. The bastards hunted anyone with power. Supernaturals who were caught were either brought in to be experimented upon or worse. Paranormals, regardless of age or social status, were killed on sight. Society feared them because their power gave them more abilities than Supernaturals, and they were the only ones who could see and speak with the dead. Since they could do so much, PSI considered Paranormals to be more dangerous than anyone else with a power. The Head of State had given PSI authority over even the most influential members of society. No one was safe from their lunacy.

Swallowing hard, it was now Tara's turn to be afraid. A Paranormal and a Supernatural standing in the house of a dead Highborn PSI agent was a dangerous recipe. Nate was right, she needed to be swift and almost dropped her holster as she pulled it out from under the dresser. With a deep breath she worked to calm her wildly beating heart.

"What's our transportation, and who do we have with us?" Tara asked as she stood and strapped the holster to her hip.

"Kevin's outside on lookout, and the car is a few houses down. Orders are to get you to Kronos's compound on the double. I caught your mark as he was about to leave. He seemed to have been in a hurry and...ah...didn't notice me until it was too late."

Tara grimaced as she dug out her emergency bag from the back of the closet. Nate had spoken as though killing were easy for him, but death was something that Tara avoided whenever possible. Paranormals had the power to sense the moment a soul left the body and communicated with the dead. Long ago her kind were celebrated shamans. Now, they were hunted like animals by everyone. A life like hers was not to be envied. The power she wielded wasn't worth the death sentence it would bring down upon her if discovered.

Avoiding death and eluding PSI assassins were only two of the challenges in a Paranormal's life. One of her more useful abilities was the power to sense the natural wavelengths that make up all forms of energy, including minor disturbances caused by human thoughts and emotions. One side effect was that this limited telepathy/empathy now forced the fresh memory of Korwin's death to invade her mind when Nate had spoken of what he had done. There was no time to shut out the vision before she saw her asset's death as though she had been his silent executioner.

Nate had been swift with his kill and the flash of a memory was mercifully short. If his involvement ended with taking her to Kronos, then Tara would be a content spy. Life was never comfortable with Nate around, regardless of how many missions they carried out together. When his emotions ran hot, the mercenary's mind opened wide and showed her more of him than she wanted to know.

Closing her eyes and shaking her head, Tara cleared her mind before she informed Nate that she was ready. "Can we at least go out the back door?" she asked. Nate laughed and the sound turned her face hot with anger. "I hate it when you throw me out a window."

"Why not?" Nate asked as his smile turned into a sadistic sneer. "Throwing people is fun." Tara was ready to punch him when he held up his hands. "Fine. If you want to take the long way then be my guest. I'll watch your six."

Letting out a sigh, Tara reigned in her emotions and prepared herself for trouble other than the infuriating Nate. With a nod to the Boy, she unholstered her gun and eased herself into the wide hallway. Alert to any change in the environment, her power showed her the various forms of energy that swirled about them in innocent patterns. Nate had cleared the house already, but under these circumstances she needed to be sure.

Tara hated the narrow servant's stairway, which led into the kitchen, but it was the quickest way to the back door. Although the stairs were kept tidy by the staff, there were two steps in the center that squeaked loudly enough when stepped upon to have been a bother. Every time she had descended them, she skipped over the center steps for practice. It was wise to have a well practiced strategy for times like these when one needed a quiet exit. How she managed to keep her balance remained a mystery. While the precaution was no longer needed, she still skipped over the squeaky steps out of habit.

"Clear," Tara said after she scanned both the large kitchen and noted the lack of life on the rest of the first floor. A void existed in the energy near the front entrance – a definite sign of a recent death. Turned out Korwin had planned to leave without telling her after all. With any luck, his spirit had moved on. Handling a live prick like Nate was more than enough for one night. She didn't need a dead prick too.

It had been a small blessing that Korwin's PSI induced paranoia hadn't allowed him to keep his personal staff in his home. Nate would have killed them too for good measure and an extra pat on the head from Boss. What were a few more casualties to a mercenary like him? Tara had a suspicion deep down that he received some perverse pleasure from ending enemy lives. Then again, Supernaturals had the luxury of not being sensitive to the same after effects she endured. For a Paranormal, killing the staff meant a house full of confused spirits and an equal number of voids to step around. No thank you!

Turning towards the stairs, she watched as her new partner put his weight upon the squeaky steps without a care. Nate knew as well as she did that there wasn't anyone around to hear them and she rolled her eyes at his smug expression. For safety's sake she preferred to be careful, even when she was sure she was alone. It was a redundancy that he always found amusing. His smile faltered when she stuck up her middle finger and then signaled that they needed to hurry.

Together they headed for the back door when the hair on Tara's neck began to stand on end. A spirit had entered the room and it wasn't hard to guess whose it was. Ignoring the entity, she first looked at the disabled security keypad and then out the window. Glancing up at Nate, Tara pointed to her third eye and shook her head. It was code which told Nate that she used a Psychic power and detected no enemies waiting in ambush outside. Nate nodded and she swung open the back door.

Korwin's spirit called out to her in confusion. A swift death ensured that victims hadn't suffered. However it tended to leave their spirit disoriented. The journey from life into death was easier to cope with if the dying were aware of the impending change beforehand. Although she had shared his bed, Tara didn't care enough about the dead man to calm his spirit. Her sole concern was not becoming one herself.

Tara ran through the back door and headed towards the high hedges that bordered the right side of the property. Expanding her awareness the moment she left the house allowed her to avoid any potential threats while she kept tabs on Nate. Reaching the hedges proved easy and they provided excellent cover with a deep shadow to hide in. Nate followed her lead and the two of them made their way to the sidewalk in silence.

Tara didn't bother to look for their Supernatural scout, with or without her power. Like Boss and Boss's father before her, Kevin had the power of invisibility. If he followed protocol, then he wouldn't show himself until he joined them at the waiting car. Her own power didn't provide her the ability to perceive the energy of the Invisible Ones, whether or not they were using their power. It was an odd exception considering all other Supernaturals generated an intense energy output that was difficult to ignore and increased as a power was mastered. It made a weird sort of sense that she lacked the ability to detect everything. Life was, after all, more interesting with a little mystery. No one knew that better than Psychics.

Once they reached the sidewalk, Tara slipped her gun into its holster and Nate put his arm around her shoulders. It was unnerving to be in close contact, and she made sure that this time she put up a small energy shield between their bodies. This defensive shield blocked out Nate's memories, which in turn allowed her to stay alert for danger without becoming distracted by his mind. Acting as though nothing was wrong, the duo pretended to be guests heading to their car.

The time may have been around 1 a.m., but that didn't mean every neighbor was guaranteed to be asleep. All of SUM's operatives were trained to play it safe and deal with discomforts. Unwanted casualties were something to be avoided whenever possible. Even Nate knew that.

When they reached the vehicle, Nate opened the door for Tara, and she slid onto the front seat with grace. A back door opened and shut at the same time as hers, ensuring a single sound echoed down the street. Turning around to face her friend, she said, "Nice of you to join us, Kevin."

Bit by bit, the African man's face became visible until his smile glistened in the light of a nearby street lamp, presenting a sharp but pleasant contrast to his ebony skin tone. "Good to see you again too, Tara." Kevin's deep voice echoed the emotions she wished she could see behind his words. "It's been too long."

Tara matched Kevin's smile with one of her own. Unlike Nate and many of the other Boys, Kevin held an air of natural contentment. Most operatives forgot how to take whatever joy life offered because of the limitations caused by their line of work. Somehow Kevin had managed this with endless ease. Tara had liked him for that since the day they met, and he had become one of her closest friends and allies. It seemed like such a waste that someone like Kevin had the same blind obedience as the other Boys. None of them were willing or able to tell her where this undying loyalty to Boss came from.

Unanswered questions were like a relentless itch that Tara yearned to scratch. Sometimes she wondered if Salvina Vinachelli took pleasure in making all of the Agents, like Tara, squirm with pesky questions they were forbidden to ask. Spies looked for answers while Soldiers followed orders. Obedience was something Tara could understand about the Boys, but mercenaries who lived more than five years were too smart to follow orders as though their leaders had their best interest at heart. That was where her understanding of their behavior ended.

Loyalty came to spies and soldiers in ways that were both familiar and unfamiliar at the same time. For every single Boy to share such undying loyalty to a prominent mob boss and terrorist leader had to be a statistical impossibility. Why were intelligent battle-hardened men so devoted to that woman? Searching for hidden answers to SUM's leader and her family lacked the usual thrill of the hunt and often left her exhausted with few rewards for her efforts.

Nate slid into the driver's seat and drew Tara's attention back to the present as they sped down the deserted avenue. Frowning at the houses they passed, she couldn't help but let out a heavy sigh. Had her extraction gone smoother than it should? Life for an

Agent was never uncomplicated. Looking out her window, she knew that Korwin's neighbors' estates weren't going to give her the clues she sought. With disgust she regarded the large ornate houses with their manicured lawns, state of the art security, and air of privilege. Nobody sleeping beyond those walls knew how good – or how bad – their lives truly were.

The yards were spacious and the homes had cost more than some Gutter Trash made in three lifetimes. Inside, lives ran on lies built upon the backs and blood of those born to a family with nothing. Trees that were kept uniform lined the center and sides of the road, while 'wildflowers' were artistically planted with care. This gave the area the impression of driving through a well maintained park while affording glimpses of Old World architecture beyond locked gates and high hedges. Beautiful to look at, but please do not touch.

From the outside, it was obvious that the town had long been reserved for Highborns; elite members of society who owned most of the cities they lived near. Most of them were horrid people with pockets deep enough to absolve them of all but the most heinous crimes. What hadn't been spent on lawyers went to the best protection money could buy, ensuring that nothing ruined the illusion that Highborns had saved humanity instead of bleeding it dry.

For any Highborn to die in such a neighborhood without raising alarms wasn't easy to accomplish, and the Boys weren't known for their finesse. Considering the man Nate killed was a wealthy and respected PSI analyst, some amount of fighting should have been involved. There was a reason high-valued targets were used rather than killed. Manipulation didn't raise suspicions if done well. Murder, on the other hand, turned the heads of too many people who needed to be blind to SUM's operations.

Something didn't sit right. The more Tara worked the night over in her mind, the more she realized that perhaps they weren't homefree yet. Before she could finish telling herself to relax, the hair on the back of her neck began to stand on end. Swearing under her breath, she did her best to ignore Korwin's spirit as he reached out for her again. Shutting out a spirit had never been easy. When she had tired of his attempts to get her attention, she spun around in her seat to face the intruding entity.

Spirits never appeared as they had been when they were alive, unlike in the movies that romanticized the phenomena. Instead they looked like they were made of grey smoke that swirled with the natural, colorful, and vibrant energy of the environment. It was the energy of the spirit itself that told her who it had once been. Looking straight at these entities was disorienting, and Tara had to watch Korwin from the corner of her eye.

:Why did you do it?: Korwin asked. Instead of using sound, spirits communicated by sending out an impression of what they were trying to communicate with what energy they had. As a result, emotions and thought-forms floated towards her, turning his question into more than mere words.

Tara turned and faced front. *:It's my job:* She said in the same manner as a spirit. *:Now, go away. I don't want you following me:*

"You OK?" Kevin asked.

Tara glanced back at him and smiled. "Yeah, why?"

"You just...you looked spooked for a second." He glanced behind them. "We're not being followed."

Tara sighed when Kevin's comment caused a small wave of concern to flow from Nate. "I'm fine. It was nothing."

Most of SUM's operatives assumed that Tara was Supernatural. Before Vincent Vinachelli had been assassinated, he had told Tara that it would be safer if her fellow operatives remained ignorant of what she could do with her Paranormal powers. To keep up the facade, she pretended to be an average level Supernatural Psychic. Kevin had been one of her closest friends, and yet he had been kept in the dark like almost everyone else. Friend or no, it was rare for her to share such potent information about herself with anyone.

Supernaturals had an almost native hatred and

fear towards anything that could make their lives more difficult. To add fuel to the fire, most of them believed the false propaganda and conflicting lies the government had put out there about Paranormals. Those same Supernaturals knew the propaganda against their own kind to be false, and this baffled Tara. While her kind were hunted by the government and its PSI teams like any Supernatural with a bounty on their head, most of those she once called 'friends' might have turned on her had they learned the true nature of her power. The Head of State had a standing kill order for any Paranormal that was found, regardless of their age or status. Tara wasn't as surprised about the government's laws than she had been about those Supernaturals who obeyed them when told to kill innocents.

The government was adept at creating hysteria so that people wouldn't care what they did to anyone, including children. Those who were born without a power believed that they were being protected and that Supernaturals and Paranormals were rare and dangerous. The irony was that most people had the Supernatural gene and therefore were born with a power that they could control. On random occasions, a Supernatural would give birth to a Paranormal. In a hospital birth such a baby would have been 'destroyed' by the very doctor who delivered her, if they performed a blood test that showed the baby had the paranomral gene. Thankfully such tests were expensive and rarely performed. A Paranormal who survived into adulthood was unusual. Tara's parents were Supernatural and had avoided a hospital birth. It was why she had avoided the fate of execution for the crime of of being born with the 'wrong' genes.

All of this animosity thrown at her own kind was one of the many signs that people had an intrinsic blindness to the truth if they are told enough lies. Society was too comfortable being fed misinformation and refused to see for themselves what was happening all around them. Tara sometimes believed that she saw the truth because her power made her aware. Their ignorance was more than annoying and unsettling. It was outright dangerous and she couldn't understand why anyone had allowed it at all.

Nate turned onto the highway and headed West. Tara looked up at him in confusion. "The private airport is in the opposite direction."

"I'm well aware of that, Tara, " he said with obvious annoyance. "We're heading to the desert, a helicopter is waiting for us there."

"Great," she muttered under her breath.

Deserts held little life energy and as a result Tara felt half blind while in one. Her ability to detect all wavelengths of energy had been with her since birth. Most of what she hadn't learned to block out had become so familiar that she expected and relied upon her Paranormal senses the way most people relied on sight and sound. If their luck held, then the lack of life pulsing around her wouldn't hinder her part in their getaway.

To her surprise, the ride remained uneventful. Tara half expected PSI agents to ambush them at any moment. Nate had said that the war had started, but not where the initial battle had taken place. Since Ms. Vinachelli was involved, it was safe to presume that she was in the middle of the fray. This implied that it had occurred somewhere near the woman's home, which sat about 600 miles north east of their position and over a mountain range. The compound wasn't much further.

Holding back a groan, Tara hoped that they weren't going to take the helo the entire way. They hadn't yet reached it and she was already dreading the ride. With a few hours of sleep and her adrenaline wearing off, it became difficult to keep her eyes open. SUM had trained her to operate with little sleep, but that didn't stop it from being a burden. Even the most seasoned operatives required rest, and it was impossible to sleep while riding a helo. Two Supernatural soldiers and a Paranormal spy weren't much of a challenge against a full PSI Team if they didn't have the energy stores with which to use their power. With enough rest, however, it would take far more than one team to take them down.

If they found themselves in a fight with the enemy

before they reached the helo, then she needed as much internal energy as her body could muster. Without it, she might not survive.

Read more in Tara's Escape: A Supernatural Uprising Novel: Book 2

Gutter Glossary

Past, Present and Future Tense

Because verbs in Gutter usually end with '-in' (for -ing), 'get', 'be', 'been', and 'done' are used to describe when something happens.

be: The word 'be' is often used to indicate something that will happen. This is quite often put near the beginning or at the very end of a sentence.
been: This word indicates something that is either currently happening, or has just happened.
done: This word often indicates something that has happened a long time ago (over 1 year)
done been: This phrase indicates something that happened a long time ago and is still in effect.
get: To do presently or soon

Slang:

ables: can

bester: best/better
babe: baby
birthed: born
block: Gutter street
bony: skinny, too thin
'bout: about
bro: brother

c'mon: come with me
chick: girl, woman

clear: safe
clue: to know or understand
curb: to prevent, to refuse

eats: food
eyes: to look for, to watch

favorin eyes: looking for, targeted
'ford: afford
'fraid: affraid

get gone: to go away, to leave
get it: to understand
get on a thing: do something
g'night: good night
gov'ment: government

heavy: hard, a lot, very
'hind: behind
hold a deal: to accept an

offer

joint: place, house, building

keep/keepin: to stay

launderin: to do laundry, to wash clothing
lil: little
lose ya mind: to act crazy, be silly, do something stupid

mind gone: to act crazy
mindful: careful
moms: mother
morer: more
musta: must have

nabbed: to be arrested.
'nother: another, other

o'er: over
one-two: a second, a short while, a moment, a minute, soon

'part: apart
pass/passin: to offer
picturin: to imagine, to picture in your head, to think
piece: gun
pissed: angry
poppers: medication, pills
pops: father
pound on: to be beaten or physically abused

rat: to tattle, to snitch
rememory: to remember
'rents: parents

riskful: increased risk or danger
riskless: Safe
'round: around
runway: runaway

s'ides: besides
s'more: some more
s'pecially: especially
s'possed: supposed
same: the same thing, alike, similar
share a story: to talk about something personal.
share words: to have a conversation
shit ton: A whole lot
sis: sister
so's: so long as
spooked: afraid, scared
'stead: instead
steady: regular, continuously ongoing
stick: to stay
sweat: to worry

tame: calm and quiet
them shits: that stuff, it, those. Sometimes the word 'shits' is replaced with another word (eg. 'them peoples')
ta: to
true: honest, truthful, real

works: a job, to work
worser: worse

ya: you
y'know: You know

About the Author

Jayelle Cochran is an independent author living with her husband and two children in Indianapolis, IN. An avid reader and writer, Jayelle has a deep love for Science Fiction and Fantasy genres. Although this series is Urban Fantasy/ Dystopia, Jayelle has plans for a post-apocalyptic series in the future.

Find more information at
jayellecochran.com